TO
Ten Things You Shouldn't Say

1. You're wearing that?

2. Something smells funny.

3. Where's the Tylenol?

4. And to think I first wanted to date your brother.

5. I have a confession to make....

6. My dad has a suit just like that.

7. That man is hot. Look at him.

8. My ex, may he rot in hell forever...

9. You're going to order *that?* Seriously?

10. You're how old?

Gena Showalter
Animal Instincts

HQN™

Recycling programs
for this product may
not exist in your area.

ISBN-13: 978-0-373-77567-5

ANIMAL INSTINCTS

Copyright © 2006 by Gena Showalter

This edition published by arrangement with Harlequin Books S.A.

® and TM are trademarks of the publisher. Trademarks indicated with ® are registered in the United States Patent and Trademark Office, the Canadian Trade Marks Office and in other countries.

www.HQNBooks.com

Printed in U.S.A.

Dear Reader,

Here's a little piece of useless trivia for you: I actually wrote this book before *The Stone Prince* (2004) and *The Pleasure Slave* (2005). It just took me a little longer to find it a home. But *Animal Instincts* was a story I had to tell, even though writing it was a huge departure for me. There are no paranormal elements in it. No aliens, vampires, or creatures of any kind. Just regular people who have fears and flaws like the rest of us (with the exception of the book's hero, Royce, who has more money than—and I'm just guessing here—God).

See, Naomi Delacroix has always been a doormat, allowing people to walk all over her. Cut her down—she would have smiled. Hurt her feelings—she might have said thank you. She's tired of living that way, though. That's why, with the aid of a self-help book, *Unleashing the Tigress Within,* she's determined to become a stronger, more assertive woman. Cut her down now—she'll make you bleed. Hurt her feelings now—she'll tell you to go to hell (and might even help send you there).

Life is good (or so she thinks) until she meets sexy Royce Powell. To Naomi, falling for him means falling back into her old way of life. To Royce, falling for Naomi means amazing sex and a lifetime of love. (Typical guy, putting sex first.) Neither wants to back down. Still, Royce is determined to make this tigress purr. Whatever it takes. I hope you enjoy reading about their passionate (and slightly bloody) journey as much as I enjoyed writing it. And for more information about my books, visit my Web site at www.genashowalter.com and my blog at www.genashowalter.blogspot.com.

Wishing you all the best,

Gena Showalter

To Kassia Krozser—for your generosity.
Okay, and your smart-ass mouth.

To my brothers—Shane Tolbert, Michael Showalter,
Matthew Showalter (aka the pimp), Josh Slovak
and the delectable Kyle Hurt.

To my good friend Mr. Johnson—
for being hard on me when I needed it most.

To Max Showalter Jr.—the sexiest man ever to walk
the face of the earth (comment offered freely
without any hint of bribery).

Acknowledgments

A big thank-you to Tom Kerstine for sharing
his time and wisdom.

Thanks also to Margo Lipschultz for her keen editorial eye.

I would like to thank Susan Grimshaw and
Kathy Baker for their continued support.

Another thank-you to Aviation Research
for answering all my questions.

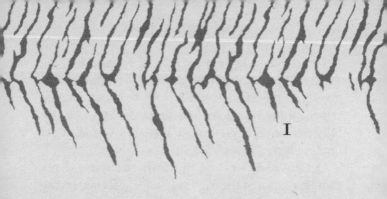

I

A true Tigress knows how to strut her stuff. She walks with her head held high, her breasts pushed forward and wears an expression that says, "I'll eat you alive."

I'M A DOORMAT.

There. I admitted it. If people want to wipe their muddy boots on the rug that is my life, I'm likely to welcome them with a smile and thank them afterward. Knowing this, some people might lose all respect for me. In my defense, let me just say I'm getting better. Stronger. More assertive.

I'm unleashing my inner Tigress.

Unfortunately, I've kept her on a tight leash today. So far the score is not in my favor. Life 5. Tigress 2.

Again, in my defense, let me say that Life is a mean, mean bitch.

I replayed the last section I'd read of *Unleashing the Tigress Within* through my mind as the chrome-and-glass building that housed Powell Aeronautics came into view. My upcoming meeting would go wonderfully, I assured myself; as a Tigress, I would allow nothing less.

Determined, I raised my chin and squared my shoulders against the cab's seat, effectively displaying my breasts to their best advantage. But try as I might, I couldn't get the cannibalistic expression down.

Of course, when you have lips as full and seemingly collagen-injected as mine—okay, maybe not so seemingly—the only expression they're good for is "I charge two hundred dollars an hour." Which, if you think about it, *could* imply I want to eat someone alive.

For Brad Pitt, I'd be willing to work something out.

For everyone else, well…I shrugged. Sorry, but all they'll get is the expression.

I pursed my lips, relaxed them. Pursed. Relaxed. Trying to find the perfect menacing facial cast. When I noticed the cabdriver staring at me through the rearview mirror, I turned my reddening face toward the window. I should have practiced at home, but I'd received an impromptu call from my ex-husband—may he die and burn in hell for all eternity—and that had consumed my spare time.

"I want to give us another try," he'd said. He usually called once a month with the same speech. He just couldn't stand the thought of a woman not wanting him. "I love you, babe. I swear I do," he'd finished.

Yeah, and my breasts are double-D delights of pleasure.

They're not, in case anyone is wondering. I'm barely, *barely* a B-minus.

I'm proud of myself. I'd told him I hoped he became intimately acquainted with a flesh-eating bacteria that ravaged his entire body slowly and painfully, beginning with his favorite appendage, and hung up. (The first point to go on my scorecard.) I suspect and hope my Tigress is as mean a bitch as Life, but I haven't interacted with her enough yet to know for sure.

Anyway, while Richard and I were together, he cheated on me. Like the good little girl I am, I let the first time slide. Fight for your marriage and all that bullshit. Boys will be boys, right? Never mind that they're male whores.

Oopsie. Is my bitterness showing?

The second time he cheated, I left him for all of four weeks. I'm embarrassed to admit he romanced me back. I mean, he tattooed my name on his ass. Who can resist that? So what that my name rests next to his first wife's.

The third time he cheated, well, I moved out for good and filed for divorce. That was six months ago. Being a divorce lawyer—aka scum of the universe— himself, he'd known exactly how to work the system and had ended up with everything while I had nothing.

If you want to know where depraved murderers get their ideas, I think I know. From scorned women. What I could have done with a curling iron and an ice pick....

Well, that's a moot point now.

Richard's call had been the perfect beginning to my increasingly horrendous day. Earlier this morning I'd been fired from one of the biggest jobs of my almost nonexistent party-planning career. All because I'd refused to give the owner of Glasston Industries a "private party"—his words, not mine—in the back of his luxury sedan.

My dismissal came after I'd already spent four weeks planning Glasston's annual employee banquet.

Four long, torturous, I-want-to-kill-myself weeks!

At the disgusting offer, my inner Tigress had emerged unbidden and I'd quickly introduced Mr. Glasston's groin to my knee. (My second point.) Needless to say, they didn't part on good terms. Before he could have me arrested for assault, I had jumped in this cab, buckled up and prepared to meet my next client. That's when I found a piece of rotten food stuck to the seat belt. At least, I hoped it was food. I did not want to contemplate what else the non-removable grease stain could be from.

Grease—or *whatever*—was the least of my problems, though. When I'd first entered the cab, I'd thought the driver had a horrible case of gas. Wrong. That noxious scent of dog poop wafting through the cab, well, it came from *my* shoes. I'd probably stepped in a steaming pile on my trek to Glasston Industries. I only hoped I'd left a souvenir on Mr. Glasston's trousers.

Is it horrible of me to wish he and Richard would rot in hell together?

Okay, wait. I'm beginning to sound bitter again. I don't want to be a bitter woman. Really. I want to be strong. Strong women are happy. And I desperately want to be happy.

Needing a mental boost, I dug in my briefcase and gripped my copy of *Unleashing the Tigress Within*. My twin cousins, Kera and Mel, had given me the book for my thirty-first birthday two months ago, and with its guidance I *was* becoming a stronger, happier woman.

A woman in control of her destiny.

A woman who didn't let a little bad luck bring her down.

Everything will work out, Naomi. Just you wait and see. The cab came to an abrupt stop. I handed the driver a ten. "Keep the change," I said, then drew in a deep breath and pushed open the door.

As I stepped onto the sidewalk, a young man grabbed the leather strap of my purse and tore off in a sprint. I screeched and leapt after him. Except, only four steps into my pursuit, the three-inch heel of my left shoe snapped and I toppled face-first. Dark strands of hair clouded my vision and air abandoned my lungs in a mighty heave. My briefcase skidded across the concrete.

It was early July and a typical Dallas morning: sweltering, dry and miserable. The heated pavement burned raw scratches on my knees.

The thief disappeared around the corner and no one even tried to stop him. I think one woman actually said, "Did you see that guy's butt? So cute!"

As I lay sprawled, quite a few people rubbernecked as they walked by; others simply stopped, stared and snickered. Cheeks burning, I jackknifed to my feet. And practically fell again when one of my injured knees buckled in protest.

It would have been nice if the cabby had gotten out and helped me. But a harried blond woman jumped over me and settled herself inside the taxi before I could even blink. The damn car whizzed away, leaving me in a cloud of exhaust. Choking, I bent and gathered my things. At least I'd left my maxed out credit cards at home. Not the case with my (now missing) lipstick and oil-control powder.

Damn it! I did not need this.

Limping and dirty, I somehow collected my wits enough to make it inside the Powell building. Despite being robbed, I had to act confident and assured. This job was too important.

Disregarding the curious stares of the businessmen and women in the lobby, I searched for and found the bathroom. Women filled the space to capacity, their loud, cackling voices more annoying than the thick haze of forbidden cigarette smoke.

I coughed and shoved my way into one of the cramped stalls, locked the door behind me and tossed my stained jacket in the trash can. I leaned my head against the cool, polished wood. A part of me wanted to sob great buckets of tears. Another part of me wanted to attack something. Just fling myself at the next person I saw and dine on the carnage.

I had to find a happy medium. Approaching a potential employer looking like a feral—but sensitive—

beast wasn't good business. Taking a deep breath, I closed my eyes and mentally chanted, *I'm in a meadow of happiness. I'm in a meadow of happiness.*

Why hadn't I kicked off my shoes and chased that purse-stealing bastard down?

I'm in a meadow of happiness.

Why hadn't I reported Mr. Glasston's disgusting proposition?

I'm in a freaking meadow of happiness!

Why hadn't I—

My eyelids popped open and my fists clenched. The meditation my stepdad had taught me was only increasing my agitation. Better to stop now before I started screaming/crying/ performing kung fu against the stall walls. My stepdad is a psychiatrist, but his methods rarely work for me. I don't know why I keep trying them.

"I can do this. I can."

Liar, my Tigress said, and I snapped, *Bitch.* God, maybe on top of it all I'm schizophrenic.

Forcing my muscles to relax, I slipped out of the stall. My gaze automatically scanned the crowded bathroom, taking in previously missed details. Every woman present wore some type of green. There were pea-green blazers, lime-green skirts, olive-green blouses.

I felt like I'd just stepped into an avocado salad.

Why green? I wondered, gazing down at my own brown, calf-length skirt. Then I uttered a dejected sigh. What the hell did it matter? Even if I'd known green was the current fashion trend, I no longer owned any clothes in that color. Lately I only wore browns, blacks and whites. Business colors. Boring colors.

Another item for my growing Why My Day Sucks list.

With the mirror overly crowded, there simply wasn't enough room to fix my hair, so I left it alone, pinned haphazardly at the base of my neck, errant strands floating down my temples. I was, however, determined to make it to my meeting without limping.

After I cleaned my disgustingly ripe shoes, I spent ten minutes banging, scraping and clawing them to a similar height. Finally they were both completely flat. I wouldn't limp, that was for sure, but I now looked like a twelve-year-old. At five-three, I needed every extra inch I could get.

The bathroom was growing more crowded by the second. Feeling the walls close in around me, I squeezed my way out. A security guard with burly shoulders and a belly that hung over the waistband of his pants stood in the lobby, just in front of the elevator entrance. When I tried to pass him, his arm shot out, blocking my way.

"Applications are at the front desk, miss," he said.

I almost said, "Thank you, I'll head over there immediately," but I stopped myself in time. *I'm confident. I'm assured.* "I'm not here to apply for a job." Actually I was, but not the kind he was talking about. I made a point of straightening my shoulders to the self-help manual's specifications. "I have an appointment with Royce Powell."

The guard snorted. "Try it on someone else. I'm not buying your particular brand of bull."

My jaw dropped, then closed with a snap. "I'm telling the truth."

"Hey, either you mail in your application like the others, or I put your name on the bad-girl list and you won't be considered for the position."

Normally I would have been cowed by such a patronizing tone. After all, I'd had years of practice with both my real father (may he twist painfully in his grave) and Richard (may he meet his maker soon and twist painfully in his grave). But, as I've already mentioned, I'm in the process of becoming a new woman. A new woman who wouldn't take this kind of crap from a man.

And, to be honest, the thought of being on that bad-girl list kind of excited me.

"Listen," I said, using one finger to poke him firmly in the chest. "This hasn't been a good day. I suggest you move before you get hurt."

He laughed. Actually laughed! "I ain't movin', lady."

"Get. Out. Of. My. Way." Every word held an iron edge.

"Not gonna happen." He gave me a cocky grin, revealing crooked, yellowing teeth. "I wouldn't let you pass now if God Himself shoved me aside."

At that moment, something odd came over me. The guard suddenly represented everything that had gone wrong today, yesterday, all of my life. Getting past him wasn't just necessary for obtaining a job. It was vital for my peace of mind. Can someone say *meow*?

"I might not be able to arrange God's intervention," I told him, "but I could certainly shove *my* foot up your ass."

Surprise flickered over his weather-roughened features a split second before he frowned. "God, I hate premenstrual women," he grumbled.

"If you want premenstrual, I'll give you a premenstrual bitch slap. What do you think of that?"

"You tell 'em, honey," someone yelled.

I turned. Almost every woman from the bathroom stood behind me, lined up like a St. Patrick's Day parade. Empowered by their support, I spun back around, absolutely certain I now wore an "I'll eat you alive" expression.

The guard took a precautionary step backward.

"You have exactly two seconds to get out of my way," I ground out, "or you're going to regret it. I spoke with Linda Powell three days ago—"

"Linda Powell?" Sheer terror clouded his eyes and he stepped aside. "Why didn't you say so? Take the express elevator. Nineteenth floor."

Shocked by my success, I could only blink up at him. The women behind me acted instantly, surging forward. Unprepared for movement, I was propelled past the guard and into the elevator. I managed to right myself before I kissed the carpet.

"*I* spoke with Linda Powell," several women shouted at once. "I did. I swear."

"Back off, ladies," I heard the guard say, just as the doors closed around me.

As I rode up the many flights, my hands began to

sweat and my heartbeat quickened. I don't hate heights. I simply hate the knowledge that I could plummet to my death at any moment. Thankfully, the elevator didn't crash and I made it to the office with a few minutes to spare, one of the advantages of being a perpetual early bird.

A woman wearing a stiff black tailored suit manned the reception desk. Her black hair was slicked back from her face, not a single strand free. The bun was so tight, in fact, her eyes slanted upward. Her pale, pale skin (even paler than mine and I'm practically albino) gave her an eerie, almost vampiric appearance.

"Is this Royce Powell's office?" I asked, just to be sure.

"Yes." The severe, frowning woman glanced up through the black fringe of her lashes. "And you are?"

"Naomi Delacroix. I'm here to see him."

She gave me a once-over and obviously found me lacking. Her frown deepened. "Applications are supposed to be mailed, not personally delivered."

Application? Lord, what was it with the people in this building? Royce Powell had called me months ago—okay, he'd called me several times over the last few months, but I'd ignored him and never phoned him back. I hadn't had the courage to face the devastatingly sexy man I'd met only once, but had dreamed about countless times. Sadly, though, I'd work with the devil at this point. (If you're reading this, Mr. Satan, I have good rates. Just FYI.)

Anyway, when Linda Powell had called me a few days ago, I hadn't ignored her, and she'd requested that I meet with her son to see if I was the "right person" to plan her sixtieth birthday party. I tried to explain this to Elvira, Mistress of the Dark. "Look, I don't need an application. I'm—"

"Honey, everyone needs one and you can pick yours up downstairs. In fact," she said, her eyes narrowing, "how did you get past Johnny?"

"I walked." For emphasis, I waved one arm through the air. "Look, I believe I explained that I don't need an application. I already have the job." Well, that wasn't a complete lie, but almost. No terms had been reached, no contract signed. "What I need now is to speak with Mr. Powell."

"There's no need to become violent."

"Uh, excuse me?" Was the woman on drugs? "I'm not violent."

"Tell that to the murderous gleam in your eyes."

I gritted my teeth. "If you'll just tell Mr. Powell I'm here—"

"For the love of God, I'll get you an application." She pushed to her feet. "Wait here. And don't touch anything while I'm gone."

"But I'm not here to apply…" My voice tapered off when I found myself completely alone. Wait. Uh-oh. What if the applications were for the position of party planner and all those women downstairs were my competition? I gulped.

Moments later, a blue packet of papers was thrust in my direction. "Here. Fill this out and *mail* it in."

I glanced over the application. Favorite hobbies. Information on last boyfriend. Sexual habits. What the hell? I was *not* filling that out. Not knowing what else to do with it, I stuffed it in my briefcase. "Is this for the party planner gig or a regular office job?"

She snorted. "That isn't an application for employment, chickie. It's for the position of Mrs. Royce Powell."

I took a moment to breathe, positive I had misheard. "Excuse me?"

"Oh, please. Don't pretend you're not here to marry him. The *Tattler* broke the story a few days ago. Women have been swarming in ever since."

"He's taking applications for a *wife?* Seriously?" What kind of man expected women to fill out a questionnaire to be his life partner? It was so unbelievably egotistical.

Contemptuous.

Disgusting.

And yet, it fit so perfectly with my day.

Like I ever wanted to get married again. Like I wouldn't rather sign up to be a contestant on *Fear Factor* and eat rotten bugs wrapped in pig uterus and smothered in a nice cow-blood sauce.

I strove for a calm, rational tone. "I'm here to discuss the details of Linda Powell's birthday party. Nothing more."

That earned me a raised brow. "Name?"

I'd already told her, but I smiled politely. Now we were getting somewhere. "Naomi Delacroix."

One long, bloodred nail (authentic coloring, do you think?) ran down a calendar printout. "Well, well, well. What do you know? You're not listed."

My smile slipped a notch. "I assure you, I do have an appointment. Monday. Eleven o'clock."

"Oh, I believe you." Her sarcasm was as sharp and biting as fangs sinking into my vein. "A magic fairy must have sneaked inside and erased your name."

Maybe her lover the devil had done it, I thought, my smile fading even more. "Please check again."

"I don't think so. Just have a seat over there," she said, pointing to a stiff, uncomfortable-looking chair. "I'll call you *if* Mr. Powell can work you in. And by the way," she added with an evil smile, "you have a streak of dirt on your cheek."

"Thank you for telling me." Bitch. "I truly appreciate it." My own smile dissolved completely, but I didn't immediately clean my face. I waited until she turned, then scrubbed both cheeks with a vengeance.

Why hadn't the cab just run over me when it had had the chance? That would have saved me a lot of trouble. Would have been more merciful, too.

Legs stiff, I strode to my designated seat and waited like a naughty child for punishment. I would have liked to go home and indulge in an extra-large, thick-crusted pepperoni pizza dripping in grease with a side of gooey chocolate-chip cookies. And a box of Krispy Kremes. And a bag of Doritos. And a large Cherry-Vanilla Coke. What did I care about cholesterol and clogged arteries when my sanity hung in the balance?

Time ticked by and my butt began to throb. I couldn't get comfortable. The chair had no padding and, each time I shifted my weight, my ass bones ground into the faux leather.

Just as I was shifting yet again, a woman with

shoulder-length silver hair and a regal air that shouted "pedigree," glided through the doorway, looking neither right nor left. An expensive, perfumed breeze brushed my face as she passed. When Elvira noticed the newcomer, she shot to her feet, her features tight with disgust. And just a hint of fear.

"No need to announce me," the older woman said in a tone that left no room for argument. "I can see myself in." With that, she sidestepped the freshly polished desk.

"I'm sorry, Mrs. Powell, but I can't let you do that." Elvira held out a hand, blocking the woman's path. "Give me a minute and I'll tell him you're here."

The two faced off. Nails were bared. Hair stood on end. If either woman's expression grew any hotter, the fire alarms were going to erupt. Right about then, I forgot about my ass pain, forgot about my sucky day. All I needed was a bowl of Orville Redenbacher's best and a scorecard. This scene had definite ass-kicking potential and, if anyone deserved to have their ass kicked, it was Elvira.

Go, old lady. Go!

"I do *not* need to be announced to see my own son," Mrs. Powell barked. She *was* scarier in person than she'd sounded on the phone. If I were Elvira, I would have backed away long before now. "Move out of my way this instant or you'll regret it."

Elvira licked her lips and crossed her arms. "I'll only take a second. You can sit in the waiting room—with the other lady who doesn't have an appointment." Without waiting for a reply, she picked up the phone. "Mr. Powell. Your mother—"

Mrs. Powell didn't wait. She shouldered her way past the desk and stalked down the hall.

Dark storm clouds settled over Elvira's features and she barked into the receiver. "It's too late. She's on her way." She slammed the phone down.

And just like that, the showdown was over, leaving me to wait.

And wait. And wait.

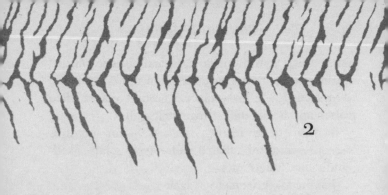

2

When two primal jungle animals come face-to-face, they will fight until the weaker one admits defeat. A true Tigress meets every challenge with wit, cunning and blood instinct.

I SPENT THE NEXT HOUR PERCHED in that stiff-backed chair from hell, reading old issues of *City Girl.* I really enjoyed the article titled Breasts: To Buy or Not To Buy. My own were small. I often called them "the Wonders." (I wondered if they were even there.) Obviously after reading the article, I was leaning toward buying.

I only wish there'd been an article on Botox. I had already passed the dreaded three-oh and was beginning to notice fine lines. I'm too young for lines of any kind. And, I admit, I like to look my best at all times. I'm not vain or anything like that. It's just, when I first found out Richard had cheated on me, I'd felt so…ugly. So unwanted and unnecessary. So *disposable*. Like a filthy piece of garbage that smelled rotten and oozed disgusting black stuff.

I didn't like feeling that way—for obvious reasons—and still had to fight for every scrap of self-confidence I could get.

I shifted in my chair yet again.

Finally—thank you, Lord, finally—Elvira, Hand-maiden of Lucifer, approached me. "Are you Naomi?" she asked, as if I hadn't already given her my name. Twice. When I didn't reply fast enough, she added snidely, "Well, are you?"

I knew she hadn't forgotten me so soon, so I stub-bornly refused to answer.

She got the hint. "Your name isn't listed," she grumbled, her pale, matte-finished lips thin with ir-ritation. "However, Mr. Powell will see you anyway."

It pained me to say, "Thank you," but I said it with a straight face. I even threw in, "I appreciate your efforts on my behalf," though it nearly killed me to utter the words in a civil tone.

I was striving so diligently to appear forgiving and professional because, as I mentioned earlier, I really needed this job. My bills were stacking up and I did not like the thought of losing my bottom-level apart-ment and having to move back in with my mom and stepdad. Especially since Jonathan enjoys psycho-analyzing my every action. Like I really need to know the reason I ran away from home at the age of sixteen was because my mom hadn't breast-fed me. I love the man, but please. I'd run away (for all of six hours) because my mom hadn't let me date Aarin Bower, the hottest boy to attend my high school. Duh.

"Follow me," Elvira said, turning in one fluid motion.

"Follow me," I silently mimicked.

She flicked me a narrowed, backward glance.

My eyes widened innocently. *What?* I mentally projected. She bared her teeth in a scowl before turning back around. Obviously, the woman had unleashed her own inner Tigress long ago.

I marched behind her, remembering to keep my shoulders squared and breasts pushed forward. Wits, cunning and blood instinct. I'd wield all three from this point on.

My shoes sank into the plush off-white carpet. A starched, almost sterile aroma clung to the air, as if the office lacked any type of personal touch. Judging from the employees I'd met so far, maybe that was a good thing.

Elvira swung open the heavy double doors, holding them forward and out of the way while I glided past. In the next instant, Royce Powell came into view—and the rest of my day tumbled straight into the deepest, darkest depths of hell. My eyes met his and my step faltered. I stumbled. (And this time, it had nothing to do with my shoes!)

I steadied myself, fighting the urge to drop everything I was doing and simply nibble on him. Really, truly nibble. As in, sink my teeth into naked flesh. Run my tongue over every inch and hollow. *This* is why I hadn't returned his calls. This is why I hadn't wanted to meet with him in person. With only a look, he sizzled my hormones and knocked me out of my comfort zone.

He probably didn't remember (or maybe he did, since he'd called me?), but we'd crossed paths six months ago at the first party I'd planned on my own. We hadn't spoken, but he'd glanced in my direction once or twice, and I'd salivated.

The man was absolutely, one hundred percent edible.

After years and years of dealing with Richard, aka Whore Hound from Hell, I liked to think of myself as immune to testosterone. But this man radiated sex like a blinking neon sign that said, "Come get a piece of this." I felt like a big, fat sexual appetizer screaming for a little down-and-dirty attention. I had the urge to slowly strip and swing from a pole. Maybe offer to give him a lap dance.

How pathetic was I?

Royce Powell was in his mid-thirties, possibly early forties. He had bronze skin. Electric, pale blue eyes— that were watching me intently. My stomach clenched. Did I still have dirt on my face? His nose was straight, his lips full, soft and completely kissable. A shadow of dark stubble lined his jaw, giving him a rugged quality that only added to his appeal. His broad shoulders were encased in an expensive Italian suit.

He was a combination of George Clooney shaken together with Josh Wald and a splash of Brad Pitt on the side. Did I mention how much I love to look at Brad Pitt? Maybe I'm not so immune to testosterone, after all.

Royce offered me a sexy smile of greeting.

My senses reeled and my mouth went dry; a lump formed in my throat. That smile…it was lethal. Pure lady-killer. *Run,* my mind shouted. *Get out of here.*

Where were my wits? My cunning? My blood instinct?

I would soon be chatting with this perfect man, maybe even shaking his perfect hand. At the thought, my nervous system kicked into high gear. How could I shake his hand when my own felt like a swamp? I had to do something to calm my nerves. But what? My stepdad's advice to "picture those who make you nervous completely naked" didn't apply here.

Royce Powell…naked….

I slapped a polite smile on my face and decided then and there to think of him as a turkey-and-cheese-on-rye sandwich. I did *not* like turkey and cheese. I hated rye.

He rose, his gaze lowering and lingering on my lips, and held out one hand. We shook. When he pulled back, he wiped his palm on his slacks before reclaiming his seat.

My professional expression never wavered.

I hoped.

I cleared my throat. "I realize I'm seeing you later than scheduled," I said, just in case Elvira, Queen of the Damned, hadn't let him know of my early arrival, "but I'd like it noted that I did, in fact, arrive on time." Tardiness was one of the biggest sins in the world, in my estimation.

His smile grew wide with amusement. "So noted."

My knees almost buckled. His smile was bad enough, but throw in that voice and good God! Its deep, husky timbre flowed as smooth and rich as expensive brandy. He'd spoken only moments before, but he hadn't spoken like this. All husky and low, as if he were lying in bed after a vigorous session of sex. Raunchy, I-screamed-my-brains-out sex.

He watched me for a long, silent moment. Then, "Please—" he motioned with his chin "—have a seat."

Nodding, I eased down and set my briefcase aside. "I hope you don't mind my asking, but where's your mom? I didn't see her leave."

He didn't seem put out by my question; in fact he appeared even more amused by me. "She went out the side door."

"Oh." Smart woman. She wouldn't have to deal with Elvira again. "I spoke with her over the phone last Friday," I said, getting down to business. *I'm calm. I'm professional.* "I'm not sure I fully understood the facts. She wants me to plan a surprise party, doesn't she?"

"Yes."

"Yet she also stated that the party was to be given in her honor."

"Don't try to understand her. It will only drive you insane." He didn't offer any other information. He just gave me another of those I'm-the-best-lay-you'll-ever-have smiles.

Was the ground shaking? "When I spoke with her, we didn't have a chance to discuss my fee." The most important matter, to my way of thinking.

"Money isn't a problem," he said, his eyes again roving to my mouth.

My cheeks heated. I had to get to a mirror ASAP and make sure I still didn't have dirt on my face. "I can't in good conscience continue until we've agreed upon— "

"Whatever the party costs," he interjected, silencing my protest, "I'll pay it."

Was he that enthused about celebrating his mom's next step closer to death's door? Or did he love her so much he wanted the woman happy, whatever the cost? "Mr. Powell, that's not a wise thing to tell a woman who hasn't yet named her price."

"True." He chuckled. "Why don't you work out the specifics and fax me an estimate."

I nodded. "Excellent."

"Good. Now, please, call me Royce. And I'll call you Naomi."

My name on his lips somehow seemed too sensual, like a mating call of some sort—a mating call my sexually bankrupt body definitely heard. I clamped my mouth shut before I did something stupid, like say out loud that yes, I'd have his babies. I managed another nod.

A high-pitched beep sounded a split second before I heard Elvira, Harpy of Doom, say, "Mr. Powell, Mr. Phillips is on line one."

Royce rubbed a hand down his suddenly weary

face. "Will you excuse me for a moment?" he said to me. "I have to take this."

"Of course. Should I wait in the lobby?"

"No, stay where you are." He picked up the phone and swiveled his chair so that I saw only its back and the top of his dark head. "Do you have the figures yet?" Pause. He growled low in his throat. "That's why you called? Yes." Pause. "The one." Pause. "Yes. Glad." Pause. "You know I'll do what it takes to win."

Glad about what? Win what? Man, listening to a phone conversation when you could only hear one side of it sucked. Bigtime.

"I'm in a meeting right now." Pause. "Yes." Pause. "Goodbye. Idiot," he muttered. He spun around and replaced the phone, his gaze on me, going all intent again. "Sorry. I'm in the middle of an acquisition, a merger of sorts." He waved his hand through the air. "Anyway, I wish I had more time to meet with you today," he said, with what sounded like genuine regret in his voice, "but unfortunately, I have appointments lined up all morning and I can't get out of them. Why don't I call you in a few days and we'll set up another meeting?"

At his words, a fine mist of red shrouded my vision. Yet despite my anger, my first instinct was to politely accept his offer and leave. Just like in the lobby, however, I squashed the urge to capitulate. I would not be a doormat. Not anymore. I'd spent cab money, had my purse stolen and had waited for over an hour. I wasn't leaving without finishing this meeting.

My fists tightened on the armrests of my chair. *I'm a Tigress.* "Mr. Powell, we haven't gone over a single detail yet."

"I want you to call me Royce, remember. Mr. Powell makes me sound like my father. And we'll have to go over the details another day."

"Royce." *Be strong. Assert yourself.* "I waited out there for over an hour."

"I only learned of our meeting a few moments before you stepped inside my office. I apologize for any inconvenience you've suffered."

Inconvenience? That red mist shrouding my vision became a boiling inferno. His apology didn't bring back my jacket or my favorite tube of lipstick. Teeth grinding together, I said, "Can't you spare ten minutes? That's all it will take. I have a list of questions—"

"My mother's visit threw me off schedule, and I'm afraid I can't even spare five." O-kay. Message received. Obviously, he was giving me the brush-off. He wasn't going to hire me and was eager to get rid of me. I found myself reaching out and lifting a notepad from the edge of his desk. I began itemizing my time, my purse, my lipstick (with twenty dollars extra tacked on for sentimental value), a new pair of shoes and, what the hell, a dry-cleaning bill.

"What are you doing?" He tapped the shattered edge of a pencil against his knee.

"I generally build the meet-and-greet into my original costs, but I'm making an exception for you. Here's my invoice for today's meeting." I ripped off the paper and handed it to him.

His eyes gleamed with curiosity as he read it. That curiosity was quickly replaced by amusement. "Lipstick?"

"My purse was stolen outside the building and my favorite tube was inside."

He frowned, losing all hint of amusement. "I'll have security look into it. That will *not* happen again."

"Thank you."

Pause. Then, "Is it okay if I mail you a check?" he asked.

"Yes." Like I'd ever see the money. "Of course."

"I'll make time for you another day, you have my word. In fact, I'll devote a full day to you and the party."

Liar, I wanted to say. "Fine," I said, giving up.

Exhibit A, my inner Tigress said. *You're a weakling. Fight. Make him talk to you now. Don't let him kick you out like this.*

"I'm so glad you'll make time for me," I added, ignoring my Tigress. "That's great. Wonderful." I handed him a business card, confident I'd never hear from him again. "Here's my number. Call me when you're ready to get together."

He took it, giving the surface a cursory glance. "On second thought, I *do* have something I want to go over before you leave."

"Won't that take up too much of your precious time?" I mentally patted myself on the back for that one, even while I kicked myself for such blatant sarcasm. The man had many influential friends who might one day need a party planner. But damn it, my knees still ached.

"For this, I'll make an exception," he said. "I have a stipulation you need to agree to before I officially hire you."

Officially hire me? I gulped. O-kay, perhaps he *did* plan to get in touch with me later on. Oopsie. "Stipulation?" I asked, breathless.

"Prerequisite. Condition. Term."

"Thank you, but I know what a stipulation is."

"While you're working for me," he continued smoothly, "I want my mother's party to be your first and *only* priority."

Every muscle in my body stiffened. I should have realized this the moment I stepped inside the office, but it just now hit me. The man is a Triple C. Corporate. Controlling. And a total Commando. "I'm sure, as a businessman, you understand my unwillingness to allow someone to take my business decisions away from me."

"Yes," he conceded, but didn't rescind his request. Make that Triple C slash Single B. Bastard. "I promise you, I'm quite capable of handling several functions at once."

"I didn't say you weren't."

"Never have I allowed one event to overshadow another." Not that I'd ever had enough events at one time to worry about it.

"I don't doubt your ability."

I nearly stomped my foot in vexation as he waited patiently for my agreement. "If you're going to insist on this—"

"I am."

"—then I suppose I'm forced to accept." I truly hoped one day soon someone would put Royce Powell in his place. Under a woman's three-inch spiked heel!

As if he read my thoughts, he flashed me a not-in-this-lifetime grin.

My blood instinct must have finally kicked in because my palm itched to slap it right off him. Jonathan, my stepdad, would have told me this rare bout of violence was because my teenage need to rebel was resurfacing, or something equally stupid.

"So we have a deal?" Royce asked.

"First, I have a stipulation of my own," I said. "I expect dou—triple my normal fee because I'll be turning clients away. It's only fair."

"Of course."

He wasn't balking? Why wasn't he balking? His easy acquiescence shocked me and nearly toppled me out of my chair. Maybe I should have asked for more. "So I'm officially hired, without having faxed an estimate and at triple my normal fee?"

"Yes. Don't forget, I have your first invoice." He waved the paper I'd given him. "Shall we triple it now or later?"

"Later is fine." I almost hugged him. Almost. "Whenever you're free, give me a call. There are certain details we'll need to go over before I can begin preparations." With nothing left to say, I stood.

He ran a finger over the calendar on his desk and frowned. "Well, damn. For the next two weeks, I'm booked. I'll be in Arizona acquiring a Piper Dakota—

an airplane," he explained, "and I can't reschedule. How about Tuesday, the sixteenth? Twelve o'clock?"

When I nodded, he added, "We'll have lunch at Mykal's."

"That's fine," I said, not the least surprised he could get a reservation at the famous Italian restaurant on such short notice. It usually took two months for the little people, if they got in at all. I should know.

He rose and stepped around the desk, holding out his hand, intending to shake.

Forgetting I now wore flats, I attempted to take the steps that brought us together. Only, the heel of one shoe knocked the toe of the other. Without warning, I stumbled straight into him.

Not again! My momentum pushed him back against his desk. I landed with both hands clutching the hard muscles of his thighs, my head perilously close to his crotch.

His arms wrapped around my waist to steady me. I should have jumped away, but I didn't. I lingered...and lingered. My gaze remained glued on the center of his pants, widening as he—no, surely not. He was *not* getting an erection. His slacks were *not* inching toward my face.

With a gentle tug, he forced me to stand, though he didn't completely release me. His hands tarried on my arms, warm and callused and oh, so delicious. The scent of unadulterated sin enveloped me. His eyebrows furrowed together and I could tell he didn't know quite what to do with me.

As reality settled in, I jolted away from him. Holy Mother of God, what was wrong with me? I'd come so close to making this man—this ultra-rich, ultra-sexy man with lots of influential friends—a eunuch. And I'd enjoyed it. I needed to be committed.

"I'm so sorry." When I noticed the papers that had been neatly stacked upon his desk were now scattered across the floor, my mortification increased. Only me. This would only happen to me.

I placed my briefcase aside and crouched down, gathering the papers and photos. All of the pictures were of women, and strangely, every woman wore green—or nothing at all.

"I'm so sorry," I told him again, chin canting to the side. Was that woman slathered in green pudding? And was she actually licking her own arm? What kind of kinky shit was this man into? "I didn't—"

"It's all right," he said, his tone pleasant, not the least put out.

I relaxed the tense grip I had on the stack of papers/porn. "Did I damage anything important?" My god, that woman was bending over and eating from a box of Lucky Charms.

"No." He chuckled. "The most important item is still intact."

I felt a blush creep from my forehead to collarbone. I forgot Royce's implication, though, when I spotted the photo of the woman naked and spread-eagle on a lush pile of leaves.

"Here. No reason for you to do that," he said. He

bent and gently swiped the items from my hands, his fingers brushing mine. "I'll get those later."

His touch startled me. Electrified me. I jolted away from him for the second time as if he were some type of radioactive waste. *Turkey on rye. Turkey on rye.* My hands shook as I picked up one of the photos still lying on the floor. In it, a female crouched on all fours, a pair of green cat ears peeking from her blond hair.

"It's my fault," I said, staring at the photo, "so I'll help pick up." What would I find next? Naked green mud wrestling?

"No. I mean it. That's not necessary." This time his answer was curt, almost angry sounding, and he ripped the picture away from my grip.

What had I done now?

It was then I realized exactly what I'd held. Applications from all of the women who wanted to be Mrs. Powell. No wonder he was trying to get rid of me. He didn't want me to see the naked candidates.

I uttered a raspy, embarrassed cough. "I guess this is goodbye, then." Straightening, I spun around and raced for the exit.

"Naomi?"

"Yes?" I stopped, but didn't turn back. Had he felt the same flare of awareness that had nearly incinerated me? Would he ask me out? I'd have to turn him down, of course. He was a client. Only once before had I dated a client. Richard. The effects of that relationship had taught me three valuable lessons I'd never, ever forget.

One: no sleeping with clients.

Two: no getting naked with clients.

Three: no doing the nasty tango all night long with clients.

Yet I couldn't stop the rush of pleasure that hit me at the thought that such a magnificent man might be attracted to me. Tense, I gripped the fabric of my skirt and waited for his next words.

"What's your favorite color?" he asked.

Unexpectedly, my heart sank. I admit it. I'd wanted him to ask me out. Just because I planned to say no didn't mean an invitation was unwelcome.

"Naomi?" he said again.

I realized I hadn't answered him. "My favorite color is blue. Why?"

"No reason." There was an edge of satisfaction in his voice.

I started for the door again.

"Naomi?"

I paused. Anticipation rushed through me. This was it. The next words out of his mouth would be an invitation to dinner. I knew it. I *felt* it. "Yes?" The word emerged as a breathless whisper.

"Don't forget your briefcase."

3

A Tigress never lets anyone get the upper hand in a conversation; she never lets someone else have the last word. Otherwise, she becomes a receptacle for her opponent's emotional garbage.

"So, WHEN ARE YOU GOING to make a move on your new boss?"

"Ha, ha," I said, giving my cousin Kera my best don't-go-there frown.

My other cousin opened her mouth to say something flippant. I knew Melody's comment would be flippant because everything out of her mouth was something only a smart-ass would say. I shot her a death-ray glare.

It worked. Actually worked. Tell-it-like-it-is Mel remained silent. Perhaps I really was getting good at that I'll-eat-you-alive expression.

I eased back in my seat. Sunlight streamed through the pink kitchen curtains, surrounding the table in a haze of warmth. The scent of coffee filled the air. As we did every Monday morning before rushing off to work, or school in Mel's case, we sat at Kera's kitchen table, feasting (or gagging) on whatever food she had prepared.

Kera owned a catering business and was trying to put together a cookbook of fresh, exotic recipes. Normally she was an amazing cook, but those "exotic" recipes of hers were pure crap and killed all hint of her talent.

On the Kera Diet, I'd lost eight pounds. And I needed all the pounds I could get. Don't hate me, but I'm one of those women who really doesn't have to watch what she eats. I'm thin, too thin if you ask me, and I always have been. There's a downside, just so you know. Being called Bones. Having small breasts. Looking malnourished. My stepdad actually counseled me on eating disorders once.

This morning we were safe with bagels and blueberry muffins. Store-bought. Kera hadn't had time to prepare anything exotic, thank God. I don't think I could have handled another breakfast like last week's. A strawberry-barbecue-and-blue-cheese ostrich egg omelet. Just the memory upset my stomach.

"Well?" Kera said. "Are you making a move on him or not?"

"I'm not attracted to Royce," I told her, hoping I sounded convincing. (I didn't.) "Therefore, I'm not making a move on him. And what's up with him and his wife applications?"

"He's eccentric and looking for love," Kera said, as if that explained everything.

Mel took a sizable bite of her bagel, chewed, swallowed. "He's a man. Men like naked photos and will do anything to get them. End of story."

Now that made sense.

Mel and Kera were identical twins, but they were different in so many ways. Kera had been born with an angel on her shoulder. Mel had been born with the devil on hers.

Mel had thick streaks of bottle-red running throughout her blond hair. She also sported several tattoos and piercings. In contrast, Kera appeared delicate, practically angelic. Both women were five-four with petite bodies and bright blue eyes.

"Did you drool over him during your meeting?" Mel asked.

"No. Of course not." Did liars go straight to hell or were they granted some sort of immunity? It wasn't like liars were murderers or anything. "Why would you ask me something so ridiculous?"

Eyes twinkling, Mel slathered cream cheese over her bagel. "You've been drooling over his picture all morning."

I gasped. "That is *sooo* not true."

"Oh please. I could bathe in the puddle you've created. A long, leisurely bath, at that." She raised our copy of the *Tattler*. "But, if you insist you're not attracted to him, I'll just get rid of this." She cast a meaningful glance at the trash can and eased to her feet.

Quick as a snap, I grabbed her arm and snatched the tabloid. "Give me that." As if I hadn't stared at it for the last hour, I studied the large black-and-white photo gracing the front page.

Royce had his arm around a leggy brunette, a slight smile curling his lips. The caption underneath read, "Son of multimillionaire Elliot Powell caught with Gwendolyn Summers. Has Royce found his bride already?"

The article vaguely mentioned the two were at some sort of charity gala for kids with cancer, and I had to wonder which was the real Royce. The womanizer I suspected him to be—wife applications, for God's sake—or the Good Samaritan who donated money and time to charity?

I sighed. To my consternation, the last two weeks had passed with amazing speed, and most of my nights had been filled with images of Royce and me cavorting like sex-starved nymphs who had only a few days to live.

I couldn't banish the man from my mind.

After getting a new driver's license and finding a new tube of Chocolate Mystique lipstick—which had taken four hours and six different stops—I should have been happy. Instead, I thought of nothing but Royce. And that made me…unhappy.

He'd sent me a check, as promised, with a note attached that said if I had any trouble finding the right lipstick to let him know and he'd have one made. How sweet was that? I wouldn't have taken him up on it, but still. I was on the road to obsession, almost to the point where Royce would need a restraining order against me.

I knew better than to let myself desire the man. Yes, Royce was handsome (okay, deliciously gorgeous), but he was a Triple C, just like Richard. Plus, he apparently wanted a wife. I never wanted to get married again.

Did my body care about that? Noooo.

Each evening before I went to bed, I made a list of the reasons why I shouldn't be attracted to Royce, why I shouldn't want to rip the clothes from his body and have my wicked way with him. In fact, I'd made several lists.

None of them helped.

"Look, even if I did drool over him," I told my cousins, "Royce is a man. That means he's only interested in women who are not boobularly challenged."

Frowning, Mel brandished the butter knife she held through the air. "Boobs so don't matter anymore. Flat is in. Flat is the new black."

My brows arched. "Then why is the implant business booming? Why are push-up bras in such demand?"

She obviously didn't have an answer, so she shook her head and said, "Forget boobs. You said he kept staring at your lips."

"I had dirt on them." I'd noticed the moment I returned home and had almost died of embarrassment. I'd also wished Royce to everlasting hell for not telling me.

"He probably wanted to lick the dirt away. The

fact is, you've got yourself a pair of hooker lips. The man wanted them all over his body, is my guess."

"I'll concede that he might, *might* have liked my lips, but he couldn't care less about the rest of me." He hadn't even asked me out after I'd fallen into his crotch. Not that I would have said yes, I quickly reminded myself.

"Sure, you're not pretty in the classic sense, but that doesn't mean you're dog food."

I almost choked on my muffin. When I regained my voice, I said, "Gee, thanks Mel. I feel so much better about myself now. In fact, my self-esteem has suddenly skyrocketed."

"You're misunderstanding." Mel sighed, the breathy sound layered with exasperation. "Your look is fragile, like a cameo. Something most women can never achieve. You've got the kind of appeal that forces a man's protective instincts to surface."

Kera grinned slowly. "She's right. And I think you're a closet sex kitten, Naomi."

Closet sex kitten. Meeeeoooow. No one had ever accused me of that before. In fact, Richard had accused me of being sexually repressed. This inner Tigress thing must be paying off. "Okay, say a miracle happens and Royce wants me like a sailor on leave. What should I do?"

"Marry him," Kera said.

"Rock his world," Mel said, "then toss him out like a piece of rotting, stinking garbage."

Kera gasped and lost her smile. "One-night stands are stupid, not to mention potentially damaging both physically and emotionally."

"She's been free from Richard the Bastard's clutches for six months now and she hasn't gone on a single date. We might as well take her to the local shelter and buy her a few cats. She needs to get laid, not wallow in another bad relationship."

"Hello." I waved my index finger at them. "Hi. I'm right here. In the room with you."

They shrugged simultaneously.

"I swear," I grumbled, "Royce had to be a hemorrhoid in another life because he's already a pain in my ass. I can answer my question myself, thank you. Royce is a client, and I do not get involved with clients. It's bad for business."

Kera, ever the romantic, piped in. "Who cares about business when love is at stake?"

"Who the hell mentioned love?"

She ignored me. "That kind of thought process might just keep you from experiencing something completely wonderful."

I gagged.

"Love is amazing," she said defensively. "A gift. I know you think marriage is an institution for the insane, but one day I'm going to willingly commit myself. I'm going to walk down the aisle with a radiant smile. And I'll be holding flowers, lots and lots of flowers. Silver-tipped roses with pink baby's breath."

I watched in horror, unable to administer a verbal vaccine as the wedding bug sunk its claws into Kera. Her eyes glazed with dreamy expectation; her lips lifted with longing. I could almost see and hear her thoughts.

Was that a baby crying?

"I wish I were in love right now," she said, confirming my suspicions.

Mel rolled her eyes. "How are we related?"

Still smiling that dreamy smile, Kera propped her elbow on the table and flicked me a glance. "Since Naomi doesn't want to marry Royce, I'm sure she won't mind hearing that I filled out one of his applications."

"What?" I shouted. "When?"

"A few days ago."

"No you did not." Mel leaned back in her chair, her expression one of complete shock. "You did, didn't you? You're not lying. Why didn't you tell us?"

"I knew you'd make fun of me." Kera's grin turned to pure wickedness. "But I couldn't help myself. That man is male perfection, and I know I could fall in love with him."

"Love," I scoffed, but my disdain was more from the image of Royce and Kera living happily ever after than from my hatred of the emotion. I was beginning to believe love had been created by the devil himself. What better way to get people to make fools of themselves?

Kera pushed a honey-colored tendril of hair from her forehead. "One day we'll all find men who love us, who we can trust with our hopes and dreams. Men who—"

My laugh cut her off. "The idea of a loving, caring, *trustworthy* male is too ludicrous to contemplate even for a second."

"Hear, hear," Mel seconded. She'd experienced her fair share of broken hearts. In fact, she'd *inflicted* her fair share of broken hearts, but that was beside the point. We were man bashing, not airing our own dirty secrets.

"There's nothing special about love. It sucks and it's messy." I hated to disillusion Kera, but she needed to know the truth. The longer she drifted through life thinking her true love waited just beyond the corner, the more she risked getting hurt.

And, to be honest, I hated the thought of Kera's sweet-heartedness being obliterated by a walking penis.

"I refuse to believe love means nothing," she said. "Just because you *thought* you were in love with Richard the Bastard doesn't mean you had actually found your true love. Your soul mate is out there, Naomi, just waiting for you to find him."

Lord, I hoped not.

However, a wave of trepidation washed over me as Royce's perfectly chiseled face filled my mind. I quickly brushed the sensation—and the image—aside. I didn't believe in soul mates. Not anymore. My mom had thought my real dad was her soul mate the entire ten years they'd been married. That's why she took him back every time he hit her. Every time he cheated on her. Still, I couldn't deny that when I'd fallen into Royce's arms, the contact had been electric; something I'd never experienced before. Not even with my ex.

But that didn't mean Royce was my soul mate.

"So, when do you see the delectable Mr. Powell again?" Kera asked.

I lifted my shoulders in a shrug, trying to act casual. "Tomorrow." Oh, God. Tomorrow. I gulped. I wasn't sure I would survive our next meeting.

Mel nibbled on the edge of her bagel. "Mmm, I'll want all the delectable details, of course."

With the word *delectable* ringing in my mind, my gaze strayed once more to the newspaper photo. I just couldn't help myself. The camera had managed to capture Royce's raw masculinity, but the film failed to reveal the blatant sexuality that oozed from his every pore.

"I can give you all the details right now," I told them, using my next words as a vow to myself. "Nothing's going to happen between Royce and me because I won't let it."

Circling a fingertip over the rim of her glass, Mel said, "Whatever you say, you dirty sex kitten."

I pinched the bridge of my nose. I wished to God I could add Royce's name to my To Be Avoided list. He was causing trouble already. Truly, a smart woman would have called him and ended all association. But with my new motto—I'll Plan a Party in Your Ass if the Price Is Right—I had to stick it out.

"I, for one, am grateful Royce entered your life. He's causing your sex drive to finally kick into gear." Mel drained the last of her juice. "About time, too."

"Hey, did you read this part? I missed it earlier." Kera suddenly grabbed the paper. She hooked a lock of hair behind her ear. "Royce actually lists the qualities he wants in his wife."

"I've read it." I grabbed another muffin, mimicking:

"She must share my interest in backgammon. She cannot complain too much. If she doesn't speak at all, even better. And she absolutely must love the color green." Disgusted, I shook my head. "That's either meant to be a joke or the man needs intense psychotherapy."

"You know," Kera said, brightening, "we need a list like this."

"A stupid one?" I asked.

Kera pursed her lips. "No, a list of requirements."

"What for? Mel's taken. I'm not looking. And you, well, all you have to do is breathe to gain a man's attention." Which was true. She and Mel might be identical, but there was an innocent sensuality to Kera that somehow personified the term *wet dream*. Men went crazy for her.

"Actually, I'm a free woman now," Mel said, not an ounce of remorse in her tone. "So I'm on the prowl."

I couldn't hide my surprise. "What happened to Harry? Last I heard, you two were hot and heavy."

"I dumped him. He kept asking to borrow my panties." She shook her head, blond hair dancing with the movement. "It wouldn't have been so bad, except he wanted them so *he* could wear them."

Nose crinkled, Kera wiggled until her legs were folded under her. "I never liked him. He was too… funky."

"What kind of name is Harry Johnson, anyway?" Mel said. "What could I use as an endearment? Woody?"

"I think Harry Johnson is a great name," I said,

deadpan. "As long as he's got a father named Peter and a brother named Dick."

Mel chuckled. "Let's not talk about Harry, Harry, the Panty Wearer, okay?"

"I'd rather talk about our list." Propping her elbows on the tabletop, Kera regarded us with expectation. "I want to make one with our top ten requirements for Mr. Right."

"That sounds fun," Mel replied dryly. She clapped her hands with mock excitement.

"A Mr. Right list has been done by every woman in America and they all say the same thing," I said, then rattled off the usual handsome, charming, blah, blah, blah. "What we need is a list for Mr. Wrong."

Silence.

"Like how to spot a loser…." Mel nodded, getting into the game. "I love it. Let's do it!"

Kera said, "We all know how much you like to make lists, Naomi, so you're in charge of writing everything down."

Getting into the spirit of things myself, I stood, gathered a sheet of paper and a pencil and plopped back down at the table. "Ready."

"I know what number one should be," Kera said. "Unemployed."

"That's so cliché." Pensive, Mel tapped a finger on her chin. "We have to think creatively." Pause. Gasp. "Number one should be a man who says we'd look great in our clothes if we'd just lose ten pounds."

"Bastard," I growled. I'd heard the opposite from Richard, but I completely understood the sentiment.

You'd look great if you'd just put on some weight, Naomi. Have you ever considered a boob job, Naomi? Your ass bone is killing me, Naomi, maybe you should get off my lap and sit over there. "That's perfect."

"The man I dated before Harry had a lazy eye," Mel said. She licked her lips, snagging a bagel crumb. "Make that number two. A man with a lazy eye."

"There's nothing wrong with a lazy eye," I said, meeting her gaze.

"There is when one eye stares at your boobs and the other at your crotch."

"Okay, okay." Kera uttered a chuckle. "Number three. A man who thinks quality time is a quickie during commercials."

I lifted my orange juice in salute. "Hear, hear."

"Number four." Mel folded her arms over her stomach. "A man who tells you he can't go out in daylight with you because he's too sensitive to the sunlight, but later you find out he only said that because he's married with four children and—"

"Whoa, there. Rein it in," I said on a laugh. She was growling with the force of her increasing fury. I eased back in my seat and propped the notepad in my lap. "I think *lying bastard* will cover number four."

She drew in a deep breath, then another. More calmly, she said, "With this year's crop, I think we need to add men who belch and scratch in public. And never shave! I hate the way beard stubble burns my cheeks."

"Excellent," I said, writing in her requirements. But I have to admit, I kind of like the feel of beard stubble. Okay, I *really* like to feel a man's stubble. It makes for some delicious friction. Maybe I'd cross that one out when I was alone.

"What about a man who can't listen?" Kera glanced around the table, waiting for nods of approval.

"That works for me," Mel said. "I once dated a man who fell asleep every time I opened my mouth. Well, unless I was using my mouth to—"

"We get the picture, and it's a bit too vivid." Kera shook her head and rolled her eyes.

Mel shrugged. "Your loss. What number are we on?"

My gaze scrolled down the list. "Seven. I've got it covered, though. A man who thinks the perfect birthday present is allowing you to put the dishes off for a day."

Both women stared over at me with wide eyes. A tinkling laugh escaped from Mel's lips. How could such an angelic sound come from such a devilish woman? "You're kidding, right?" she demanded.

"I wish."

"Did Richard the Bastard give you that extra special gem of a gift?"

"On more than one birthday."

"How has that man's karma not killed him?" Scowling, she pounded her fist on the tabletop, causing glasses to shake and juice to splatter. "In Naomi's honor, I say we add any man whose name begins with *R*."

That eliminated Royce, I thought happily. I was *not* upset. Really. "I second that," I said, adding it to the list, circling it and putting three stars beside it.

"I third." Kera tapped her chin with a manicured finger. "I also say we add a man who refuses to wear a condom because it inhibits his pleasure."

"Oh, that's good. That's very good." I gave the list another glance. "Okay," I said, "we need one more requirement, then we'll have ten." When no one answered, I said, "What's it gonna be, girls?"

Mel jumped up. I could practically see the light-bulb shining over her head. "I know! A man who leaves you unsatisfied in bed, concerned only with his own orgasm."

I smiled. "Well, I do believe we've just eliminated every man on the planet earth."

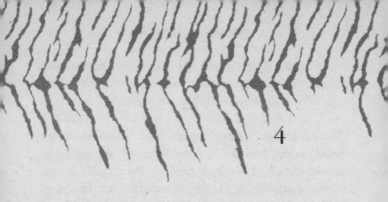

4

*A Tigress marks her territory and cuts down any-
one who dares enter. Poachers must learn the error
of their ways or they will continue to enter the forbidden land, hoping to find a wounded cat to en-
slave. Fight. Never give an inch.*

THE RESONANT VIBRATO of the doorbell sounded, cap-
turing my attention.

Who could that be? Because I'd agreed not to take
on any new clients, I had nothing to do for the rest
of the day and had decided to work out to my favorite
T-Tapp DVD (I hoped to build some muscle tone), so
was dressed in cutoff shorts and a sports bra.

Frowning, I padded across the shiny wood floor. I
didn't want to deal with guests.

The bell sounded again. And again. And again. My

frown became a scowl. Did people really think ringing the bell over and over like that would make me open the door faster? All it did was irritate the hell out of me.

I glanced through the peephole. When I saw who stood in the hallway, the breath caught in my lungs. I froze. Shit. *Shit!* Royce Powell was here. Visiting me.

"Oh, my God," I gasped out, hand tightening on the doorknob. What was he doing here? I looked horrible. No makeup. Hair a wreck. "Shit."

He rang the doorbell again, but I didn't open the door. I'd let him think I was gone. Yes, I decided, nodding. That was a good plan. He'd go away.

"I know you're there, Naomi," he said on a laugh. "Open the door, you little potty mouth."

I ducked away from the peephole, realized what I'd done and straightened. He could hear me, but he couldn't see me. I gazed through the hole again and gulped. Had he appeared so rugged and sexy the last time I'd seen him?

A shiver stole over me, and I forced myself to think of a turkey-and-cheese on rye. My diversion tactic didn't work. A hard knot formed in my throat, even as a delicious warmth spread through my stomach.

How pathetic was I? Acting like a sex-starved… Hey! I *was* a sex-starved woman and he was total eye candy, so I had every right to lust after him. All it meant was that I was a normal, healthy woman. Nothing to be ashamed of. Nothing to get in a panic over. I straightened my shoulders. What did it matter if he saw me looking my worst? Seeing disgust in his eyes as he looked at me might do me some good, help rid me of my growing obsession with him. At least I didn't have dirt on my face this time.

I pasted on a false smile and opened the door. The scent of man and sandalwood instantly wafted to my nostrils. My eyes gobbled him up. Royce wore a dark blue suit that probably cost more than I made in a year. No predictable tie hung from his neck. Instead, the top two buttons of his shirt were open, revealing a small patch of dark, bronzed skin.

A casual appearance, really, on any man except Royce.

His midnight brows winged in amusement. "Do I pass inspection?"

That hard knot of embarrassment fell from my throat and into my stomach, obliterating all hint of tingling warmth. "I wasn't staring at you," I said, scouring my mind for a plausible explanation. "I was lost in thought about something completely unrelated to you." *Genius, Naomi. You idiot.*

His eyes gleamed bright and he coughed. Hoping to cover a laugh? "I see."

I scowled. "How did you get my address? And what are you doing here? Our meeting isn't today."

His gave a casual shrug. "It's not hard to find someone these days, and my schedule cleared. I'm not due back in the office until tomorrow and thought we could spend the day together, as promised. Talk business." With a pointed stare, he asked, "Are you going to invite me in?"

Royce. Inside my home. Alone. With me. A resounding *No!* almost roared past my lips. I bit it back. There wasn't a polite way to refuse him.

Damn it.

"Fine. Whatever." I sighed, letting him know—discreetly, of course—that I wasn't exactly pleased with the idea.

A wide smile lit his face. "Well, which is it? Your tone says no but your lips say yes."

It didn't bode well for either of us that I wanted to strangle him and de-pants him at the same time. In lieu of an answer, I stepped back, allowing him to breeze past me. It was only then, as his body brushed innocently against mine, that I realized my nipples were hard. Really hard. As in, could-poke-his-eyes-out hard. And because of my sports bra, he would have to be blind not to notice.

Royce wasn't blind.

I barely managed to stop myself from cursing. I slapped my hands over my breasts as if the desperate action could make me magically disappear. "I'm not dressed properly."

It was such an obvious statement, I expected him to give a flippant "no shit" reply.

Instead, he turned and flashed me another wicked grin. "I noticed. Don't change on my account." His eyebrows wiggled suggestively in a way that would have made me laugh in a different situation. "I like you this way."

Then his gaze turned bold and assessing, and my heart hammered in my chest as if a little elf had suddenly decided to use the organ for drum practice. Royce didn't look disgusted by my appearance as I'd hoped—and dreaded, I admit. No, he truly did look admiring.

My knees almost collapsed. "I'll just be a moment," I muttered, pivoting. I paused. With my back to him—I didn't have the courage to face him again—I motioned to the left with a wave of my hand. "Have a seat in the living room."

A light pad of footsteps echoed behind me as I stomped to my room. I peeled off the spandex and shorts, letting the ultra-tight material sink to the floor. As fast as my hands could work, I pulled on a pair of black slacks and a tailored white blouse.

I anchored the long length of my dark hair in a tight, no-nonsense twist. As a lowly party planner/former doormat, I wasn't generally seen as a serious entrepreneur, so I used every trick I knew to make myself appear stern and unbending.

My gaze scanned my room, searching for my black shoes. I only had one pair, and at the moment, they were nowhere to be seen. I darted about, furthering my search. After a few minutes, I gave up. I didn't like leaving Royce unsupervised, and I refused to wear brown shoes with black pants. A fashion diva I wasn't, but even I had standards. I'd go barefoot. At least my toes were painted a pretty metallic blue. Yes, blue. I'm not the pink-polish kind of girl.

I headed back into the living room, not ready to face my nemesis but knowing I had no other choice.

"Royce," I said, my tone just as no-nonsense as my hair. He was seated on the couch, looking decadent against the red satin pillows. I claimed the chair across from him. "I don't mean to be rude, but you shouldn't be here. This is my home, not my place of business. Besides, our appointment is scheduled for tomorrow."

He leaned back in a carefree pose, watching me, studying. "I decided to change it."

No, no, no, I thought, *I won't have any of that Triple C behavior in my house.* "You can't just change your mind at whim," I told him, exasperated. "What if I had other plans today?"

"Do you?"

Not wanting to answer, I glanced away. My eyes focused on the Mr. Wrong list sitting mere inches from Royce's view. Crap! Had he read it? My cheeks heated at the thought.

"Well?" he asked.

"Well, what?" What I really wanted to say was "If you read that list I'm going to flay the skin from your bones and feed your organs to my neighbor's cat."

"Do you have plans today?" he asked again.

"Yes." *No.*

"Try again, T-Tapp. You planned to stay in, admit it."

I uttered a soft growl. "It doesn't matter if I did or didn't. Our appointment is tomorrow."

"I know, and I'm sorry." His relaxed stance never wavered. He looked as if he had every right to lounge on my couch like a king expecting his every sensual command to be heeded. "I spent the last two weeks trying to work a deal that never panned out, and I'm on edge. I thought spending the day with you would help wind me down."

Wind him down? What, was I so boring that being with me acted as a sedative? "You could have called first," I said sweetly. Okay, I had grumbled, and I wasn't sweet about it. "A little warning would have gone a long way."

He chuckled. "Your enthusiasm is touching. It really is. I don't think I've ever felt so welcome."

"I'm sorry," I said on a sigh. I really needed to show this man I possessed *some* professionalism. So far, he'd only seen my worst.

"You were desperate to go over your list of questions last time we were together, so I assumed you'd be happy to see me." He rose from the couch, closed the distance between us in three quick strides and knelt at my feet. Suddenly we were eye to eye.

I straightened in my seat. Red alert! *Turkey on rye. Turkey on rye.*

He clasped my chin in his deliciously calloused hands and tilted my head up. "Your schedule is clear, Naomi, and so is mine. I didn't think it would be a problem. If you want me to leave, tell me to leave and I'm gone."

Up close, he was even more handsome. Bright blue eyes that were flecked with ribbons of darker indigo. Lush, soft lips that would look even better attached to my body. Long, spiky lashes that cast shadows on his cheeks, blending with his slight beard stubble. My defenses melted. Client? Who cared. Triple C? Bring 'em on. Royce just, well, he smelled so good. So masculine.

A deep, primal part of me responded to him, wanted

more of him. A part of me *did* miss the touch of a man, the kissing and the tasting. The heat and the passion.

No, I didn't want him to leave.

I cleared my throat. "You're the boss, right? If you want to work today, we'll work today." Jerking from his touch before I did something stupid like jump into his arms and demand he find my nearest G-spot, I swiftly maneuvered to my feet.

"Let's go to the kitchen," I said. The dangerously small width of air that separated us wasn't nearly enough for my peace of mind. "Would you like something to drink?" I didn't wait for his answer. I just strode away, forcing him to follow or be left alone.

He followed.

Once the kitchen counter stood between us, I felt myself begin to relax, regain control. Even when he sat at the bar stool, watching me, filling me with an achiness I didn't want to acknowledge, I didn't lose my calm.

I concentrated on rifling through the drawer stuffed with miscellaneous items. When I found a blank notebook, I set it in front of me, almost as a shield.

"As you mentioned, I do have a list of questions—"

He cut me off. "Why don't you sit over here?" He gave the stool beside him a pat. When I didn't move, just blinked over at him, he added, "That way I won't have to strain to hear you."

"Your hearing is fine."

"What was that?" he asked, cupping his hand over his ear.

"I said your hearing is fine."

"Speak a little louder." He was clearly struggling not to grin. "I can't hear you."

I regarded him for a long, silent moment. "You are such a faker," I uttered on a sigh, dragging my feet to the chair, making sure our knees didn't touch. Making sure no part of us touched, for that matter. I scooted back as far as I could go. Why he wanted me to sit by him, I didn't know. Was he just trying to be friendly? Did he hope to relax me? Was he attracted to me?

I cleared my throat. "Question one…"

He didn't cut me off this time. Oh no. My words simply tapered off, lingering unfinished in the air as he leaned over, diminishing the distance between us. He sniffed the air at my neck.

"What are you doing?" I asked, hating the breathless quality that had entered my voice.

Instead of answering, he asked a question of his own. "What's that smell?"

I froze. What? Did I really smell so distasteful he had only to lean in my direction to catch a putrid whiff of me? I stayed the urge to break his freaking nose for pointing out my stinkiness.

He sniffed again. "I can't place it."

"How bad is it?" I asked, my cheeks heating.

"It's good. Some kind of flower."

My first thought: Hurray! I don't stink.

My second: Ohmygod!

Was he making a pass at me? Cranky, bitter little me? Yes, had to be. Excitement unfurled through my veins—not that I'd acknowledge it. This was shocking, really. Maybe my hooker lips truly were irresistible. Maybe—

Wait. Hold everything. I was studying Royce's features. They were blank, no hint of a leer. No hint of desire. Only curiosity. I must have misread his intentions. My (unacknowledged) excitement died a slow death. According to the *Tattler*, he might have a girlfriend. Gwendolyn Summers, to be exact. Of course he wasn't hitting on me.

"Does the perfume have a name?" he asked.

"I'm not wearing perfume. You either smell my shampoo or my deodorant." I bit my lip as soon as the last word left my mouth. Maybe saying he smelled my deodorant was tantamount to telling him he smelled my BO.

The notebook balanced on my knees plopped to the ground, providing a much needed distraction. I bent down and picked it up, never once looking at him as I settled back into place. I clutched the notebook to my chest. "Okay, let's get to question one."

"Your eyes are silver," he said suddenly, as if the color were some kind of surprise. "A liquid silver, really."

I gulped, hard. Shook my head. Okay, what the hell was going on here? One minute it seemed like he was hitting on me, the next it didn't and the next it did again. Was he or wasn't he? "They're gray," I finally responded.

"They're beautiful."

"Thank you," I said, my heart skipping a beat.

Turkey on rye. "Now, question one. How many guests do you plan to invite to your mother's party?"

He watched me silently for several seconds and must have decided I'd cut off his most precious appendage if he uttered another compliment, because he shrugged and said, "Fifty. Maybe a hundred or two."

"Well, that certainly narrows it down, doesn't it?" I replied dryly, making a notation. "I'll need a list of each individual name and address."

"How soon do you need it?"

"Sometime within the next few days would be great. You know," I said as a thought occurred to me, "once we go over the details, should I call your mom for approval of our choices?"

"Absolutely not." His tone was firm, unbending. "She'll second-guess everything."

"Technically, she *is* the one who hired me."

"I *tried* to hire you, but you never returned my calls. More than that, I'm the one paying you."

I ignored the censure in his tone about the unreturned calls. "That's good enough for me. She'll never hear a peep from me." Moving on. "Is there a specific caterer you'd prefer?"

"No. Whoever you normally use will be fine."

"Excellent." Deep breath. Let it out. We had a nice business rhythm going, those trickles of sexual attraction dissolved. I'd ask Kera to cater the party on the condition she use only the food items I approved. Which meant nothing exotic would be on the menu. "What about decorations? Will your mom want something simple, elegant or traditional party style?"

He rubbed his temple and sighed. "Elegant, most likely."

That had been my guess, though sometimes clients surprised me. I once planned a bachelorette party for a seventy-three-year-old woman. She'd wanted strippers, condom hats and zucchini trays. "Is there a particular symbol or theme she prefers? Anything she collects? Loves?"

"Jewelry. She can't get enough of it."

I paused, pen poised over notepad, as images drifted through my mind. "You know, I could make the location look like a jewelry box." Last time I'd shopped for decorations, I'd seen giant faux diamond rings. They would make excellent centerpieces.

Royce's dark brows arched, hiding under the inky fall of hair on his forehead. "You can do that? Really?"

"I can do whatever you want."

His eyes flashed with sudden heat, and I kicked myself for uttering such a suggestive comment. Any man would have reacted to it. It wasn't *me*.

"Let's leave the decorations open for right now," he said. "While I like the jewelry box idea, I'm not one-hundred-percent sold on it yet."

I nodded, making another notation. I really, really wanted this party to be my best ever. Something people would remember and talk about for months afterward. I tapped the pen on my bottom lip and said, "All right, next on the list is location." Another tap. "Have you decided where you'd like the party to be located?"

He didn't answer.

Another tap. "Royce?" I looked up and my tapping

stilled. His gaze was fastened on my mouth. Had the pen left a smudge? Was a crumb from breakfast hovering on the edge of my lips? My tongue slipped out to wipe away whatever it was. No taste of ink. No crumbs.

His eyes flashed with blue fire again.

Maybe…maybe it had nothing to do with ink or crumbs. Maybe Mel had been right before, and he wanted my hooker lips all over him. I inhaled a shaky breath, pretending the strange heat growing inside me didn't exist.

He started leaning toward me. Closer. Closer still. He's probably dating that supermodel, I reminded myself. "Royce?" I asked again, a bit hoarse. Where was my inner Tigress when I needed her to claw out a man's eyes? Surely I hadn't caged her and thrown away the key. "Royce."

He blinked, but didn't remove his gaze from my mouth. "Yes?"

"Have you decided where you'd like the party to be located?"

When he still didn't answer, when he tried to close the space between us a second time, I said, "Royce!" I snapped my fingers in front of his face. "You need to stop that."

"What?" He paused.

"Staring. It makes me uncomfortable."

"Sorry," he grumbled, at last removing his gaze and directing it over my head. "Just for the record, I wasn't staring. I was thinking about something totally unrelated to you."

My mouth fell open. He was lying, just like I'd lied to him earlier. That meant… Good Lord, that meant he'd almost kissed me. My nipples hardened at the thought, and I had to clear my throat. What about his supposed girlfriend, the whore of Babylon? Was he hoping to cheat on her with me? To have a fling with me, then marry the girl he found worthy of him? Bastard!

My fingers tightened around the pen, nearly snapping it in two. "Have you thought about where you want to hold the party?" The words emerged clipped, layered with a hint of anger.

"No," he said, seeming a little surprised by my vehemence, "I haven't."

Great. With this type of *help,* the party was sure to be a success. "There are several places I've used before. I'm positive you'll find one of them satisfactory."

"I'm sure I will."

"Give me just a moment," I said, jolting up. "I've already made a list. It's in my room."

My steps hurried, I sailed to my bedroom and rooted inside my briefcase. After finding what I needed, I rushed back into the kitchen and plopped onto my seat. One by one I tapped off the names listed.

"The botanical gardens."

He shook his head. "No."

"The Mansion on Turtle Creek."

"No."

"Omni at Park West."

"No."

"The Adolphus."

"No."

"The Hilton. The Hyatt Regency. Four Seasons."

"No. No. No."

My jaw clenched so tightly I felt the burn all the way to my teeth. "None of these places will work?"

Again, "No."

Why the hell not?

"If you'll put together a list of places *you* find suitable—" damn him "—I'll visit each one and let you know which will work for a party the size you're planning." Not that I knew what size party it was going to be with an answer like *Maybe fifty, or a hundred or two.*

"Then," I finished, "I'll put together another list, as well, and we can compare."

"Sounds good." He paused and studied me, his eyes blank, giving no hint of his thoughts. "I have a question for you now."

I almost shuddered. The last time he'd asked me a question in that tone, I'd had to promise to turn other clients away. "Shoot."

"What's your home number?"

I frowned. "I keep my business and private life separate. It's the reason my home number isn't listed on my card. My cell phone is always turned on during business hours."

When he remained silent, I added, "There's no reason for you to have access to my personal line."

"I disagree. Since I'm paying triple your normal

rate, I expect you to be at my beck and call. If I need you to look at a potential location at four in the morning, I want to be able to get a hold of you."

The only place I could think of that was open at four in the morning and equipped for a party was the all-nude, all-the-time strip club a few streets over. "Very well," I answered, even though I knew a true Tigress wouldn't have acquiesced so easily.

Just because I gave in didn't mean I did it grace-fully, though. With jerky movements, I wrote down the required number and shoved the pad and pen at him. "I'll need your home number as well. Just in case I need to get a hold of you at four in the morning," I added with a false, bite-me smile.

He didn't balk as I expected—but then, when did he ever? He grinned as if I'd given him exactly what he wanted and plucked the pen from my hand. His fingertips brushed my knuckles. Slivers of sexual awareness pulsed the length of my arm and sparked electric currents through my veins.

He didn't seem the least affected by the touch, I noted irritably.

"This is a direct line." He tore the bottom half of the page from the notebook and handed it to me. "You can reach me without having to go through Ms. Carroll."

"Who?"

"My assistant."

Ah, Elvira, Mistress of the Dark. I almost French-kissed the number. "Thank you."

"You're welcome." He scanned the paper I'd

handed him, nodded and tucked the sheet of paper in his jacket pocket. "Any other details we need to go over right now?"

"No." Now he would leave, I thought, and wanted to jump and shout with joy. Okay, that was a lie. I *still* wasn't ready for him to leave—even though he might have a *girlfriend*. He was fun to talk to, with a dry sense of humor I enjoyed. Plus, I liked looking at him.

"Good." He stood, took my hand and tugged me to my feet. "Now that business is over, let's get something to eat. I'm starved. Do you like Chinese? We can call in an order and have it delivered."

"Eat?" With Royce? Here? Alone? My stomach growled at the same time an ache throbbed between my legs. A *yes* from my stomach and a *yes* from my libido. "No." From my common sense. We could sit and chat, but a meal provided a sense of intimacy I knew I wasn't ready for. "No, thank you. I don't think that's a good idea," I said with a bit more force than necessary.

At least a small part of me recalled my rules.

Royce was so close I feared he might hear the wild rhythm of my heart. He grinned. "I heard your stomach growl. If you were any hungrier, I'd worry you were about to gnaw off my arm."

"You're hard of hearing, remember? My stomach did *not* growl. Your ears must have been ringing because of your inner-ear problem. And just so you know, I had a big breakfast." As a preventive measure, I eased out of his grasp and shifted out of reach.

"Really big." My stomach chose that moment to growl again. "So big I may not be able to eat ever again."

He crossed his arms over his chest, causing his shirt to tighten over his well-defined, corded muscles. Holy Lord, he had the body of a Trojan warrior. I shivered. I'd always felt small around men. Now, standing in front of Royce, that feeling jumped to the next level. I felt as if I were a tiny speck consumed by the raw power he emitted. We weren't touching, yet his broad shoulders all but surrounded me.

"Either you don't like Chinese or you're pretending not to be hungry so you won't have to eat with me." His voice dropped to that husky whisper. His eyelids lowered to half-mast. "Which is it?"

"I don't like Chinese?" I hadn't meant to phrase it as a question.

"Then we can cook something here."

I gulped back my panic. "I don't like home cooking, either. It upsets my stomach."

His brows arched. "If I asked you to have drinks with me, you'd say…"

"I don't drink. Alcohol makes me loopy."

"I was referring to water."

"I'm allergic. Besides, I have a ton of stuff to do."

"Like what?"

"Just stuff. Lots and lots of stuff."

His eyes narrowed. I watched a strange, unreadable light enter them, giving the blue a deep, greenish hue that seized attention. He surprised me by stepping toward me, leaning down and whispering in my ear, "I think you're afraid I plan to kiss you."

Royce's words rocked my already shaky composure. "Do you?" I asked on a wispy catch of breath, my gaze searching his.

He slowly smiled. "Yes. I do."

Ohmygod. Thinking that he desired me was completely different from actually hearing him admit it. Different and horrible and heady and mind-boggling and amazing. That delicious heat sprang to life again and my mind instantly recognized it as dangerous. *Fight it. Fight it, damn you.*

"What about your girlfriend?" I gulped.

He frowned. "I don't have a girlfriend."

"Gwendolyn Summers," I reminded him.

He waved away my words. "A friend, nothing more. Now *you*, I'd like to be more."

My stupid, dumb-ass knees weakened. He didn't have a girlfriend…he wanted me to be more than a friend…he wanted to kiss me. All of that combined had my equally dumb-ass hormones screaming for a taste of him.

"Now," he said, his voice dropping to that husky whisper, "about that kiss."

"I've already made a list of why we shouldn't," I rushed out, then cringed, realizing I'd just admitted to pondering such an event. Conclusion: all of me is a dumb-ass.

His features lit; obviously he'd caught the implication of my words. "What's reason number one?"

"We work together."

"So do lots of couples," he said. "Two?"

"It wouldn't be wise."

"The best things in life never are. Three?"

"I'm not interested in getting involved with you or anyone else right now." Rotten, rotten lie. I wanted to get naked with him ASAP, and that was pretty involved, to my way of thinking.

"I don't believe you," he said.

Smart man. "Believe what you want. That doesn't change the facts. I don't want you. I never will."

"You're lying again," he said in a singsong voice. "I can tell."

My mouth dropped open and I gazed up at him with incredulity. "You can't tell. There's no way you can tell."

He ignored me. "Let's make a new list, hmm?" He leaned toward me and his breath caressed the sensitive hollow of my cheek.

My knees weakened again. I would have stepped away from him, but I would have fallen. "About what?"

"Exactly why we *should* kiss. I'll help you with reason number one."

I barely had time to register the fact that Royce's mouth was descending to mine before he was there, kissing me. Slowly at first, simply exploring and testing. His tongue brushing mine, rolling over it, pushing against it. He tasted so freaking good, like heat and man and something all his own.

Of their own will, my arms skidded up his incredibly strong, corded-with-muscles chest and anchored around his neck. My fingers inched into his silky hair. The world around me faded. I knew only the heady throb working through my body, pooling between my legs. Had the good Lord suddenly summoned me to heaven? I wondered, dazed. How else would I have reached the corridors of paradise so quickly?

"Your lips are softer than I imagined," he said, low and husky.

"You imagined them?" I couldn't help but ask.

"A thousand times these past two weeks. A thousand more if you count the last—" He stopped.

"The last what?" Snared by his sensual appeal as I was, I nuzzled his nose with mine, breathing in his scent, absorbing his heat. I couldn't force myself to move away.

"Nothing." His tongue swept inside my mouth as his arms caressed their way down my waist, locking me in place, arching my hips forward. When I liquefied against him, his grip tightened, held me up and let me sink even deeper into his embrace.

"Oh, my God," I said as his erection rubbed against me.

"No. Royce."

The kiss gained speed, going from sultry to wild in mere seconds. I moaned. My nipples—my ever traitorous nipples—hardened and I meshed them into his chest. The strength and warmth of Royce radiated from his clothing and nearly singed every inch of my body.

It had been so long since I'd been kissed. *So damn long.* But never like this. Never with this intense yearning for more. This need. The past six months had been difficult, and at times, lonely, but I had coped, had thought I'd properly insulated myself against man's dangerous allure.

Now I wondered why I'd so stubbornly fought my hormones.

Royce's mouth continued to take possession of mine. One of his hands tangled in my hair, the other gripped my butt and pulled me deep, deep into the hard length of his erection. My excitement expanded, nearing the point of eruption, and my breathing became shallow, erratic.

"Oh, my Royce," I breathed with a smile.

He chuckled against my mouth. The slight pause in our kiss nearly caused me to scream in frustration. No more teasing, no more joking. I ground myself against him, worked his tongue with mine.

He licked and nipped, and his beard stubble tickled me, sending delicious sensations down my spine. "Next time I promise to shave," he said, his breath fanning my skin.

I didn't know why he thought he needed to shave, but Lord, I hoped he didn't.

He groaned low in his throat. "I meant to go slow with you. Damn it, I'm *going* to go slow if it kills me." He sucked in an uneven breath before his lips found mine again, slow and gentle this time. Reverent. Worshipping.

This was a kiss of promise, the kind women dreamed about, but rarely experienced. I'd never experienced it, that was for sure, and it scared me. He suddenly tasted like turkey and cheese on hated rye.

I cupped his jaw and pulled away. My semi-panicked gaze searched his face. I saw passion, tenderness and growing concern.

"Is something wrong, sweetheart?"

My eyes widened. Sweetheart. He'd freaking called me *sweetheart*. A cold sweat broke out all over my body. Why would he call me sweetheart, unless... "I didn't fill out an application," I said, my voice trembling.

A blank screen suddenly shuttered over his eyes. A silent moment ticked by, then another. He stepped away from my touch and crossed his arms over his chest. He was going for a pose of casual disregard, but a bead of sweat trickled from his temple, ruining the effect. Too, the lines around his mouth were taut. Desire still held him in its clasp.

"That's good," he said, no emotion in his voice. "I didn't ask you to."

A shudder, this one having nothing to do with desire, racked me. He didn't want me to fill the damn thing out because—I could only guess at the answer, and I didn't like it. Either he viewed me as so far beneath him I was non-bridal material, which offended me in an ironic sort of way, or he already knew he wanted a commitment from me.

Commitment...just the word made me want to vomit. Commitment with a client—I think I really did throw up in my mouth a little. Being tied down to someone wasn't what bothered me. It was the thought of being tied to someone who would one day treat me badly, one day lose all interest in me, one day stop loving me.

One day make me feel like I was worth less than garbage.

Richard had treated me very well in the beginning of our relationship. He'd catered to my every need. He'd done everything in his power to ensure my happiness. How quickly that had faded once he had me tied to him.

Maybe I was assuming too much here, though. Maybe Royce called every woman sweetheart. Maybe he didn't see me as bride material, but as the perfect candidate for some sort of bizarre sexual ritual he'd picked up on his many travels. A ritual I was perfectly willing to experience.

Wasn't I? I was so confused at the moment.

"What do you want from me?" I asked softly.

He gave no reply. But a muscle ticked in his jaw, I noticed.

"You're a handsome man, Royce, and you have money. You can have any woman you want. Why make them fill out applications? Are you that desperate to get married?"

The ticking branched to his eyes. Combined with the fury now flickering in his gaze, it made him appear truly menacing. A man who made his enemies tremble with fear and his lovers shiver with desire. "That's not your concern, Naomi." Pause. "Is it?"

Undeterred, I persisted. "A new reality show? You wanted to build a portfolio of naked pictures? You're tired of online dating?"

Silence. Heavy, stilted silence.

Finally, watching me all the while, he said, "Maybe it was forced on me. Maybe I offered up a challenge— think you know so much about what I need, then find me the perfect girl—and someone took the initiative. Maybe, when the applications started pouring in, I realized I'm getting older and I've never been in love. Maybe," he ended in a quiet tone, "I saw my chance."

My blood alternately turned hot and cold. Even if he hadn't liked the situation at first, he'd just admitted he was seriously considering those stupid applications now. That he *was* looking for a wife. "So you really mean to do it? You really mean to choose a bride?"

He shrugged. "Maybe. Maybe not."

I gulped. "Either way, I'm not the one for you." My head fell forward and I stared down at my hands. "I don't want your love or a ring. And I—" *Come on. Just say it.* "And I don't want your kisses."

His expression darkened, and his lips edged into a fierce frown. "I don't recall asking for your love or your hand in marriage."

Ouch. "I've been in love before," I explained, to ease the sting of my words. "I didn't like it."

He reached out slowly, giving me every opportunity to run away. Stupid me, I didn't. One more touch would be okay. I could handle one more touch. His fingers closed around my wrists gently and tugged, maneuvering me back into a kissable position.

"I liked the taste of you," he said. "A lot." He trailed feathery kisses along the length of my jaw and I liquefied again. Even my Tigress purred her enjoyment. He licked the seam of my lips. "And I think you liked the taste of me. A lot."

A sharp lance of desire warred with a cold knot of regret. "No," I forced myself to say. "No."

He looked disbelieving and aroused and oh, so tempting all at once. "Yes," he said quietly. "You want my kisses."

"Despite what you said, I think you want more than a kiss. I can't give more." Each point of contact between us sent heated blood pounding through my veins like an awakened river.

Thankfully he dropped his arms to his side and shoved both of his hands into his pockets. "You wanted to give me more. I felt how your body responded. Another minute or two and we would have been on the floor, naked."

I didn't refute it. Couldn't, for that matter. He would have seen the lie in my eyes had I tried. Desire this intense couldn't be hidden, and I knew it. "So what?" I said, suddenly defensive. "A girl has the right to change her mind."

"You're right," he said, using that quiet tone again. "A girl can change her mind."

Smart, smart man. Diabolical, but smart. He'd just issued an invitation I had trouble resisting: change your mind again and kiss me.

"I'm sorry." I swallowed, forcing the words out. "I'm truly sorry I let things get out of hand. I am not a tease, really." I twisted the hem of my shirt between unsteady fingers. "I'm not sure what happened to me; I've never acted like this before."

He pushed a hand through his hair, his body relaxing. "Finally, words I like."

I frowned. "What does that mean?"

His lips inched up in a smug, half grin. "Figure it

out. If you've never acted this way before, it means I'm the only man—"

I slapped a hand over his mouth, cutting off his words. Damn me and my big mouth. Why not just admit I was desperate for him, too, while I was at it?

He pried my hand from his face and I saw he was still grinning. His fingers curled around mine, squeezed, then released me. "If I did it once, you can damn well count on me doing it again."

I felt the color drain from my face. He was right. Shit, he was right. Before I had time to work up a good panic, he added, "Get used to the idea of me kissing you, Naomi. Looks like it's inevitable."

"Wanna bet?" my Tigress growled before I could stop her. Well, well, well. She'd finally decided to do something besides purr.

Challenge gleamed in Royce's eyes. "You enjoy losing, Naomi?"

"I wouldn't know," I said with bravado. "I've never lost."

A wicked glint lit his eyes. "Well, sweetheart, I'll try to make your first experience as pleasurable as possible for you." His sultry threat rang in my ears long after he strode away and slammed the door.

5

A Tigress eats, sleeps and breathes power, for it is power alone that sustains her. In the jungle of life, it is kill or be killed. Surprise attack if you must, but kill. Always.

AS IF MY DAY COULDN'T GET any more surreal—Royce Powell desired me, for God's sake—I later found myself blindfolded. And not for any type of kinky love play. Kera and Mel had arrived at my apartment and ushered me into the living room, where I'd been commanded to stay until given permission to leave.

I had refused to obey, of course. So they'd wrestled me to the ground like little monkeys, tied my arms behind my back, blindfolded me and led me to the couch. Here I sat. And sat. For half an hour, at least. With every little noise—was that a fire I heard crackling, or Twinkie wrappers?—my curiosity increased.

"What are you doing in there?"

Kera: "You'll see."

Mel: "If you ask one more time, I'll leave you tied up and give Royce Powell a call. Maybe he can come over and rescue you."

She'd do it, too. I scowled, deciding then and there not to tell them about Royce's impromptu visit and the earth-shattering kiss he'd planted on me—or my own involvement in said kiss. That would only increase their desire to phone the man.

"You have to let me go," I said. "I'm starved. Famished. Practically comatose. I'm on the verge of death here."

They laughed, the evil wenches.

"If you die, can I have your bed?" Mel asked. "You know how I love cherrywood."

"This is my apartment. I have every right to know what you're doing. Notice I didn't ask this time, I simply stated a fact."

Kera: "You'll just have to wait and see."

Mel: "When did you become so impatient?"

"When you two decided to hog-tie and blindfold me and hold me captive while you do God knows what to my apartment."

"Have you ever considered hormone-replacement therapy?" Kera again. "You're a live wire lately."

"Really, Naomi. You're beginning to remind me of Aunt Fredia—after the sex change."

I clamped my lips shut. Everyone knew our aunt Fredia (formerly Uncle Fred) was a real bitch.

Finally, my cousins relented. Mel untied me and I rubbed my wrists.

"You can remove the blindfold now," Kera said.

Without a word, I whipped the material from my eyes. My jaunt into utter darkness was over as sunlight flooded my vision. I blinked, trying to help my poor little ocular lobes adjust.

When they did, I gasped.

"What—" My lips opened and closed as I drank in the sight before me. Colorful streamers dripped from the wall. Crepe paper lined the coffee table, which was piled with multicolored gifts. Glitter sparkled from the wood floor.

"What is this?" I asked, awed.

"A party, of course." Kera grinned at me.

"A party? For me?"

"Yeah. Who else?" Even Mel was smiling. "You're always planning them for everyone else, so we thought it'd be nice to throw one for you."

I really, truly wanted to cry just then. This was the sweetest thing they'd ever done for me. "It's not my birthday," I managed.

"So?" Kera locked tendrils of hair behind her ear. "If we want to have a celebration in your honor, we don't have to wait for your birthday to do it."

"But why?" I asked, still in shock. "I don't understand."

Mel shrugged. "We love you. After hearing about your putting-the-dishes-off birthday present from Richard the Bastard, we wanted to do something special for you."

"Thank you so much." Eyes now completely filled with tears, I hugged them both. "You guys totally rock."

"We even have presents." Kera clapped her hands in excitement.

"Wait till you see the cake!" Jumping into action, Mel ran to the kitchen. Moments later, she returned holding a rocket-shaped cake.

Wait. No. Not a rocket. The cake was shaped like a penis. The flesh-colored frosting gave the cake a very real appearance. I choked down a laugh, then decided what the hell? I laughed until my side hurt.

"Oh, you guys. I love it. This is the best non-birthday party ever." I wiped the moisture from my cheeks. "Did you make the cake, Kera?"

She nodded. "Like I'd order *that* monstrosity from a bakery."

"What do you want to do first?" Mel.

"You have to ask?" Ecstatic, I rubbed my hands together. "I want to open presents. Duh."

"That's what I was hoping you'd say." Mel's giddiness was almost a palpable force. She ushered me to the coffee table. "Open this one first. I want to see your reaction."

Uh-oh.

If Mel was this excited about me unveiling the contents of the box, I shuddered to think what was inside.

Mel confirmed my fears by commanding Kera to grab a camera. Swallowing, I picked up the rectangular box she'd pointed to. Shook it. Heard only a slight shuffling noise.

"Don't be such a weenie," Mel said, biting her lower lip. "Start tearing."

Unable to hold back any longer, I took her advice and tore the wrapping apart. When the box was open, I stared down at a...vibrator? Yes, a giant green vibrator.

And that was only the beginning.

When all the presents were opened and the gifts were strewn around me, I felt like I had somehow been transported to a pleasure palace that had been sneezed on one too many times.

Everything was green.

A green miniskirt. A tight green dress. Green panties (camouflage). Green feathers. Green chains. Hiding my dismay behind a smile, I said, "Are you trying to tell me something here? Like I'm sexually frustrated *and* a bad dresser?"

Mel stared at me dead-on. "You need to take these items and put them to good use. Let loose for once. Just go for it with Royce. I'm telling you that with the right motivation, that man will be panting for you."

She was wrong. He hadn't needed any motivation, and he still wanted me.

"I agree with Mel," Kera said, nodding. "Although it's my hope the relationship will develop into something more than sex."

I still wasn't ready to talk about the kiss, so I said, "You guys—"

"No, don't say anything now," Mel interjected. "You're near death from hunger pains, remember?" She grinned. "Who knows? Maybe the cake will put you in a good mood."

Kera chuckled. "Let's feast."

I nodded, deciding simply to enjoy. Eat now, argue about Royce later. "Okay. But I get the balls!"

6

A Tigress is a predator and by definition a preda-
tor is one that preys and destroys, feeding on oth-
ers to sustain strength. Don't just take a bite of
your opponent. Devour him whole.

THE NEXT AFTERNOON, I strode into Cinderella
Catering. Kera was behind the only desk, looking as
fresh and pretty as a summer bouquet as she spoke
with a customer about appropriate finger foods for an
anniversary party.

I motioned that I'd wait. She nodded, and I claimed
a seat at the couch. I gazed out the shop window,
watching people stroll by. Mainly businessmen and
women, with the occasional hand-holding couple
thrown in the mix. My chest was *not* aching with
jealousy. Nor was I imagining Royce holding my hand.

A few minutes later, Kera and I were alone and she joined me at the sitting area.

"Weren't you supposed to have lunch with Mr. Wonderful today?" she asked.

"His name is Mr. Unacceptable, and we had a change of plans," I said, answering as vaguely as I could. I still hadn't told my cousins I'd met with Royce yesterday instead. After the non-birthday party—and after I'd eaten enough penis cake to give me nightmares for a year—I'd waved them goodbye and rolled myself to bed, intent on forgetting all my troubles.

I hadn't, of course. No, I'd dreamed of Royce. Dreamed of *his* penis (bad Naomi), a flesh-and-blood penis, not sugar-and-vanilla, and all the things I wanted to do to it. All the things I wanted it to do to me.

Sometimes I'm such a naughty girl.

When I'd taken my morning shower, I'd pictured Royce there with me, lathering me with soap. While I dressed, I pictured Royce playfully trying to remove each item. With his teeth. While I ate a bowl of chocolate ice cream for breakfast, I pictured myself eating it off his chest. While I strolled down the sidewalk to this very shop, I pictured him tugging me to a secluded, shadowy corner and ravaging my breath away.

Why was I letting that diabolical, evilly sexy man affect me so strongly? It wasn't as if I'd never been kissed before. It wasn't as if I'd never seen a handsome man before. Uh, hello, I'd watched every Brad Pitt film ever made. Several times each. Who the hell did Royce think he was, anyway, barging into my home, playing a round of tonsil hockey, then storming away with a delicious, I'll-kiss-you-again challenge?

"Lord, I'm so jealous of you," Kera said, a wistful edge in her voice. She drew her knees to her chest, and rested her elbows on them and her cheek on her upraised palm.

"You? Jealous of me? Whatever for?"

"Whatever for?" my cousin repeated, her wistfulness twisting into incredulity. "Because you're working for the most beautiful man in the world, a beautiful man determined to pop the question to a lucky lady in the very near future. *You* have access to him, which gives you the edge. Women everywhere would peel the flesh from your bones and feast on your rotting carcass for a chance like that."

"One, that's gross. Two, there's no edge to being the party planner. I'm the hired help. And three, I'm not going to bore you with all the reasons I gave you before for not wanting to be with him. Reasons that still stand."

"Whatever. I've just never seen you this affected by a man. Your cheeks flush every time his name is mentioned, and your eyes glow. Literally glow. I think Royce could be the one. *Your* one."

I fought the urge to cover my ears. "Don't say that. Not ever again."

"I bet he meets every requirement on the list. The Mr. Right list every woman supposedly has," she added, "and not the Mr. Wrong list we thought up."

I pushed through my growing panic and hurriedly changed the focus of our conversation. "Speaking of Mr. Right, are you still on the lookout for the future Mr. Kera Gellis?"

"Of course," she said, allowing the change without protest. "I even have a prospect in mind."

My back straightened and my brow furrowed. "Who?" If she said Royce, I was going to hurt her. "As of yesterday, you weren't seeing anyone."

"I'm still not. But George Wilben has caught my interest." He was Kera's next-door neighbor and (in my opinion) not the best choice of man for Kera. Not that she was too good for him, but she was a social butterfly and George would never be able to keep up. "He copped a feel this morning."

"Of what?"

Kera's large blue eyes sparkled with mischief. "My butt."

"He didn't!" George looked like the quintessential computer nerd. Glasses. Tall, lanky body. Mussed brown hair that always blocked his vision. The only difference was, George knew nothing about computers. He was an actor for the local community theatre.

Go figure.

"He most certainly did," Kera said, smiling. "He took a squeeze, too. I knew he'd cave in and go for it sooner or later. I feel his gaze on me every time I walk by him."

"We're talking about the guy who hasn't taken off his sweater vest since the great heat wave four years ago, right?"

"That's the one."

"He squeezed your ass? Really?" I still couldn't picture it.

"Well, maybe I turned around and asked him to do it," Kera said with a smile.

I chuckled again. "You're incorrigible, you know that?"

"Absolutely." Kera's grin widened. "Mel must be rubbing off on me." She sighed, losing a little of her humor. "If George doesn't ask me out soon, I'll have to ask *him* out."

"You're *that* interested?"

"Well, yeah. I like the way he looks at me. More than that, I realized that I like the way I feel when he looks at me."

I knew her, knew what she was really saying. She wanted a man who made her feel worshipped. She deserved it; so did every woman, for that matter. Was something like that possible, though? I didn't think so. I'd never seen it. Even the most passionate of marriages usually ended in divorce. The hotter the spark, the quicker it died, right?

With that cheerful thought, I decided it was time to get down to business. "How's your schedule looking for the third weekend in September?" I asked.

"Open, why?"

"I want you to cater Linda Powell's party. I already have Royce's approval."

"Cool." Thoughtful, she twirled a strand of hair around her finger. "You know, in the last six months, I've had more business than my parents ever did. And they ran this place for twenty years."

"It's because you're the best caterer in town." When she wasn't trying new, exotic recipes, that is.

"No." She shook her head. "It's because you send all your customers my way."

"And they love me for it. You've never disappointed." I reached into my briefcase, withdrew three sheets of paper, saw that one was the application packet for Royce's bride, and hurriedly shoved it back inside. Cheeks heating, I handed the correct papers to Kera. "Here's a list of possible themes, as well as a list of acceptable food items. You'll notice the Powells are very adamant in their desire for plain fare," I added quickly.

Her features fell, giving her expression a cute little pout. "Are you sure? I've got a new recipe—"

"I'm sure!"

She shrugged her shoulders daintily. "There's no accounting for taste," she said, her gaze traveling over the list. "You and Royce are considering going with a jewelry-box theme?"

"Considering, yes. Royce says it's the one thing his mother loves." I paused, hesitant. "Do you like it?"

"No, I don't like it. I love it," she said, making me smile in relief. Her features brightened, illuminating the angelic roundness of her face. "Perhaps I can make hors d'oeuvres that look like necklaces and earrings."

I nodded my approval. "That's the spirit, though we're not one-hundred-percent settled on that theme yet. Give me a couple of days to firm it up."

Kera folded the papers and stuffed them in her apron pocket. "I hate to change the subject back to the one you want to avoid, but I'm dying to ask. Have you filled out an application to become Mrs. Royce Powell yet?"

"No." I glanced away from her. "Of course not."

"Do you plan to?"

"What kind of question is that? Absolutely not."

"Then why do you have one in your bag?"

My cheeks heated so much I might have set off a fire alarm had one been nearby. Damn it, I hadn't wanted anyone to see the application Elvira had given me—but I hadn't had the strength to throw it away. "Royce's assistant gave it to me by mistake, that's all."

Watchful, searching, she made a *tsking* sound under her tongue. "You kept it when you could have thrown it away. Why did you keep it, Naomi?"

As if I wanted to analyze myself that deeply. I didn't know why I was having trouble parting with the stupid thing, and I didn't want to know. The answer might scare me. Perhaps that meant I was the kind of person who pulled the covers over my head if I heard a strange noise in the middle of the night instead of calling 911, but I didn't care.

My cell phone chose that moment to burst forth with a string of high-pitched rings, saving me from having to answer her. God bless technology.

"Hang on a sec," I said, leaning down and unsnapping the front flap of my case. I withdrew my phone and placed it at my ear. "Events by Naomi."

"Where are you?" an angry male voice ground out.

"I tried you at home. Many times. Obviously you weren't there."

Recognition came instantly, as did the tingling surge of excitement. The warm rush of desire. Royce.

"I'm at Cinderella Catering," I told him, commanding my heart rate to slow. "Good news. They've agreed to cater the party."

"What are you doing there? You were supposed to meet me for lunch. Have you forgotten?"

"No." Frowning, I glanced up at Kera, who was watching me with unconcealed interest. "We met yesterday instead. I thought—"

"So don't think. We met yesterday in *addition* to our lunch today. I expect you to be at my office in ten minutes."

"But I—"

"Ten minutes, Naomi."

"Will you just listen to—" I needn't have bothered trying to explain myself. The other line had already clicked, signaling its abrupt disconnection.

My teeth ground together in annoyance, anticipation and disgust at my reaction to simply hearing his voice. I threw the phone back in my briefcase, wishing it were Royce's head so I could toss it to the ground and stomp on it. Maybe even give it a hard kick between the eyes (while wearing steel-toed boots) for good measure.

I liked to think it took great lengths to shatter my composure. (Hey, there's nothing wrong with lying to oneself.) Yet it seemed as if Royce had only to open his mouth and my patience immediately flew out the window. Damn Triple C.

I directed a disgruntled look to my cousin. "I've got to run. Duty calls."

Her features were lit with interest. "Bachelor of the Year?"

"None other," I said with a grimace.

"So you met with him yesterday, hmm?" She crossed her arms over her chest and stared over at me, eyes narrowed. Her lips twitched, ruining her efforts to appear angry.

"Yes. I met with him." I offered no more.

"I don't recall hearing anything about this."

Giving Kera a quick hug, I said, "Should we have your ears tested, then?"

"You better spill the details tonight. Try to clam up and I'll sic Mel on you."

I gave a mock shudder. "What a cruel, cruel woman you're becoming."

"Hey," she said, eyes twinkling with the same wicked glint Mel's sometimes had, "you didn't happen to bring your green handcuffs, did you? Mel will be disappointed if you don't use them soon."

"No, I didn't bring them." Thank God. "I didn't know I'd be seeing Royce today."

"Keep them in your briefcase. That way, you'll always be prepared."

My brows arched as I pretended confusion. "Think I'll need to perform a citizen's arrest for his bad attitude?"

She snorted. "Hello, you can cuff him to his desk and have your naughty way with him."

I had to completely blank my mind before delicious images invaded. Images of Royce lying on his desk and me crawling over him, running my tongue over every inch and hollow. Damn it!

Gathering my composure, I stepped outside, throwing over my shoulder, "I'll see you tonight." As the door closed, I glanced at my wristwatch. I only had nine minutes and five seconds to get to Royce's building.

Realizing it would be faster to cut through the city streets on foot rather than let a cab maneuver through traffic, I raced down the pavement. My slightly heeled brown shoes thumped against the ground. The sound echoed loudly in my ears. Why was I rushing around like an idiot?

Jump through the fiery hoop, little kitty, Royce mocked inside my mind.

Can I do it naked? my hormonal doormat responded, while the Tigress in me growled, *Why don't I kill you both, instead?*

Along the way, I rammed into a portly gentleman holding a box of doughnuts. Uttering a hasty apology, I helped him rescue the now dirty pastries, then picked up my bag and hurried on.

I hate, hate, *hate* being late. Always have. I think the need to be on time had been ingrained in me since birth. My mom, who was always late, said I'd arrived two weeks ahead of schedule, that I'd walked and talked early and that I'd begun my terrible twos—whatever that meant—when I was only one.

Knowing each step brought me closer to Royce made my stomach churn with anxiety. It wasn't that I feared he would fire me. Quite the opposite, at this point. All too well I recalled his assurance that he planned to kiss me again.

With twenty-three seconds to spare, I rushed into the chrome-and-glass building and pushed my way through another green-clad crowd of women. I wondered briefly if I was the only one wearing camouflage panties and a green satin bra. Probably not. I wouldn't doubt that some of these women had a tattoo of the Jolly Green Giant.

This time, the guard let me pass without a word. I wanted to stick my tongue out at him and shout, "Ha! Ha!" but refrained. I was a Tigress, not a child. Sometimes. I headed straight for the express elevator.

A resonant chime signaled my arrival to the nineteenth floor. I stepped past the sliding doors, trying to prepare myself for the battle I knew was to come. For strength, I took a deep, fortifying breath. *I'm a Tigress, I'm a Tigress, I'm a Tigress.*

At the front desk, I faced down Royce's assistant. Ms. Carroll, aka Bride of Satan. Elvira's dark brown eyes clawed me like talons, all the more menacing in light of that vampiric complexion.

"I need to see Mr. Powell," I told her, using my most competent tone.

Matte gold lips twisted in feigned affability. "Do you have an actual appointment this time?"

"Yes."

"Well, what do you know?" She smoothed a hand over her perfect hair. "Once again your name isn't on his agenda. Would you care to explain this phenomenon?"

Not again! Why hadn't Royce told her I was expected?

"If you'll let Royce know I'm here," I said, each syllable crisper than the last, "I'm sure he'll be happy to explain this 'phenomenon.'"

"Royce, hmm?" She stood, fingers splayed wide across her desk. "When did you two become so close? Or are you his flavor of the week and I just didn't know it?"

Flavor of the week? I wanted to ask Elvira just how many women she'd seen come and go in Royce's life. The more women, the more he would remind me of my ex. And my dad. And the less tempted I would be by him. I didn't, though. Instead I said, "Just tell him I'm here. Please."

"Go to hell."

My inner Tigress crouched into attack position and I found myself saying, "I have a question for you." I placed my hands on the desk and inched forward. Eye to eye. "Are you jealous because you're three hundred years too old for him or are you simply a spiteful woman?"

"How dare you?" She gasped, my words having pushed her over the edge of tolerance. "I'll have you know I've worked here for six years. You'll be gone soon. Your kind always is. But I'll always be around."

"My kind? Just what the hell is that supposed to mean?"

"Cheap. Easy. And completely forgettable."

Now my Tigress spread her claws and growled low in her throat. I ran my tongue over my teeth and leaned even closer to Elvira. "You actually think he likes your type better? Cold. Evil. And leader of the undead."

"Why you little bitch." Her teeth bared, she flew around the desk, meaning to launch herself on top of me.

I fisted my hands, waiting, readying to strike.

"That's enough, Ms. Carroll," a male voice suddenly boomed.

Elvira stilled abruptly. She blinked, collecting her wits—if she had any, that is. Her pale complexion turned ashy as she backtracked to her desk. I whipped around.

A handsome man in his early thirties faced me. The rich baritone of his voice held an edge of unmistakable steel. With jeans that hugged his hips and a too-tight white T-shirt, he looked rugged and completely out of place in the formal office setting.

"I'm sorry, Mr. Phillips," Elvira said.

Phillips...the name was familiar to me. Wait, wasn't he the one Royce had spoken to on the phone the first day I'd come in? They'd discussed some sort of merger.

Mr. Phillips gave her a look that clearly said, "I'll deal with you later," then turned his attention to me. I applauded anyone who could intimidate the indomitable assistant.

"No need for you to have interfered," I told him. "I had the situation under control. Ms. Carroll wouldn't have hurt me."

"It wasn't *your* life I feared for," he muttered, glancing from Elvira to me. "On behalf of the staff here, I'd like to apologize for what just happened. I promise you, we do not usually act so unprofessionally or physically threaten our guests." His tone became scolding.

Lately I'd been the queen of unprofessional. Elvira had nothing on me.

"Come on." He placed a hand on my lower back and led me to a secluded corner. His gaze raked over me before settling on my lips. I was used to being sized up by businessmen, but I wasn't used to all this blatant attention to my mouth. Most people tried to be discreet.

He grinned slowly, causing his green eyes to crinkle at the corners.

In appearance, his appeal rivaled Royce's. He possessed the same strength, the same inner power, except for some reason this man didn't have any effect on my senses. Why? I mused. Why was that? How could my testosterone immunity be vanquished to the point that I wanted Royce (desperately) but not this equally handsome man? It made no sense.

He held out his hand and we shook, and I was glad to notice I wasn't swampy today. Nor did I experience the electric shock I received every time Royce touched me. "Colin Phillips," he said.

"Naomi Delacroix."

"I know. You're the one driving the big guy crazy." His smile became sheepish, revealing even, white teeth. "It's a pleasure to finally meet you in person."

When he didn't seem inclined to let go of my hand, I gently extracted it from his grasp. "I'm not driving anyone crazy who wasn't already insane."

Colin tilted his chin to the side as he considered my words, amusement in his gaze. He nodded. "Good point." His gaze raked over me once more. "I can see what's had Royce so wrapped up for so long. You've got a classic charm."

My ears perked at that. Not at the compliment, though that was nice. "Wrapped up for so long? How long? Wrapped up in what way?"

He ignored my questions. "I apologize again for Ms. Carroll's rudeness. I'll personally make sure she's let go."

In all honesty, I would have loved to see that bitch punished. However, as much as I hated to admit it, the woman had bills to pay just like I did. I couldn't be responsible for putting another human being in the poorhouse—which begged the question: was she even human? No matter. "It's fine. Really. *I'm* fine."

He chuckled, a warm, rich sound. "Were the situation reversed, she would demand your head on a pike. You realize that, don't you?"

"Actually, I think she'd demand my limbs removed one by one while she watched, but hey, you know her better than I do."

He pressed his lips together to smother another laugh. "I'm sure you don't recall, but we've met—no, *met* isn't the right word. We've been in the same room together. Before today."

A complete switch of topics, but I could handle it. I flipped through my mental files and drew a blank.

He must have read the confusion in my eyes

because he added, "About six months ago. You planned my sister's wedding reception."

"The Phillips-Howard wedding, right?" There, that was much better than saying, *I don't remember seeing you. Ever.* The reception had been the very first event I'd planned on my own, as a business owner. I remembered seeing Royce there, the first time I'd laid eyes on him in person. I'd been newly divorced and my gaze had eaten him up. Many times. He'd been as sexy then as he was now, and I hadn't been immune. But this man… I honestly didn't recall seeing him.

"Yes," he said. "That's the one."

"How is she?" I asked. "Your sister, I mean." Over the past few months, Daisy Phillips—Daisy Howard, I guess she is now—had sent several other clients my way. I was beyond grateful. Hell, I was grateful she'd hired me in the first place. I was an unknown but she'd heard me talking to Kera at Cinderella Catering, had (thankfully) liked what she'd heard and asked me to put a list of ideas together. I did and she signed me on. One of the best days of my life.

"Blissful," he said. "She just found out she's pregnant."

A little pang swept through my chest, but I tamped it down. Once, I'd wanted children. "That's wonderful. Tell her congratulations for me."

"I'll do that." With barely a breath, he added, "Is there something I can help you with, or do you need to see Royce?"

"Royce, I'm afraid. I'm helping with his mother's birthday party." Then, realizing what I'd just admitted, I clamped my lips tight. The party was supposed to be a surprise. Had I just blown it?

Stupid, stupid, stupid.

"Don't worry," Colin said, catching my distress. "I'm on the guest list."

My dismay faded and I grinned. "Thank God."

"Daisy *still* talks about how wonderful you are. So does Royce, for that matter," he muttered.

I blinked. "What was that?"

"Daisy. She sings your praises all the time."

Had he or had he not just said Royce talked about how wonderful I was? I hadn't thought Royce noticed me that night. Not the way a man notices a woman he wants to bed, that is. He sure hadn't acted like it that first day in his office. Yes, he had called me a few times after the reception, but that had been strictly business. Hadn't it?

My chest constricted with…hope? Fear? "You said something else," I insisted. "Something about Royce."

He shook his head. "No, I didn't."

Yes, he had, but I decided to let it slide. I didn't know if I truly wanted to hear the answer.

Perhaps I'd set Mel up with Colin. He seemed nice enough, and she'd go wild for his non-lazy eyes. I thought Kera was more his type, but she was now interested in her neighbor.

Just then, a hard, uncompromising form came up behind me. Two hands anchored on top of my shoulders. I didn't need to see who it was to know. I *felt* who it was, experiencing warm, electrical currents through my entire body.

Royce.

My clothes and skin soaked up the delicious heat of him, the erotic scent of him.

"I said ten minutes, Naomi. Not eleven. Not twelve. You're late." He didn't wait for a reply, just sailed past me and inside his office, forcing me to follow.

"Please tell Daisy I said thank you for all her praise and recommendations," I told Colin over my shoulder. What was wrong with Royce? I didn't understand that man. Not even a little bit. "That means a lot to me."

"You bet," Colin said.

With that, I nodded goodbye, pasted a professional smile on my face and curbed the urge to flip Elvira off as I skipped past her astonished face.

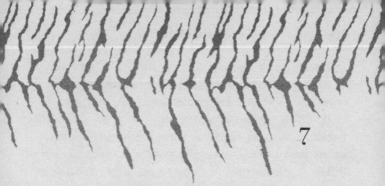

7

Animals of every species sense those who are weaker than themselves. They sense it—and attack. A Tigress must never let down her guard. She must realize danger lurks behind every bush, deep in every shadow and around every corner.

SHAKING WITH THE FORCE of my sudden nervousness, I slowed my pace as I entered Royce's office. Why was I nervous? I thought in the next instant. The man was, well, a man. He wasn't God (as he'd reminded me himself yesterday) or even a superhero. Unless he rescued small children from burning buildings and I just didn't know it. With his Triple C attitude, though, that was highly unlikely. However, I could easily picture him ordering said children to jump out a window, landing mat optional.

Anyway, he didn't decide the fate of my world.

He stood at the bar. Not a flicker of emotion crossed his features as he said, "Have a seat." His tone was stiff. With a wave of his hand, he indicated a chair. Even his motions were stiff.

Watching him warily, I smoothed my skirt and eased down.

He shifted from one foot to the other (stiffly), then poured himself a drink (even more stiffly), downed it (still more stiffly). Poured two more. "Would you care for anything?" Yep, stiff.

"No, thanks." The slightest bit of alcohol always went straight to my head. Probably because of my "delicate bone structure," as my mom would say. Or, as my stepdad would say, because of my "horrendous eating disorder."

"I'll drink yours, then." He gulped back both drinks, slammed the glasses on the bar and bowed his head. He stayed that way, silent, unmoving, for a long while.

"Next time, please tell your assistant I'm expected," I said, just to cut through the tension. I tried for a professional tone, rather than censuring.

"I told her *this* time," he replied, confused. Still stiff, though.

My eyes narrowed. That bitch! She'd lied to me about not being on the precious list. I should have told Colin to go ahead and fire her.

"I didn't mean to shout at you," Royce said, finally, blessedly relaxing. He sighed and his shoulders slumped slightly. "I...apologize."

The apology sounded strained, a bit forced, but I didn't care. I was surprised he'd even made the effort.

Disciples of evil that they were, most men wouldn't have. "Apology accepted."

He pivoted on his heel and stalked to his desk, where he sat on the corner, his gaze locking with mine. I shifted in my seat. His expression was curiously blank, as if masking an emotion he didn't want me to see. Anger? Disinterest? Irritation?

"What do you think of Colin?" he asked mildly. "The man you were flirting with outside my office."

Forget anger, disinterest and irritation. The man was positively livid with jealousy. Jealousy. About me. His eyes blazed with it, the blue irises resembling vivid sapphires. I shook my head in amazement, feeling just a little giddy.

No, not giddy, I told myself sternly. I was angry. Definitely angry. I forced myself to frown as I crossed my legs and folded my arms together. "I wasn't flirting." Did I sound properly offended he'd imply such a thing? "And just so you know, he seems very pleasant."

"Pleasant?" Royce growled. "What does that mean?"

"Exactly what I said. Pleasant."

"Pleasant agreeable or pleasant I want to go on a date with this man?"

"What does it matter?"

"Answer the damn question."

"I did." *Don't laugh, don't laugh, don't laugh. You're pissed, remember?* "I said he was pleasant and that's what I meant."

Royce clenched the edge of his desk and his knuckles turned white. "What. Kind. Of. Pleasant? You should know, the man likes women and lots of them."

"That makes him better suited for me than you." My traitorous lips twitched at the corners. This situation called for fury, damn it. I mean, how dare he question me about my intentions toward another man. Royce and I had kissed once. That didn't give him exclusive rights to me.

I still wanted to smile.

"He's never been in a lasting relationship."

"Good for him." I paused, savoring my next words. "I liked him."

"You liked him?" The words left his mouth with so much force I almost flew backward.

"Yes. He was nice. And pleasant."

For a moment, I thought I saw Royce's eyes glow bright red, thought I saw steam coming from his nostrils. Then he scrubbed a hand down his face. "You're doing this on purpose, aren't you?"

"Listen," I said, determined to stop this line of conversation before I started dancing on his desktop. Maybe stripping. "I'm not interested in dating him. Really. But I'm not interested in dating you, either, remember?"

His hands dropped to his side and he frowned. "Why not?"

"We went over this yesterday. You're just not my type, okay?" God, I was such a liar. Lately I lied to everyone. My cousins, Royce. Myself.

"I'm honest, honorable and not looking to simply get laid. When I kiss you, you burn up. What part of that is not your type?"

Yes, Naomi, do tell us the answer to that, my hormones

piped in. "There's one quality you didn't mention, and it immediately throws you out of the running."

He crossed his arms over his chest, tightening the fabric of his jacket over his biceps. "And what's that?"

"You have a penis," I said, squirming in my seat. Just saying the word in front of him made me hot.

"A penis? Baby, that's something you should be thanking me for."

Typical male response.

He worried two fingers over his jaw. Yet, even with the movement, there was something so...still about him. "Is this your way of giving me the brush-off?"

"I'm not trying to throw you over for Colin, if that's what you mean. If I was attracted to him, I could have asked him out months ago at his sister's wedding reception." Which I still didn't recall seeing him at. "You attended that party, too, by the way."

He lost his air of irritation and his expression became guarded again.

"Don't worry if you can't remember seeing me there." Bastard. "You were too busy helping your—" whore "—date put the tissue back in her bra."

He almost choked at that bit of information. When he stopped coughing, he said, "I remember you," surprising me.

As if. "You don't have to pretend. It won't hurt my feelings if you don't remember me."

"Ha! Seriously, work on the lying. You suck at it. I remember you, okay?"

My gaze slitted up at him, narrowing my field of vision to him. Only him. "Prove it."

"Okay." His expression darkened in challenge. "You had the saddest eyes I'd ever seen with dark shadows under them. And you kept glancing at the door, as if you couldn't wait to get away from the crowd. You were wearing a light green dress that hit just below your knees. Your hair was pulled back in the same twist you're wearing today. You spent over an hour making sure all the kids were having fun, and you made sure every woman had a dance partner. Every woman but yourself."

My mouth dropped open in shock and I think my heart skipped a beat. He *did* remember me. The knowledge was astonishing. Surreal. Almost more than I could take in. And so utterly wonderful I couldn't quite catch my breath.

"I nearly approached you that day," he said softly.

My eyes widened. He'd wanted to talk to me? Me? "Did you want to talk to me about…your mom's party?"

"Please." He crossed his ankles, the action casual, but the intense gleam in his eyes was anything but calm. "I wanted to talk to you just to hear your voice. I even took a step toward you, but you saw me coming and bolted."

I gasped. "I did not bolt."

"You did, too." A deep, rumbling laugh escaped him. "I've replayed it in my mind a thousand times."

Those words were familiar. He'd said them to me before…when he'd kissed me, that he'd imagined my lips a thousand times. I gulped. This conversation was having a strange effect on my equilibrium. Had I been standing, I would have collapsed to the floor.

If I wasn't careful, I'd offer this man my life, my heart and my soul on a silver platter, room service available 24-7. He and his confession were *that* dangerous.

"Were you afraid of me?" he asked. "Is that why you ran?"

"I'm telling you, I did not run."

"Whatever you say, Jackie Joyner," he said, his singsong tone contradicting his words.

I stomped my foot, drawing on frustration and anger to distance myself. To strengthen my resolve. *Richard the Bastard had been sweet in the beginning, too, saying all the right things. Remember that.*

Royce grinned slowly, smugly. "You want that drink now?"

"You obviously suffer from a severe brain disorder because your memory is warped. I did not run away from you."

"Naomi Delacroix, afraid of me. Then. And now." Features pensive, he tapped his chin with his finger. "I wonder why. Intense attraction? Unquenchable desire?"

If he only knew the truth of those words. I *had* run from him that night. There. I admit it. I'd seen him walking toward me—though I hadn't thought he actually meant to talk to me—and everything inside me, everything I'd thought bludgeoned to death by Richard the Bastard, had sparked to instant life. Attraction, yes. Desire, most definitely. Both more intense than anything I'd ever known. My mouth had gone dry, my limbs had begun shaking. My blood had heated, swimming through my veins and burning everything it touched.

I'd run. As fast as my feet would carry me.

I hadn't been able to handle him then. Hell, I was barely handling him now. I didn't want him to see me as a coward, though, therefore I would never, ever admit that I'd purposefully escaped him. Right now, I wanted this man to see me as a strong, capable woman who met her challenges head-on.

One day, that description might even be true.

"So, why did you want to see me today?" *Good. Bring it back to business.*

He tilted his chin, silently acknowledging my abrupt change of subject. Half turning, he reached out and grabbed a small square item. He thrust it at me. "Here. This is yours."

I gazed down at it, confused. "What is it?"

"A state-of-the-art BlueJay PDA. I almost bought you a Palm Pilot, but I decided to go this route instead. I'll be able to call you and send you e-mail with it. Plus, I've taken the liberty of programming appointment times for us, and this will give you periodic reminders." His eyes gleamed brightly. "You'll never forget a meeting again."

"How…sweet of you to get this for me." Without giving it another glance, I stuffed the stupid thing in my briefcase—where it would most likely remain for the next few months. "Is that our only business today?"

"No." Royce searched through the papers strewn across his desk and lifted a solitary sheet. I wondered if I could sneak a peek at some of those applications/porn. Why I cared to see them, I didn't know—okay, I hoped to incinerate them with my eyes. I leaned to the side…could almost see…

"This," he said, turning back to me and holding the page out, "is a list of possible locations for the party."

I straightened quickly and tried to appear innocent. I hadn't seen a single application, damn it.

He smiled and rubbed a hand down his jaw. I couldn't help but notice how clean-shaven it was. "I know how much you appreciate lists," he said.

"Thank you." I clasped the offered page, recalling I had something for him as well. With my free hand, I rooted through my briefcase. When I found what I was looking for, I slid it out. "Here's my own list of locations, just as promised. We might have some of the same places marked." I gave his list a once-over.

A startled gasp parted my lips. What the hell? "A cabin in Colorado?" I gazed up with wide eyes. "A resort in Maine? A cottage in Connecticut? But I only work in the Dallas area."

He shrugged innocently. "My mother will only turn sixty once, and I want to celebrate right."

"Surely you can find a place here. What about *your* home? Or Linda's?" I asked, a desperate quality entering my voice.

"I'll consider my place if the sites I have listed don't pan out. We need to check them out ASAP."

"Okay, well, I'll make a few calls, search the Internet, and—"

"No, I believe in a personal touch. So we'll visit them personally. Starting with the cabin in Colorado."

"And just how do you plan to get us there?" *Don't say we'll fly. Don't say we'll fly.*

"I'll fly us, of course."

"Of course." My fingers curled around the arm of the chair, clenching so tightly my knuckles turned white. All color drained from my face. "What do you plan to fly us in?" *Don't say airplane. Don't say airplane.*

"A Cessna Turbo 210," he replied, a proud grin lighting his features. "It's the Ferrari of small aircraft."

"How—lovely." I swallowed back bile.

Dread. Panic. Terror. All three blasted through me. I hated planes with a passion. Always had.

He caught my alarm, paused and studied me. "Is there a problem, Naomi?"

I felt a scream of fear lodge in the back of my throat but somehow managed to silence it. "Can't you be content with one of the hotels I've mentioned?" My voice was weak, shaky.

"Don't look so scared." He reached out and squeezed my shoulder, his hand strong and hot and infinitely tender. "I've had my pilot's license for years. I'll get us there and back safely."

"Why don't you view the cabin alone?" I gulped. "You can take pictures while you're there, maybe measure the dimensions. I'll go over your notes and let you know if it will actually work."

I didn't add that the sites he'd listed would be suitable over my cold, dead body. The only location I would approve was in Dallas.

"I don't think so." He went behind his desk and eased into his seat, a satisfied glint in his sexy blue eyes. He looked as calm and relaxed as a man who'd just finished a vigorous bout of lovemaking. Destroying my sense of safety must make for a real orgasmic moment.

"You have to go with me, sweetheart," he said. "What if I forget something?"

I straightened hopefully. "I'll make you a list of the things you need to do. That way, you won't forget anything."

"There's no need for a list. Not when I have you."

"I see."

"No, you don't, but I'm not going to explain it at the moment."

"You're willing to put my life at risk just so I can look at a stupid cabin?"

"Yes. We leave on Saturday. Six sharp. I expect you to be ready."

Triple Cs needed to rot in hell for all eternity. "How long will we be gone?" I ground out.

"One night." He grinned, and that single action was loaded with all kinds of sensual meaning. "Two if you insist."

One night.

With Royce.

In a cabin.

Alone? Together?

I shivered. If I survived the plane crash I knew was coming, I'd never be able to resist him. He'd try to kiss me, judging by that wicked twinkle, and I'd offer my lips on a bed of silk, judging by the ache between my legs, and then we'd tear each other's clothes off and do all kinds of naughty things to each other. I bet he'd even bring a wall harness and try to tie me up like the kinky little sex puppet I suspected he was.

What woman could truly say no to that?

His gaze raked over me. "Why do you still look so pale? Are you going to be sick?"

Deep breath in. Slowly let it out. I needed to find a calm center, my meadow of happiness. No, I needed my inner Tigress. Where the hell was she? This entire situation could be resolved with a little of her clawing, growling and screaming. Was the bitch taking a nap?

"I'll need my own room in the cabin," I said.

"Of course." He worked a hand over his jaw. "But that's not what has you worried. I've never seen you so pale. Besides being afraid of how I make you feel, you wouldn't happen to be afraid of flying, would you?"

My entire body stiffened. "I'm not afraid of anything."

"Okay, so you're afraid of flying." He shrugged. "Why?"

"I'm not afraid," I insisted. "It's just that flying is for birds, angels and drug users."

"I'd never let anything happen to you. If I thought for a second that it was dangerous, I wouldn't let you step foot inside a plane. They're safer than cars, honey."

"I'd still prefer to drive."

"No, I'm going to prove to you just how safe planes really are."

Asshole.

"Before I forget," he said, "here are the names and addresses of the party guests, as you requested." He handed me a stack of papers.

Fifty to two hundred guests turned out to be 375.

"Do you really want to fly this many people to another state?" I held up the list as if it were exhibit A. "You need to rethink this trip."

"No, I don't, and yes, I will fly that many people to another state if I want," he said, silencing my protest. "I don't want to hear anything else about it. I'll pick you up at six and you'll be ready just like a good little girl. I've already programmed this into your BlueJay."

Scowling, I stuffed the stupid list in my briefcase. "My fee increases every time I get on an airplane. Did I forget to mention that fact?"

"Yes, you did." A lazy, crooked smile slanted his lips. "But it's not a problem."

"Do you ever have a problem?" I grumbled.

"Actually, yes. Failure to comply with my orders is a major problem."

Typical of a Triple C.

I shook my head in exasperation and lifted a large book from my case. I wanted to change the subject before I really did throw up. "I have a book of sample invitations for you to go over." As I spoke, I flipped through the tract, revealing page after page of invitations. "As you can see, there are many colors and fonts to pick from, as well as designs."

He groaned. "Can't *you* pick something? I know nothing about fonts and colors and designs unless they come with propellers or a jet engine."

I liked, really liked, damn it, that this gorgeous, put-together man so easily admitted he lacked knowledge about something. My ex—may he soon discover tiny worms have invaded his body and are slowly eating him alive—once told me God made men so perfect because He'd wanted to make up for the inadequacies of women.

Richard the Bastard had said this the day after our divorce had been finalized, and I'd fallen on my knees in thanks that I'd gotten out of that living hell when I had. I'm pretty sure my real dad said something similar to my mom. Many times. While cheating on her. Sometimes I wasn't sure what was worse. Richard's cheating, or my dad's. To both men, family had meant nothing.

"What if I make the wrong choices, Royce? Linda is your mother. I don't know her, therefore I don't know her tastes."

"I trust you." He held up his hands, palms out. "I'll love your choices, I swear."

"But will Linda? I mean—"

"Naomi," he said, beseeching.

I sighed. "All right."

One of his eyebrows quirked in the middle and his grin returned. "All right what? Let me hear the words."

"All right. I'll do it." I uttered another sigh. Giving in did *not* mean I'd reverted to former doormat behavior. I was simply doing something nice for my (sexy) client. "We need to firm up the theme. Jewelry box is first on the list."

"What else is on the list?"

"Something elegant. Something nostalgic."

"Nostalgic." He rubbed the back of his neck and sighed. "Like what?"

"What if we recaptured her youth with an 1800s setting?"

"That'd be great, except she grew up a hundred years after that."

"Whatever. I could do the Care Bear party she never had as a child." If Mrs. Powell had ever been a child, that is. She might have sprung fully formed from the devil's thigh. "I could do something romantic like *Arabian Nights,* with veils and magic lamps. I could do a jungle theme, even, with animal prints and drums."

"I like the *Arabian Nights* thing," he said. "And yes, I'm man enough to say that."

He was *all* man. "Will your mother like it, though?"

"She'll love it. That's the one. It has my approval."

My heart gave a strange little leap. Already I pictured the scene in my mind, loving the bold colors, the bed of satin floor pillows—with Royce lounging on them, eating grapes from my hand—and the thought of magic at every corner.

"Will the guests have to dress up?" he asked, a hint of something wicked in his eyes.

"As in, formally?" I stared up at him, trying to figure out what he was thinking. "Or in costume?"

"Costume."

I bit my bottom lip, letting it slid from my teeth. "Do you want them to?"

"That depends. Will you come as a belly dancer?"

"No." I pressed my lips together to keep from smiling. I should have known his thoughts were lascivious.

"Then, no," he said on a sigh. "No costumes."

My gaze swept over him. Perhaps I'd spoken too hastily. I could very easily see him in a sheik costume, king of the desert. I'd be his harem girl, of course, and he'd command me—*Whoa, girl. Don't go there. Not here.* I cleared my throat. "Once you decide on a location, I'll print a sample invitation for your approval."

"Sounds good." He stretched his legs out in front of him, right beside my legs. So close I could feel the heat of them. "Now, tell me about the caterer you've chosen."

"Cinderella Catering." I smiled slowly as an idea formed. I'd forgotten about the caterer. "You should know they're located solely in Dallas," I said. "They have no other affiliations and will be unable to work in another area. Especially out of state."

He covered his mouth with his hand. Hoping to hide his grin? "You're tenacious, I'll give you that. But I refuse to be concerned about losing the caterer until that time comes."

"There may not be another caterer available by the time you decide, and if that happens, I am *not* throwing a few pizzas in the oven and calling it good."

"Once again, we'll be concerned about that when and if the time comes."

Determined, my life at stake, I persisted. "The

longer you wait to choose the party's location, the harder it will be to hire a new caterer *and* book the site."

"That's why we're leaving this Saturday."

Damn him! He had an answer for everything. "For the record, I want it noted that I do not agree with this plan of action."

"So noted," he said behind his hand. Yep. He was definitely hiding a grin. "Now, that's enough talk about the birthday party for today." He cast a glance to the wall clock. He dropped his hand, revealing his lips and a smile, but the smile quickly vanished. "Unfortunately, it's too late to go to lunch."

"So eat in."

"I don't have time." He leveled me with a frown and glanced at his watch. "I have a meeting in ten minutes."

My back tensed and straightened at his I-blame-you tone. "That's not my fault."

"It is," he grumbled, "but I forgive you."

I choked out a dry laugh. "Gee, thanks, Royce. I wouldn't have made it through the rest of my day without knowing you forgave me for something that wasn't my fault."

He chuckled, his good humor restored for a reason only he understood. "Ah, I love a woman with spirit. What do you have on under that jacket?"

"Excuse me?" The abrupt switch of topics gave me a momentary pause. My fingers sought the lapels of said jacket and drew them tight.

"What do you have on under that jacket?" he repeated.

I frowned and shifted in my seat. "Nothing."

"Mmm," he drawled, a teasing light making his eyes sparkle like sapphires. "Very interesting. And unexpected. But I must admit, I like it. There's something so sexy about a woman daring enough to go in the buff underneath her clothes."

I shifted again, becoming more turned on by the second. "I meant I have on nothing that concerns you."

"Interesting interpretation."

If I didn't stop this line of conversation, I'd soon be offering to *show* him what I wore under my jacket. The most daring part of me, a part I hadn't known existed until he'd entered my life, was responding to his words, making me ache and tingle, begging me to go for it. "We need to keep this meeting strictly professional."

"Like we can't be professional naked."

My lips pursed in pure vexation. He spotted the action, and the teasing light fizzled from his eyes as a hot, blazing fire kindled in their blue depths. "I swear I get hard every time you move your lips."

I watched, transfixed, mesmerized, as his gaze traveled over my body in a bold assessment, stopping for a long moment at my bare calves. It felt as if his hands rather than his eyes skimmed over me. And I knew what was coming next. Oh, I dreaded, craved and hungered for what was coming next.

"C'mere," he said, the word a seductive whisper.

Remain strong! my inner Tigress cried.

Where have you been? I mentally shouted at her. Everything about Royce, from the look on his face to the way his body leaned forward as if poised to attack, was a guarantee he planned to kiss me senseless. Again.

I might hate myself later, but I couldn't allow it. Our first (shatteringly exquisite) kiss had been our last. He was too sexy, too potent, and he wanted too much from me. More than that, I wanted him too much.

"I can't," I said, trying to impress upon my sex-starved body the importance of those words. "Besides, you don't have time. Your meeting, remember?"

"Yes, you can," he said, his voice a throaty, heady murmur that seduced me. Lured me. "And I'll always make time for this."

So will I, I thought, my lids lowering to half-mast.

What are you doing? my inner Tigress snapped. *Think about the consequences of your actions. Triple Cs are trouble. Pure trouble.*

My body said: *I don't care. Kiss Royce. Pleeeease.*

Royce clicked under his tongue. "If you won't come to me, I'll come to you." He rose. Before taking the steps that brought us together, however, he strode to the door and clicked the lock in place.

Uh-oh. I gulped.

My mind and body continued their war, and I didn't know what to do. Well, I knew what I should do. It was just a matter of doing it, of getting my ass out of the office and away from Royce.

"I gave you plenty of time to run," he said, stalking toward me. "Yet here you remain."

My eyes followed his every movement with horrified fascination and, seconds later, he was in front of me, reaching down and clasping my hands. In one gentle tug, he pulled me to my feet. Even now, I didn't try to escape, didn't utter a protest, but kept my hands cradled in his.

Leap out the window, my inner Tigress cried. *You aren't ready to face such a powerful Tiger.*

I frowned. *I thought a true Tigress never backed down from a fight.*

Don't you know anything? When she's in heat, she avoids everything male. Now run!

If only being with him like this didn't feel so right. If only his hands weren't so warm, so callused. Did he work on the planes himself? The thought of him dressed as a mechanic, oil streaking his arms and face… Holy Lord, fantasy overload.

"What type of flowers does your mother like best?" I asked in one last desperate attempt to prevent what I knew—and secretly hoped—was coming. I'd already proven I didn't have the willpower to run. Words were my only hope. "Maybe I'll scatter petals across the floor and tables." And maybe he could have sex with me on those petals. I uttered a nervous laugh. "They'll fragrance the air very nicely."

"Use orchids." His voice became a husky whisper, deep, low, seductive. "I finally figured out what you smell like. Orchids and honeysuckle."

His seduction was melting my resolve, drugging me. *Kiss me,* I beseeched with my eyes.

Stop that, I commanded them. No beseeching!

"Every time I'm near you, I drown in your scent," he muttered. "But I've told you that, haven't I?"

Lick me.

Shit.

"Did I tell you how sexy your lips are? I can't keep my eyes off them. I want them all over me."

Bite me.

Damn it all to hell.

He nuzzled the side of my cheek with his nose. Nipped with his teeth.

Oh, yeah. He nipped again. *Just…like…that.*

I sighed, melting. Lust zinged through me, hot and wild. My body trembled, totally and completely winning the battle against my mind. I really, really wanted Royce to kiss me again.

I knew how he affected me, so I knew to guard my emotions. Right? Yes. Right. That meant I could allow myself to kiss him again. Maybe then I could finally get him out of my system and walk away a stronger woman—Tigress—better equipped to resist him later. Right? Yes. Right.

In a hidden corner of my mind, I admitted I'd been waiting for this moment since I had stepped into his office, uncaring of the consequences. He drew me, tempted me.

"You still haven't run," he said softly. His hands slid up my arms, onto my waist and to the small of my back, enfolding me. I sank into him, my chest pressing against his, my legs cradled by his.

His warm breath fanned my cheek until finally his mouth settled over mine. His tongue thrust out, licking, tasting. He teased me with flicks and nibbles, and it wasn't enough. I needed hard and rough and pure passion.

I bit his bottom lip; I coasted my hands up his back, gripped his head and ground him against me. He got the point. His mouth slanted over mine, his tongue thrusting deep, thrusting as hard as I desired. I purred, kissing him with all my pent-up longing. My tongue battled his, retreated, then went back for another delicious skirmish. His coffee-flavored taste intoxicated me.

Royce's sultry attack continued until my head felt wonderfully groggy from lack of air. My nipples were hardened little points, and my heart was thundering inside my chest, erratic and undeniably fast.

He jerked his mouth from mine. I growled my disappointment, my need. I wasn't finished with him. This was the last kiss I was going to allow between us, and, by God, it was going to last a long, long time. My hands tightened on him, holding him, locking him in place.

"See?" he panted. "We're good together." Between each word, he planted hot little kisses along my cheek, my jawline and my neck. "So good."

"No." I had to deny his words. The principle of the matter and all. "We suck together."

"What a little liar you are. I like your idea, though. We should do more sucking." His strained chuckle breezed against my lips, but his laughter soon ceased and he gave me another earth-shattering kiss. "I want you, Naomi."

His words were even headier than his kisses.

"Let's forget the rest of the world and go to my place. Just you and me."

"What about your meeting?"

"I'll cancel."

"I—" My refusal, or agreement, wouldn't form as I battled the seductive fog woven through my every thought.

His movements clipped, Royce set me at arm's length, an emotion I couldn't decipher shining in the depths of his eyes, lines of tension tightening his features. He waited. Simply waited for my agreement. He wouldn't do more, wouldn't touch me again, until I uttered my capitulation.

I opened my mouth, but no sound formed. Why couldn't I say yes? Why couldn't I say no? I wanted both options too much, damn it.

He continued to look at me. He knew exactly what his silence did to me, too. It gave me time to imagine all the things we could be doing to each other. Stripping slowly. Touching and tasting. Shuddering with an exquisite, I've-found-the-gates-of-paradise orgasm. Or two.

A sultry shiver racked my spine, and I fought the urge to grip his chin and jerk him back to me for another kiss. *Better leave now—you're already too far over the edge.*

"I need to go home," I said, finally finding my voice, though it was no more than a desperate whisper. "My home. Alone."

His phone suddenly buzzed. "Mr. Powell. Donovan is here to see you."

Royce stormed to his desk and jabbed a button. "I need a few more minutes." He released the button and said to me, "You want me. I see the desire in your eyes."

"So?"

"So?" he asked, incredulous. He stepped around his desk, closing the distance between us again. "So you want to walk away from that? Pretend there's nothing between us? Well, I won't let you."

He must have changed his mind about waiting for my consent because he suddenly reached behind my head, clutched the hair at my nape and, in one swift movement, jerked me back into his embrace.

I didn't try to deny him. I couldn't. Our tongues met in a tangled clash, hot, wet. Wild. The kiss went on and on, pure passion.

It was a mistake, unbuttoning his shirt, but I did it anyway. Was helpless to do anything else. I had to touch him. My hands dipped inside the material. Warm skin. A small patch of soft, downy chest hair. How could I have known he'd feel so good? So much like a warrior? All muscle, like velvet poured over hot steel.

With a rough push, Royce sent my jacket whipping to the ground. The brown material pooled at our feet. Next he jerked at the buttons on my blouse, shoved the folds aside and got his first glimpse of my green satin bra.

He rumbled low in his throat, primal, eager man. He looked at the bra. Looked at me. Looked at the bra. All the while, the blaze grew hotter and hotter in his eyes. "Green. Yes, you want me." He shoved the satin aside, exposing the peaks of my nipples. His breath caught. "You have the most perfect nipples I've ever seen. They're pink and ripe as little berries."

I licked my lips. "Stop saying things like that."

"Why? Because they excite you?" With a sultry chuckle, he kissed me, cupped one of my breasts, kneaded it, rolled the nipple between his fingers. At the first expert touch of his palm, I groaned. I couldn't believe we were doing this in his office, where anyone outside the door could hear us.

His lips tore from mine, and he arched me backward, letting his hot tongue tantalize my nipple. One hand moved over me, skimming the swell of my hips. "Don't think of anything except how I make you feel," he murmured against my heated flesh.

I wasn't.

He sucked my nipple into his mouth. My body jerked and I almost came right then. My hands slid through his hair, clasping him to me in a tight, you're-not-going-anywhere grip.

"Royce, I—"

He sucked harder.

I gasped, arching my back farther, wanting more, needing more—until the phone buzzed, allowing a single, solitary thought to slip unbidden into my mind: *This is more than a kiss, Naomi. You're about to step straight into a sexual relationship. With a client.*

"Mr. Powell," Elvira said.

My blood went from molten to ice cold in mere

seconds. How could I have let this happen? I'd thought to allow myself one last kiss, yet this was so much more. I'd known better, known this would be the result, but I hadn't let common sense prevail.

I wrenched away, disengaging from him completely, panting. "I, um, have to stop now."

The phone buzzed. "Mr. Powell?"

The fine lines around Royce's eyes and mouth were already taut, but they tightened further. I could tell he wanted to grab me, to tumble me back into his embrace. But he must have read my determination to resist him in the hard stance of my body.

"I'll let you go for now, but we're not finished, Naomi." Aroused fire beamed from his eyes as he took a menacing step toward me. Another. "In fact," he purred dangerously, "we've only just begun."

With shaky limbs, I whirled away from Royce and righted my clothing. I picked up my jacket from the floor and slipped my arms through the openings. "Lucky us, we found the beginning and the end in the same day. I just…I can't be with you," I said. It was a plea for him to understand.

"Can't." His expression lost some of its heat. In fact, he looked positively arctic. "Or won't?"

The phone buzzed yet again. "Mr. Powell?"

He stormed back to his desk, slammed a finger into a button and barked, "I said I need a goddamn minute. I'll let you know when to send him in."

"Well?" he said to me.

He wanted to hear that my lips ached for the return of his, that I felt lost and unsure without his arms around me. It was true, but I couldn't say it aloud. If he knew how close I was to giving in, he'd pounce and I wouldn't be able to deny him. And I could wave my rules goodbye.

I didn't turn to face him when I said, "Won't."

A heavy pause.

"I don't understand you," he said, exasperated and angry. "I don't understand how you can be so hot for me, then turn so cold."

This time, I did face him. I whirled, glaring, pointing at his chest. "That's right. You don't understand me because you don't know me. You don't know my life. You don't know my past. I won't get involved with you, Royce."

His features softened just as the sunlight streaming in from the window hit him at the perfect angle, casting him in a glowing halo. "I know you're strong and honest and you fight for what you want. Well, fight for me."

I almost—almost, damn it—capitulated then and there. I swear, I was changing my mind lately more than I changed my underwear. Those words of his…that quiet beseeching…I don't think I'd ever heard anything quite so beautiful. He was the first person ever to call *me* strong. And I responded to that on a primal level.

"I can't," I whispered, and saying it was even harder than pulling away from him had been.

"Why not?" He threw his hands in the air. "Help me understand, so that I can help you accept what's between us."

How easy he made it sound. How tempting. *Work through your concerns and we can be together.* I closed my eyes, as one horrible fear after another flitted through me. The way men cheated and lied and lost interest in their woman. The late-night phone calls, the "business trips."

"Tell me," he said softly.

If I told him about Richard the Bastard's infidelity, I'd also have to admit to my own stupidity. My own weakness. How many times had I taken Richard back? How many times had I allowed him to treat me like garbage? Royce had just admitted he thought of me as strong and capable, a fighter. I absolutely did *not* want him to change his view. Did not want him to see me as a doormat.

"There's nothing to tell," I said, staring down at my intertwined hands. "I'm just not interested."

"Is this a game?" He scowled over at me. "Are you playing hard to get, trying to tie me in knots so you're all I can think about? If so, it's worked. I admit it, you're always on my mind. I dream about you, crave you constantly."

I wanted to cover my ears. I wanted to run. I wanted to stay. "Don't tell me that." I shook my head, strands of hair falling at my temples. "Don't say stuff like that."

"Why not? It's true."

"I'm unavailable to you," I said, desperate to believe anything but what he was saying. Capitulation was not an option for me. Not with this man, and not about the future. Because he affected me more than even Richard had, that made him far more dangerous. "You're simply responding to the challenge. That's all."

"You're wrong. I want to marry you. And that has nothing to do with you being a challenge."

My stomach dropped. I think my vision went black for a moment. My throat closed up and all I could say was, "You want to marry me?" The words emerged as nothing more than a croak.

"Yes."

"You've only known me a few weeks, and you want to marry me?" Louder now. "You've never been on a date with me, and you want to marry me?" Louder still.

"Yes." He said it so simply, so easily. "I've dreamed about you for six months, Naomi. After Daisy Phillips' reception, I called you to ask you out. You never returned my calls. So I admit, in a moment of desperation I had my mother ask you to plan her party. It was the only way I could think of to get you in my life."

Dear God. I covered my face with my hands, trying to drag air into my too-tight lungs. A loud roaring filled my ears; my stomach cramped. What kind of sick, alternate world had I slipped into?

Things began to click into place. That day in his office, when he'd spoken on the phone about "the one," who he would win, he'd been talking about me, I realized. A merger of sorts, he'd said, meaning marriage.

"Do—do you love me?" I asked, unable to face him.

Another pause, this one heavier, deeper. Then, "Yes. I do."

"This is crazy, Royce. You have to see how crazy this is."

He crossed his arms over his chest and tilted his chin to the side, regarding me, studying me, gauging exactly what he would reveal. "This company thrived under my father's care, yes, but I doubled its profits by acting on my instincts. They've never steered me wrong, and right now I know, *know,* you're the woman for me."

"You're just desperate to get married. Any woman will do."

"Is that so?" He ran his tongue over his teeth. "Then why the hell haven't I chosen one of the applicants?"

I placed a trembling hand over my mouth and simply blinked at him. Yes, I'd known he desired me—the way he kissed me was proof of that. Hell, the erection he still sported was proof of that. I'd even suspected, yesterday in my apartment, that he wanted a commitment from me. Hearing it, though, having it confirmed... This was ludicrous. Love?

"Royce—"

He cut me off with a stiff shake of his head. "Don't say no. Just say you'll think about it."

Think about it? I'd be able to think of nothing else for the rest of my life. Any decision I made would be the wrong one, and I suspected I'd always wonder what would have happened if I'd gone the other way.

"I want you in my life, Naomi, and I'm willing to do whatever it takes to convince you of that fact."

His sweetness, his willingness to fight for me, beat at my resolve harder than anything else had. But— *No!* my mind screamed in the next instant. *He's dangerous. You'll get hurt. He's a man. He'll cheat.* I had to combat him, had to continue to resist, and there was only one way to do that. I couldn't think of him as Royce Powell, sexy man of my dreams. I had to think of him as simply a man, a cheating, lying bastard of a man.

"I-never-want-to-get-married," I shouted. "Never ever, ever." For emphasis, I stomped my foot. "Never!"

Unperturbed, he shook his head. "You don't mean that."

"Like hell I don't. I wouldn't get married if aliens invaded our planet and the only way to escape a deep body probing was to marry the leader. Do I make myself clear?"

"You're exaggerating, trying to push me away for whatever reason. I can still see the fear in your eyes."

"What will it take to make you realize the only way to get me down an altar is to carry my cold, dead body in a casket?"

He regarded me silently for a moment. "You're telling me you have no interest in love? No interest in a white gown, a diamond ring and a church filled with family and friends oohing and aahing?"

I nodded with determination. I didn't even have a slight pang of doubt. "That's right." Been there, almost killed myself because of that.

"You won't mind if I laugh in your face, will you?

I know women, and I know they dream about a splashy wedding, about having an adoring husband and bearing his children." He held out his arms, a wide open invitation for me to peruse him at my leisure. "Well, here I am, willing to give you those things. And you still want to tell me no?"

"That's right," I said again, unwavering.

"Unbelievable." He shook his head in exasperation.

"This has all been very interesting," I said, smoothing down my skirt. "You've given me the men are from Mars example I've always wanted, so now I'll give you a women are from Venus example. I promise you on all that is holy that I'm not holding out for a ring. In fact, I don't even want to be a bridesmaid."

He shook his head. "I don't believe you."

How could I explain it in terms he'd understand? "I do not want a man. Period. No men. Men make me sick. Men bad. Gag, gag, gag."

He regarded me, his eyes growing wide. "Wait. You don't like men?"

Finally. Contact. "No."

"Well, why the hell didn't you tell me that sooner?"

"We work together, for one thing. Personal business isn't something co-workers need to discuss."

"I didn't realize." Shaking his head again, he fell into the chair behind him. "I'm sorry."

"Yes, well, now you know the truth."

"Have you always felt this way?"

"No," I answered, again opting for the truth. "Just the past six months."

"There were no signs. I mean—" he plowed a hand

through his hair and glared at me in accusation. "You kissed me. Twice. I thought you liked it. You seemed to like it. It's the blondes, isn't it? The twins in the pictures on your coffee table. I should have guessed. But how could I have known?"

Had we just entered the twilight zone? "What the hell are you talking about?"

"You prefer women to men," he said. "It's nothing to be ashamed of, I just didn't realize. You seemed to like— Oh, shit."

Argh. This was too much. Both of my hands, which were now fisted, went to my waist. He thought I was seeing two women, twins at that. What was it with men and twins? "I'm not gay, Royce. If a woman isn't interested, it doesn't mean she's gay."

A long, protracted silence filled the space between us. His features gradually relaxed. "So you're not…"

"No."

"Damn it," he said, suddenly losing all traces of relaxation. "You said you wanted nothing to do with men, that men made you sick. Earlier you mentioned hating everything with a penis. What else was I supposed to think?"

"Maybe that I'm not interested in a relationship, like I've been trying to tell you. Or maybe that I want to live alone, without a man's interference. Or maybe I simply want nothing to do with romance. Especially with a Triple C."

A glaze of puzzlement washed over him, halting the tirade I knew was coming. "What the hell is a Triple C?"

"Corporate. Controlling. And completely wrong

for me." Okay, so it had been *and a total Commando,* but this was my phrase and I could change it if I wanted.

His brows arched, almost hitting his hairline. "I'll admit to being corporate. But controlling? Wrong for you? I don't think so. I happen to be a WHP."

I crossed my arms over my chest and rolled my eyes ceilingward. "Explain please."

"Willing. Horny. And Perfect for you."

Not to mention egotistical. "Is that so?"

He crossed his own arms over his chest, mimicking my battle stance. "Yeah, that's so."

"This isn't a game, Royce. I'm truly not out to catch a man. Any man. Even a WHP. That's all there is to it."

His lips lifted in a slow, knowing grin, his eyes sparkling like sapphires. "Now, I happen to know that's a lie." He studied me in an openly assessing way, like he possessed X-ray vision and could see to my very soul.

I shifted uncomfortably from one foot to the other. "You keep saying you know when I'm lying," I said, hating how my voice trembled. I knew I was lying, that I wanted him in a very bad way, but there was no way he could know it. Right?

"Your list. I might have forgotten about it for a moment, but now that I've remembered—"

"What list?"

"Do the words *what to look for in Mr. Wrong* ring a bell? If you're trying to avoid Mr. Wrong, you're trying to find Mr. Right."

Sparks of anger lit inside me, but those sparks died

a quick death as amusement grew. I laughed. I just couldn't help myself. The situation was too funny. Too sweet. My gaze zeroed in on his clean-shaven jaw, and I laughed even harder.

"You shaved," I said. The knowledge sent me doubling over as another wave of laughter swept through me. "I get it now. Number four. Mr. Wrong never shaves his beard."

Royce stiffened and his gaze slitted. "What's so funny about that?"

"Nothing, if it were my list."

"Of course it's yours. It was in your home."

"No. Sorry." More laughter. "It belongs to my cousins, Kera and Mel. The blond twins in the photo."

The clock ticked. Four minutes of complete silence passed. Okay, so I was still laughing and the sound of it echoed off the walls. The man had made a sweet, sweet fool of himself. I was entitled to a little amusement.

Royce ran a hand down his face. He pushed out a deep breath and peeked at me over his fingers. "Are you sure that isn't your list?"

"Swear to God."

"But I fit none of the requirements for Mr. Wrong."

"Not my list," I said again, still grinning.

"I can't believe this is happening," he muttered. "Are you absolutely one-hundred-percent positive it isn't yours?"

"Yeah," I answered again.

"But you love lists."

"That's why I was the designated writer. For the twins."

"Wonderful. Just fucking wonderful. I stood a chance of winning the list's owner. Now, well— Shit."

In a flash, I froze, losing my burst of humor. What if… No. I didn't want to contemplate such an event. My mind wouldn't let the thought die, however.

I gulped back the sudden lump in my throat. "Since you're so fascinated with that list," I said, judging my words carefully. I gazed down at my shoes, using one to scrape the toe of the other. "You might be interested in knowing that Kera, one of the twins, sent you an application. She's smart and beautiful and she's looking for love." Rigid with an emotion I didn't want to name, I waited for his reply.

"Sounds great." His tone didn't reveal a hint of his inner thoughts. Nor did his now blank expression. "I'll put hers at the top."

I didn't want to analyze why my heart suddenly squeezed painfully in my chest.

8

Sometimes, to properly stalk her prey and learn its habits, a Tigress must stealthily approach, watch and gauge before exploding into a rush of amazing speed and attacking. With carefully timed maneuvers, she can deliver the killing blow without her prey ever knowing she was there.

"WHAT DO YOU THINK of this one?"

I glanced up from the rack of black, brown and navy-blue dress suits. All were ankle length, plain and would conceal every inch of skin, protecting it from a man's naughty gaze. When I saw my cousin's selection, I frowned. "I am *not* wearing that…that… X-rated napkin."

"What's wrong with it?" Mel gave the green mini-dress she held a once-over, even brushed her fingers down the split bodice.

"The hem won't cover the edge of my panties and the bodice opens to my belly button. You might not know this, but I'm not planning to make a few extra bucks on the side while I'm gone."

It was Wednesday night and we were hitting the bargain department stores instead of the night-clubs—Mel liked penny beer—all for the sake of my upcoming trip to Colorado with Royce. Apparently, a new shipment of green clothes had arrived only the day before. When Mel and Kera learned of this, they had demanded we go shopping. Being the meek, mild woman that I am, I relented. And my capitulation had nothing to do with wanting to look good for Royce. I swear.

Did the old "fingers crossed" thing still work?

"Try it on, at least," Mel persisted just as the BlueJay in my purse erupted in a series of beeps. "And for God's sake, turn that thing off."

"I can't." Scowling, I dug inside my purse and pounded the stupid thing front and back. It beeped every hour, reminding me of my upcoming trip. Royce, the diabolical son of the devil, had pro-grammed it in such a way that I couldn't turn it off or turn down the volume. Too, the screen continued to flash crap like, "You'll have fun on our trip, I promise."

Once the beeping stopped, I surveyed Mel's choice of ho-wear again. "I'd feel better covered in body paint."

"Now there's an idea," she said with a sly grin.

I rolled my eyes, but couldn't stop my own grin. "Even if I was willing to parade around like a living porno ad, I don't want to wear anything green. I'd just look like a lumpy bowl of pea soup. Or worse, an overused snot rag. I don't care how much Royce likes the color. I'm. Not. Wearing. It."

"What about this one?" Kera held up a conservative mint-green pantsuit. "It's fifty percent off."

"And it's still green," I said, my voice heavy with exasperation. Did they never listen to me?

"Sister dear," Mel said, "she's flying to Colorado—with Royce Powell, I might add—not a summit for sexually repressed librarians."

Kera chuckled. "You're right."

"Think ski bunny," Mel said. "Sexy," she continued. "Wild. Uninhibited."

"I'm not trying to seduce him," I told them.

"Oh, please," both said in unison.

"I'm not. Really." How many lies could one woman tell in a single day before God could no longer forgive her? When I was a little girl, my mom used to tell me the limit was 490 times a day. I think I was dangerously close to reaching that.

"You may not allow yourself to try," Mel said wickedly, knowingly, "but you want to. Bad."

I didn't try to deny it, but I didn't audibly agree with her, either. She took my silence for refusal.

"I thought you had a brain in that skull of yours," she mumbled. "If you don't want to seduce him, we need to get you a prescription for Viagra for women ASAP."

"Maybe we should take her in for a CAT scan," Kera suggested.

"Guys, I'm a hardened bitch with relationship scars.

That's all there is to it." I ran my fingertips down the lapels of a wool jacket. "No amount of drugs or medical testing will change that."

"True." Mel.

"You're right." Kera.

Hey, weren't they supposed to defend my character? Weren't they supposed to assure me that I might have internal scars, but an entry in the Bedroom Olympics would do me some good?

"Still," Mel finally said, "I think the whip and feathers we gave you at your non-party will go a long way towards helping you overcome your bitchiness."

An image of Royce tied facedown to my bed, his naked body bared for my viewing pleasure while I whipped him then soothed the ache with feathers— or my tongue—filled my head. My nipples instantly hardened and the juncture between my thighs ached.

"Well, hello ladies." Mel laughed. "Something I said got through to your hormones." She flicked a pointed glance at my breasts.

Cheeks heating, I quickly covered them with my hands. I should have worn a padded water bra—yes, I owned one and I wasn't ashamed. Small-breasted women had to do what small-breasted women had to do to fill out their shirts properly. That would have kept my traitorous nipples hidden.

"So you aren't as immune to him as you would have us believe." Kera lifted a green floral sundress and held it to her petite frame. "Why else would you have kissed him? Twice."

"Shut up," I said.

"We aren't the *Tattler.* You don't have to deny, deny, deny with us."

"It's obvious you two want each other," Kera continued. She twirled around, the dress she held dancing at her knees. "So what's the problem? Seduce the man, and get it out of your system. Sex doesn't have to be a major commitment."

I knew she didn't believe those words, just as I knew what she was trying to do. Kera thought if I slept with Royce, I would fall in love and suddenly decide I wanted to marry him.

What if she wasn't far off the mark? *That's* what scared me most. Still, that was no reason to tell the man to read Kera's application. Bad Naomi.

"Sex *is* a major commitment to Royce," I said. I snatched the dress from her and hung it back on the rack. No green.

"Just because of that article?" Mel asked doubtfully, flipping through another mound of napkins/dresses. "It could have all been a joke, you know. Or even an exaggeration. The media always distorts the news."

"The press was right this time. I know because—" Jeez, it was time I came clean and revealed exactly what was going on. I hadn't told them everything, and they deserved to know. "He proposed. To me."

"Proposed?" In the next instant, Kera grabbed me by the shoulders, spinning me around to face her. "As in, he asked you to marry him?"

I bit my bottom lip. "Well, yeah."

My petite, delicate cousin shook me once, twice. "So what did you say?"

"No, of course."

"No, of course, she says." Kera threw up her hands and swung to face Mel, her blond locks whipping me in the face. "Did you just hear what this foolish woman said? Can she possibly be related to us? Naomi turned down a man who looks like Colin Farrell, is richer than God and finds her so desirable he can't live without her."

"Now wait just a—"

"I'm having trouble believing it myself." Mel tsk-tsked under her tongue. "It's one thing to *say* you're never going to get married, but it's quite another to actually reject such a man's proposal. Naomi, Naomi, Naomi. Do we need to have you committed for being mentally unstable?"

"I never said anything about him being unable to live without me. *He* never said anything of the sort, either." Well, he kind of did. He'd said some of the most wonderful things to me, things that continually swept through my mind, weakening my knees. He'd thought about me for six whole months. He'd dreamed about me. He loved me.

"He implied it with his proposal," Mel said. Hooking her red-streaked bangs behind her ear, she leveled a pointed stare at me. "If you won't consider the marriage thing, at least say you'll think about that wild affair with him."

How could I not think about it? My body craved the man like a drug. I leaned against a rack of slacks and the hangers dug into my back. "He'd probably expect to fly to Vegas the moment we slept together."

Mel gently pushed me aside so she could study a pair of hip-huggers. "Just because he expects it, doesn't mean you have to say yes."

True.

"Why don't you introduce him to me?" Kera shifted her weight from one high-heeled foot to the other and eyed me with the same purposeful intent Mel had earlier. "I don't have a stupid rule about dating a client, and I am *so* ready to fall in love and get married."

My stomach tightened. The same sick, yucky feeling that had washed over me in Royce's office washed over me now. I didn't want Royce for myself, but I damn sure didn't want anyone else to have him either. Not even Kera, whom I loved.

What was it about that man that tied me in so many knots?

"Trust me," I said, trying to act nonchalant and breezy. "You don't want him, Kera. What type of husband would he make, anyway? He obviously travels a lot. He's bossy, arrogant, egotistical, tyrannical and possibly vainglorious. And what happened to George? I thought you were interested in him."

"Maybe I'm more interested in Royce." She expelled a dreamy (fake?) sigh. "He's *sooo* hot."

Yes. Yes, he was. And his kisses slayed me. Enthralled me. Had me panting for more. Maybe, after I finished planning his mother's party, Royce and I *could* have some type of fling.

My chin tilted to the side as I considered that scenario. Hmm…sex on the beach. Sex on a balcony.

Sex in every room of my apartment. Sex, sex, sex. Would he be interested in an affair? He was a healthy man, and he'd said he wanted me in his life. If I made it clear sex was all I could give him, surely he'd relent.

I'd never had a purely sexual relationship before, a relationship where emotions were taboo. Could I handle one? Surely I could. Surely my fears about falling in love with him if we got naked were unfounded.

I had to admit, the thought of touching him at my leisure appealed to me. Tasting him, too. Letting him touch and taste me. A sultry heat invaded my veins, and I licked my lips. A few nights of hot, dirty (unemotional) loving would surely cure me of this obsession for him. Of my need for his naked body straining against mine, slipping and pumping erotically inside me.

Yes, I decided then, already eager to begin. I would seduce him after the party. For my peace of mind, if nothing else. I would sleep with him and keep my heart well guarded. When the passion was sated, he and I would part. Simple. Easy. No one would get hurt.

"Kera," I said. "I want Royce, so you can't have him."

She grinned slowly, as if that was what she'd wanted to hear all along.

Mel muttered, "About time."

In all of my life, I'd been with a total of two men. Number one: Jase Waldren, my high-school crush. After several months of "going steady," he'd taken my virginity in the back seat of his rusty yellow truck and had never called me again. Not that I'd cared. I'd been about as close to orgasm that night as I was to buying a pair of Dolce & Gabbana black leather stiletto boots right now.

Number two: my ex-husband. I'd just started working for a local party-planning business, and Richard the Bastard had strolled in looking all suave and self-assured, needing help with a business function. He was a divorce lawyer and ten years my senior. Caught in his charismatic snare, I'd requested that I be assigned to him. I don't know why, but he'd taken an instant liking to me, as well, and had romanced the hell out of me.

We married soon after.

Right after the ceremony, he'd hinted that I needed to quit my job. He hadn't said it in so many words, but he'd wanted me to devote every waking moment to him. So I stupidly did it. I'd loved him and wanted to make him happy. And a small part of me had liked the thought of taking care of him. How romantic it had seemed. Give up everything for love and all that crap. Yeah. Right. I'd known better. My mom had given up her life for my dad, as well.

What had my let-me-please-you personality won me? A husband who had sometimes ignored me, always taken me for granted and never found me good enough. A husband who'd found me lacking and hadn't minded telling me so.

A husband who'd preferred to spread his love all over Texas rather than sleep with his own wife. Yep, I'd known better.

After our divorce, no one had wanted to hire me. I'd not only slept with a big-name client, I'd walked away from a job without notice, as well. What's worse, I'd deserved the lack of confidence from potential employers. How much more stupid could I have been?

I'd been forced to start my own business with what little money I had. I was glad for that now, of course, but six months ago I'd been an emotional wreck, scared of failure and nearing bankruptcy. Perhaps I could have done something different, taken a menial job I'd hate, but I had no skills other than party planning and honestly couldn't see myself doing anything else.

Was history repeating itself? I suddenly wondered.

Here I was again, lusting after a client and determined to have an affair with him. Like Richard, Royce had developed an instant attraction to me, something I just didn't understand. It was too rare. Most men preferred the lithe beauty of Kera or the wild, untamed personality of Mel.

I massaged the muscles in my neck and pretended to study the clothes in front of me. What was it with me and men with names that started with *R?* If a man's first name started with *R,* was I destined to find him irresistible?

"Uh, Naomi. Hello?"

Kera's voice penetrated my thoughts. I shook my head, forcing myself to concentrate on her and not the past. "What?"

"You were in some sort of sad, I'm-about-to-cry-or-kill-someone trance. I asked what you were thinking about."

"Richard. Royce. My own stupidity." I waved a hand through the air, effectively cutting off that line of conversation. "It doesn't matter. Mel," I said, "there's a guy I want to introduce you to. He's very cute. Tall, dark hair. Good sense of humor."

Mel's vivid features brightened. "Who is he?"

"His name is Colin Phillips and he works for Royce." I recalled what Royce had told me about the man, that Colin was a love 'em and leave 'em kind of guy. That made him perfect for Mel, who never lasted more than a few weeks in any romantic relationship. She talked a good talk, wanting *me* to take the marriage plunge, but when it came to herself she was just as anti-marriage as I was.

"Hey." Kera turned away from us to scrutinize a bubble-knit shirt. "I've met Colin. He was at the wedding I catered for that girl, Denise...Danny? What was her name?"

"Daisy." I nodded. "That's the one. His sister."

"You'll like him, Mel," Kera said. "He's more than cute. He's scrumptiously sexy."

Mel crossed her arms over her chest, her red mani-cured fingernails tapping on her slender biceps. "If he's so sexy, why didn't either of you go out with him?"

"He didn't ask us," I said.

"That's not a point in his favor. In fact, that proves he's a very foolish man."

"You happen to like foolish men," Kera reminded her.

Mel smiled. "You're right. When do I get to meet him?"

"Don't know," I said. "I'll have to work it out somehow."

We resumed our shopping and I soon found a pair of pants I knew both my cousins would approve of. Extra-tight and black, with ribbons of red, pink and yellow orchids sewn up the bottom left seam. I wanted them. Badly. And not because Royce thought I smelled like orchids. They were pretty, that's all. *And easily removable.*

"This is so cool." Kera clapped her hands, jumping up and down in a little dance. "Oh, I'm so excited for both of you. All right, girls," she said when she settled down. "We came here to shop and that's exactly what we're going to do. Now that Naomi's hormones have decided to come out and play, we need a few more items for her seduction arsenal. Let's get to work."

LATER THAT NIGHT, I lay in bed and considered the outfits I'd purchased—one green sundress (Kera insisted), an ice-blue miniskirt with matching tank top, and a blood-red pantsuit—as well as a red lace nightie. And the black pants, of course.

What would Royce do when he saw me wearing them? Would his eyes heat like they did when he wanted to kiss me? Would he become desperate to tear the clothes off me?

The image had me aching again, hungry. I rolled to my side and stared out my bedroom window, drawing in cleansing breaths. The night sky was as black and silky as velvet, the stars tiny pinpricks of diamond light. So beautiful and peaceful. But sometimes I hated these nights alone with nothing to do but think.

I wanted to talk to Royce, to hear his sexy, seductive voice, but that was tantamount to relationship behavior so I nixed that idea immediately. I'd sleep with him, yes. Entrench him in my life and rely on him, no. I wanted to hear his voice so badly, though, that I started trembling. My blood heated, growing hotter and hotter. I moaned.

I decided to call my mom. Yes, my mom. If anything could get my mind off naked bodies and phone sex, *she* could. Leaning over to my nightstand, I palmed my cordless phone and quickly dialed her number. As I settled back into the covers, she answered.

"Hello?" My mom sounded grumpy and sleepy and wonderful all at once.

I smiled, feeling calmer already. "Hello to you, too."

"Naomi?" There was a pause and I pictured her jolting up. "Is something wrong? What's wrong? I know something's wrong."

"Nothing's wrong, I swear. I just wanted to hear your voice."

"Gloria, what's going on? What's wrong?" my stepdad said in the background.

"It's Naomi. She says she's just calling to chat."

"To chat? At this hour? Something's wrong. What's wrong?"

My mom sighed. "I don't know. Give me a minute to find out."

"Fine, but I want to talk to her when you're done."

I rolled my eyes. Ah, this crazy couple could always usher me back to a sense of normalcy.

"Now, why don't you tell me what's bothering you, darling," my mom said to me. "You never call this late."

"I need your advice." The words tumbled out of me before I could stop them. "How can a girl know if a man will treat her right? If he'll be faithful to her?"

She gasped with excitement. "Are you thinking about getting married again?"

"No, nothing like that," I rushed out. "I'm just curious about how you knew Jonathan wouldn't turn out like Dad." Slap her around. Cheat on her. Verbally abuse her. How did she ever place her trust in another man's hands?

"I didn't," my mom said. "I couldn't. I could only hope."

I gasped this time. "Mom, I expected you to give me a pep talk. To tell me there's a man out there who will love me and treat me right and never cheat on me."

"You didn't let me finish. There *is* a man out there for you. Will he treat you right? Not always. Will he cheat? Only time can tell. Things happen and people do change." Her voice raised bitterly. "Even Jonathan and I have our problems."

Every muscle in my body froze at the implication of her words. Was she trying to tell me something? She and Jonathan rarely fought. Mom had probably meant they were having problems about who should do the dishes or something equally innocent. That's all. Over the years, Jonathan had proven himself to be a good guy. Even though I'd accused him for so many years of just pretending. I'd expected him to one day morph into a beast, but he never had. Gradually, my body relaxed.

"Now, Gloria. Naomi doesn't need to know our problems." Static filled the line as my stepdad claimed the phone. "Naomi, Jonathan here. Marriage is a wonderful thing. You know I don't believe in divorce and always discourage my patients from taking that route."

Yes, I'd heard his thoughts on the matter a thousand times over the last few months. He thought I should give Richard the Bastard yet another chance. Maybe I should have told him everything Richard had done to me. Maybe I should have explained just how deeply I'd been hurt. But I hadn't. Yes, I'd given him and my mom a glimpse, but never the harshest of the reality. I hadn't wanted the people I most respected to know how stupid I'd been. How utterly foolish.

"Are you considering going back to Richard?" he asked.

"My answer is the same as the last time you asked me. Hell, no."

"Oh," he said, disappointment loud and clear in his tone.

My hand clenched on the phone and a spark of fury sprang to life. "You're so eager for me to take him back, but you didn't live with him." Perhaps I *should* forget my pride for a moment and give Jonathan more than a glimpse. "You didn't have to endure total humiliation at his hands. What if I told you Richard had tried to kill me during our marriage?" My tone was hard, unbending, and for the first time in my life, I actually felt like a true Tigress.

"I'd—I'd say you had every right to leave him," Jonathan blustered. "But he didn't. Richard is not a violent man."

"He didn't try to kill me physically, no. He simply tried to kill my emotions. My self-esteem. He cheated on me, Jonathan. Over and over again. He left me broke. He made me feel worthless. Isn't that just as bad?"

Jonathan sputtered. "I'm—I'm sorry, Naomi. I didn't know."

My anger drained away. This man really did love me. He'd raised me from nine on and he'd always treated me like a daughter. He did want what was best for me.

Another burst of static erupted as my mom grabbed the phone. "Naomi, dear. I heard what you said. You did the right thing leaving Richard. I hope he rots in hell."

"Thank you, Mom. That means a lot to me."

"Have you found a new man, then? Is that the reason for this call?"

"No," I lied, and that single word settled like lead in my stomach. Royce *was* a new man, a new temptation. A new everything.

"I can always tell when you're lying. Your voice gets higher. Meet me at Holy Grounds tomorrow.

Eight a.m." She sounded like a drill sergeant, expecting absolute compliance with her orders. "We need some mother-daughter time."

"I will." I didn't even think about refusing. Besides, I wanted to see her. I loved my mom and didn't spend enough time with her. "G'night, Mom."

"Night, dear."

I hung up the phone and flopped onto my bed. I blinked up at the ceiling. All right. Well. Now my long, sleepless night could officially begin.

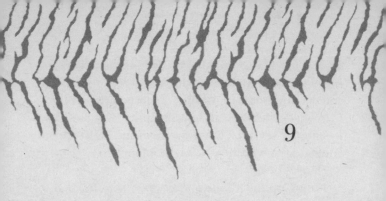

9

A Tigress must always be on her guard against a Tiger. These male animals sense fear, smell it, and will try to use it against you to get what they want from you.

THE NEXT MORNING, A LITTLE before eight, I found myself sitting alone at the coffee shop, waiting for my mom. I'd left that damn beeping BlueJay at home. I was *this* close to flushing it down the toilet. "Stupid BJ," I muttered. *That's* the name it really deserved.

Vanilla and cinnamon flavored the air, blending with the scent of fresh baked breads. I swirled a spoon in my mocha latte and watched as people sauntered past my table.

I didn't want to be here. Last night I'd wanted to see my mom. Today I didn't. God knows I didn't want to answer questions about my love life, didn't want to discuss the merits of love and marriage. And that's why she'd called this meeting, I knew it was.

Why in the world had I opened that topic for discussion?

Was I an idiot?

Wait, maybe I shouldn't answer that.

Mom had called me early this morning to make sure I remembered our meeting. She'd done it on purpose, making sure I was too groggy to think up a good excuse to avoid her.

Smart woman, my mom.

Finally, she arrived, only fifteen minutes late. Better than usual. My mom had no concept of time, really. Throughout my childhood, she'd made me late for everything. Birthday parties, cheerleading camp, hell, even school. I'd always gotten lukewarm, leftover food at the parties, missed exciting games and never learned the right cheers. Come to think of it, maybe that was when my obsession with punctuality had started.

"Why are you wearing that color?" was the first thing she said, taking the seat across from me. She was an attractive woman in her early fifties. Short brown hair, eyes that were a mix of brown and gray— and filled with a kind of sadness and vulnerability I hadn't seen in a long time. Her slight build and petite height gave her a damsel-in-distress vibe.

"Are you all right?" I asked, concern growing.

She waved away my words and the action wafted a sweet fragrance of lilies in my direction. Lily was her favorite scent. Every time I'd cried over a boy, she'd wrapped her arms around me comfortingly and that smell had surrounded me.

"You should be wearing green," she said. "To match your eyes."

"In case you never noticed, my eyes are gray."

"Never mind that," she said, once again waving my words away. "That brown washes out your skin tone."

Why was she so concerned about my clothing choices? That was completely unlike her. "I like to look washed out," I said dryly. "Otherwise people are intimidated by my glorious beauty."

Her lips pressed together to prevent a smile. "Do you sass everyone this way, or just me? Never mind. I'm just glad you're doing it. I was afraid Richard had killed your spirit. Anyway, we were talking about your clothes and the fact that you should be wearing something green."

My eyes widened as it suddenly hit me. I almost groaned. She knew about Royce. That was the only explanation for this bizarre behavior.

She confirmed my suspicions with her next words. "Why didn't you tell me you're working with Royce Powell?"

Because I didn't want to, I silently answered. To her, I said, "How did you know about my job with Mr. Powell?"

"Mr. Powell, is it?" She tapped her pink oval fingernail against the table surface. "That's not what the *Tattler* says you call him."

I jolted to a perfectly aligned position any chiropractor would have applauded. "The *Tattler* has an article about me and Royce?"

"That's why I'm late. I saw the tabloid at a newsstand and almost died." Her pretty face scrunched with distaste. She pulled the tabloid from her purse and slid it across the table. The front page glared up at me.

It was a picture of me walking out of my apartment building. I looked…bad. Really bad. My face was all puckered up like I'd just sucked down two dozen lemons without a breath in between. My hair was anchored back in my usual twist, except my shadow made the twist look eight times larger, reminding me of Marge Simpson.

The caption read Has Royce Powell Been Brainwashed by Alien Female?

Mortification washed through me and I wanted to slink down in my chair. My cheeks reddened. My only hope was that I looked so hideous in the picture that no one would recognize me in person.

"Really, Naomi. Couldn't you have smiled at the photographer or something? You look…I don't even want to say it."

Not wanting to draw undue attention to myself, I kept my voice down. "I didn't know anyone was taking my picture."

She frowned and shook her head. "Sweetie, you need to be more aware of your surroundings. It's dangerous to be so oblivious to what's going on around you. A thief could run off with your purse or something."

As if I didn't know that.

"Don't feel bad," my mom added. "You're not the only poor female caught on film with Royce."

My shoulders straightened. "What! What other woman?" That bastard!

She blinked. "Well, this one." She tapped the corner of the paper and my gaze darted there. Royce stood next to Gwendolyn Summers, the gorgeous, leggy brunette he'd been photographed with before. They were in formal wear, looking fancy. Perfect together. Pieces of a well-matched puzzle.

What were they doing together yet again? Was Royce dating her? He'd told me she was only a friend. It was none of my business if he *was* dating her, but damn him to the hottest fires of hell! He'd asked me to marry him. He'd kissed me. Twice. He said he loved me. What a scum, rat, dog bastard. I wouldn't sleep with him now if I was dying and the only thing that could save me was a penis injection from him.

The sound of crumpling paper filled my ears and I realized I was gripping the tabloid too tightly. I also realized another photographer could be here, too, waiting to snap another shot of me. Immediately I pasted a pleasant, I'm-so-happy-and-not-a-hideous-monster smile on my face. I glanced around the room, showing that smile to everyone who looked in my direction.

My mom eyed me as if I'd suddenly sprouted braided nose hair. "What are you doing?"

"Nothing," I said, still gazing around the coffee shop, trying to spot any suspicious characters. No one seemed out of the ordinary. No one sported a camera.

"Naomi, sweetheart, your face looks…I don't know, frozen. And that's the fakest grin I've ever seen."

I would have glowered at her but I didn't want to spoil my nonchalant expression. "What did you want to meet me for? And don't tell me it's because you were worried about me. I've already told you there's nothing wrong."

"Can't I see my daughter for no other reason than that I miss her?"

No. There was always a reason. I decided to turn this around and aim the spotlight at her. Still smiling, of course. "Why don't you tell me why you look so sad, hmm?"

"I do *not* look sad." She assumed an airy pose, though it clearly took a concentrated effort on her part. "I was just curious about your social life, is all. You call me in the middle of the night, asking about love and marriage, and now I learn you're working for Royce Powell. Are you considering marriage to him?"

"Not even if it would save my soul from roasting in hell!" *Smile,* I reminded myself. I bared my teeth in what I hoped was a happy grin.

"Well." Her pointed stare bore into me, probing deep and completely unnerving me as only my mom could. "Are you? Be honest this time."

"No." *Smile, damn it.* "Of course not."

"Why not? And stop smiling like that."

I allowed my facial features to relax, but only slightly. "You know why."

"Because you saw him in a picture with that

Summers woman? Or because of Richard the Bastard?" She scowled. "Jonathan might not have seen the way Richard changed you, but I did, and every day I curse that lying scumbag to everlasting hell for what he did to my baby's hopes and dreams. You're a beautiful, intelligent woman and you should be—"

A waiter appeared, cutting off the rest of her sentence. What had she been about to say? That I should be comfortable with the idea of marriage? If so, I didn't know what I could say in response. Once, I *did* have dreams of marriage, children and happily ever after. When Royce said every girl pictured herself in a wedding dress, walking down the aisle to pledge herself to the man she loved, he'd been right in my case, though I'd never admit it to him. I'd wanted those things at one time, very badly. Now I wanted to rely only on myself. I wanted to be happy because *I* made myself happy.

I sipped my latte while my mom ordered an espresso. The second the waiter moved away, she picked up our conversation but maneuvered it down a different path.

"I have something to ask you, Naomi, and I want you to tell me the truth. I won't be upset, I swear."

Oh Jeez. This didn't sound good. "All right," I said, bracing myself for impact. "I'll be honest with you." Maybe.

She sucked in a breath, paused, then swallowed. Sucked in another breath. Swallowed again.

"Out with it," I cried.

"Are you gay?"

"Mother!" My mouth dropped open and I sat for a long while in stunned disbelief. Only the thought that someone could take a picture of me looking like that snapped me out of it. "Why would you ask me something like that?" First Royce and now my mom. What kind of come-and-get-me-ladies vibe was I putting out there?

"I'm just curious, sweetie. Since your breakup with Richard the Bastard, you've become a dating recluse. Jonathan tells me this is a definite sign that you hate men."

Little Johnnie was a regular pain in my ass. I think he lived for analyzing every moment of my existence.

"Jonathan also says Richard the Bastard was a smoke screen," my mom finished.

"A smoke screen?" I asked, not sure I wanted to hear the reasoning behind this little gem.

"You know." She motioned with her hands. "A device used to fool those around you into believing what you want them to believe, and not what is the actual truth." That was a direct quote from Jonathan, I knew. I could almost hear his "helpful" voice while my mother spoke, as if she were channeling him.

Sweet Jesus, this was too much.

"I'm not into women, Mom. I really do like men."

Doubtful, she gazed down at the table. "If you're sure—"

"I'm sure. I want to have sex with men." God, I couldn't believe we were having this conversation.

"All right," she said on a sigh, "I believe you."

Her coffee was delivered, and she stared down at the cup for a long while. Another sigh slipped from her lips a split second before her face crumbled. "I think Jonathan is cheating on me."

The blurted words hit me like a disco globe falling from a domed ceiling. I'd expected this type of announcement in the first several years of their marriage. Not now. Fury blazed a hungry path through every part of me, even hotter and darker than when I'd first found out about Richard. For my mom's sake, I didn't allow it to emerge. Not yet. She needed comfort right now, not rage. "I'm sorry, Mom. I'm so, so sorry."

"I don't know what to do." Tears gleamed in her eyes, making the hazel irises look like swirling pools of brown and silver.

"Why do you think he's seeing someone else?"

"It all started when he bought me that damn lamp for my birthday. What woman wants a practical household item as her present?"

"No woman I know."

"He should have known better. But I think I nagged him about it too much because after that, he started coming home late. And he's been making secret phone calls. I know because he slithers out of bed when he thinks I'm asleep and goes into another room with his cell phone. Some evenings he even stinks of some musky bouquet-type perfume. You know I'd never wear anything like that. I wear lilies. Lilies!"

I somehow managed to retain a neutral expression.

Inside, however, the fury bubbled and churned with greater force. I was a seething cauldron, ready to erupt. The late nights, the secret phone calls, the different perfumes…those had been the early signs with Richard.

"Maybe I drove him to it, it's just—it's just—" She wiped at her tears with a shaky hand. "I never thought he'd be like your father."

At first, I'd allowed myself to make excuses. Working late. Business emergency. A freak perfumed breeze that stuck to his clothes. When the excuses no longer worked, I'd blamed myself. I wouldn't let my mom do the same. Not this time, anyway. If he hadn't died of a heart attack, my mom would still be with my real dad.

Reaching out, I covered her hand with mine. "There's not a reason good enough for a man to cheat. Ever. It's his fault, his lack of integrity. Not yours."

"What should I do?" she whispered brokenly. "I can't go through this again."

"You need to hire a private investigator ASAP and catch him in the act."

"I don't know." She shifted uncomfortably in her seat, refusing to meet my gaze. "What if I'm wrong?"

"There's only one way to find out."

"I don't know," she repeated.

"Will you have any respect for yourself if you do nothing? You did nothing with Daddy. You saw what Richard's affairs did to me. Don't let this beat you down. Be strong and take action."

"I—I just…"

I knew what that wavering meant, so I pounced on

it before she could completely absolve the man. "If you don't want to hire a private investigator, don't. But I'm going to follow him."

She frowned and finally faced me. The tears were gone, at least. "Really, Naomi. Be serious."

"I'm dead serious." I was going to nail the bastard in more ways than one. Lie to my mom, would he? Cheat on my mom, would he? He'd picked the wrong girls to screw with. Detective Delacroix. That was me.

My mom pressed her lips together and reached out with her free hand, skimming her fingertips over my jaw. Tenderness shone from her features. "I've always thought of myself as the strong one for what I survived, but it's you. You're the one with true strength. Look at you, ready to defend my honor."

I glanced down at the table surface, beading with rings of moisture from our cups. Her praise caused my chest to constrict. She was wrong, but her words pleased me nonetheless. "I'm trying," I said.

"No, not trying. You *are* strong."

If she kept it up, I was going to bawl like a baby. I clasped her hand in mine and gave a gentle squeeze.

"Jonathan expects you at the house tonight. Seven-thirty. He wants to counsel you on your relationship choices. Can you come?"

How ironic. Relationship counseling from a cheater. I didn't think I was ready to see the rotten creep without scratching the skin from his bones, but I'd do it. I'd use the opportunity to sneak around the house like a goddamn Scooby-Doo disciple and find clues.

"I'll be there," I said with a firm nod.

"I love you, sweetie." She kissed my cheek, stood and glided away.

I FORCED MEL AND KERA TO GO with me to Jonathan's "relationship therapy" session that night. After he was finished dispensing his advice, they were going to distract him while I searched the house. Thankfully, my fury had lessened and I felt in control enough not to attack the cheating bastard with a whip and blowtorch. I loved the man, but I still planned to castrate him.

Maybe I wouldn't have been so upset if not for the picture of Royce and Big-Boobed Gwen. Nah. I'd still be pissed. Cheating was cheating.

Mom greeted us at the door. She brightened when she spotted her nieces. "Mel, Kera! I'm so glad you came. It's been too long since I last saw you. How're you doing, girls?"

"Fine, Aunt Gloria. Just fine," they answered simultaneously, and hugged her.

"Come in, come in," my mom said. I followed behind Mel and Kera, but when I tried to move past my mom, she grabbed my arm and tugged me aside. "You look ready for war." She spoke behind her hand and didn't meet my eyes. "What are you planning?"

"It's better if you don't know." I kissed her cheek, savoring the fragrance of lilies, and sailed past her. "Where's Dr. Johnnie?"

"You know he hates when you call him that." Mom waved toward the back of the house. "He's waiting for you in the den."

We followed the trail of floral-scented candles. The den was spacious, well-lit and fairly bursting with elegant bird figurines of every color and breed. Jonathan collected them. If I were analyzing him, I'd say he collected them because he's a cheating bastard who thinks it's okay to trample over a woman's self-esteem and ruin her ability to trust for the rest of her life.

That, and perhaps he wishes he could fly.

My stepdad was sitting on a big, cushy recliner, smoking a pipe and reading a book. He had a thick head of silver hair and a neat, trimmed beard.

Over the years, this man had counseled me on everything from eating disorders to shopping addictions. My entire childhood had been spent digging into my inner core, learning why I behaved as I did.

Maybe that was why I was so screwed up.

A pretty woman in her mid-twenties occupied the room's only other recliner. She, too, was reading a book and didn't notice the new arrivals. I gave her a once-over and frowned. Red curls framed her round, pleasant face. Her brown eyes tilted upward and her lips were small and shaped like Betty Boop's. She wore a fitted pink T-shirt and red-striped pants.

Could *this* be Jonathan's new love interest? Was he screwing around with a woman less than half his age? My frown became a hot scowl. How dare he bring her into my mom's house? How dare he! He was probably trying to pass the redheaded Boop impersonator off as a "friend." I'd met a parade of Richard's friends, aka whores, tramps and sluts.

"Hello, Jonathan," I said, both words measured carefully. Cheating bastard. Rot in hell!

He glanced up from his book and smiled, completely unaware of the fact that I was planning his death in my head.

"Naomi. So good of you to come." He placed his pipe in the ashtray, smoke wafting around him like a misty cloud. "You'll be happy to know I've been studying primitive mating rituals, hoping to help you with your problem."

Mel snorted, and I had to pinch her arm to keep her from saying anything.

"What problem?" I asked.

He didn't answer. "I see you've brought the twins," he said, brightening. "Excellent. Excellent. I'm sure this will be beneficial for everyone."

"Who's your friend?" I motioned to the redhead with a tilt of my chin. I didn't mean to sound so rude, but my blood pressure had escalated several more points.

The woman in question stood and held out her hand to shake. "Hi, I'm Jennifer. Jonathan and Gloria's neighbor."

Neighbor…was that the word for "whoring tramp" nowadays? "So nice to meet you," I ground out. I didn't take her hand.

She blinked over at me, obviously startled by my seemingly unwarranted ambivalence. "Nice to meet you, as well."

"I'm Kera." Kera shot me a what's-wrong-with-you frown before reaching out and clasping Jennifer's hand in a friendly shake. "And this is my sister, Melody. Everyone calls her Mel."

"Jennifer is joining us for the session," Jonathan said. "I thought it would do her some good, too."

I just bet you did, I thought darkly.

Mel, Kera and I settled on the couch. My mom eased onto the armrest beside Jonathan. Jennifer began to reclaim her chair, but Jonathan said, "No, no, Jennifer. You sit beside Naomi."

I tensed, not wanting the tramp anywhere near me.

"I'm fine here," she said, casting a wary glance in my direction.

"To the couch." Jonathan pointed.

I scooted over to make room and Jennifer obligingly sat down. She smelled good, like roses and baby's breath. I made a mental note to hate that scent for the rest of my life, as well as to check Jonathan's laundry for any hint of roses.

"I can feel everyone's eagerness." Jonathan rubbed his hands together in a show of delight. He lived for this shit. "That's the first step toward recovery, you know."

What were we trying to recover from? Being related to cheating male whores?

Get a hold of the bitterness, Naomi. There'll be time enough for that later. I pasted a fake smile on my face. In the past I'd always put up with these therapy sessions because they made Jonathan happy. He'd done his best to make me feel loved, so I'd done the same for him. Now, today, I only wanted it over.

Using a remote control, Jonathan turned on the

stereo. Soft new-age music floated and hummed from the speakers.

Kera rolled her eyes at me and I shrugged.

"Now then, girls," he said. "I want you to relax."

Like that was possible. My bones and muscles felt tight and strung out, brittle, ready to break.

"Close your eyes." He was using his I-am-in-a-happy-place voice. "That's right. Relax. Find your meadow of happiness. Melody, close your eyes please. Good girl. Naomi, you, too."

Though we'd all endured many therapy sessions over the years, I guess none of us had realized that failure to do as Jonathan wanted only prolonged the experience.

"Really, Gloria," Jonathan suddenly sighed. "You're casting shadows over my notes."

"Oh, goodness. I'm sorry." My mom moved to stand in the corner.

I watched the whole thing through slitted eyelids and came close to launching myself across the room and bitch-slapping the man. No one told my mom to get out of their way! This was not a normal interaction between my mom and Jonathan. He was acting strangely, just like my mom had said, and I didn't like it.

One point in Royce's favor was he'd never spoken to me so dismissively, as if I were a pesky fly to be swatted away. Still, the man liked leggy brunettes, and that made him just as bad as Johnnie.

"Better," Jonathan said. "Now, where were we? Close your eyes…check. Meadow of happiness…yes, there." Once again his voice went soft. He sounded like an idiot when he did that. "Imagine yourself in a meadow. A lush, green meadow swaying with wild-flowers and lit by sunshine."

Kera squeezed my knee.

Mel smothered a chuckle.

Jennifer had yet to move. In fact, I barely heard her breathing.

"While you're in this safe, happy place, I want you to consider my next words. Picture them, even. Rela-tionships are like maps. When you first meet someone new, you set a course for yourself."

Yada, yada, yada.

He continued. "Sometimes, the wind will blow you off course. But that doesn't mean your map is useless. That just means you need to readjust your route. Do you girls understand what I'm trying to tell you?"

"I do," my mom said, her voice hard.

"Not you, Gloria."

I bit the inside of my cheek to prevent myself from snapping the man's head off.

"Girls, do you understand?"

I nodded stiffly and nudged Kera and Mel. They, too, nodded.

"Good. Now it's time to picture the man—not the woman—you plan to marry."

How subtle.

"Remember, no choice is wrong." He cleared his throat. "Who do you see, Kera?"

She glanced to me, her expression saying, *Do I really have to answer?*

Again I nodded.

"I see someone I love dearly," she said. "But I can't make out a face clearly."

"That's okay. At least you know your map is going to lead you to love. And you, Melody? Who do you see?"

"Actually, I see four men."

"Four?" he gasped out.

"One for every divorce."

"Perhaps we need to readjust your map." He uttered a nervous chuckle. "I'll work with you privately on that." Now he turned his attention to me. "And who do you see, Naomi?"

At that point, I decided I'd had enough. I wasn't in the mood to convince my stepfather that I liked men.

"Well, Naomi?" he persisted.

"I see Jennifer," I told him. "I've been hot for her since I walked into this room." With that, I leaned over and planted the woman a big one.

Surprisingly, she responded.

"How was I supposed to know Jennifer's gay?" I whispered fiercely.

Kera, Mel and I were in the kitchen, supposedly preparing everyone a drink. The therapy session was over and it was now social hour.

"Did you see the look on Dr. Johnnie's face?" Mel asked, laughing. "That was priceless."

"Yeah, come here and kiss *me,* lover girl." Kera puckered up.

I covered my face with my hands. Guilt hovered

over my shoulder for the way I'd glared and snarled at Jennifer, thinking she was Jonathan's secret lover. "What else was I supposed to do?"

"I don't know, but I'm ready to sign up for the next therapy session he wants to give us," Mel said. "I've never laughed so hard. Maybe next time he'll tell me a man's penis is like a flute. Blow it hard enough and you'll make music."

A choked laugh bubbled past my throat. "Just take him a drink and keep everyone busy. I've got some snooping to do."

FIRST, I SEARCHED MY MOM and Jonathan's bedroom. Needless to say, the whole thing creeped me out. I didn't need to know that they slept on red silk sheets and had mirrors on their ceiling. I didn't need to know about the sex toys in the drawer next to their bed. Most of all, I did *not* need to see the Strokia Sex book—whatever the hell that was—under Jonathan's pillow.

Cringing, I rifled through the dirty clothes hamper and the scent of sweet perfume wafted to my nostrils. Floral and musky, yes, but not lilies. Mom was right; that was not a scent she'd ever wear. I checked Jonathan's shirts for lipstick stains and stray hairs. Nothing. Not a smudge, not a strand. The man was immaculate.

Of course, a cheater needed to be immaculate to properly hide his clandestine activities.

With Richard the Bastard, I'd had to count condoms. He hadn't thought to buy a new box but had used the one from our home. The supply would get low—and they hadn't been used with me. My mom was postmenopausal, so that would be no help.

Where should I look next? Mom had said Jonathan sneaked away to make secret phone calls. I needed to get a hold of his phone bill. Every number dialed and received would be recorded there.

My heartbeat drumming in my ears, I padded quietly to the office. It was small, but crammed with books. Mostly psychiatric mumbo jumbo. His desk drawers were locked, I noticed, eyes narrowing. He probably kept kinky pictures of the other woman in there.

I leaned back in the plush, black leather seat and considered my options. I could jimmy the locks open with a letter opener, but then he'd know I'd been here. I could search for the key, perhaps not find it and waste precious time.

There was no choice, really. I had to risk wasting time by searching for the key.

My gaze circled the room. If I were Jonathan, where would I hide my keys? A place my poor, un-suspecting wife wouldn't think to look for them, that's where. Richard had kept his on his person or in his briefcase 24-7. I doubted Jonathan would be that paranoid. He was a mind doctor, therefore he would assume he could outsmart anyone who entered his domain.

The picture of him fishing on Lavon Lake…no. A hollowed-out book…no. Too cliché. My gaze contin-ued to search, considering and discarding items as I came to them. Then I noticed a small, seemingly innocent blue-and-yellow parakeet. I lifted the item in question and turned it in every direction, wondering why my I'm-so-sophisticated stepdad owned an ugly, plastic figurine.

The answer hit me, and I smiled slowly.

"Of course you'd hide the key in plain sight," I whispered, pressing the bird's beak. A key instantly snapped out. My hands shaking with excitement and nervousness, I quickly unlocked and searched the desk drawers.

My teeth bared when I spotted photos of a plain, conservatively dressed woman in multiple stages of movement. In some, she was holding a cute, dark-headed toddler. My jawbone almost snapped with the force I used to bite down. Did Jonathan have a love child? Of course he did. Why else would he hide the picture? That sugar daddy dickwad!

I found his cell-phone bill, too. There were too many numbers to write down, so I folded the papers and stuffed them in my pocket. Hopefully, he'd just think he lost them.

Smoldering with anger, yet giddy with my triumph, I locked the desk and replaced the key, then strolled into the den. I breathed a sigh of relief when no one took notice of my arrival. Mel and Jonathan were facing off, arguing over the prevalence of divorce. Kera, Jennifer and my mom were seated demurely on the couch, discussing the merits of good skin cleanser.

Watching them proved to be a surreal experience. I'd gone from snooping to finding incriminating photos to happy domesticity in less than seven minutes. I almost wished I was dreaming.

"Time to go," I said, my voice tense.

Everyone's attention snapped to me.

"Are you feeling better, sweetie?" My mom pushed to her feet, her expression concerned. At her sides, her hands twisted the material of her slacks. "Mel said you were sick."

"No, uh, I'm not feeling better. I'm very sick." I coughed for good measure.

"I thought it was your stomach," Jonathan said.

"Throwing up probably scratched her throat," Mel said helpfully.

"Yes, that's right." I rubbed my stomach and gave another cough. "I hate to leave so early, but I need to get home."

A look of relief washed over Mel and Kera's faces, and they raced to my side, wrapping their arms around me and pretending to hold me up. "Let's get you home and put you to bed," Mel said. "You look awful. Just awful."

Gee, thanks. I allowed them to lead me toward the front door.

"Did you find anything?" Kera whispered.

"Phone records."

"I'll ring you tomorrow and see how you're feeling," my mom called after us, a wealth of meaning in her words.

Just as a Tiger searches for and uses your weaknesses against you, you must find and use his against him. Exploiting a weakness can make the difference between victory and defeat.

I SPENT THE NEXT DAY, Friday, on the phone.

Royce called me. Richard did, too.

I told Richard to die and go to everlasting hell. I hung up on Royce without a word. He called me back, and I said, "Nice photo of you with Gwendolyn. Your non-girlfriend. Did you ask her to marry you, too?"

He laughed. Actually laughed. "She's a friend, nothing more. We do the charity circuit together. I'd love for you to be my date from now on. Are you interested?"

He sounded so sincere, but then, Richard had always sounded sincere as well.

I told Royce, "No thanks," and ended the call, not knowing what to think. Should I believe him? And why the hell was I so concerned? We weren't in a relationship—I'd made sure of that.

I avoided my mom's "did you find anything" call. I avoided Jonathan's "how do you feel" call. I did answer Jennifer's "would you like to go on a date" call and explained the kiss I'd planted on her. She took it well.

Through it all, my BlueJay never shut up. It continued to beep and beep and beep.

Finally I drop-kicked the little bastard out the window, taking immense satisfaction when I heard it shatter. Feeling better, I dialed every number on Jonathan's cell-phone bill, giving everyone the same story, "Your number was on my caller ID. Who are you and why did you call this number?"

The responses were wide and varying. Only two disturbed me, however. Jonathan had called Nora Hallsbrook, his secretary, numerous times during the middle of the night. He'd also phoned a local beauty salon six times. Body Electric. That meant only one thing: the lying little prick was having phone sex with his slutty secretary, then paying for her beauty appointments.

How cliché. How infuriating! I knew he hadn't called the salon to book an appointment for my mom. She wouldn't have been able to talk about anything else.

As mad as I was at my stepdad, though, I was also deeply hurt and feeling unbelievably betrayed. He was supposed to be different than my father. He was supposed to guard our family unit. He was supposed to love my mom, cherish her. He was supposed to love *me*.

I pinched the bridge of my nose. I would have liked a copy of Johnnie's Visa bill to see exactly what he'd purchased for Nora. Tanning? Laser body hair removal? Total body rub to assuage the guilt she felt for helping destroy a marriage?

I'd seen Nora on numerous occasions. She was a semi-attractive woman in her early forties with big, ratted hair and lots of makeup, but she wasn't the woman I'd seen in those photos, the young woman with the child. Could Jonathan be seeing two women on the side? It wasn't too far-fetched. Richard, may he fall into the ocean and be torn apart by a pack of wild, vicious, man-hungry sharks, had had booty available in every apartment building and housing unit in every city in the United States.

God, what was I going to tell my mom? Nothing, I decided in the next flash. Not yet. I shouldn't go to her without concrete proof. Otherwise, she might blow off everything I said. Make excuses for Jonathan and wallow in disbelief.

Like I had done for so many years. Like she had done before.

Jumping up, I raced to my kitchen and grabbed my phone book. Proof. Oh yeah, I'd get her proof. I looked up the address for both Nora and the salon. Just as I finished writing them down, my phone rang.

Caller ID showed Powell, Royce. I grabbed the phone and barked, "What?"

"I've decided whether or not you go with me, I'm not going to escort Gwen to any more events. I only want to go with you."

My skin tingled at the sound of that rich, husky promise. His words shouldn't matter, but they did. I might be an idiot (again), but I believed him (kind of). *Dumb ass,* my Tigress said. Was I just like my mom?

"Are you hungry?" he asked.

"No, sorry," I said, regret pounding through me. "I'm busy."

"Doing what? Working on my mother's party?"

"Actually, no. Now isn't a good time to talk. I'm on my way out."

"Where's your BlueJay? I programmed a meeting today and it should have been beeping all morning. You should be on your way to my office."

"Hmm, well, I haven't heard a thing." A knock sounded at my door. I pushed out a frustrated sigh, hating to end the conversation, but knowing I needed to, and walked into the living room. "I'll talk to you later. We need to discuss tomorrow's trip to Colorado and the fact that I still don't want to go." I hung up before he could utter a single protest and tossed the phone on my couch.

From the coffee table, I snatched up my keys and purse—I had yet to replace the stolen one, so I had to make do with this old, ugly white one. Right now I wore brown pants and a white top. Brown sandals, perfect for the two-mile walk ahead. My hair was in its usual twist. Hopefully I presented a completely un-noticeable and unmemorable package.

Without stopping to check who wanted to visit with me, I jerked open my door, ready to send whoever it was scurrying.

I stopped dead in my tracks instead.

Royce smiled down at me. He wore jeans and a black T-shirt. The material clung deliciously to his biceps and pecs, outlining every ridge and peak. I'd never seen him dressed so casually, and the sight made my mouth water. My nipples immediately took notice, jumping up to say, *Hi, Royce. We love you and really want to introduce ourselves to you properly.*

"I worked late last night, and I took the day off because I'd planned to meet with you today," he said, pocketing his cell. Still smiling—perhaps because he'd caught a glimpse of my naughty nipples—he said, "I'm going with you, wherever it is you're going in such a hurry."

I fought a shiver of anticipation. The thought of spending the day with him appealed to me in so many ways. I'd get to hear his voice, feel his warmth, even stare at him if I wanted. I'd also get a distraction that I, Detective Delacroix, couldn't afford.

"No, you're not." I scooted around him, doing my best not to touch him, and locked the door. Not sparing him a glance, I stalked toward the main lobby. I loved having a bottom-level apartment. No stairs or elevator for me, thank you.

"Where we going?" He was barely a step behind me.

As I pretended to ignore him, I felt the heat of him all the way to my bones. I stopped before going outside. The scent of sandalwood taunted and teased my nose. "You're not going to get rid of me," he said, before I could tell him to go away.

"Royce—"

"Naomi. I'm coming. End of conversation."

If I didn't invite him to come with me, I realized, he'd follow me and draw all kinds of unwanted attention my way. He was just too damn noticeable with that sexy, recognizable face of his. I'd rather deal with a distraction than the possibility of being spotted by my prey.

"Can you be sneaky, Royce? Can you blend into a crowd?"

"Yes," he answered, his forehead furrowed in confusion.

"Do you have a car with you?"

"Yes."

"Fine, you can come." Silver lining: I wouldn't have to walk, nor would I have to pay for a cab if I changed my mind about walking. I hated cabs, hated buses more, but I didn't yet have the money to fix my jalopy. "We're going to a salon on Main Street. Body Electric."

"The joy in your voice is making me feel all warm inside."

"Then my day is complete," I said with a sarcastic edge.

He snorted.

Lord, he was even sexy when he snorted. I felt

myself melting, my bones liquefying in anticipation of a touch. Already my hands itched to explore him. Itched to touch his skin, itched to wrap around his—

"What are you having done at the salon? You're perfect just the way you are."

I tossed him a frown before pushing open the door. He was doing it again. Being sweet and irresistible, making me go disgustingly gooey inside. "Don't be nice to me, okay?" I'd already established I couldn't resist him physically, but I really needed to resist him emotionally. He made that extremely difficult with his devilish, charming personality.

"What?" He gave a choked little laugh. "Why?"

"Just because." Bright sunlight and sweltering heat hit me full force, and I was suddenly thankful he'd insisted on coming. I would have hated to spend more than a few seconds in this heat.

Beside me, bushes swayed together despite the fact that there was no wind. Odd. But then I spotted the shattered remains of my BlueJay, forgot about the ghost bushes, and steered Royce away, trying to direct his attention somewhere else. "Uh, to answer your first question, I'm not having anything done. I just want to look around. Where's your car?"

Without a word, he sauntered to a black stretch limo and opened the passenger door. Such wealth and luxury appeared odd in front of my modest apartment building, with its un-mowed, brittle grass and peeling stucco.

Royce waved me inside. "After you."

I remained in place, floundering in a puddle of

shocked awe. "Are you trying to impress me? Because it's working."

"Actually," he said, a sheepish grin on his gorgeous face, "I just wanted my hands free."

Yippee, my nipples cried.

I hope he plays with us first, my thighs chimed in.

"Damn it!" I muttered. I had to get my thoughts under control. I might—might—believe him about Gwendolyn Summers, but I was on a mission to save my mom. Nothing else mattered at the moment, not even pleasure.

"What?" Royce asked, all innocence.

"You better keep those hands to yourself." I slid inside the car…and felt like all my troubles instantly melted away. Luxurious air-conditioning enveloped me. The seats were so plush and perfect I couldn't help but revel in their delicious decadence. Soft as clouds they were. I could have sunk into a coma of bliss.

Royce scooted inside until our shoulders brushed. A shiver rolled down my spine.

"Body Electric," he told the driver. Seconds later, the limo eased into motion. "Want to tell me what's bothering you?" he asked me. "You've got shadows under your eyes, and you're unusually pale."

I didn't want to talk about my cheating stepdad, so I said, "Did you see the article about me in the *Tattler*?"

"Well, yeah. I think everyone in Dallas saw it."

"They called me an alien. I should sue."

He uttered a short, booming laugh. "On what grounds?"

"I'm sure my attorney could think of something."
My head lolled back on the pillow rest. "I'm surprised no one was waiting outside my apartment,
snapping pictures of us as we walked out."

"They were."

I jerked upright and stared wide-eyed at him.
"What!"

"There was a woman behind the bushes. She had
a camera aimed right at us."

"And you didn't say anything? Argh. I can't believe
this." I slapped his thigh. "You better do something.
Pay her to give you the film or threaten to get her
fired. Just do something. Anything! I do not need
another hideous picture of me circulating. The last
one nearly killed my mother."

Royce wrapped his fingers around mine and leaned
toward me, bringing with him that delicious sandalwood scent. "I'll take care of it, okay?" He kissed my
temple before settling back in his seat. "No worries."
He didn't release my hand.

That single kiss affected me deeply and unequiv-
ocally, but the fact that he kept our fingers linked
meant more. I yearned to melt into him, to absorb his
strength, his complete ease with our being together.
But I remained where I was. I would not rely on a man
for anything. Especially not comfort. That's where
dependency began. I didn't allow myself to consider
the fact that I was relying on him to fix the little
unwanted photographer problem.

"Thank you," I said stiffly.

"You're very welcome," he replied, using the same

rigid tone. "Now, why don't you tell me why you want to look around this salon."

I shrugged. "I want to see what type of services they offer." It was the truth. I didn't tell him that I also wanted to speak with the employees and find out if Nora had visited.

"Why?" he persisted.

Ignoring his question, I shifted and faced the opposite window. Trees and cars whizzed past. The people in those cars strained, trying to see inside the limo, but the darkened windows blocked us from view. "Do you think you could get me a list of their employees?" If Nora *wasn't* the other woman, that employee list would give me somewhere else to look.

"Absolutely," Royce said. "Just tell me why you want it."

"Well," I said, turning to him, a lie forming in my mind, "my mother is a twin, and they were separated at birth. She's been searching for her sister all her life and I suspect one of the employees is that twin. And now, with my mother dying of cancer—" I pretended to wipe away a tear "—I want to give her this gift."

"How tragic," Royce said dryly. "Did you know your voice creeps higher when you're lying?"

Damn it, my mom had warned me about that betraying fact. I crossed my arms over my chest and frowned.

"Maybe a better gift for your *dying* mother would be grandchildren," he suggested.

My lashes sprang up and I was given a full-on view of his amusement. "You are so not funny." But I was covered in a cold sweat by the time the limo stopped in front of a white stucco building.

"We're here." Royce didn't wait for the driver, but opened the door himself and emerged. He held out a hand for me.

The dry heat clamped tight fists around me as I stepped out.

"Do we need to be incognito here?" he asked. When my brow crinkled in confusion, he added, "Before we left your apartment, you asked me if I knew how to be sneaky."

Oh, yeah. "I don't want them to know my name, but they can know yours."

He nodded. "Let me do the talking."

We entered side by side. A long desk loomed in front, manned by several young, attractive women. Too young for Johnnie, that was for sure. While he might be willing to destroy his marriage, I didn't think he'd be willing to destroy his practice for an underage hottie.

But what did I truly know about men?

"How can we help you?" the only blonde asked.

"I'm Royce Powell, and I need to speak with the owner." He voice reeked of suave authority. "My fiancée isn't sure which salon she wants to use the day of our wedding. I'm here to see what type of services can be provided so my little sugar bottoms feels extra special that day."

My stomach dropped at the word *fiancée*—then twisted at *sugar bottoms*. Sugar bottoms, indeed.

"Money is not an object," Royce continued. "We'll want the works, of course."

I could be mistaken, but I think dollar signs flashed in the blonde's eyes.

"Right this way," she said. "Brenda is in her office, and I know she'd love to speak with you."

"While my dear, sweet snookie-wookie is busy chatting," I said, "I think I'll have a look-see around, 'kay?" Without waiting for consent, I sailed past the desk and down a long hallway.

"I'll come with you," one of the girls said, at my side in the next instant.

For the next twenty minutes, I scoped out the entire salon, meeting and speaking with the employees. The masseuse, the aromatherapist. The nail tech, the facial tattoo artist. The tanning specialist. I asked all of them the same question: "Is my Aunt Nora, Nora Hallsbrook, a client here? Because if she's not I want to get her in ASAP. She'd love this place."

Confirming all my fears, each one answered, "Yes, she's a regular."

Jonathan the Jerk was paying for Nora's days of pampering while he treated his own wife like a bothersome insect. He was going to suffer. I was going to make him suffer. Once I returned from Colorado, I would follow him with a camera and catch him in the act. Then I would help my mom take him for everything he owned.

Fucking bastard!

When my tour ended, I strode to the front entrance. Royce was waiting at the door, and the pert receptionist was flirting with him, running her fingertip over his arm as she spoke. She was wearing a green bracelet, I noticed with a scowl.

To my surprise, Royce discreetly moved his arm. He even stepped away from her. His shoulders were stiff, and he radiated a discomfort that helped extinguish the raging fury in my blood.

"Snoogie bear," I called. "I'm back."

His gaze snapped up, colliding with mine, and he smiled with relief. "Sugar bottoms. Did you see everything you needed to see?"

"Yes." I tried to walk to him, but I suddenly couldn't move my feet. They were frozen in place. As I stood there, my gaze still locked on Royce, something…odd welled up inside me. Something sad and vulnerable. Tears sprang into my eyes.

In three quick strides, Royce was at my side, his arm slipping around my waist. I let him wrap himself around me. I hated all men at the moment, but I let him. My Tigress seemed to be on hiatus, and I didn't have the strength to protest or push away his comforting touch.

Maybe, deep down, I didn't really want to protest. Royce wasn't like Richard the Bastard. Royce wasn't like Jonathan the Jerk. Royce said sweet things and wanted to be around me. He didn't flirt with pretty receptionists. Royce called me just to hear my voice and made me feel important and needed.

"Come on," he said gently. "Let's get you home." He led me to the limo. We didn't speak the entire drive. I was grateful. I didn't know what was wrong with me, didn't know why my emotions had chosen that moment to overtake me.

"We're here, sweetheart."

I pushed open the door and tried to step outside, but he stopped me with a hand on my wrist. He held out the list I'd wanted with the other hand.

I grabbed it and ran inside the building before I burst into tears.

I CRIED MOST OF THE NIGHT, and my tears only made me angrier. At Jonathan. At myself. At Royce and Gwendolyn. I believed Royce one moment, I didn't the next. Did that make me as foolish as my mom? Worse, did that make me the same foolish Naomi I'd been before?

No, surely not. None of the above meant I trusted Royce completely.

Cheating... Why did men do it? Why did any man think it was okay to trample on a woman's heart by lying to her and giving the best of himself to a woman other than his wife? It wasn't okay. It wasn't acceptable. It was disgusting and disrespectful, vile and wretched.

When Royce arrived the next morning, my eyes were still red and puffy. I hated that I was leaving town. There was so much I needed to do: follow Nora, take pictures of her with my stepdad and, of course, the most important item on my list, kill Jonathan.

Maybe I needed this trip, though. Royce always proved a good distraction. Plus, my mom kept calling me, and I kept ignoring her. I'd even turned off the ringer. I couldn't lie to her and tell her I'd found nothing, but I couldn't tell her what I *had* found. Not yet. Not while she could deny it.

I pulled open the front door to see Royce. He held

out what must have been four dozen orchids, a mixture of yellow, white, pink and blue petals. Blue? Caught off guard, I was momentarily incapable of speech.

"For you," he said. "I know blue is your favorite color, so I had some of the petals dyed."

I'm sure my expression was horrified as I accepted the bouquet, holding it in my hands like it was a stink bomb about to go off. Richard the Bastard always brought me flowers—always red roses—when he'd done something wrong.

My heart fluttered, though, because this felt different. Royce had gone to so much trouble, had thought about my individual tastes. And he'd done it to make me feel better, I suspected, not to throw me off the scent of his bad behavior.

"I had to search the whole damn state for those," he told me.

"They're beautiful," I said softly. "Thank you."

"If you start crying, I'll be forced to cut out my heart and give it to you. How are you feeling?"

"Better." I pushed out a breath and gazed down at the dewy, sweet petals. "Thank you for, well, everything."

He grinned, a bit of self-deprecation hanging at the edges of his lips. "I was going to give you a list of to-do chores, but everything on the list was raunchy and I'd rather wait until you're receptive to give you something like that."

I laughed; I just couldn't help myself. And it felt good, forgetting my troubles, releasing my tension and simply enjoying him.

"Are you going to invite me in?" Royce asked gently. "I have another present for you."

"Oh, sure. Come in. What kind of present?" I couldn't hide my excitement.

He brushed past me, turned, then placed a brand new BlueJay in my free hand. "For you."

Damn it all to hell!

"I noticed yours had sprouted wings and flown itself out of your window, so I thought you'd like another one."

"Gee, thanks."

"You ready to go?"

"Let me put these in water first." Without a backward glance, I strode away.

Once in the kitchen, I stuffed the BlueJay under a stack of magazines (never to look at it again!) and arranged the orchids in my favorite crystal vase. A fresh, dewy scent washed over me. I closed my eyes and savored it, holding my breath for as long as I could, then releasing it.

I liked that Royce had gone to so much trouble for me. But I hated it, too. I was beginning to feel all mushy inside.

Frowning, I practically shoved the arrangement onto the table as a centerpiece, then moved the pink carnations my stepdad had sent me this morning to the counter. I don't know why I'd kept them. To remind me he was really a turkey-on-rye sandwich hidden in a Krispy Kreme coating, perhaps. The note attached had congratulated me on landing such a lucrative job and hinted that I needed to fill out an application for the position of Mrs. Royce Powell. He also apologized for pushing me to get back together with Richard. How could he be so sweet, yet treat my mom so badly?

"Who sent you those?" Royce asked from behind me. He was suddenly so close I could feel the heat of him. His arms reached out and anchored on the counter in front of me, trapping me with his body. Surrounding me.

I swallowed. I shivered.

I licked my lips and perhaps—and this is not a confession—arched my back slightly and allowed the best part of him to rub against the crease of my bottom. Tendrils of desire unfurled, wrapping and winding around me. My defenses were down, and I didn't know whether it was because I'd been through an emotional wringer the last few days or because I was destined to respond to Royce no matter what. Either way, I wanted him.

Maybe I needed to rethink my sexual time line. Maybe being with him *before* his mom's party wasn't such a bad idea.

"Who, uh, sent me what?"

He leaned forward, his sandalwood fragrance wafting around me as surely as his heat. He pointed and said, "Those," in a tone that reeked of anger and attitude.

What was this? Another bout of jealousy? "None of your business," I said, turning my head to see how my words affected him. Right before my eyes, Royce's seemingly casual facade mutated into black fury he couldn't hide.

"Who's sending you flowers, Naomi? Are you seeing someone else?"

I studied the hard line of his jaw. He'd been jealous at the thought of me flirting with Colin, but this was different. This was more potent. Raw. Like before, a part of me reveled in the thought that this man, this wonderfully sexy man, felt strongly enough about me to harbor feelings of possessiveness.

Maybe I was playing with fire by goading him, but I kind of liked the thought of being burned. "Like I told you, Royce, it's none of your business."

"Who is he? I have a right to know. Are you seeing someone else?"

I pressed my lips together, refusing to answer. A pulse ticked in Royce's temple. If his teeth clenched any tighter, I feared his jaw would break. Was it cruel of me to enjoy this so much? My ex—may he become stranded on a deserted island, his only companion a legion of man-hungry bees—had been a jealous man, but it had been an accusing, projecting I-know-you're-cheating-on-me jealousy, not a possessive one.

Feeling bold and dangerous, I plucked a petal from one of the carnations and breathed in its scent, pretending fascination with the flower. "They're beautiful, aren't they?"

Royce clasped my arm and spun me all the way around, effectively gaining my undivided attention. The petal floated unheeded to the floor. Heat fairly sparkled in his eyes.

"Are you seeing someone else?" he asked again, each word bit out.

"And if I am? You've been seen with Miss Summers."

"That's not an answer, and I explained about Gwen. I've already called her and told her I won't be escorting her again. Now, are *you* seeing someone else?"

"No," I sighed, inexplicably relieved he'd done as promised and told Gwennie goodbye. "Are you happy now?"

He released me, suddenly relaxed and completely at ease. "Who are they from?" he asked curiously, as if he hadn't been on the verge of eruption.

"My stepdad."

"Good." He tucked a stray tendril of dark hair gently behind my ear; his fingers lingered at the rise of my cheek, caressing the skin there. "I refuse to share." Then, "Get your stuff and we'll head out." He didn't give me time to disagree, he simply exited the kitchen.

He refused to share me.

I gripped the counter behind me and frowned. That was just the kind of thing a domineering Triple C would say. How macho. How revolting.

How sweet.

I heaved a deep exhalation. *You don't like to share, either, Naomi. Remember? And there will always be other women vying for Royce's attention. How long do you think he'll retain this attraction to you and you alone?*

My frown deepened into a scowl and I stomped to my room. I shouldn't want to be with him, not this much, and his legendary conquests shouldn't matter to me. Again, not this much.

As I gathered my bag and briefcase, a sense of unease stretched and awoke inside me, obliterating all other thoughts. I was about to board a plane, aka a flying instrument of death. My stomach bottomed out, leaving a hollow ache in my side.

A bit shaky, I trudged through the apartment in search of Royce.

He was lounging across the bright red cushions on my couch, looking at home as he waited for me. His expression warmed when he spotted me. "All set?"

I managed a convincing nod. I'd rather face the burning pits of hell than step one foot inside an airplane. Maybe I should have had Jonathan hypnotize me for this. Not that it had ever worked before, but I was desperate.

"You're going to have fun, I promise," he said.

With the erratic pounding of my heart, the ride to the airport proved maddening. Royce talked the entire time, asking me about my fears, trying to comfort me with statistics and a list of requirements for all his mechanics and planes. He'd even brought charts for me to view. I didn't say a word. I was simply too nervous to make conversation.

When we reached our destination, a quiet ring sounded in my ears. I shook my head to clear the noise, but it persistently remained. I hadn't brought that stupid BlueJay, had I? "What's that ringing?" I asked raggedly. "Do you hear ringing?"

"No. Sweetheart, it's going to be okay," Royce said. "I promise. I hate that you're so afraid."

As we walked down a winding corridor hand in

hand—I didn't even try to pull away—I cast a sidelong glance at his profile. He seemed in perfect control. Our steps echoed throughout the empty hangar. The closer we came to the plane, the stiffer I became. I squeezed his hand, hoping to make him stop, or at the very least, slow him down. I thought I could do this.

I couldn't.

The ringing in my ears increased in volume, a frantically rising crescendo of string instruments. "Please, Royce. Choose somewhere here in Dallas to host the party."

He didn't stop, didn't pause for that matter, just continued to guide me down the corridor. "We've got to conquer this fear of yours. I have to travel, it's part of my job, and I want you to be able to go with me. Once we're in the air, you're going to love it. I know you will."

"Please," I repeated, a bit more desperately.

"Sweetheart," he said, glancing in my direction. "Do you trust me? You have to know I would never let you get hurt."

"Can't we drive? I'm sure it won't take us long." Sweat beaded on my forehead.

He laughed, a husky laugh he tried to squelch. "That's a twelve-hour drive. No," he said, shaking his head, "we'll fly." That said, he tossed me a wink.

As if winking at me solved all my problems!

"It'll be fun," he said. "You'll see."

I knew I'd have more fun strapped naked on top of a cab going two miles per hour through downtown traffic.

"Once you've flown in a plane like this one, you'll never want to touch the ground again."

He didn't understand. I had to make him understand. The only word to escape my constricting throat, however, was "Please." The ringing in my ears was so loud now, I could barely hear myself. The desperate plea finally stopped him in his tracks. There was an edge of disconsolateness in my voice this time, along with cold-blooded fear.

He looked down, his eyes filling with concern. "It's going to be okay," he repeated. And I knew he kept repeating the same phrases to drill them into my mind. "I'd never let anything happen to you."

"You're right, okay, about me being afraid. I—I hate planes," I whispered. The knuckles clasping my overnight bag turned white with the force of my grip.

"I can see that." Using the tip of his finger, he lifted my face until our gazes locked. "Want to tell me why?"

Where was my Tigress when I needed her? I bit my lip, hard, the action close to drawing blood.

"If you don't stop that, I'm going to kiss you so I can ease the sting your teeth are inflicting."

Looking away, I said, "It's not the plane. Not really. It's the fear of crashing."

He enfolded me in his arms, causing the ringing to subside. I buried my head in the hollow of his neck. His hands caressed my back, offering comfort. "You're more likely to be in a car accident than a plane crash."

"You told me that before, but now I want you to tell that to everyone who's ever been in a plane crash."

"Have you ever flown before?"

"Yes. Once."

"And you didn't die."

"No, but the wheels twisted on takeoff and we had to fly around for hours, getting rid of fuel. I've never been so scared in my life."

"But you did land safely."

"Yes," I admitted.

"With me as the pilot and having checked the plane myself, nothing bad will happen this time."

"I—I just can't. I had to be heavily sedated last time, and even that didn't stop my panic."

"It's okay to be afraid. I'll be with you. Right beside you the entire ride."

"I can't do it."

"Yes, you can." Pulling away, he left one arm draped possessively around my shoulders. He began walking again, slowly this time. I didn't protest, just let him lead the way. "The best medicine for fear is confrontation."

Confrontation. That word made me queasy. Still, I pushed a puff of air past my lips. "You're right," I said. "I know you're right, but that doesn't stop me from wishing you were wrong."

He didn't reply, giving me time to overcome my riotous fears.

"I'll do it." I forced myself to say the words. "I will. I'll do it."

The hand at my shoulder tightened. "Good girl. Come on," he said, quickening his pace and forcing me to keep up. "It's not as bad as you think." Unfortunately, we had reached the plane. The death trap.

How could something so heavy stay in the air? Small as it was, it looked like it weighed a gazillion pounds, with a heavy white metal body and wide expanse of wings.

"Let me prove how safe it is. You'll love every second in the air so much you'll beg me to take you again."

Not in this lifetime.

The terror I had managed to set aside while snuggled in the crook of his arm reared its ugly head again, stronger than before, mocking my determination to push onward. That terrible ringing erupted in my ears once more, so loud I almost screamed in fright.

Blood rushed from my head, running like ice through my veins. The overnight bag I held fell from my cold, clammy fingers and thumped to the ground. For the space of a heartbeat, the world around me disappeared, replaced by bright, blinking lights. Then the blackened tar beneath my feet shifted, consuming my vision, squelching all hint of light. Why did I feel like I was falling slowly, falling down?

The next thing I knew, I was flat on my back, everything quiet. I searched through a dark mist for Royce.

"Naomi," I heard him call. It sounded as if he stood at the end of a long, narrow tunnel. "Talk to me, sweetheart."

The heavy shroud around my mind began to recede and the fog clouding my thoughts thinned. Suddenly, I saw Royce. He was staring down at me, his features drawn tight with worry.

Why was he worried? I blinked in confusion. Slowly comprehension dawned. And with it came mortification.

Holy Mother of God, I'd fainted. Never in my life had I done anything so childish. My inner Tigress finally decided to show herself, only to roar in displeasure. Displeasure with me, not Royce. *Weakling,* she said.

"Come on. Talk to me," Royce said again.

"I'm all right," I assured him, my voice little more than a whisper.

When I tried to sit up, he gently held me down. "Not yet. You shouldn't move. I'm calling the paramedics. Hang on."

"No." Stronger now, I squeezed his hand. "I'm fine. Really."

"I don't believe you." The anxiety darkening his eyes warmed me. Seeing it made me feel as if a blanket had been placed over my body, heating my flesh, giving me strength. Tentatively, I reached up, touched the side of his cheek with my fingertips.

"I'm not hurt. I promise."

After a terse nod, he replaced his cell phone in his bag and helped me to my feet. Thankfully, I felt no ill effects from my rendezvous with the ground. I tried to smooth the wrinkles from my slacks.

"We can stay," he sighed, surprising me.

I brightened instantly. "Really?"

"Damn it." He jerked a hand down his face. "It was like watching you in slow motion as your knees buckled and you plummeted to the ground. I wasn't able to do anything except catch you and lower you the rest of the way." He massaged his neck. "I'll get your bag and take you home."

"No." The intensity of that one word shocked him, as well as myself, but something had just hit me with the force of a jackhammer. I was acting like the old Naomi, the doormat afraid of the world. I wasn't that woman anymore, and that meant I had to be strong. "I can do this. I can. It's time to conquer my fear, just like you said. Besides, my inner Tigress will kill me if I don't."

That gave him pause, and he blinked down at me. "Your inner Tigress?"

"That's right." A slow smile spread, and I was sure it lit my entire face. "My inner Tigress. She's fierce and bloodthirsty and brave."

He spread his fingers over my head, feeling for a bump. "I think you hit your head a little too hard."

"Careful, or I might have to scratch you to death."

"I might let you, but it depends on where you want to scratch me," he muttered. He frowned and shook his head. "I'm taking you home, Naomi. No," he said when I opened my mouth to protest. "The thought of watching you faint dead away once more makes me shudder. I'll help you overcome your fear another way."

"Please, Royce."

"I said no arguments. That means no pleading, begging, crying or cajoling. And no wetting those luscious lips."

I planted my fists on my hips, my determination increasing with every second that passed. "Either you go with me or I pay someone else to take me and go alone. That's your choice."

"Damn it, Naomi." He let out a forceful breath. "How do you feel about riding in a large company jet instead of a small aircraft?"

I mulled it over, then nodded. I could pretend the large jet was a hotel room and hopefully forget I was soaring thousands of feet in the air, ready to crash at— "Uh, much better."

"My crew can have it ready to go in half an hour if you don't mind waiting."

The force of my relief was almost tangible. "But what about you? Do you mind not being the pilot?"

"I mind—I wanted to impress you, but I'll live through it."

He hustled me inside an air-conditioned room, then made a quick call.

It didn't take the thirty minutes he'd predicted. His flight crew had the Gulfstream ready in twenty. And, God help me, I boarded it.

ONCE INSIDE THE LARGE CRAFT, Royce gave me a tour. I couldn't help but gasp at the luxury. A soft, ivory wraparound couch graced the front entrance. A large-screen television was positioned overhead, perfect for viewing from a reclining position.

There was an office fully equipped with chairs, table and drawing board. Next, I entered a bathroom that was larger than mine at home. And last…the bottom of my stomach dropped out. My eyes widened as I took in the bedroom. It had a small, comfortable-looking mattress and glossy headboard with silk sheets and a soft comforter. The room was used for napping, I was sure, but that didn't matter to my brain.

I pictured Royce there, naked and beckoning me over with a seductive motion of his finger. I'm pretty sure I spent more time imagining Royce naked than I did anything else. If only I could get paid for fantasizing about him… Oh well. On with the fantasy: His bronzed skin glistened against the soft, white sheets. His entire body was hard. Hot. Ready. He continued to motion me over with a crook of his finger, wicked intent in his eyes.

I gulped.

"Let's get ready for takeoff." The real-life Royce placed one hand on my waist, and the contact sent currents of desire down my spine.

I didn't move. Couldn't. My gaze slashed up and collided with his. How could I get so worked up, so quickly?

He sucked in a breath. "Or if you'd rather wait and do other things," he murmured, "I'm all for that."

We stayed completely still for a moment, each lost in our own thoughts, thoughts that were too naughty to voice. Thankfully—and with much effort—I collected my wits. This wasn't the time; this wasn't the place. Distance. I needed distance. I stepped back, trying to act annoyed, though I was tempted to take what he offered. Always tempted.

"Not on your life," I managed. "I want to get this flight over with."

His fiery stare lingered on my lips for a long while. "Too bad. Maybe next time."

Taking my hand, he led me to the wraparound sofa and latched my seat belt into the proper hook. My body began to tremble. I was careful to keep my expression blank, passive, lest he tried to halt the trip. I *had* to prove to myself that I could do this. That fear didn't rule me.

"It takes courage to face your fear," he said. "I'm proud of you."

"Thank you." I was proud of myself, too.

After several minutes, the engines roared to life and the plane jostled, going slowly at first, then picking up speed as it moved down the runway. The captain said something over the speaker. My ears were ringing again, so all I heard was "Mmmm-mm mmmm-mmm."

"If the plane collides with the ocean, there's a very good chance the sharks will eat me alive."

"We're not flying over an ocean. We're flying over mountains."

"Even worse! Mountains have bears." I clutched Royce's hand and stiffened—if it was possible to become any more rigid than I already was. I looked ahead, knowing my complexion grew greener by the second. Silver lining: green was Royce's favorite color. I probably seemed like a goddess of beauty to him. "What if the pilot doesn't see one because the snowcaps look like clouds and he slams us right into it?"

"Then I swear to God I'll fire him." Royce clasped

my chin and lowered his head. His lips met mine; his tongue swept inside without waiting for permission.

Hmm, delicious. My fears slowly diminished as thoughts of crashing were replaced with thoughts of sweaty bodies, tangled limbs and gasping pleasure. Royce tasted like pure sin today, hot and masculine with a dash of the forbidden. Maybe his saliva possessed an addictive chemical and that's why I couldn't get him out of my mind.

It was possible.

Within minutes, we were soaring through the air. To be honest, I barely noticed that we had taken off. Who cared, anyway? If I died today, it would be with a smile on my face. Royce certainly knew how to kiss.

Oh, did he know how to kiss.

He used his entire body. His hands. His chest. His legs. His masculinity consumed me, making me feel as if his whole existence was centered around me. Maybe it was. What a refreshing change from Richard's how-far-can-I-get-my-tongue-down-your-throat-before-I-can-get-into-your-pants kisses.

His hand moved to my breast, plumping and kneading. He groaned. I moaned. The sounds traveled over me, heating my blood. How easy it would be for him to shove down my pants and take me, I thought dazedly. How easy…and how wonderful. I spread my legs, about to beg him to touch me there. I ached so, so much.

He suddenly tore away, completely releasing me. His hands fisted at his sides. His breathing was shallow, quick, just like mine.

"One day soon, Naomi, I'm going to show you just how much pleasure I can give you. And neither one of us will be able to walk for a week."

II

Be aware. Always aware. A Tiger will create a distraction on one side of the jungle to better attack you on the other.

UNFORTUNATELY, WE WERE STILL on the plane half an hour later. Silence stretched between us. It had been like that since our kiss had ended, and I didn't know why. I didn't know why he had pulled away, why he was now ignoring me. Had I done something wrong? Did he know something about the plane that I didn't?

Fear slowly began to take root in my mind again. I couldn't fight it. I was soon squeezing my eyes shut, refusing to look out the windows behind or in front of me. Images of blood and death poured through my mind. I jerked completely upright. We were on a path to certain death. Royce remained stiff at my side. He knew the plane was about to crash, the sick bastard, but didn't know how to tell me. That was why he was still so tense.

We were going to die! I just knew it. Big breath in. Big breath out. Big breath in. Big breath out. Dizziness assaulted me.

I forced myself to calm down before I had a major panic attack. I tried to meditate, to imagine a tranquil meadow with lush green foliage, just like Jonathan had taught me. It had never worked before, but this time I actually felt a summer breeze caressing my skin like the brush of a feather. A small measure of peace settled over me—until the aircraft careened and rattled. A loud popping sounded.

I immediately lost that peaceful center. My eyelids flew open; I gripped Royce's forearm, afraid if I didn't, I would fall out the window and spin out of control as I slid down, down, down to the hard surface of the earth.

"Everything's fine," he said. "We hit an air pocket, that's all." He wrapped his arm around my shoulder, but ruined the "calming" action by trying to unbuckle my seat belt.

Panicked, I glued my hand over his. "What are you doing?"

"Getting you comfortable."

I slapped at his wrist. "That will never happen if you don't get your hand off my safety harness."

"Safety harness, hmm?" He chuckled. "Naomi, if the plane were to plummet—"

I gasped. He zipped his lips, but it was too late. The damage was done.

"Oh, my God, oh, my God, oh, my God." I couldn't breathe. Wait. Did I smell smoke? Ohmygod, Ohmygod, Ohmygod. The plane was plummeting and was about to become a fiery ball.

He nuzzled my neck. I didn't relax this time. I couldn't. Everywhere I looked, I saw my own death.

"This worked before," he said.

"Well, it isn't working now."

"There's no reason to worry," he said against my ear. "Nothing bad will happen. I promise."

"How can you promise something like that? Are you psychic?"

"No."

"Then shut the hell up."

He did. Probably because I wore an I'll-eat-you-alive-expression. Happy meadow, happy meadow. Where was my freaking happy meadow? *I'm not going to die,* I chanted. *I'm not going to die.* I had to kill Jonathan first. Surely God would let me live long enough for that.

After a while, I began to calm down again. Tranquil waters, a happy meadow. I was a strong woman and the plane was gliding smoothly through the air.

Royce must have sensed my new state of serenity because he motioned with a tilt of his chin to the window. "Go on," he said. "Take a peek. This will be like therapy for you."

I'd had all the therapy I could take, thank you, but knew he was right. It took five long, agonizing minutes to work up the courage to look down—with my heart pounding sporadically in my chest all the while—but I finally managed to do it. I looked.

A gasp escaped me and I squeezed my eyes shut. Opened them. Cars lolled along city roads, reminding me of ants meandering atop a hill. Buildings appeared like little more than specks on the horizon.

I wondered where we were so I could chart a rescue mission in my mind. I didn't ask, too afraid I'd jinx myself.

"Okay, that's enough," I said, easing back. "I'm cured."

He chuckled. "While we've got this time to ourselves, why don't you tell me what made you decide to open a party-planning business."

I knew he was only trying to distract me, but I was perfectly willing to go along with his plan. "Nothing glamorous," I said. I wiped my sweaty hands on my slacks. "I was never any good at schoolwork. I hated math, hated writing research papers and studying of any kind, but loved all social events. One day I saw an ad in the paper for an assistant planner, and I knew it was the job for me. And since I'd worked at my aunt and uncle's catering business, it was a good fit." I sighed. "I was developing a good name for myself just before I left the business for a few years."

"Why did you leave?"

"I foolishly thought I needed to be available for my husband twenty-four hours a day. Anyway," I said, not wanting to go down that road, "after my divorce, Kera had taken over the catering business and things just worked themselves out."

"I'm very glad that they did."

"What about you?" I asked. "Why fly instruments of death?"

He shrugged. "At first, it wasn't the planes. I was eight, maybe nine, when my father first took me with him to Powell Aeronautics. I watched the employees jump to do his bidding and knew I'd found my calling. I wanted everyone to take *my* orders."

"Somehow I'm not surprised," I said dryly, though a chuckle underlined my tone.

"After my first time in a cockpit, bossing people around stopped being my first priority."

"Besides flying planes and bossing people around, what is it that you actually do?"

"Mostly I buy and sell airplanes. My company also sells parts, does title searches and generates daily aeronautic reports. That kind of thing."

"I can't imagine having enough money to buy an entire airplane. A seat belt, maybe, but not much else."

"I always make back double my initial investment, so it's no hardship."

Yeah. No hardship. I could hear the buyer/seller interaction now:

Buyer: *You only want a million for the plane?*

Seller: *Yeah. I paid four mil, but I just don't like the thing anymore.*

Buyer: *(Chuckles) Well, do you take checks?*

No hardship. Yeah, you can bite me.

"Are you purchasing a plane anytime soon?" I asked.

"There's a SJ30-2 I've had my eye on. In fact, you

can fly to Florida with me at the end of the month and check it out."

"No thanks." I meant it with every fiber of my being.

A slow grin lifted the corners of his lips. "I might just decide to hold the party in Florida. Then you'd *have* to go."

"That might put you on my Must Kill list."

His grin became wicked. "I'd rather be on your Must Seduce list."

He was. He was the only name on that list, but he *was* on it. Not that I'd admit it out loud. "This is a milestone for me, you know. I don't even like to stay in a hotel room that has a balcony. I've never understood my fear of falling, but I've learned to live with it. I'm proud of myself right now. This is the first time I've ever done anything so…scary."

"Except for the fact that you've almost squeezed my wrist off every time the plane jostled and left me with a bloody stump, you've done great."

I snorted.

Soon afterward, we arrived at a private airstrip on the outskirts of Eagle Airport. Thankfully, the plane landed with no complications. Had anything gone wrong, I felt certain I would have done serious damage to the inside of my cheek instead of simply biting it raw. I think I'd already lost enough blood to warrant a transfusion.

With stiff limbs, I stepped out of the death trap and onto the ground. Thank you, God! Royce grabbed my bag, threw it over his shoulder. He shuffled me inside a waiting limousine.

"Now, that wasn't so bad, was it?" He settled in beside me.

"It was quite enjoyable, actually."

A smug gleam lit his features.

"*If* I were a masochist," I added.

"Ha, ha." Grinning, he shook his head. "We've got a half hour drive ahead of us. The cabin has already been stocked with everything we'll need. All we have to do now is relax."

"Is the cabin isolated?"

"Technically, no. It just seems that way at times. It's about a mile from Mountain Lodge. A resort," he clarified when my expression turned questioning.

"What's the square footage of the cabin?"

"Two thousand."

"Hmm." I pictured his guests squeezed inside that amount of space, one standing on top of the other. "Forget the cabin for a moment and concentrate on the lodge. Does it have any areas designated for large gatherings?"

His eyes narrowed, blocking out the sudden, suspicious darkening, but he answered me anyway. "Yes."

"Well, the lodge sounds better suited for a party than the cabin does. Let's go there."

Now he frowned. "I prefer the cabin."

We were safely on the ground and my thoughts were clear, focused. So I wasn't taking his crap. "Still," I said, "I'd like to view the resort first, if you don't mind."

"I do mind."

"I didn't want to fly here, but I did. The least you can do is stop at the lodge."

"Damn it, Naomi."

Silence.

I wasn't backing down, wasn't going to rescind my request.

"Damn it," he said again. "We'll stop at the lodge." He massaged his neck and gazed up at the car ceiling. "I don't know why the hell I'm putting up with your bossiness. I'm in charge here. You work for me."

"I work *with* you. There's a difference. And just so you know, you're seriously starting to piss me off."

"Well, just so *you* know, this is the last time you're getting your way."

Jeez, what a sore loser.

"So, what do you think?" Royce asked.

I regarded him for a moment. We were in a secluded corner of a smoke-filled bar, drinking wine and listening to the hum of a saxophone in the background. The area was dim, lit only by candles. We had finished our tour of the lodge only a short while ago.

I didn't want to argue with him, but realized I might have no other choice since the information I was about to give him wasn't what he wanted to hear. "As lovely as this place is," I said, "it simply won't do."

"Have you already made a list as to why not?" Amusement glinted in his eyes. He wasn't angry, at least.

I exhaled a relieved breath. "As a matter of fact," I told him, "I have."

"This, I need to hear."

"This building isn't large enough, for one, and the cabin, which is smaller, won't be, either."

"And two?" He tried to cover his smile with his palm, but I caught the action.

His levity should have ruffled me. After all, if he truly wanted the party here, I had no other choice but to comply. Instead, I felt strangely at ease. The wine, perhaps? Or the company?

"Two," I said, "this is too rustic for our *Arabian Nights* theme."

"So we'll make it *Arabian Nights* meets Urban Cowgirl."

"Three," I said, acting as if he hadn't spoken, "I don't want the party held here."

"That's not a reason."

"It is to me. What about flying the guests here?"

"They'll love being flown in my jet, I promise you. And my mother will adore the clean mountain air."

"You can't fit three hundred people in your death trap of a plane."

"We'll cut down the list. Make it a small, private gathering."

He had an answer for everything.

Loud, raucous laughter suddenly rang out. A thirty-something man with long, wavy brown hair stood onstage, tapping on a microphone. "It's time for the karaoke entertainment hour," he said, his voice booming throughout the bar. "I know we've got some eager beavers out there, dying to get up on this stage and belt out a few tunes. Well, tonight's your lucky night. We've got a great selection."

The crowd cheered. Several people even raised their glasses.

"Who's first?"

One young man stumbled to his feet. His constant swaying and glassy-eyed expression made it obvious he'd had a little too much to drink. "I'll do it." His words were slurred, almost unrecognizable. The girl at his table giggled hysterically, urging him on. "I want to sing a sappy hong."

More giggling.

"Anyone else. Please," the man onstage begged, an edge of desperation evident in the tense profile of his body.

Silence.

I looked around and noticed that everyone else was doing the same. An instant later, I heard, "I dare you."

I whipped around, staring over at Royce. Surely he'd misspoken. He wouldn't have said—

"I dare you." He gave me a devilish smile.

I wasn't someone who usually responded to dares. I mean, who wanted to run outside naked screaming, "The sky is falling?" I also knew Royce didn't think I'd accept his dare.

My own devilish sense of humor—or maybe the simple desire to prove to him that I truly did possess an inner Tigress—rose within me, insisting I leap out of my seat and pole-vault onto that stage.

I tapped a finger on my chin and regarded him intently. "What do I get if I take you up on your dare?" I asked.

He held out his arms in invitation. "Me."

I should have expected such a reply. Smiling, I shook my head. "Good try. But that prize doesn't appeal to me." Lie. "Name something else."

"A night of wild sex."

"Nope." Bigger lie.

Royce stroked his jaw with deliberate slowness. "Hmm. What will tempt you, Naomi Delacroix?"

"Probably nothing." Biggest lie of all. I refilled my glass and sipped at my wine, savoring the robust flavor, relishing the comforting warmth it gave me. And the courage. "Try and tempt me. Just try."

"What if I promised the party won't be held anywhere that requires stepping inside an airplane?" he said. "Does *that* appeal to you?"

No more plane rides? I almost did a table dance right then and there. He'd chosen the one prize I could never refuse. Was the embarrassment of missing a note, of watching him snicker at my attempt to sing worth it?

I didn't have to think about it.

"You've got a deal," I said. Then, before I could talk myself out of it, I held out one hand to shake and seal the bargain. His big hand dwarfed my smaller one and his calluses sparked a delicious friction.

"Good luck." He shot a glance through the restless crowd. "This doesn't look like a receptive audience."

He was trying to dissuade me, anything to win the bet. I surprised him by pushing to my feet. "I'll do it,"

I said, loud enough for the man onstage to hear. I made a face at Royce. Ha! I might make a fool of myself, might have to endure jeers and snickers and catcalls, but I'd be damned if I'd leave this bar a loser.

All at once, the crowd quieted. Every eye in the room found me, riveted by the spectacle I must surely make. My knees began quaking.

A slight brush of Royce's palm against my hip drew my gaze back to him. "What? Wishing you'd kept your mouth closed?" I asked.

His brows rose in mock salute. "Are you sure you want to do this?"

"A bet's a bet, and I simply can't let you win." With that, I pivoted on my heel and strolled to the stage, unwinding the twist in my hair and letting the long, dark tendrils cascade down my shoulders and back.

Though my hand shook, I took the microphone from the announcer's outstretched hand. "Do you have 'Achy Breaky Heart'?"

He offered me a relieved grin. "Never have karaoke night without it."

A few seconds later, music blasted from the speakers, penetrating the sudden silence. The sound continued to climb in volume. Words appeared on a screen just in front of me.

Deciding simply to have fun, I assumed a laugh-with-me-not-at-me pose: one hand on my hip, silly grin on my lips. I began to sing. When the first note left my mouth, all movement in the audience stopped. Even the drunk guy stared up at me like I belonged in an institution.

But I worked the stage like a pro, flipping my hair, copping an attitude and, at last, someone chuckled. That was all it took.

"Oh, yeah," a man yelled. "Give it to me, baby. My heart is hurtin'."

"You can break me anytime," another called.

All around, hands clapped to the beat, urging me on. I went for it, giving the performance my all. I'd never admit it aloud, but I had the time of my life on that stage, belting out the lyrics and strutting my stuff.

When the end arrived, my voice slowly tapered to quiet. I waited for a reaction. Suddenly applause erupted and loud, buoyant cheers peeled like bells. Catcalls and whistling abounded.

I resisted the urge to stick my tongue out at Royce. I'd done it. Really done it. I had won my bet with him. Na, na, na, na, na, na. Take that, Mr. Royce Powell, god of the airplane world and superhero of sexiness.

No more airplane rides!

My grin became a smirk as I looked to Royce. He saluted me with his wineglass.

Intending to gloat, I descended the stage and strolled to him. When I reached the table, he helped me settle into my chair, but didn't wait around to let me wallow in my victory.

"I'll be back in a moment," he said. And before I could protest, he sauntered away. He didn't even send me a backward glance. My lips pursed. How dare that sore loser not lavish me with compliments.

A few minutes later, my shock and anger at Royce's

abrupt departure dissolved. I was too busy praying God would make me invisible. A very untidy, very intoxicated man was stumbling my way.

"Hey, baby." He was in his late thirties or early forties, and smelled like he'd just bathed in Jack Daniel's best for at least an hour. He breezed into Royce's vacant chair. His clothes were rumpled, his eyes glassy and red. "You really rocked onstage. I thought you were a real singer or something."

At least he was coherent. Kind of. "Thanks," I said.

"Can I buy you a drink?" While he spoke, his gaze locked onto my breasts, small targets though they were.

"No, I'm not thirsty," I answered. And neither were my breasts. Actually, I really was parched, but I didn't want to invite this man to stay any longer than necessary. Where the hell was Royce?

My unwanted visitor didn't get the hint. He threw an arm over my stool, as if he had every right to invade my space. I'm surprised he didn't try the yawn-and-grab routine. He gave me a lecherous grin, and I shuddered. There was something black lodged between his front teeth and I really, really hoped it was food.

"What's your name?" he asked

"Naomi." I fanned the air in front of my face before I passed out from the fumes.

"Naaaomi," he said, sounding it out. "Na-oh-me. I'm Doug." He paused. "What's a pretty thing like you doing all alone?"

I tried not to cringe. Really, there was only one way to get rid of a guy like this. "I'm so glad you came over here, Douglas." I planted my elbows on the table and gazed over at him as if he were the most beautiful sight I'd ever beheld. "I've been dying to talk to someone about all the things that have been going wrong in my life lately. My ex-husband Richard, may he choke on his own tongue, get an STD and win a free one-way ticket to everlasting damnation, called me the other day and asked me to get back together with him. As if I need another cheating bastard in my life. One at a time, thank you very much."

Doug tried to interrupt me, but I kept right on talking. "You're probably thinking that the other cheating bastard in my life is my stepdad, and you're right. I do have plans to castrate him, though, don't you worry."

All color drained from Doug's face.

"I bet you're wondering why I haven't done it yet. Killed and castrated him, that is. Well, the answer to that is simple, really. First I've got to find the perfect knife. A regular household blade simply won't do. I really hate cheaters, Douglas, and I think—"

Just as Doug cut into my speech to mutter, "Excuse me, I think I see someone I know," Royce returned. He watched Doug race away through slitted eyes before sinking back into his seat.

"Where were you?" I demanded. "Five more minutes and I might have had to ask Dougie Boy to be the father of my children in the hopes of scaring him away."

"I was getting a room. I don't want to make the drive to the cabin tonight."

My anger faded, replaced by dread—and anticipation. I shook my head. "Wait a sec. Getting *a* room? As in *one?*"

"That's right." He reached under the tabletop and slowly, oh so softly, grasped my thigh.

I nearly jumped out of my skin.

He grinned slowly.

"What are you doing?" I asked in a scandalized whisper, looking all around to make sure no one watched us.

"Seducing you." The darkened atmosphere and the corner placement of our table guaranteed privacy from everyone except the person walking directly by. Which happened to be Doug. He stumbled past once, twice, staring at me with jaundiced suspicion.

The third time, he actually stopped at the table. "She plays with knives," he told Royce before racing away.

"She's vicious, I know," Royce said, keeping his eyes on me. "You were adorable onstage."

"Thank you." I tried to push his hand away; I didn't push too hard, though. It felt too good.

He merely moved those naughty fingers of his higher, to a better place. "Where'd you learn to sing country music like that?"

"In the shower." My blood heated, and I so wanted to open my legs and invite him to feel all he wanted.

"We've been building to this point and you know it," he said, getting to the heart of the matter. "Ever since I picked you up this morning, I've wanted to strip you down and taste you. All over."

I swallowed. Hard. There was a reason I needed to

tell him no, to wait until after his mom's party, but at the moment I couldn't think of what that reason was.

"I have this fantasy of us in my mind. You ride me and your hair tickles my chest. Your breasts are pushed forward, and you keep screaming my name."

"Do I, uh, have an orgasm every time I scream?" The words escaped on the barest whisper and I was unable to stop them.

He nodded. "Oh, yeah."

My nipples hardened and my heart began a frantic *boom-boom* rhythm.

"Once we make love, Naomi, you'll only want more," he promised. "Much, much more."

No. He was wrong. I couldn't let myself want more.

He came closer to me, his gaze stroking my face like a caress. "I'll touch you here." He palmed one of my breasts through the fabric of my shirt.

The fingers covering my thigh inched down my calf, not stopping until they reached bare skin. Those naughty fingers tunneled underneath the flare of my pants, then started going higher. Higher still. The material tightened at my knees, not allowing him to go farther.

I almost shouted a string of curses.

My breath hitched in my throat as he abandoned my knee and moved his hand to the waist of my pants, unsnapping the button. His pushed his hand inside, his fingers making dead-on contact with the lacy fabric of my panties.

"I'll touch you here as well," he said, gently stroking the material. Of their own accord, my hips rocked slightly with his touch. "And you'll beg me to take you over the edge."

"I've already decided to sleep with you," I admitted in a whisper. "After the party."

His nostrils flared. "After. Before." Pause. "Now."

Now…so tempting. God, I wanted him. I did. I needed him. "I haven't changed my mind about a relationship." Unlike the way men treated women, I didn't want him to misinterpret what was about to happen. "We can sleep together, but that's it. Nothing more."

His fingers stilled, and I nearly moaned. "Maybe you didn't want a relationship," he said, his expression fierce, "but you're in one, anyway."

"No." I had to stay strong, had to fight my body's needs until he agreed. "I want you. I do. Just—" breathe "—nothing else."

"Well, I want everything. And I want you against a wall." His fingers began their tormenting search again, this time bolder, moving up and down over the now-damp material. "Have you ever fucked against a wall, Naomi?"

He was deliberately being crude, I knew, trying to force me to admit I wanted more than a hard, emotionless screw. It had the opposite effect, however. I ached all over, and hearing him talk like that increased my excitement. Maybe, at heart, I was a bad, dirty girl. A closet sex kitten, like my cousins had said.

"Have you?" he demanded.

Slowly, I shook my head. My experience was

limited to the back seat of a Chevy and a cold, forgotten mattress. Don't get me wrong. I've had orgasms and even enjoyed the sex. But *this* was something altogether more pleasurable.

"I'll press your back against the wall and brace your legs around my waist."

Breathless, I glanced at a wall and pictured exactly what he described. Two naked bodies, straining together, standing up and tangled. My throat constricted. The scene was carnal. Primal. Raw.

I'd die if I didn't experience it.

"All right," I told him, my voice hoarse with longing. "Now. Before the party."

He paused, his eyes widening with disbelief. He hadn't expected me to agree. "What did you say?"

"I said yes. I'm willing to do it against the wall."

A blaze of heat caught fire in his irises, sparking blue flames. Those flames licked at me. His gaze moved over me with blatant possessiveness, and I licked my lips. His nostrils did the flare thing. Royce clasped my hand and jerked me to my feet. I hurriedly buttoned my pants.

No longer concerned about those around me, I raced behind him through the bar, past the reservation desk and into the elevator. Royce quickly punched a button. The doors slid shut. In the next instant, he had me pinned to the corner, plundering my mouth with his tongue, rubbing his erection into the crevice of my legs.

I almost climaxed right then.

A bell sounded. The elevator doors slid open.

It required a conscious effort to tear my mouth from Royce's. He grabbed my hand and dragged me into the hall. "I got the lowest floor I could," he said.

A shiver of anticipation slipped down my spine. Helpless to do otherwise, I kept moving. Okay, so I nearly beat him to the door. Big deal.

He jabbed the passkey into the electronic box. The green light winked its assent. Royce shoved open the door, hustled me inside and let the heavy wood slam behind him.

We were finally alone.

I raced to the bed, trying to shed my top along the way. It took a few minutes for me to notice Royce hadn't followed. I turned and faced him. He had his back to the entrance. He was watching me, a predator-like gleam in his eyes. Without taking his gaze from me, he clicked the lock.

"Now," he said.

"Now," I agreed.

He advanced. I didn't move, just let him come. When he reached me, my head fell backward with the force of his kiss. His tongue dove immediately inside. It was a hard and demanding caress, not meant to be gentle. But then, I didn't crave gentleness. I craved the weight of his body, the sear of his lips, the domination of his hands.

He couldn't be stopped.

I couldn't be stopped.

We were wild for each other.

His hands sifted through my hair and fisted it before he began working at my bra. Next he tackled my pants. Those, too, pooled at our feet. The lights were on. I tried not to let it bother me. I was so thin. Royce didn't seem to mind, though.

He was all over me. I loved every second, every squeeze of his hands, and returned the favor. He was caught in the avalanche of my lust. Again, he didn't seem to mind.

Just when I thought I might collapse, I was lifted in his arms and placed on the bed. The soft mattress cushioned my back.

"Wait!" I shouted. Had he forgotten? I cast a meaningful glance to the wall. A large floral picture hung in the center. I could almost feel the ridges pressed into my back.

Royce gave me a slow, wicked grin of agreement and nodded. "Oh, yeah. The wall."

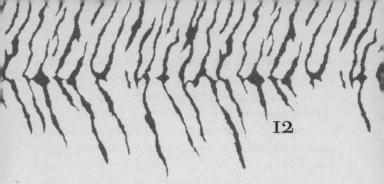

12

A true Tigress will fight for what she wants with every weapon available. Manipulation? Absolutely. Screaming? Without a doubt. Fists, teeth, legs? Get in her way and find out.

ROYCE HEAVED ME UP and carried me to the wall. The second my back hit, the hotel picture crashed to the ground. He dropped my feet so he could kick the frame out of the way, and pushed me harder against the cold paneling.

I gasped at the sensation. Our hands were frantic, our breath choppy.

But then, all of a sudden, Royce slowed down. He ceased the frantic need of our kiss and brought it to a leisurely exploration. With one hand, he caressed my neck, my collarbone and my breasts. With the other, he skimmed downward, over the taut hollow of my stomach.

"I want to take off my panties," I gasped out. "Help me take them off."

"I knew you were sexy, but I don't think I realized exactly *how* sexy until this moment," he said, gazing down at me. His voice strained with suppressed ferocity.

"Mmm." Who had time for conversation? I didn't. I wanted to come now. Right now. It had been so long, too long. I ripped at his shirt buttons. "Take. Panties. Off. Me."

He stilled my hands. "Not yet."

"Do you want to have sex or not?" His fingers glided over my hard, waiting nipple. I jerked at the deliciousness. Everything in me was coiled and poised for release. I was so close to the edge, so unbelievably close.

"I want to savor you."

"Savor later." I arched against him. "Climax now."

He closed his eyes. A bead of sweat trickled down his temple. "Not yet." The words were more strained this time, barely audible.

I was burning up and he said "not yet"?

"What's the problem?" I breathed. Everywhere he touched, heat rippled under my skin, but not deep enough to make a difference. "Stop being lazy and kick it into gear."

"Lazy? Honey, you're going to thank me for my laziness when I'm done with you. I promised you that first day that I'd go slow with you, and I'm damn well going to go slow."

I reached between our bodies, opened his pants and slipped my hand inside. I clasped the long, thick length of his erection in my hand. "So you want to go slow? Fine." I moved my palm up, down with agonizing slowness.

He groaned, the vibration touching me all the way to my toes. "Think you're smart, do you?" he said, doing exactly as I had done. His hand dipped inside my panties and he pressed his fingers against my clitoris, circled, pressed again.

Actually, I thought I was a freaking genius. His actions were just enough to make me come. I screamed. I spasmed. Bright stars winked behind my eyelids. Fire swept through my blood.

"Look at me," he commanded.

My eyes refused to open.

"Look at me. See *me*."

I forced my lids apart. With his gaze never leaving mine, he buried two fingers deep inside of me and I clenched around him. His other hand gripped my hips. Pulling me up, helping me imitate the rhythm of sex. Once. Twice. He pushed inside. Over and over, pulling back, sinking in, making my climax last forever and ever.

And that easily, he had me ready for another round.

"See, Naomi," he said. "I can give you pleasure. You could have this for the rest of your life. *I* could have this for the rest of *my* life."

"Just a few nights." I barely managed to say it, much less breathe.

He growled. "You're too damn stubborn. Maybe

I haven't shown you just how good it can be between us."

"Then do it. Show me." One orgasm wasn't enough. I wanted more, needed more.

The tips of his fingers grew bolder, pushed deeper, teasing and taunting. I writhed beneath his hands, sensation eclipsing time.

"I'm going to taste you," he said.

I turned his command into a command of my own. I was in charge of this show, after all. "Yes. Do it. Now."

His scowl said he knew what I was doing, but he immediately dropped to his knees.

He jerked my panties down, and I quickly stepped out of them. He slid his hands up my calves, gripped my knees and urged them apart. It was a little disconcerting, being naked with such a sexy man poised between my legs, but I was too excited to worry much.

Richard had never, ever done this to me. No man had. I wanted it so badly.

Royce's warm breath tickled me before I felt the first stroke of his tongue, the heat of it. The pleasure. He licked, caressed, moved his mouth against me, creating a dizzying friction. My bones liquefied. My nerve endings sizzled. I moaned, low and hungry, and the sound filled the room.

"Mmm…" I couldn't speak, could only moan. The room around me ceased to exist. My second climax ripped through me, this one even stronger than the first. Making me arch and clench and scream. I flew back to the stars.

How long until I returned to earth, I didn't know.

"I came twice," I said, awed by that fact. Royce was standing now, staring down at me with fire in his eyes. "I came twice."

"And that was only the appetizer," he promised.

I could barely stand, but Royce released me and stalked toward his pants. "What are you doing?" I asked. "Get back here. We aren't done." Pause. "Are we?"

"Condom," he said, suddenly holding me up again. "Not done, but can't savor anymore. Too… much…" With a roar, he buried his cock inside me.

Pure pleasure rocked me, intense, consuming. I wrapped myself around him. He began to move deep, deeper still, lifting me up, pulling me down. Little by little, his rhythm began to quicken.

"I had no idea you'd be this wild once I got your clothes off." His breath stroked my ear. "Thank you."

I couldn't help a grin as I rotated my hips, taking more of him inside. Oh, yeah. I gasped. "Well, I knew *you'd* be this good."

His hand reached down between us and pressed. His fingers moved in a circular motion; his body slipped in and out of me, increasing in speed, increasing in urgency. Yes, faster and faster. Sure enough, my sensitized body responded, dampening, aching for another orgasm.

I clawed at his back, bit the cord of his shoulder and tugged at his hair. I was an animal, a Tigress, my true, wild nature suddenly released. He surged once more, hard, and I propelled over the edge. As my body spasmed for the third time, he growled low in his throat and surged deep, so deep. Deeper than I'd thought possible. His body stiffened and he roared my name.

"Damn, Naomi," he panted. "I think you almost killed me."

With what little energy I had left, I sighed happily. Take that, Richard the Bastard.

WHEN ENGAGED IN A WILD, no-strings fling, how many times in one night was the couple in question allowed to make—uh, have sex? Once? Twice? Three times or more?

Hopefully the latter because Royce and I had just finished round three. On the bed, this time. I lay limp as a rag. Royce was beside me, the heat of his body like a warm blanket. A dewy sheen of sweat caused our bodies to cling and stick to the other.

I was naked, not an inch of covering over my body, and I realized I might never regain the strength to do anything about it. I knew my hair was a tangled mess, knew that my lips were slightly swollen. Knew, too, that pink scratches lined my breasts from his beard stubble. I probably resembled a beat-up prostitute. And there was no better way to look, to my way of thinking. A satisfied smile curled my lips.

I don't smoke, hate cigarettes actually, but I would have liked one right then.

Royce anchored his weight on one elbow, hovering above me, his eyes heavy-lidded and seductive. Silver moonlight surrounded his tousled hair. I smoothed several strands from his face and stared up at him.

"Thank you for tonight," I said.

His turquoise gaze suddenly glowed like the clearest ocean. "I'm the one who should be doing the thanking."

I grinned. "You're probably right."

Chuckling, he rose from the bed. "Cocky girl." His chuckle became a grimace, and he rotated his shoulders. As he padded into the bathroom, he said, "I think you did major damage when you threw your legs around my neck."

"Big baby." A cool blast of air wafted around me, and I forced my jelly-like arms to grab onto the sheet and pull it up to my chin. I heard a splash of water. Then silence.

He exited the bathroom with a wet washrag in his hand, saw me, and paused. "*Now* you're shy?" he teased.

"Now I'm cold," I said. If I were honest, I *was* beginning to feel a little self-conscious. This man had slept with some of the most beautiful women in the world. Models. Surgically enhanced heiresses. And now imperfect me.

"You're the most beautiful thing I've ever seen," he said, as if reading my mind. He grunted with pleasure as he settled beside me, then spent the next several minutes cleaning both of our bodies. Once the towel was discarded, he cuddled me to him, his body half covering mine.

I'd never been a cuddler. Hated it, in fact. I always felt pinned down, shackled—and not in a good way. But…I found that I loved it with Royce. The tenderness. The illusion of caring. I didn't want to move, could have stayed in his arms forever.

And that suddenly scared the living shit out of me.

My heart kicked into overtime, pounding sporadically in my chest. Being here with him like this felt too good, too…right. Was I…could I be— No. *No!* I absolutely refused to believe I was falling in love with him. This was a fling. Only a fling.

Emotions were not allowed.

Emotions meant a relationship. A relationship meant marriage. Marriage meant trusting, giving my heart totally and completely. And giving my heart eventually meant hurt, pain and perhaps betrayal. Not even my mom's marriage was going to survive, and I'd thought their union unbreakable.

A cold sweat broke out all over my body; my breathing became shallow, ragged. I began to feel claustrophobic. A wave of dizziness assaulted me. A deafening ring filled my ears and my stomach cramped. I had to get out of here. Had to get away from Royce. Right. Now.

"I have to use the bathroom," I blurted.

He untangled his limbs from mine. "Hurry back."

I raced away. When the door locked behind me, I sucked in a panicked gulp of air. What was I going to do? I couldn't stay here all night, but I couldn't pick up my clothes from the floor and take a cab home, either.

I collapsed onto the toilet lid and hunched over, putting my head between my legs. *Breathe. Just breathe.* There was no reason to panic. I'd think of something.

How long I stayed like that, I don't know.

"Are you okay in there?" he called.

"Fine," I croaked.

When the ringing and dizziness subsided, I forced myself to stand and splash cold water over my too-pale face. "You don't seem to worry when he's inside you," I told my reflection. "So get him inside you again and your worries will melt away. He's your sex toy. Nothing more."

With a deep breath, I stepped out of the bathroom and sashayed toward the bed. Royce was splayed out, rumpled and sexy, looking satisfied but concerned. My chest constricted at the sight of him. His torso was lined with scratches and bite marks.

"You sure you're okay?" he asked, his tone dripping with worry.

"Yeah." *He's my sex toy. Nothing more.*

"Come here." My sex toy patted the empty space beside him.

"Do you want me again?" I asked hopefully.

"I want to hold you."

Well, crap. I dragged my feet. Slipped in next to him. Wanted to snuggle up to him—what the hell was wrong with me—but remained a short distance away. *He's my sex toy.* I frowned and turned my back to him. My stomach began to churn again. My palms began to sweat again. *He's my sex toy.*

"Naomi?"

Please don't ask me if I want to spoon. "What?"

"Is this about the condom?"

I paused. "What do you mean?"

"It broke that last time."

My mouth went dry. My blood mutated into ice. Total and complete silence surrounded us as my world crumbled. Ohmygod. Oh. My. Freaking. God. My lungs quit working and another rush of dizziness slammed into me. "Tell me you're joking. Please, tell me you're joking."

"I wish I could."

I twisted to face him, meeting his gaze. "How the hell. Could that. Have happened?"

"Hey, I'm healthy. No reason for so much worry."

"I'm glad to hear it, but what about the other thing, huh?" At the moment, I couldn't say the *B* word. Couldn't even think it.

He ran a hand down his face. "Aren't you on the Pill?"

"No, damn it!" A horrible thought raced into my mind and my nostrils flared. "Is this your way of trapping me in a relationship? Because if so—"

"Hell, no." He jolted upright, pinning me to the bed with the fierceness of his gaze. "I don't have to resort to that kind of tactic to keep a woman."

I believed him. I'd even known it, deep down, before the words had rushed out of my mouth. Some of my anger and panic eased, and I was able to identify another emotion, the barest glimmer, underneath the surface of everything else. An emotion I didn't yet want to name.

My hand fluttered over my mouth, then dropped to my heart. "I'm sorry," I told him. "I shouldn't have said that."

"I understand." He nodded stiffly and eased down beside me. He tangled a hand through his hair. "I'm sorry, too. This has only happened to me once before."

I licked my lips as images of Royce playing blocks with a child, another woman's child, filled my mind. The tabloids had never printed a story about him being a father, but that didn't mean it hadn't happened. "Did the girl get—you know?"

"No."

"Maybe you're sterile," I said hopefully.

"Thanks a lot." Reaching behind himself, he folded his pillow in two and created a higher rest for his head. "Listen, I didn't mean to spoil the mood, but I thought you knew. And if you didn't, you needed to."

"You're right," I sighed.

A pause.

"I really enjoyed being with you, Naomi."

The words dangled like a lifeline, and I grabbed onto them for all I was worth. I didn't want to even consider diapers and the *things* that wore them—I still wasn't saying the *B* word. And I still didn't want to identify the ridiculous emotion swimming so determinedly through my veins.

"You roared so loudly," I said, "I think every person staying in this lodge knows you enjoyed yourself."

He chuckled, easing more of the tension between us, and pulled me into his arms. "Before we got in the plane, you mentioned an inner Tigress. I've been dying to question you all day."

A topic I could handle. "What do you want to know?"

"What exactly *is* it?"

I shrugged. "A Tigress is the part of a woman that is strong, self-assured and brave, able to do anything, say anything and always come out the winner. And—" I leaned toward him, lifted my hand and tapped him on the end of his nose "—a Tigress isn't particularly fond of Tigers."

"Hmm…" He took my fingers and kissed them, sucking them one at a time into the wet heat of his mouth. "Is there anything a Tiger can do to gain favor with a Tigress?"

As a delicious shiver ribboned through me, and even with the condom thing looming over my head, I knew I'd let him take me again. Like I'd realized in the bathroom, I didn't worry about anything but pleasure when he was inside me. Not emotions, not consequences.

"There is *one* thing," I said.

His dark brows slashed together. "And what's that?"

"He has to obey her every command."

Royce's deep, rich laughter echoed off the walls. "C'mere, kitty, kitty, and give me a command."

I leaned toward him, saying huskily, "You're going to let me kiss you right here." My fingers circled his cock. "And then you're going to pleasure me until I'm incoherent. You're going to pleasure me until I'm so sated I can no longer move." No longer think or worry.

"As a dedicated patron of the animal arts," he said, cupping my jaw, "I consider it a matter of pride to heed such a command."

We met in the middle. Our lips meshed together and our tongues collided. All worries forgotten. He tasted so good, like passion and heat and forbidden desire. My hands slid up his chest, the hard strength of his muscles covered by velvet-smooth skin.

When his lips moved away from my mouth, he placed a wet, hot caress along my jaw. "I really like this Tigress thing."

"You're about to like it even more." I inched my way down his body and took him in my mouth. He was big, very big, and my jaw stretched wide to accommodate him. I sucked him up and down, loving the heat and feel of him.

"Shit," he growled. "I'm going to come."

"Meeeooow," I said, a hint of wickedness in the undertones, then swallowed the taste of him.

AN HOUR LATER, WE HADN'T MOVED from the bed. Rumpled linens had sprung from their corners and fit untidily around us. After two more rounds of intense sex, I didn't have the strength to race to the bathroom and have another mini-panic attack. I liked where I was, and even though that still scared me, I wasn't moving.

I'd allow myself tonight. Nothing more. Tomorrow I'd fight my attraction to him. *Tomorrow* I'd worry about possible consequences.

"I know you've told me you don't want to get married," Royce said, cutting through the silence.

He was lying on his back, hands propped behind his head. I was curled beside him, arms splayed over his chest. Every muscle in my body tensed at his words. If that was the beginning of our next conversation, I needed to seriously reconsider my decision not to move from the bed.

"But..." He hesitated here. "Did tonight change your mind?"

I tried not to cringe, tried not to scream in horror. I couldn't handle this, not right now. I'd told Kera and Mel this would happen. Damn it! Why couldn't he have waited until tomorrow?

When I didn't answer, he rolled over and braced himself on his elbows. He gazed down at me. "I want to marry you. You know that."

"I told you before, marriage is not for me."

Slowly he eased off the bed. "Tonight didn't change your mind?"

"No."

"We're amazing together." He tangled a hand in his hair. "You can't deny that."

"Maybe not." Despite the renewed roaring in my ears, the new bout of dizziness in my head, and the sick, cramping feeling in the pit of my stomach, I managed to remain calm. "But I'm never going to change my mind. Not for any reason."

He leapt into a fast back-and-forth pace, and his muscles rippled beneath his skin with every movement. "Have you already forgotten the way you clung to me, the way you moved beneath me and screamed my name?"

"Just because we had sex," I told him, "doesn't mean we need to—you know." I didn't even want to say the word. It was as foul to me as the *B* word. My heart was already pounding against my ribs and the ringing in my ears was growing louder.

"What do you have against marriage?"

Everything. "It's not for me, that's all."

"It could be." He softened his voice; even his gaze softened as he stopped and regarded me. "We're perfect together, sweetheart."

I tried not to shudder. "No. I'm sorry."

"Help me understand." His pacing renewed. Step by step, his feet sunk into the plush rose-colored carpet. And step by step it was clear his determination intensified. "Help me understand what's brought you to this point. Please."

The ringing reached a fevered pitch, and my next words exploded from my mouth. I couldn't stop them. "You really want to know? Well, here it is. My ex-husband didn't get the memo about fidelity. He preferred other women, and lots of them. He professed to love me while he nailed everything that breathed. Maybe I could have written that off as Richard's depraved moral character and the fact that he's a male whore, but I can't write off my stepdad. He's a decent, hardworking guy and he's cheating on my mom. I will never willingly give my heart to another man only to have it thrown back in my face. How's that for an answer?"

By the time I finished, I was huffing. My hands were shaking. And Royce wore an expression of utter shock. I tried to calm myself down with a few deep breaths, tried to picture myself in my meadow of happiness.

A bit more rationally, I added, "I need to leave now. I need to be alone."

"You're staying here, Naomi." He ran a hand down his face. "Even if I have to lock you in the bathroom."

"Royce—"

He shook his head, his features dark and fierce. "You're going to hear me out. I'm not your ex, okay. I've never cheated on a woman, and I swear to you now I never will. I know what I want, and I want you. And, baby, you'd better understand now that I can be ruthless when it comes to getting what I want."

I threw my hands in the air. "There's nothing special about me." Why couldn't he understand that?

The distant rustle of wind sliced through the sudden silence. A thin layer of mist clouded the unadorned window. The mountainous landscape just beyond our room looked as harsh as Royce's face.

"Nothing special about you?" He stalked to that very window, gazing out at that very scenery. "Honey, I told you how you affected me at that party. And when you stepped into my office that first day, everything inside me went on alert. Your hair was messy, you had a streak of dirt on your face and when you sat down I saw the scrapes on your knees. And you know what? I'd never seen anything more beautiful. One glance at your lips, and I knew I had to have them all over me."

My cheeks reddened and I swallowed the lump in my throat. "You're just saying that because you're desperate to get married."

"You've said that before. I didn't answer you fully then, but I will now. I want to get married, yes, and I want a family. I want to belong to a woman and for her to belong to me. I want a woman to come home to—the same woman every night. I want our children running through our house. I want to know I have a partner who only wants the best for me, who will love me through everything. I want that with you. It's always been you."

The beauty of his words was shattering, and something lurched inside me at the happily-ever-after he described. Something that had nothing to do with panic, nothing to do with my hatred of marriage. "You've received thousands of applications. What if your Miss Right is in the stack, waiting for you? What if you find her after you've committed yourself to me?" I asked, softly speaking one of my deepest fears.

"I threw all the applications away the day you came into my office."

"But—"

"No buts. My mother ran the story. We were arguing, again, about my lack of dating. She said you obviously weren't interested in me and decided to introduce me to women who *were* available. I refused to date any of the applicants, and even talked her into having a birthday party with you as the planner." Royce turned toward me, his gaze clashing and locking with mine. "There's no other woman who has your spirit, Naomi. Your humor. Your ability to set me on fire."

I covered my face with my hands. If he'd said this to me six years ago, I would have caved. I would have been all over him. Now, I bore too many scars.

I couldn't give Royce what he wanted. I just couldn't put my heart on the line like that. The thought of permanent, legal ties made me nauseous. I wasn't ready. Hell, I might never be ready.

"I'm sorry, Royce, but my answer is still no."

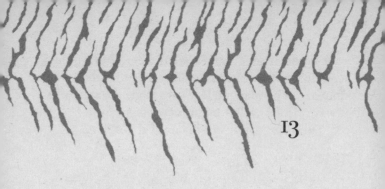

13

The only absolute in life is death. A Tigress knows this and avoids anything that could render her own absolute, be it physical or emotional.

EVEN THOUGH ROYCE SLEPT in another hotel room, I tossed and turned all night, confident I'd made the right choice one minute, hating myself for making the wrong choice the next. I was so confused. Maybe I'd acted hastily. Maybe I shouldn't have told him no so quickly.

I wanted to be with him sexually—truth. I didn't want to see him ever again—truth. When I looked at him, I melted inside—truth. At the same time, when I looked at him, I panicked—again, truth.

Would he agree to a phone relationship, maybe?

I discarded that idea as quickly as it formed. His voice was as sexy and mesmerizing as the man himself. Maybe I just needed to kick him out of my life for good, party be damned.

Great, now I wanted to cry.

When subtle, golden rays of sunlight peeked through the window, I gave up trying to rest and lumbered out of bed. This was exactly why I hadn't wanted to get involved with him in the first place. I hated the confusion, the insecurity.

I took a much needed shower, lingering in the steamy water, allowing the wet heat to relax me. Afterward, I dried my hair, brushed my teeth and dressed in my new black pants with ivy and flowers sewn in the seam and a matching blouse.

To my surprise, Royce was waiting in my room when I emerged from the bathroom. He sat in the cushy recliner, watching the news on TV. I stilled, my heartbeat picking up its pace. He looked delicious. His deep tan was displayed perfectly by the black pants and shirt he wore.

Now that I knew exactly what was under those clothes, I found myself picturing his hard, tanned muscles bunching, coiled and ready for my touch.

"Are you ready?" he asked, barely sparing me a glance. His cold, hard expression cut me deeply, but I should have been prepared for it. Should have been glad for it.

"Yes."

"We still need to drive to the cabin. We'll look around, then fly home."

"Just let me get my things." I turned, went to the divan and lifted my bag. Then I followed him out the door, my gaze boring into his back. Did he hate me?

We stayed at the cabin for less than an hour before driving to the airport. The plane ride home passed in agonizing slowness. Neither of us spoke. I sat still, eyes closed, not wanting to face Royce or the land so far below. At that point, I wasn't sure what would have been better. Crashing and dying or carrying on a conversation with Royce.

After we landed, he drove to my apartment building. The same uneasy silence filled the car. I hated it. We'd been so comfortable with each other before, and I already missed that. Had he decided that I wasn't the right woman for him after all? My hands tightened into fists, the thought not sitting well with me.

Yes, I realized how contradictory my thoughts were, how silly I was acting, but I had no control over my emotions. I had no control over the way this man made me feel. I constantly swung to both sides of the pendulum: I wanted him, I didn't. I needed him, I didn't. One part of me constantly battled the other.

When his luxury sedan came to a stop just outside my apartment, he removed the key from the ignition. "I'll help you inside."

"That isn't necessary," I told him, deciding to get as far away from him as possible so I could think about all that had happened. "I can get myself in."

"I'll carry your bag."

"I told you, I can get myself in."

He frowned. "Let me do this, Naomi."

"Fine."

I held my head high as I emerged from the car. And even as I unlocked the front door, I kept up the casual facade of a woman who cared about nothing more important than the weather.

When the lock clicked, Royce leaned forward. His chest brushed my back as he held the door open and out of my way. I stepped inside, away from him, and turned, blocking any move he might make to come inside.

"If you'll set my bag down," I said primly, "I'll get it the rest of the way in."

A muscle ticked in his jaw. "I don't know what gave you the idea that I'd let a woman of mine leave me outside without any kind of goodbye, but I assure you, it's the wrong idea."

My heart skipped a beat, and I opened my mouth to respond. No sound emerged.

"We're not finished, sweetheart, and you can't get rid of me so easily. If you think you can shove me aside because you're afraid of the past and the future, you need to readjust your thinking. And I'm more than willing to help you with that."

"H-how?" I didn't know what else to say.

He shrugged and leaned in a little closer to me. "You'll just have to wait and see."

I gulped. His words were innocent, but his tone was so suggestively sensual a tremor swept through me.

"Right now," he said, "there are some things I

need to discuss with you. We can have the discussion out here, for all your neighbors to hear, or you can invite me in."

The man was simply too tempting, a smooth talker who could easily charm me out of my clothes. "I can't let you in."

He took a step closer to me. "I don't have a single qualm about making a scene guaranteed to keep your neighbors entertained for weeks. Who knows? Maybe the *Tattler* wants to snap another picture of you."

"You wouldn't," I gasped.

"Try me."

There was a hard edge of determination to him that I'd only seen a few times before. Yeah, he'd do whatever was necessary to get inside. I moved out of his way. He brushed past me and set my bags beside the couch. He plopped down on the oversize cushions and motioned for me to take the space next to him.

I ignored his gesture and stood off to the side. One whiff of him and I might crumble like a condemned house. Before he could speak, I said, "I don't think we should discuss last night. It would be best if we just pretended it never happened."

"Maybe you can do that, sweetheart, but I'll never forget how you screamed my name so many times."

"Perhaps we should stop working together, as well," I continued, as if I hadn't heard him. I needed the money, yes, but I needed my sanity more. "I can put together a list of planners suited to y—"

He cut me off. "You agreed to help me with this, Naomi. Quit and I'll sue you for breach of contract."

I crossed my arms over my chest. "Why don't you go ahead and try it. We never signed a contract."

"You don't really want to fight me on this. I can be a bastard when I have to be."

"Like that's news," I muttered. If I were honest, though, I was immensely relieved he hadn't taken me up on my offer. I don't know why I'd even suggested it. The thought of never seeing him again rocked me to the core. In a horrible, horrible way.

"By the way," he drew out. "I want to know if you're pregnant."

I shook my head, trying to block out the *P* word and ensuing thoughts of the *M* and *B* words. "I'm not."

"You can't be sure."

"I'm just not, I tell you." But what if I was? A little thrill worked its way through me, the same kind of thrill I'd ignored last night, giving precedence to my panic and fear. I might not be ready for the *M* word, but the thought of the *B* word, a baby—there, I'd thought it—didn't make me panic nearly as much for some reason.

The thought of having Royce's baby suddenly made me feel all warm and tingly. God knows when I'd know for sure. My periods had always been irregular.

"Are you psychic?" he asked.

"I've been known to correctly guess the future," I lied.

He rolled his eyes. "Your voice got higher. You really need to work on your bluffing skills."

I stomped my foot and slitted my gaze at him. "Damn it—"

"You *will* let me know if—"

"—I told you—"

"—you're pregnant because I—"

"—I'm not—"

"—have a right to know."

"—pregnant."

He stared me down, and long minutes passed in silence.

"Fine," I finally said. "Yes. I'll tell you." Maybe.

Before I could protest, he rose and placed a hard kiss on my forehead. My lips puckered of their own accord, hoping he'd kiss them, too. "You still work for me, Naomi. I won't let you quit."

"Fine," I said again. "I won't quit."

"I'm not leaving until I have your word."

"I said okay, and I meant it. On both counts." Making a shooing motion with my hands, I said, "Now leave. I need to unpack."

"Tell me truthfully, first. Did you enjoy being with me?"

"I guess," I grudgingly admitted.

"And you'd like to be with me again?"

Damn him. "Yes, but that doesn't mean—"

"Yes," he said smugly. "It does." He strode out the door with a smile on his face, all hints of his dark mood gone.

What the hell kind of lame-ass Tigress was I? I

couldn't lie worth a damn, and I hadn't told Royce to get the hell out of my life.

I decided to order a pizza and call it a day.

I GORGED MYSELF ON PIZZA and worked on Mrs. Powell's party invitations. Which, I had to admit, were pretty amazing. I'd decided to go with something new, something different. The top portion featured a woman's bright emerald eyes, a paste-on jewel between them, and covering what would have been her nose and mouth but was actually the wording was a thin, wispy pink veil.

Sometimes I amazed myself.

When that was done, I had a long chat with my inner Tigress about her too frequent disappearing acts, then threw pepperonis at the old newspaper article about Royce that I'd saved, and decided I might—would probably—was destined to—sleep with Royce again. He was right, damn him. We weren't done.

I had needs. He had needs. I'd had a taste of him, and like an addict, I wanted more. Already. He was *that* potent. I'd just have to fight harder to keep my emotions under control—and *his* emotions, as well.

I sighed.

It was time to call my mom. I'd keep it casual. See how things were going. What I really wanted to know was what Jonathan was up to. I picked up the phone and dialed.

She answered on the second ring. "Hello."

I jumped right into the conversation as if she'd said, *What can I help you with, Naomi?* "Tell me what

Jonathan's been up to these last two days." How was that for casual?

"Darling," she said with a nervous laugh, "now isn't a good time."

"Is he in the room?"

"Well, yes."

"Move to another room or talk in code."

Pause. Several moments passed in silence. Then I heard, "Where are you going, Gloria?"

More nervous laughter. "I have to change my tampon, dear."

Dead silence. "Uh, take your time," Jonathan said.

"All right," she whispered a few seconds later. "I'm in the bathroom."

"Please tell me you weren't telling the truth. That you're only in there to talk to me privately."

"What do you think? I've already gone through menopause, silly. I doubt your stepdad will recall that fact, stupid man." With barely a breath, she continued more sternly, "Have you been screening your calls, young lady, because I've called and I've called and you haven't answered."

"Mom, concentrate. Tell me about Dr. Johnnie."

She tsk-tsked with her tongue. "Last night he came in three hours late." Her voice shook with the force of her frustration and disenchantment, and I actually thought I *heard* tears in the undercurrents. "He told me a client needed extra therapy. Well, obviously that client likes to rub gardenia-scented massage oil on his—"

"Information overload. Stop right there. Did you say anything to him?"

"No. I didn't know what to say. I came close to punching him in the nose, though."

"The action of a true Tigress," I said. "Why didn't you?"

"I keep thinking that I'm blowing this all out of proportion. What if he really was working late with a patient? He's not like your father. He's really not."

Had I sounded like this at one time? Had I sounded so needy and sad and hopeful? So wrong? "Don't lie to yourself." I purposely made my tone hard and unflinching. "You're a better woman than that."

"Did…did you find anything when you were here?"

I hadn't wanted to tell her anything until I had solid proof, but she needed to know something was going on, that her first instincts were correct. "I found pictures in his desk. Pictures of a woman and child."

"Oh, is that all?" My mom exhaled a deep sigh of relief.

"Is that all? Uh, hello. Can you say secret lover and illegitimate child? What do you mean, is that all?"

"I wanted to tell you about this," she hedged, "but Jonathan didn't think it would be a good idea."

My confusion soared. I gazed up at the ceiling, hoping for a little divine intervention. "Tell me what?"

"A few months ago, Jonathan learned he has a daughter and that daughter has a daughter of her own. She's been searching for him, isn't that neat? He didn't want you to think you were being replaced in his life, so we didn't mention it."

Okay, I totally hadn't expected to hear that. "That's...wonderful," I said. "I'm happy for him." And I was. Still, a hint of jealousy swept through me. Jonathan was my stepdad, but he was the only father I'd ever really accepted and I didn't like the thought of sharing him with another woman, no matter how much I hated him at the moment.

What was with my emotions lately? They were unpredictable. They were erratic. They were so damn stupid. I rubbed my temples in a vain effort to ward off the oncoming ache. "What's her name?"

"Rachel."

I cursed the name in my mind. So he had a daughter named Rachel. Fine. That explained the photos, but not the after-hour phone calls to his sec- retary. Not the perfume on his clothes. Not Nora's trips to Body Electric.

"I still think he's cheating on you, Mom."

"You may be right." She sighed again. "I heard him talking on the phone a little while ago and he told whoever it was that he was closing the office Friday morning. He never goes in late. He's just like you, an early bird. I think he might be spending the morning with *her*."

Friday huh. Well, I would be there, camera in hand.

"Gloria?" Jonathan's muffled voice crackled over the line. "I just realized something. You shouldn't be having a period."

"Oh, is that so?" she said with another of her nervous laughs. "Silly me. He remembered," she whispered fiercely into the phone.

"If you're bleeding, we should take you to the hospital."

"I'm not bleeding. Who said I was bleeding?"

"Then why were you wearing a tampon?"

"To, uh, double my pleasure?" To me, she whispered, "I've got to go, darling."

The line went dead just as my doorbell erupted in a series of chimes. I shook my head at the chaos that was my life and placed the phone in its receiver. I strode into the living room, trying not to think about Jonathan and his real daughter. Rachel.

"Rachel," I sneered. My nose crinkled in distaste. I was pissed enough at the man to want to use him as live bait during a shark-fishing expedition, but still… He was *my* dad.

After a quick peek through the peephole, I opened the door. Kera swept inside, her expression determined. She dropped her purse on the foyer table and twirled around. "You'll never guess what happened."

You made insane love with your client—several times—told him to get lost, then decided you wanted to sleep with him again? Wait. That was my news. You think your stepdad is cheating on your mom, you hate him, but you don't want him to have a daughter of his own that he might love more than you? Wait, me again. You might very well be knocked up with the aforementioned client's baby?

Damn, me again.

"What happened?" I asked her.

Smiling as if her fondest desire had just been

granted, she splayed her arms wide and twirled again. "I met the man of Mel's dreams."

I blinked. "Who?"

"Colin Phillips. Mel is pretending she's not interested in him, though."

Hey, wait. "When did you two meet him? I hadn't set anything up yet."

"Friday we were bored, so we sneaked into Powell Aeronautics. We just wanted to get a look at Colin, you know, but the security guard chased us up the stairs. Thankfully, we lost the jerk and managed to get to the nineteenth floor."

Mouth agape, I threw my hands in the air. "I can't believe you guys went to Powell Aero."

"Don't worry. Colin wasn't mad."

That was the least of my worries.

"He was so sweet about the whole thing. Even thanked us for coming."

"What's the rest of the story? The part about Mel pretending she's not interested in him?"

"I'm telling you, they clashed right from the beginning," Kera said, radiating amused glee. "Mel called him a corporate dust bunny."

"A what?"

"Someone who's always at the office, but doesn't do anything except sit around and pollute the air. Don't feel bad. I didn't know, either."

"How did you get past Elvira?"

"Who—oh, you mean the assistant. What a sweet, sweet woman. She just told us to go straight back to Colin's office."

What? No dirty looks? No superior attitude? Bitch.

"Anyway—" Breezily, Kera waved a hand through the air "—Colin wanted her, and she wanted him. You were right—they're perfect for each other. I could feel the sparks."

"But?"

She ran her bottom lip between her teeth. "But they were acting like silly children and I was afraid they'd never get around to actually dating. Not without a little help, that is."

Kera the matchmaker. Jeez. "What'd you do?"

"I, well, asked him on a date myself. Mel almost tackled me, even though she claimed she didn't want him. She's reminding me a lot of you lately."

I gave her a good frown to let her know I didn't appreciate her barb. She padded into the kitchen and snatched a soda from the fridge. I followed.

"He said yes," she added with a grin.

"First, what about George? Second, if Colin is willing to date you, even though he likes Mel, he's a bastard and not worth Mel's time."

"First, things are going very well with George. He asked me out, and I said yes. Second, I didn't say Colin and I were dating. I just said he agreed to go out with me. We talked about Mel the entire night. I think he's going to pursue her," she said, clapping happily. She twirled, spilling dark liquid all over my (formerly clean) kitchen floor.

"You know how Mel is. When she doesn't like someone, she's a mean, mean bitch." I loved her, but that was a known fact.

"That's why I'm going to make her miserable and jealous and let her think I'm after the man. She won't be able to get him out of her mind then."

I shook my head. "I thought Mel was the twin with the devil on her shoulder, but it's been you all along. You pulled this crap with me, too, didn't you? Pretending to want to date Royce."

She laughed. "Everything I do is for your own good. Mel's, too. She's too stubborn. Like you. So anyway, how was your trip?" She settled at the table and gazed expectantly at me. "You, Royce, together. All night. Did you share a room?"

"No." And that was the truth. We *hadn't* shared a room. He'd left in the middle of the night. "Everything went very well." Without meeting her eyes, I grabbed a paper towel and mopped up the spill.

"If everything went so peachy, why is your jaw clenching? Why is your eye twitching? Why is your voice so high?"

Had everyone known about my being deceitfully challenged but me? "All right, all right, all right." I popped to my feet and slammed the wet paper towel into the trash. I needed to work through at least *one* of my troubles. "The more time I spend with Royce the more confused I am about our…relationship." I almost gagged on the last word. "One minute I'm positive I never want to see him again, the next I'm wishing he were with me so I could rip off his clothes."

"That's called being human, sweetie, and I know just what to do." She leaned over and flipped through my basket of magazines. When she found the one she wanted, she held it up for me to see. "When Mel gets here, we're all taking a relationship quiz."

Oh joy.

MEL ARRIVED SOON AFTER and Kera dragged us into the living room, where she proceeded to give us assigned seats. "Naomi, you sit here. Mel, you're there." She pointed, forming a circle on the floor.

She sat between us and opened the latest issue of *City Girl*. "We're taking the Keep Him or Cut Him Loose test. It's just what we need to see where we stand romantically." There was a mischievous twinkle in her eyes. "I think we'll all understand ourselves and our men a little bit better after this. Are you ready?"

"Yes." Me.

"Uh, whatever." Mel. "I don't have a man."

"You will in the future," Kera said confidently.

"As if."

That didn't dim Kera's enthusiasm. "Okay, here we go. Question one." She read, "Your man is going out of town. Do you A) throw a party in his honor. B) cry. Or C) take up a new hobby to keep your mind occupied."

None of those sounded right to me. So I said, "What about D? Drink yourself into oblivion because you aren't sure what you want to do." Now that seemed like the perfect solution.

"You can't make up your own answers. That defeats the purpose." Kera frowned. "My answer is B. If Colin left," she said, aiming her words in Mel's direction, "I'd be too upset to do anything except cry."

How had I never seen Kera's acting potential before?

Mel stiffened. "As much as D appeals to me," she said through a tight jaw, "my answer is definitely A. Party time."

"Commitment-phobia must be contagious, because I swear you both suffer from a severe case," Kera said with a shake of her head.

"Yes, but I enjoy every second of it. Now, question two." Mel swiped the magazine and read, "Your man has just given you an expensive gift that you hate. Do you A) jump up and down with excitement because he only wanted to make you happy and keep the gift. B) toss it in the trash and call him a bastard. Or C) exchange the gift for something else."

I recalled the orchids Royce had given me, and my chest constricted. "B," I said. "Toss it in the can so I won't have to look at it and remember how he has no business being so sweet to me."

"I would exchange the gift, no question," Mel said. "There's no need to toss a free item. Ever. And Naomi and I both know what your answer is, Kera. You'd pee your pants from excitement." There was a sullen quality to her voice.

"Very funny," Kera said, grinning. Then she frowned. "Hey, is anyone keeping track of our scores?" She jumped up and raced into the kitchen. Several minutes later, she returned with pen and notebook in hand. She immediately jotted down our previous answers. "All right. We're all caught up. Let's move on."

Mel tossed me the magazine. "It's your turn to read."

I lifted the pages between my fingers as if they were nuclear waste. "Question three. You've just finished making love. Do you A) relax beside your man and enjoy the rest of the night. B) try to slither away in the dark. Or C) see if you can generate the world record for number of sexual positions attempted in one night."

I already knew my answer. At least, the only one I could say out loud.

"B," Mel and I said in unison. I didn't mention that Royce and I had *lived* C. Nor did I mention that after our second marathon, I hadn't been so eager to get away.

Kera: "I'm A."

"Too bad for Colin," Mel grumbled, a hard glint in her eyes. "What's the next question?"

"I'll read." Kera swiped up the quiz. "You're dating one guy, but another, super-hot guy asks you out on a date. Do you A) turn him down—after all, you're perfectly content with the man you have at home. B) accept and tell your man you're going to see your sick aunt Ruby. Or C) accept and tell your man you thought you had agreed to see other people.

"A." Kera.

"C." Mel.

"D. Never get involved in the first place so you don't have to worry about this type of situation." Me.

Kera pursed her lips. "I thought we discussed not making up your own answers."

"All right. All right. I'll take A." I could never, *never* do to a man what had been done to me. I'd never be able to live with myself if I made someone doubt their appearance, their personality and their intelligence.

"Now," Kera said. "It's time to calculate our scores." She flipped open the calculator. Five minutes later, she smiled. "Naomi scored a five. Mel, an eight. And me, a fourteen."

"So what does that mean?" I asked.

"Let's see." Kera flipped a page in the magazine. "If you score a ten to fifteen—that's me," she said, then read, "your man is a keeper. Did you hear that Mel? Colin is a keeper. What's more, *you* are a keeper. You are highly motivated to succeed and care about those around you."

"What's it say about me?" Frowning, Mel grabbed the magazine and read, "If you scored a six to nine you need to readjust your priorities. Spend a little time thinking of all the wonderful things others have done for you because *you* may not be worthy of your man." She tossed the magazine to the ground. "That's the worst bunch of shit I've ever heard. I think of others all the time."

I couldn't wait to see what the stupid quiz had to say about me. Maybe I'd get the answers I needed and would know what to do about Royce. "My turn." I swiped *City Girl* from the floor. "If you scored a one to a five," I read, "seek professional help."

I looked up.

"What else does it say?" Kera asked.

"That's it." I couldn't believe it. That was the advice the quiz had for me? Seek help? What kind of dumb-ass advice was that? The stupid kind, that's what. It was like telling a burn victim to put salve on their wounds.

So I needed professional guidance. So what. I'd known that already. Dumb quiz.

EARLY FRIDAY MORNING, I wolfed down two blueberry muffins and made a list of everything I wanted to get done that day.

1. Call Royce and ask to borrow his car and a camera.
2. Follow Jonathan and snap photos of him acting like a male whore.
3. Take Mrs. Powell's invitation mock-up to printer so I could present a sample for Royce's approval.

After a moment's consideration, I scratched out number one. Added it back. Scratched it out again. I should avoid that man like the plague. However, I scowled and picked up the phone, hurriedly dialing his number.

It wasn't like this was a social call. I needed his help and, by God, I wouldn't be afraid to ask. Wouldn't be afraid to hear his voice. I would control my hormones or die trying.

And you know what? As the phone rang, I heard that stupid BlueJay beeping from the trash can. I ignored it. Royce finally answered, his voice scratchy with sleep. A shiver snaked down my spine, and an image of him lying in bed, naked, swept through my

mind, his mouth finding my breasts, and his fingers—
I growled. Damn hormones.

"Uh, hi Royce. It's Naomi."

"Hey, sweetheart. Something wrong?"

Another shiver. If only he hadn't uttered the endearment with such warmth and tenderness. "Can I borrow one of your cars?"

Pause. "Why?"

"I have to do something."

"What?"

"Can I borrow one of your cars or not?"

Another pause. "With me in it?"

"No."

"With me in it?" he asked again. "And you better answer it right this time, because your answer is the same as mine."

"Yes." Stubborn man. "Do you never have to work? You'll have to take a couple hours off if you go with me, because I need the car this morning."

"I'll call you right back," he said and hung up on me.

Openmouthed, I stared down at the phone. "No you did not," I muttered and redialed his number. He didn't answer. That decoded piece of—

The phone rang. I almost jumped out of my skin. "What?" I barked into the receiver.

"Done. I'll be there in fifteen minutes."

My pulse fluttered at the thought of seeing him again. "Bring your camera. And wear a hat. And sunglasses."

"And a fake beard?" he asked on a husky laugh.

"If you have one," I said in all seriousness. "Drive your cheapest, most unnoticeable car. No limo today."

"What's going—"

This time, I hung up on *him*. I'd clue him in when he got here. Time to get busy. As I strode into my bedroom, I stripped. I belted a pillow over my stomach. The condom incident with Royce had given me an idea for a disguise. Dr. Johnnie would never know the pregnant woman following his every move was actually his stepdaughter, Detective Delacroix.

I slipped the largest dress I owned over my head and shimmied it down the rest of me. The plain, light blue material was tight around my middle, emphasizing my rounded belly. I ran my hands over the pillow and a thought occurred to me: This image might actually become a reality in the coming months. My heart skipped a beat.

Don't think about that, Naomi. For God's sake, don't think about it.

As I slipped into comfortable shoes, I stuffed Mrs. Powell's party invitation in my purse. I twisted the long length of my hair under a hat, then locked up my apartment. Fighting a sense of eagerness, I headed outside to wait for Royce. Thankfully, no *Tattler* reporters were behind the bushes—I checked—nor was anyone waiting beside the building.

Fifteen minutes later, I was a hot, sweaty mess—and still freaking waiting outside. Did no one believe in timeliness anymore? Royce finally eased his shiny, expensive sedan in the parking slot right in front of me. I would have preferred something less expensive, less noticeable, but this would have to do.

I slid into the passenger seat, sighing as the cool, conditioned and sandalwood-fragranced air washed over me. Lord, he always smelled so good. I slammed the door with a flick of my wrist. When I turned to Royce, I noticed he was staring at my belly in open-mouthed astonishment.

As I'd requested, he was wearing a hat, sunglasses and even the fake beard. He was also wearing yellow-pink-and-blue golf pants and a yellow T-shirt. The sight of him made me go all weak and needy inside. He looked so cute, and he'd done this for me. Just because I'd asked. How sweet was that?

"What the hell is going on?" he choked out. "Is that some kind of hint?" He pointed to my puffy belly.

"We're going to follow my stepdad, and I didn't want him to recognize me. Did you bring the camera?"

"It's in back." Brow furrowed, Royce reached under my skirt and smoothed his hand up my calf, my thigh, and onto the pillow.

I gasped at the sudden liquid heat pooling between my legs. Before I begged him to go ahead and give me an orgasm while he had his hand up my skirt, I slapped his arm away. "Stop that."

"I had to feel for myself."

I cleared my throat and pulled at the collar of my dress. "Yes, well, thank you for rearranging your schedule for me, but I wish you'd worn jeans or something. Everyone will notice those pants."

"I had no idea what we were doing. You hung up on me, remember? Besides, the pants go well with the beard and your, uh, belly."

I had to clear my throat again. Shifting in my seat, I rattled off my parents' address. "We need to hurry. Jonathan always leaves the house at eight-thirty."

Minutes later, Royce and I were speeding along the highway.

"I could hire a P.I. to follow him," he suggested, keeping his eyes on the road.

"That's not necessary. I'm perfectly capable of catching him in the act." Plus, it was horrible of me to admit, but I was taking a perverse sort of satisfaction in doing the investigating myself. I hadn't done anything like this with Richard. I hadn't had the courage. So, in a way, this was kind of like therapy for me. And Jonathan was big on therapy.

"Naomi," Royce said, then stopped himself. He gripped the steering wheel with one hand and massaged his neck with the other.

"What?" I stiffened. He'd sounded…upset. "Tell me."

"Remember that trip to Florida I mentioned? I'm flying out tomorrow. I'll be gone for a week."

I immediately began to analyze the situation, last night's quiz replaying through my mind. If your man goes out of town, what would you do? Did I want to throw a party? Cry? Or take up a new hobby? I was pretty certain I wanted to go with B, like Kera, and cry like a goddamn infant. I frowned, my lips pulled down so tightly my jaw began to ache.

"You want to come with me?" he asked.

Yes was the answer that first leapt to the surface. "No. No, thank you." I *did* want to grab him by the shirt and command him to stay. After all, a true Tigress knew how to fight for what she wanted and keep what she won. The thing is, I had never really fought for Royce, which meant I hadn't really won him. I'd all but pushed him away.

What if Royce found another woman in Florida?

What would I do then? The quiz hadn't given simple answers for that question, but I suspected I'd do more than cry. *You have told him over and over you want no claims on him.* Damn non-relationships. They sucked ass.

14

*Turn your back, and you will be attacked. Guard
yourself constantly. Never relax. Not even while
you're alone. At any moment a Tiger, or even another Tigress, could be planning your demise.*

JONATHAN LEFT THE HOUSE right on schedule, and
Royce and I were right behind him. Mom's eaves-
dropping proved accurate; he didn't go to his office.

He drove to Nora's.

"That blatant bastard," I growled, reaching for
Royce's digital camera.

Nora answered the door wearing jeans and a tank
top. Her eighties hair was ratted at her temples, and
she wore enough makeup to send a cosmetic
company's stock through the roof. She didn't kiss
Jonathan when she saw him, but she did hug him and

step aside. I snapped a few pictures of Jonathan entering the house.

"That isn't his sister, I take it?" Royce asked.

"His secretary."

"Not all men are like that, you know."

I snorted. "Can you prove that?" Without waiting for his answer, I pushed my way out of the car. I stalked toward the small but well-maintained house. I heard another car door slam, heard Royce mutter under his breath, and knew he was following me. It was a workday, so most of the neighborhood residents were gone. No one was mowing their lawn. In fact, the only person out in the open was a young woman on a morning jog.

I smiled hello to her, rubbing my belly to show her I was merely an innocent pregnant female having a nice stroll, and continued on my path to the house, the camera gripped tightly in my hands. I didn't go to the front door, but stalked to the nearest side window.

A dog barked and growled, the sound so menacing I jumped and whirled around, my gaze darting in every direction. There, behind the chain fence, was a Chihuahua. He continued to bark and growl at me.

"Shut up, or you'll be breakfast," I whispered fiercely.

His ears flattened, but he went silent. I breathed a sigh of relief and turned my attention back to the window. The curtains were lacy and split down the middle. By pressing my eye to the glass, I had a perfect view inside. Unfortunately, the living room was empty.

Had those horny cheaters already adjourned to the bedroom?

"I can't believe you're doing this," Royce said from behind me. "I can't believe you dragged *me* into this."

"I can't believe those two don't even have the will-power for a conversation before jumping into the main event. And dragged you? Please."

Just then, Nora rounded a corner, Jonathan close at her heels. "Wait," I said. "They're coming this way." Nora carried three clear bottles filled with... oil? I gasped. "Those sick, perverted shits. I think they're going to massage each other."

"Come on, sweetheart. You don't need to see that." He tugged on my arm, but I resisted.

"Oh, no. I'm not leaving."

The couple sat on the couch at the far wall, facing me, and I snapped several pictures through the lace curtains. Nora held up one of the bottles and Jonathan sniffed. His nose wrinkled and he shook his head. Nora rubbed some on her arm and he sniffed again. They repeated the exact same action with the other two bottles.

I watched as Jonathan ran a hand through his hair, his expression frustrated. His mouth was moving, but I couldn't hear what he was saying.

"Uh, sugar bottoms," Royce said. "I think we need to go."

"Not yet. They're about to do something. I can tell."

"Sweetie. Maybe you didn't hear me. We need to go."

"Just a min—"

"What are you two doing?" a scratchy female voice snapped.

I whipped around. In my haste, my camera slapped against the window glass with a loud *clang*. An elderly woman wearing her bathrobe and rollers stood in front of us, her hands on her hips. Her wrinkled eyes were narrowed and her lips were pulled taut. My heart almost leapt out of my chest. I stood frozen, not knowing what to say, not knowing what to do, only knowing that at any moment Jonathan and Nora were going to come sprinting out of that house.

"Nora!" the old woman called. "Nora, get out here. You got peepers."

"Run," Royce shouted. There was laughter in his voice. He grabbed my wrist and we took off in a mad dash.

I was hooting with my own half hysterical, half disbelieving laughter as I grabbed my hat to keep it from flying off my head. My belly bounced up and down with every step.

We jumped into the car—which he'd wisely left running—and peeled out, the tires squealing all the way down the street. From the rearview mirror, I watched Jonathan and Nora stop abruptly in front of the old woman, who was pointing in our direction.

"That was close. Too close," I panted. Another chuckle slipped out. My blood was pumping at lightning speed, and my breath emerged ragged and shallow.

Royce's smile grew wider. "Did you get the evidence you wanted?"

"No. They were doing some sick, pre-sex ritual, I think. Five more minutes and I would've nailed him."

Royce shook his head, causing his fake beard to fall and hang at one side. "Maybe he's not cheating."

"Not cheating!" I lost all traces of humor. "What was he doing at that woman's house, then? Why did he lie to my mom about his whereabouts?"

"Okay, he's cheating. Want me to beat the shit out of him?"

I plopped against the seat rest. "Let me get back to you on that."

On the way home, we stopped at the printer and dropped off the invitation. We received several odd looks because of our attire. "It'll be ready for your approval when you return from Florida," I told Royce.

We arrived at my apartment soon after, and he walked me to my door. I was eager to load the pictures onto my computer and see if there was something in them I had missed at the scene.

"Naomi," Royce said, an odd note in his voice.

I was just about to insert the key in the lock, but I stopped and turned to him. "Yes?" Our gazes locked. He'd removed the beard and his lips were slightly lifted at the corners. I loved—no, hated—loved—*hated* the way his scent and heat surrounded me every time he was near.

"I'll miss you while I'm gone."

I gulped. I'd miss him, too. Horribly. He made me laugh, made me ache, made my hormones spike. He made me crazy, made me ache, made me feel so wonderfully alive. He confused me, made me ache, branded me, made me ache. Did I mention he made me ache?

He leaned down and lightly brushed his lips over mine. The kiss was soft and sweet and oh, so tender. Filled with promise. I shivered, desperately craving more. Maybe…maybe I'd just invite him in and show him my bedroom. I mean, saying goodbye properly would be okay. If I didn't allow myself to linger in his arms afterward, surely my emotions would be safe. I'd already decided to sleep with him again. Hadn't I? I couldn't remember, I'd changed my mind so many times.

My fingers fisted around the fabric of his shirt, and I opened my mouth to ask him if he wanted to stay.

"I'm dying to have you again," he said, cutting off my words, "but I'm going to wait until you realize this isn't a sexual relationship. This isn't—what did you call it? An unemotional fling."

I frowned.

"I want your affection. I want your trust. You don't have to worry about me," he said. "Ever. There isn't a woman out there who compares to you on any level. I'm not going to be with someone else while I'm gone. I'm not going to have a one-night stand or any type of sexual relationship in Florida."

"How can I be sure?" I asked softly. Dare I admit, desperately?

"It's called trust, baby, and you're just going to have to give me yours. You're the only woman I want. Think about that while I'm gone."

He left me standing there, my fingers tracing my lips, his heady, intoxicating words ringing in my head.

FOR THE NEXT SEVERAL DAYS, I worked feverishly on the decorations for Mrs. Powell's party, despite the fact that Royce still hadn't approved a location. I didn't think about him—and how he'd abandoned me to go on his trip, how spying on my stepdad had been fun because *he'd* made it fun. I didn't think about Jonathan, either—and how the pictures revealed nothing sexual had happened at Nora's. Nor did I think about anything related to either of them—like the fact that both men had me tied in knots.

I concentrated only on the party, on the vivid blue, green and violet table drapes, the multi-hued satin pillows I planned to scatter over the floor, and the perfect exotic lanterns I'd rent.

On the fourth (lonely) morning after Royce's departure, I went to Kera's for an impromptu breakfast (at Kera's insistence) only to learn my cousin had prepared one of her new, exotic recipes. Some kind of fried meat with a disgusting egg sauce. I should have called in sick. I was destined to be sick anyway, if I ate that crap.

"So what's going on with you?" Kera asked after taking a huge bite of her meat. She chewed as if it were one of the most delicious things she'd ever eaten. "You've been ignoring us for days."

I started with business. "What kind of food can you make for an *Arabian Nights* party?"

"Hmm. Let's see…what about ashta with honey, baclawa, kounafa, mafrouki and stuff like that?"

"I'm not sure." I had no idea what any of that stuff was. "They aren't new recipes of yours, are they?"

"No, dummy. They're Lebanese."

"Do you think Royce's trip to Florida was his way of giving you the boot?" Mel asked suddenly, cutting into our conversation.

Business forgotten, my stomach dropped. I hadn't considered that.

"I would sob if Colin dumped me," Kera said, fighting a smile.

"We know." Mel sent me a will-you-shut-her-up gaze.

"No boot," I said firmly. All right, hopefully. Royce had said he wouldn't be with another woman while he was gone. He'd said that he wanted me, that no other woman would do. He'd proven himself trustworthy so far. "I like Royce," I told them, swirling milk in my glass. "And I miss him. I do. More than I should. He's an amazing lover and I—"

Kera: "Wait. Back up. Amazing lover? You told us you'd kissed him, and that's all. You've slept with the guy and this is the first we hear about it?"

Mel: "I should have guessed from the way your skin is glowing."

I plopped my elbows on the tabletop and dropped my head into my upraised hands. "I'm sorry I didn't tell you. I just…I don't know. I wasn't ready to give details."

"Why? I always share my details." Mel again.

"We know," Kera and I said in unison. Over the years, we'd heard all about Mel's love life in vivid description. Way too much description. The girl liked it wild, no doubt about it.

"What if he finds someone else while he's gone?" Mel asked, pouring more of the yellow gravy mix over her meat. "In fact, what if the man comes back married?"

Again, I hadn't thought of that. Nausea churned in my still bottomed-out stomach.

I must have gone seriously pale, because Kera said, "Don't listen to her. The man is obviously in love with you. He asked *you* to marry him, not some other woman. He'll come back to you. Single," she added with a firm nod.

"So what should I do?" My voice cracked. How long would Royce be content to wait for me? "I'm not ready to give him up. Should I marry him like he wants? He said he won't sleep with me again until we're committed."

"The bastard," Mel said.

Kera's shoulders hunched as she considered my words. Her lips dipped into a soft, little frown. "I honestly don't know what you should do."

Life sucked.

"We need to think about this," Kera added. "Why don't we spend the rest of the day and night thinking about Naomi's problem, and we'll meet back here in the morning."

THE NEXT MORNING:

"Okay, I've thought about it." I sat across from my cousins, buttering a piece of toast.

"See, I knew a day and night of reflection was all you needed." Kera passed me the strawberry jelly. Praise the Lord, she hadn't cooked today. "What have you decided?"

I closed my eyes, opened them, preparing myself to remain strong. "I'm going to seduce him until he forgets about any type of commitment issues."

Kera rolled her eyes. "Good luck with that." She munched on a bite of her cereal, thoughtful as she chewed. "In theory, I'm sure ignoring his desire for a commitment seems feasible. But in actuality, you'll start to feel guilty."

"She's right." Mel nodded. "You're better off ending things now."

Now they offered advice. *After* I'd spent the night agonizing. "I hate how complicated this is."

"You're such a complainer, Naomi." Mel pushed her bowl away. "If *Royce* were to ask me for advice, I'd tell him to never see *you* again."

"And that would be the best advice you've given all week," I said with a frown.

"Well, I think you're in lu-ve," Kera sang.

"Me, too. What's so bad about marrying Royce, anyway? I know you think you're not ready. But hey, if it doesn't work out, get a divorce. It's as easy as one, two, three." Mel snapped.

"Divorce isn't easy. It's hard and it hurts and it can turn into a blood bath. Hello, did neither of you pay attention during my divorce from Richard?"

Kera: "If Colin asked me, I'd already be at the altar."

Mel: "Will you shut up about Colin, Kera? I'm sick to death of hearing about him. You're dating him, but he calls *me*. Comes on to *me*."

Kera smiled, barely managing to hide her gloating. "He's probably got you confused with me."

"Maybe *I* should marry Royce," Mel snapped. "Then this entire conversation would be moot. I'd never have to hear about Royce or Colin again, and I could go back to my peaceful existence."

I stiffened, not liking those words at all. "You can't marry Royce. The two of you would never get along."

She ran her tongue over her teeth. "Oh, really?"

"Yes, really."

"Why not?"

"Because you don't play backgammon, that's why. The article in the *Tattler* specifically stated that Royce wants a woman who plays backgammon."

Mel chuckled. "You'll have to do better than that, Naomi. *You* don't know how to play backgammon, either, and he asked you to marry him."

"That's not the point."

"What about green?" Mel asked. "Green is my best color, or so I've been told. And Royce's favorite color is green."

"So what?" I said defensively. "He prefers women who don't talk back. You're disqualified for that alone."

Kera tapped her fingernails on the tabletop. "So are you, Naomi. I mean, you could tear the flesh from someone's bones with that razor-sharp tongue of yours. Especially recently." To soften her words, she smiled. "Maybe we should get Jennifer's opinion about your tongue. She would know better than any of us."

We stared at each other for a moment before bursting into laughter. Tears trickled from the corners of Kera's eyes, she laughed so hard.

"Look," Mel said between chuckles. "The point I'm trying to make here is that you don't like the image of Royce with other women. So there's your answer. You want him all to yourself. So take him before it's too late."

Wise words. Could I do it, though? Risk everything?

"Hey!" Kera exclaimed. "Why don't you take on another client? That'll keep your mind off of Mr. Sexy."

"I can't," I said after swallowing a bite of toast.

"Why not?"

"Royce dictated at the very beginning that I couldn't work on another project while planning his mother's party. Which makes it impossible to bury myself in work." My legs kicked out and rested on the empty seat across from me. "You and I have discussed the menu. I've ordered the flowers, reserved a DJ. I've already ordered some of the decorations and drafted an invitation. There's nothing left to do now except wait for him to contact me once he's back in town."

"Don't wait for him to call. Take the initiative. Pick up the phone and call him. You have his cell-phone number, right?" Mel downed her glass of apple juice. "Men love phone sex."

I rubbed a hand down my face, considering the idea. "You know, before walking into Royce's office, I had my life mapped out. No men. No relationships. Then Royce rocks my world—several times—and it's changing everything. The jerk."

"Yeah, a real bastard." Kera rolled her eyes. "How dare he change your life for the better."

"Hey! Let's TP the asshole's house tonight," Mel suggested. "We haven't done something like that in years."

Grinning, I shook my head. "I am not toilet papering his home."

"Then we're going club hopping tomorrow night and drowning our sorrows in beer and sexy men."

"Now that I can do," I said.

MY PHONE WAS RINGING when I walked into my apartment. I hurried into the kitchen and picked it up. "Hello."

"Why didn't you tell me you were pregnant?" my mom demanded.

"Wha—What are you talking about?" How did she know about that?

"There's a picture of you in the *Tattler* with a very large, very pregnant stomach. The article says you're having triplets. The next words out of your mouth had better be that you're getting married, young lady."

"Mom, I'm not pregnant," I said, wishing I knew the truth of those words. "Nor am I getting married." I wished to God I knew the truth of those words, too. "I've got to let you go now. I'm going to sell all of my vital organs on eBay."

15

*When the jungle's leaves and bushes are too thick,
quickly chop them down so that you can see your
path more clearly.*

MUSIC BLARED FROM SPEAKERS hanging overhead. Undulating bodies littered the floor as men and women clanged together. Smoke and chatter wafted all around us. We'd been here only ten minutes and I already wanted to leave.

Why had I agreed to come?

Desperate for a little alone time, I made a quick trip to the ladies' room, where I attempted to force my skirt to elongate. Mel had given me the dress at my non-party. It was short, tight and green, and it barely concealed my ass. I felt like a piece of candy on display at a day care. Worse, I felt as if I had a neon sign around my neck that read Free, Take One.

Several men had already attempted to take me up on the unintentional offer.

The bathroom was growing more crowded, women flocking inside to check their hair and makeup. With a sigh, I maneuvered back to the table and reclaimed my seat. Mel and Kera were surrounded by admirers. Nothing new. Men loved the whole idea of twins. Double the love, or something like that.

Colin stood watch at both girls' sides, frowning at any man who glanced their way. He sometimes looked to the door, as if he couldn't wait to leave. Kera had invited him to join us, much to Mel's chagrin.

Women brushed against him, flirted with him and smiled at him, but he ignored them. And that surprised me. The only woman he seemed to notice was Mel. He didn't just notice her, either. He watched her through eyes filled with longing and desire. Mel pretended not to notice, but she constantly darted stealthy glances his way.

"Colin," Kera said. "Why don't you ask Mel to dance? She could use the exercise."

Mel ignored her and pushed a shot glass in my direction. Her red bangs appeared ultra-bright in the strobe light. Her top was cropped just under her breasts, showcasing her tanned, flat stomach and the tattoo of stars around her belly button. "Drink."

I shook my head no. Ginger ale was my drink of choice tonight—for reasons I wasn't sharing with my cousins. I grabbed onto my half-full (bet you expected me to say half-empty) glass. "I've already got a drink."

"You need alcohol. You look like Death in a Green Dress."

"Then why the hell did you insist I wear this?"

"I thought it would look good on you. I can admit when I'm wrong." She pushed another drink at me, and I shook my head. "If you won't drink, eat something."

My stomach growled at the word *eat*. I *was* hungry. Famished, actually. I hadn't eaten since breakfast and the thought of buffalo wings made my mouth water.

I waved the waitress/bartender/whatever the hell she was over and ordered two dozen. The wings arrived soon after. Thick red sauce dripped from each boneless delicacy. I ate the first one slowly, the tangy flavor exploding on my tongue. The rest, well, I shoveled them in like a Hoover. Mel tried to steal one, but in my starved haze, I stabbed her hand with my fork. The men at our table cheered me on.

"Maybe you've had enough, Naomi," Kera said, grinning. "You've got sauce around your lips."

Cheeks reddening, I rubbed my napkin over my mouth. A man chose that moment to scoot in beside me. "What's your name, sugar?" he asked.

Why did men insist on calling women by food endearments? Sugar. Sweet cakes. Honey pie. Richard the Bastard had called me by other women's names. Royce called me sweetheart, as if I actually held a special place in his heart, so it meant something when he did it. I think my inner Tigress would have preferred Sex Goddess of Wet Dreams, though. That had a nice ring to it.

I cast a glance in my new admirer's direction. "You may call me Your Highness," I said. "Or Empress Beauty."

He chuckled. I wasn't kidding.

"I love a woman with a healthy appetite." He leaned into me, pretending he couldn't speak over the loud music. "The way you ate those wings, well, it turned me on. You're not going to run to the bathroom and throw them up, are you? Some women do that."

I studied his face and frowned. He was cute, with brown hair and big puppy-dog brown eyes. He was a little older than most of the other people in the bar, I noticed, which screamed *midlife crisis*. Suspicious, I peeked at his left hand. His fingers were wrapped around a beer and the beer was resting on the tabletop. Sure enough, his fourth finger possessed the telltale white band left by a ring, where the skin around that *symbol of lifelong commitment* had tanned. Either he was recently divorced or he'd removed his ring for tonight.

My inner Tigress suddenly roared to life, demanding that I claw out the man's stomach and present it to the women at my table for consumption. Ah, she'd become vicious. I liked that.

"Where have you been?" I muttered to her.

Midlife Crisis heard me and assumed I'd been speaking to him. "I've been waiting for you, sugar."

"You married?" I asked him innocently.

He had the audacity to stare me dead-on and say, "Never wanted to take the plunge. I guess I just never met the right woman." His voice dipped as low and seductive as he could make it. "You?"

"I haven't met the right woman, either."

He blinked, but then his lips stretched wide in a grin. "You like women? Well don't worry, I'm open-minded. I'm all about equality."

"I'm not sleeping with you," I snapped.

"No, she's not," a deep, rich, *familiar* voice said.

I spun in my seat, my eyes going wide, my heart racing.

"Royce," Colin said, relief heavy in his tone. "About time you got here."

Royce shot Midlife Crisis a pointed stare. "If you want to live, I suggest you leave."

Midlife paled and scampered away.

Royce was here. Actually here. Shock and pleasure wound through me, tightening around every limb, cell and hollow of my body. Richard had never come home early for anything, had never acted eager to see me.

I stood, my knees unsteady. "What are you doing here? Why aren't you in Florida?"

His arm wrapped around my waist, as strong and warm as I remembered. He pulled me into his side and kissed my temple. "I came back early. Colin called me and told me you were coming here. Since I love the music," he said dryly, "I decided to come, too."

"The music, hmm." I bit my lip, wanting to prompt him for more of an admission. I couldn't help it; I loved his sweetness and I wanted him more in that moment than I ever had before. "That's all?"

His eyes flared with heat and fire and possessive-ness. "Maybe the real reason is I missed you like hell."

I leaned more snugly against him and breathed in his sandalwood scent. "How was your trip?"

"Miserable. Like I said, I missed you." He nuzzled my cheek with his nose.

A shiver stole through me, warm, delicious. "You didn't get married or anything like that, right?"

"I thought about you every second of every day, and ended up walking out on a roomful of buyers in the middle of a meeting. What do you think?"

God, I wanted him. Reaching up, I caressed a fin-gertip down his cheek. He sucked in a breath.

I think Kera said, "How adorable." I think Mel chimed in with, "Do it on the table, why don't you. I don't mind being a voyeur."

"Let's dance," Royce said on a husky chuckle.

He led me onto the crowded dance floor, maneu-vering us through bumping and grinding bodies. Colin dragged Mel onto the dance floor, too, I noticed, and she didn't protest. She actually slid her arms around him and pressed her body into his.

Smoke wafted around us, arms flew toward us. The music belted out a fast, writhing rhythm, but Royce held me tightly and we swayed slowly. I loved being in his arms.

"I'm glad you came," I admitted.

Gently he smoothed my hair from my temples. Another of those wonderful shivers raced through me. "I do believe that's the first time you've ever admitted to any type of affection for me."

"Yeah, well. Don't get used to it."

His fingers trailed down my shoulder to the curve of my waist, stopping at the hem of my ultra-short dress. "It drives me crazy when you wear green," he said, his voice dropping an octave. "The only thing I like better is when you're wearing nothing at all."

I stared into his eyes, those gloriously blue, heart-warming eyes. This man was tearing me apart inside, but I couldn't walk away from him. "What am I going to do with you, Royce?" I whispered.

His arms tightened around me and smoothed a path up my bottom and to the small of my back. "Love me. Trust me."

I shook my head almost violently. My stomach cramped with enough force to make me gasp. I stilled. My blood went cold even as my skin heated several degrees. "I think I'm going to be sick," I said. I flattened a hand against my stomach, trying to tamp down another cramp.

He frowned. "What I said wasn't *that* bad."

"No, really. I think I'm going to be sick," I said, then hunched over and threw up boneless wings all over his expensive Italian loafers.

LOUD, NEFARIOUS RINGING penetrated the darkness blanketing my mind—and it wasn't from my hidden BlueJay. The screeching thundered in my ears with deafening intensity. I hadn't drunk any alcohol, but I felt hungover.

The ringing continued.

Damn phone. I blindly reached out, meaning to

pound it into a thousand tiny pieces, but I found nothing but air. By the time I sat up, my lips bared in a scowl, the ringing had ceased, going silent. With a sigh, I laid my heavy head back on the pillow and burrowed deeper in the covers.

God, my brain ached. My stomach still felt queasy. "Death by chicken wing," I muttered. I had already spent most of the night hunched over the toilet, throwing up. I wanted to die, but sometime during the night, I'd decided to be brave and live. I thought now that I had made the wrong choice.

Another bout of ringing erupted.

Jumping up from the bed—anything to make the noise stop—I tripped over the tangled sheets. It had to be another reporter from the *Tattler.* They'd called me all night long, in between bouts of vomiting, wanting to know about my (alleged) relationship with Royce, when my triplets were due and if Royce and I had set a date for our wedding. I hadn't spoken with them myself, but had heard their questions over my answering machine.

I'd had enough. I planned to tell this reporter exactly what he could do with himself. Rot in hell! Sprawled out across the floor, I made a grab for the receiver. "Hello." My voice was croaky, as if I'd spent the night sucking on Brillo pads.

"Naomi, darling? That you?"

Mom. If I hadn't felt like killing myself already, I would have then. "Yeah. It's me," I said. "Barely."

"Darling, you sound horribly sick."

"I am."

"Oh, dear. I'd thought you were lying when you said you were sick at my house, but you were telling the truth, and now you're even worse, and that makes me the worst mom in the world for—"

"I *was* lying," I interjected. "I'm just a little out of sorts right now."

Pause. "Good, then. I won't keep you long. I just have to get a few things off my chest before I burst. Now that you know about Rachel, Jonathan really wants you to meet her. I'll let you know when and where. And—and I've decided we were wrong, that Jonathan just isn't the type of man to cheat on me."

"Mom, that's—"

"No, no. He's an honest man. And so sweet. He brought me flowers yesterday and we spent a romantic evening together, dinner, wine, the works."

Most likely the romantic night had been born of Jonathan's guilt. Why couldn't my mom see that?

My stomach chose that moment to cramp again, and I moaned. "Do you see what that kind of talk does to me, mom? It makes me want to throw up."

"Want me to come over and take care of you? I'll bring soup. I think I have a can of chicken noodle here. If not, I'm sure I have tomato."

"Oh, God." I pressed my lips together to keep from barfing right then and there. "Are you trying to kill me? No soup. No mention of soup ever again. I'll be fine. People don't die from food poisoning."

"Yes, they do," she said matter-of-factly. "All the time."

Great. "Thanks, Mom. I really needed to hear that."

"Are you sure you don't want me to come over?"

"Positive."

"I'll let you get some rest."

"Wait." I fought through the pain long enough to say, "I know you want to think the best of Jonathan. So do I. But I also wanted to think the best of Richard."

"This isn't the same thing. They aren't the same man."

"That's where you're wrong. They are the same man. Every man ever born is the same man." Except Royce. Maybe. "Don't you remember Daddy? I was only a child, but I remember his late nights, his 'female business associates.'" While my mom pretended not to notice. "And you saw how I made excuses for *my* husband. You saw how I suffered, so why are you putting yourself through the same thing?"

"We have no proof," she said defensively.

"I saw him, okay. I saw him with a woman."

Silence. A horrified gasp. A sob. "Who? What did they do? What did she look like?"

I scrubbed a hand down my face. This was not a good time for this conversation, but there was no help for it. "It was Nora Hallsbrook, his secretary."

"What did they do?" she repeated brokenly.

"Talked, smelled oils."

"That's...that's all? Nothing sexual?"

"No. Not this time, but—"

My mom cut me off with a shaky, relieved breath. "Well, then, there you have it. He's not sleeping with her. They were working."

"At her home? With massage oil?"

"They are not sleeping together," she said, a desperate edge to her voice.

"Mom—"

"I've got to go, dear."

Click.

I stared down at the phone and shook my head. Why did women in love insist on making excuses for their men? Even women who'd been burned in the past, like my mom had?

"Your mom reminds me of mine."

I spun around, which was a mistake. My stomach cramped yet again, doubling me over. I clutched my side, croaking out, "What are you doing here?"

"I couldn't leave you, not like this," Royce said. "I tried to turn your ringer off, but your phone resisted me every step of the way. Stubborn, like its owner. And I didn't want to answer and give the *Tattler* something more to talk about. Come on, I'll help you back into bed."

He closed the distance between us and curled his arm around me. He'd actually stayed to take care of me. Only men in movies did that. Richard would have taken off, claiming he couldn't afford to catch whatever I had. In that moment, I slipped a little further under Royce's spell.

Unemotional fling. Apparently I'd still never had one.

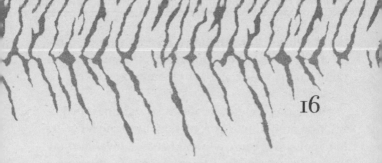

16

When your paws get muddy, emotionally speaking, clean them on your opponent's finest fur. This reveals your complete power, as well as intimidates, and the more intimidated your opponent is, the less likely they are to attack you again.

ROYCE TOOK CARE OF ME all morning, making tea, holding my hair out of the way when needed (i.e. when I vomited) and covering me with blankets while I lay in bed. Despite my abject humiliation and the fact that I was freakishly sick, I loved every minute of it. He was so much better *everything* than I ever could have predicted. So much more wonderful. So much more giving. So much more kind.

Today, we almost seemed like an old married couple. That should have caused me to puke yet again, but it didn't. I liked that he'd taken a shower at my place. I liked that he'd washed his clothes here—never mind that it was to get rid of stains and smells I'd caused.

His clothes were in the dryer, so right now he was walking around in a pair of sexy black boxers. Did food poisoning cause a fever? Because I was burning up just looking at him. His stomach was ripped with muscle, his skin bronze and beautiful. His legs were long and lean.

I'd seen him naked before, but at the time I'd been looking at him with sex on the brain. Now, without the energy to jump his bones like a wild cowgirl, I could appreciate him like an art connoisseur. And appreciate him, I did. Fluid strength, he was, and all man.

He strode to the edge of my bed and gazed down at me, warmth and tenderness in his blue eyes. His black hair fell at his temples in complete disarray. "You need anything?"

Now there was a loaded question, and one I could interpret in so many ways. "I could use some company," I said.

A hint of satisfaction curled the edges of his lips. "I found your BlueJay under a bunch of magazines— which, by the way, have some great quizzes on relationships. You should read them. Anyway, I left it on your kitchen table. Uncovered."

"You're too good to me," I said dryly.

"You know, we could see this sickness as a sign."

"That it's my time to die?"

He laughed. "That you're pregnant."

I stiffened. "Not another word on that subject," I said. "I don't need the stress of that now."

Slowly he sobered. "Would it really be so bad?"

"I'm not going to answer that." Because if I said yes, I'd be lying. And I didn't want to say no. That would lead to a whole different conversation.

Sighing, he eased down, propping his weight over my legs and onto his elbow. Without his tall, strong body blocking the view in front of me, I was afforded a glimpse of myself in my dresser mirror. I gasped, horrified.

"I'm a hideous beast monster." My hair was messy and tangled. Black mascara smudges coated the skin under my eyes. "You have to leave," I told Royce. "You have to leave right now."

"Don't worry," he said on a laugh. "I'm not going to sell pictures of you to the *Tattler*."

The entire world could see me like this, but not Royce. Anyone but Royce. "Seriously, you need to go."

"Naomi, sweetheart, you threw up all over me. I think it's a little too late to be worrying about appearances."

Please Lord, I thought then, let me be one of the lucky souls who actually dies from food poisoning. I tossed the cover over my head, shielding my haggard features from his view. "I look so ugly."

He tugged the covers out of my kung-fu grip and cupped my jaw in his hand. "You look like you need me, and I think that's one of the most beautiful things I've ever seen."

Oh. My chin tilted to the side and I found myself feeling all dreamy and goo-goo.

"I got you a present while I was in Florida. You'll have to come to my place if you want to open it, though."

No way was I going to his house. Too personal. Too…tempting right now. What if I never wanted to leave?

But…

"A present? For me?" A shaft of warmth speared me. Like any normal human, I loved receiving gifts. "What is it?" A necklace? An airport snowglobe? A ring?

"I'm not telling. You'll just have to see for yourself." His hand climbed up my leg and onto my stomach, gently rubbing away any lingering pain. "I found your Tigress book. It makes for some interesting reading. To be honest, I think you've already unleashed yours."

I closed my eyes as I savored the feel of him next to me, touching me. Offering me praise. I simply enjoyed. "What makes you think that?"

"You're strong. You don't take any crap. I'm willing to admit you've left me in a bleeding heap on more than one occasion. I doubt you'd ever let me take you for granted."

I was feeling sublimely peaceful, something I hadn't felt all night. What little sleep I'd had had been constantly interrupted with bouts of sickness and phone calls. Royce's voice drifted in and out of my mind, soft one minute, a little louder the next.

I wasn't sure, but I thought I heard him say, "But even tigresses have mates."

It was the last thing to float through my mind before I sank into a deep slumber.

How many hours passed, I didn't know. I only knew that Royce had taken care of me as I slept another day away, and that my phone was ringing again. So was the BlueJay that had been placed on the nightstand beside my bed. Where was Royce? Groggy, disoriented, but no longer in pain, I lifted the receiver. "Hello."

"Miss Delacroix, please," a sweet female voice said.

I woke up a bit and rubbed the sleep from my eyes. "This is she."

"This is Hannah Carroll from Powell Aeronautics."

"Who?"

"Mr. Powell's assistant."

Elvira, I realized. "Yes?"

"I've been instructed to ask how you're feeling," she said.

My glance shifted to my bedside clock. Nine a.m. I blinked in confusion. I'd slept for nearly the entire weekend. It was no longer Sunday. No, it was now Monday morning—breakfast with the twins. I'd already missed it I realized with disappointment. "I feel fine," I said. And I did. My stomach was empty, and I was a little weak, but that was the extent of it.

"I'm so glad to hear that." Her agreeable tone morphed into one of contempt. "Since you're feeling better, I've been instructed to confirm your appointment with Mr. Powell today at ten-thirty. If, however, you feel bad, I've been instructed to tell you to stay home." Now she sounded hopeful.

"You're mistaken." I rolled to my back, stretching my legs. "I don't have an appointment today."

"You're the one who's mistaken. I actually have you down in the appointment book this time."

"But isn't Royce here, at my place?" I searched every direction, looking for any hint of him. All that remained was the lingering scent of sandalwood.

"No, he is *not* at your place," Elvira growled. "He's here at the office. Where he belongs."

"Good for him. Goodbye, Ms. Carroll." I inched forward to replace the phone in its cradle, but her frustrated what-kind-of-monster-are-you yelp stopped me. Phone back at my ear, I said, "What now?"

"Because Mr. Powell just arrived back in town, today's schedule is tight. I absolutely cannot squeeze you in at any other time." She added grudgingly, "And he was adamant that he see you today if you were feeling better."

I sat up and propped my elbows on my knees. The thought of seeing Royce again made my heart leap and my blood heat. Sighing, I rested my head in my hands. "I'll be there," I said.

Which didn't give me long to get ready, and I wanted to look my best. I *needed* to look my best, if only to make up for the fright show I'd been yesterday. If I didn't blot that image out of his mind, I might as well end our association now.

I threw down the receiver, popped out of bed and climbed into the shower. The hot, steamy liquid cascaded over me, washing away all hints of sickness.

I brushed my teeth three times and rinsed my mouth with burning, antibacterial mint wash for over two minutes. The bottle claimed thirty seconds would do it, but I wanted to make sure all germs were annihilated.

After I applied makeup, I blew dry my hair until it shone like an evening star, and I hurriedly shimmied into a dark red dress that hugged my curves and hit just below my knees. Not too business-like, but definitely sexy. To be daring, I forfeited a bra.

Surely a braless woman could replace the memory of a hideous, puking beast monster. Still, I didn't want the rest of Powell Aeronautics to see me braless, so I pulled on a dress jacket. I checked out the finished product in the mirror and nodded with satisfaction. As good as it was going to get.

Time to confront Royce Powell.

SOMEHOW, AND LORD ONLY KNEW how, I managed to make it to Powell Aeronautics with ten minutes to spare.

Elvira spotted me and glared. She looked immaculate behind her desk, as cold as stone and just as hard. She seethed with…jealousy?

Ohmygod. She wanted Royce for her own, I realized. I don't know why I hadn't figured it out earlier. Maybe because she didn't look like the kind of woman who had hormones. Or blood. Or a heartbeat. Still, she obviously viewed me and any other woman interested in him as a threat.

I couldn't help but wonder if she and Royce had

ever had a relationship. Office affairs were the most common, after all. If they had, well, I'd—I'd—I didn't know what I'd do. Royce and I had slept together, yes, and he'd asked me to marry him. But I'd said no, so I couldn't really demand he fire his assistant and hire a fat old woman who smelled like mothballs and cheese. Better yet, a fat old *man* who smelled like mothballs and cheese.

Still, I knew how it felt to yearn for the attention of a man I couldn't have. (See any and all mentions of my marriage to Richard the Bastard for proof).

Be nice, be nice, be nice. Polite smile in place, I glided past her. "Good day to you, my good woman." Her features lit with astonishment, but she didn't try to stop me. I didn't knock on Royce's office door, but swept inside.

When I saw him seated at his desk, head bowed, I came to an abrupt halt. "I believe I have the ten-thirty appointment."

His eyes lifted from the papers on his desk and our gazes met. Blue against gray. Pleasure against pleasure. He offered me a warm, sexy smile. "I'm glad you could make it."

God, he looked good. Really, really good. Instead of skin and boxers, he wore a suit, minus the tie. His white button shirt was open at the collar. His hair looked like rumpled black silk, as if he'd just rolled out of bed.

"How do you feel?" he asked, setting the papers aside. He leaned back in his chair and rested one of his elbows against the armrest.

"Much better. Thank you for taking care of me."

"That was my pleasure."

Pleasure…yes, pleasure. I needed more of it. As I stared over at him, all my desires, all my body's needs, leapt to life. My (braless) nipples hardened, my mouth watered. I had to have this man again—and soon.

I wanted Royce in my life. I did. I'd already promised myself I could seduce him, but in that moment I admitted I wanted a sexually exclusive relationship. For as long as I could have him.

"My God," he suddenly breathed.

"What?" Automatically, I stepped back.

"Your dress."

So he'd noticed. Grinning inwardly, I twirled. The red hem danced around my knees. "Do you like it?"

"Darlin'," he said in a delicious Texas accent. "I don't think I've ever seen anything more beautiful." Standing, he propped his palms on the desk. "You're driving me crazy—you know that, don't you?"

"I'm glad."

"Glad?" he asked, incredulous. "You should be apologizing. I left an out-of-state meeting to see you. I think about you all the time. I dream about you."

"Well—" I licked my lips and gathered my courage "—you're driving me crazy, too. Where's *my* apology?"

"I'm willing to give you anything you want, sweetheart. I just wish you'd ask for more than an apology."

"All right. I have a question for you and I'd like an honest answer," I said, settling in a chair. I set my briefcase at my feet and folded my hands together in my lap. Very prim, very proper. "Have you and Elvira ever slept together?"

His face wrinkled in confusion. "What are you talking about?"

"Your assistant. Have you ever slept with her?"

"Hannah? God, no."

Truth lay in his surprise and intensity, and I found myself breathing easier. "I know it's not any of my business, but—"

"Of course it's your business. Just like any other men in your life are my business." He paused, daring me to contradict him. When I didn't, he added, "There aren't any other men, are there?"

"No, of course not. I can barely tolerate you."

He plopped back into his seat with a snort.

Before the conversation delved into any talk of rings, flowers or babies, I hurriedly changed the subject. I had the information I'd wanted. "Did you sign me up for this appointment because you wanted to give me my present?"

"No." He slowly grinned. "I told you, you have to come to my place for that."

My shoulders slumped a little. "I'm here for business, then. All right, well, I know you're busy, so let's get this over with." I reached in my briefcase, pulled out two pieces of paper and handed them to him. "As you can see I've made an itemized list of things I need to be reimbursed for and things I still need to purchase, with estimated cost, as well as a list of businesses requiring deposits from you. For the first list, I need money. I accept all types of cash. Small bills, large bills, wadded bills. Extra-crisp bills. For the second list, signed checks will work."

Without protest, he opened his wallet and handed me every piece of green paper in it. I inhaled deeply. Ah, the smell of real money.

"That's eight hundred dollars. A little more than you're asking for on your list, but you never know if something will cost more than estimated."

He trusted me with his money, the dear, sweet man. "You'll notice that I need to make a down payment to the caterer as soon as possible so we can concretely reserve the desired date. However, I can't do that until you've decided on a location. Which brings me to my next point of business. Location. Have you chosen yet? The sample invitation is printed and ready for approval." I pulled my notebook from my bag, flipped it open and lifted the invitation. "All it's missing is the address."

He took the sample from me and gave the burgundy coloring and gold lettering a thorough in-spection. "Wow. You're good. My mother will like it, too," he added, knowing I'd ask. "As for the location, I don't know yet."

"Why not?" I shoved to my feet, fearing his next words.

"I want to visit a cabin in Oklahoma."

"Out of the question. It's too late in the game."

"We leave in four days. I've already made arrange-ments."

"But—but—"

"Don't worry. We'll have fun."

"I'm not flying again. I won our bet in Colorado, and you swore I wouldn't have to step foot in another plane. Is that correct?"

"Yes. That's correct."

"Then I don't have to go to Oklahoma. You can't make me."

His lips lifted in another slow smile, this one a wicked grin of pure pleasure. "I *can* make you. We're driving. It's only a three-hour drive, sweetheart."

I crossed my arms over my chest. I did *not* want to rough it in some primitive cabin. How sexy could I look then? "My answer is still no."

"I'm afraid you don't have a choice. I'm paying you triple, remember?"

"I refuse to go. Do you understand me?"

"Great. Try to be ready by three on Friday."

17

An apology is a curse word to a Tigress. By admitting guilt, you are saying your actions were wrong. A Tigress is never wrong.

I SPENT THE NEXT SEVERAL mornings shopping for table centerpieces. Finally I found shiny, to-die-for "magic" lamps. I bought bags of fake gemstones and planned to glue them around the lamps' bellies.

In the afternoons, I waited at Jonathan's office and followed him on his lunch hour. He and Nora had lunch together only once, and they hadn't done anything sexual, hadn't even kissed. I couldn't decide whether I wanted to snap his neck for that or hug him. Whether he was cheating or not, I just didn't know anymore. Why continue to lie to my mom, though, if he was an innocent man?

I had tried to listen to his conversations with Nora, but I just hadn't been able to get close enough to them.

Wednesday afternoon, I followed Jonathan to a nearby park. He met his daughter, Rachel, and his granddaughter there. I recognized them from the photo I'd found. The three of them played and talked and laughed, appearing to all the world like a happy family. But seeing them together made me sad. I'd never had that with my real dad. He'd lived and died a bastard. I'd never really had that with Jonathan, either, because, even though I loved him, I'd always set myself a little apart from him.

The next day I actually met Rachel in person at a nearby park. As trees swayed around us and children laughed and played on the swing set, we sized each other up. Jonathan sat on a bench, silent (for once), letting us have this moment to ourselves.

"So," I said. I eyed her. She had dark hair and a vivid emerald gaze. Pretty, conservative. Every man's dream daughter. Gag. "How'd your mom hook up with Jonathan?"

"They went to school together," Rachel said stiffly.

"And she never mentioned you to him?"

"No." Now she sounded defensive. I think she was as *happy* to meet me as I was to meet her. "But we're together now, and that's all that matters."

"I'm glad for you," I said. And I tried to mean it when I really wanted to say, "he's mine!" Kind of. I guess.

She bit her lip and glanced away. "My mother

passed away a few months ago and left me a note about him. I hunted him down and you know the rest."

Hearing that she'd recently lost someone dear to her, I softened. "I'm sorry for your loss."

She softened, too. "Thank you."

For a long, silent moment our gazes met and held, gray against green. "I guess this means we're sisters now." To be honest, I'd always wanted a sister. Someone to talk and laugh with. A playmate.

"I've always wanted a sister," she said wistfully, parroting my thoughts. I grinned slowly. And that was all it took.

After that, we were able to relax around each other. To really talk. We spent more than an hour together, discussing our culinary likes and dislikes, the men in our lives (she was a single parent), Jonathan's therapy sessions and promised to stay in touch. Jonathan beamed the entire time. I left the park feeling light-hearted, like I truly *had* made a new friend. A friend I hadn't wanted but had, perhaps, needed.

I SPENT THE EVENINGS all that week on the phone with Royce, caressing my BlueJay as if it were my favorite toy. I never asked, and he never asked, but I wanted him to come over. *Needed* him to come over and rock my world again. But every phone call was the same.

Me: I think we should have sex again.

Royce: Bad idea.

Me: Why?

Royce: I want more from you than sex.

Me: Goodbye, you prudish bastard.

We'd switched rolls, Royce and I. He was the waiting-for-marriage woman and I was the let's-hop-into-the-sack man. This morning, while I lingered in the hot, steamy shower, I realized my only recourse was to talk him into being my—God, I felt juvenile saying this—boyfriend. We'd try that out, see how it went. It wasn't marriage, but it was close to it. That's what he wanted (kind of), and I wasn't so selfish (I hoped) that I couldn't at least try the give-and-take thing. We talked on the phone every day, anyway. Why not spend the holidays together? Why not go on romantic dates?

We'd have lots and lots of exclusive, amazing sex. I wouldn't tell him I loved him or anything like that, but I would try—try, mind you—to act like a proper girlfriend.

FRIDAY ARRIVED TOO QUICKLY and not soon enough.

As we soared down the highway, I found myself buckled in yet another car of Royce's, this one a plush, dark blue Jag. "Are you sure you don't want to have sex with me?" I asked. "We could pull over and do it right now. I'm willing."

He flicked me a heated glance, and that glance lingered on my bare thighs. I'd purposefully worn a short pink skirt I'd borrowed from Mel, knowing it would rise every time I sat down. I wasn't without my wiles.

"I want to make love to you." His voice emerged hoarse, a little raw. "Believe me, I'm close to combustion."

"But you tell me no every day." Could I sound any whinier? "And you haven't made a pass at me this last week."

"Remember what I told you before I left for Florida? Remember what I told you on the phone? I meant it. No sex until we're committed."

"I'll be your girlfriend, okay, and you'll be my boyfriend," I grumbled. "That's a commitment."

Everything went still, silent. He kept his eyes on the road, but I noticed his hands were ultra-tight on the wheel. "What about being my fiancée?"

"One thing at a time. Girlfriend is all I can offer right now."

He sighed, but it was a happy sound. "Fair enough." Reaching over, he clasped my hand in his. "This is a big step for you. I know you never planned to be in another relationship."

So big a step I could hardly believe I'd said it out loud. "Maybe we should lay some ground rules."

"No rules."

"But—"

"No rules."

"But—"

"Rules are for the military and naughty children. The only restriction we need is fidelity. No seeing other people."

Hearing him say that warmed me in and out. "No asking for my hand in marriage, and no asking my stepdad for my hand in marriage."

The corners of his lips twitched. "Those sound like rules to me."

"You stated a rule, so I got to name some."

"Fair enough," he repeated.

"So I guess we're a couple."

"The enthusiasm in your voice is awe-inspiring. It really is," he said dryly. His eyes twinkled with mischief, happiness and heat, all at once.

I twisted in my seat, facing him more fully. The sun created a bright halo around him, and my throat suddenly constricted. "So you can rock my world later. Right?"

"No." He shook his head in regret and pushed out another sigh. "Sorry."

"No? No! What do you mean, no? I said I'd be your girlfriend."

"I'm saving myself for marriage."

I bared my teeth in a scowl. "Why you dirty little sneak. I take back everything I said. I'm not your girlfriend. I'm your worst enemy."

"You can't take it back." He pressed his lips—his gorgeous, pleasure giving, traitorous lips—together to keep from laughing. "You'll respect me more this way."

My eyes slitted. Fine. He wanted to play this game, I'd play it. But I was fighting dirty. When we arrived at the cabin, I was going to seduce him right out of his pants! Deciding to take our relationship to the next level really had been a huge step for me, and I expected—no, I *deserved* a reward.

Just you wait, Royce Powell.

An hour later, he eased the Jag down a gravel driveway and I had my strategy mapped out in my mind. Show skin, say wickedly sexy things and tease him at every opportunity. We'd just see who caved first.

The cabin came into view. It was small and homey, and overlooked a large body of glistening, crystal water. The car stopped completely. Without a word, I threw open the passenger door and jumped out.

"Leave your stuff," he said when I walked around to the trunk. "I'll take care of it."

Being a girlfriend did have some advantages. I strode away, making sure my hips swayed with every movement. Sharp gray rocks bit into my soft-soled shoes. The air was fresh and clean, like pine and summer sky. Trees swayed in the light breeze. At the door, I gave the knob an experimental turn, surprised to find it unlocked. Taking a deep breath, I forged inside. And gasped.

Sensual, perfect, and every woman's most erotic dream, the cabin appealed to me on every level. A large Jacuzzi sat in the main room, already filled, the fireplace only a few feet away. Supplying a breathtaking view of the lake was a large paneled glass window that covered the entire back wall.

It was the perfect spot to watch the sunset.

It was the perfect spot to relax.

It was simply…perfect. I smiled slowly. Royce would never be able to resist me. Wait for marriage, would he? We'd see about that.

"What do you think?"

I whirled around. Royce stood in the entry, holding my overnight bag in one hand and his own bag in the other. "What do you think?" he asked again.

"I love it. It's like a paradise hideaway. It won't work for the party, of course, but I love it."

His brows arched. "You can tell already?"

"Do you really think you can fit three hundred people in here?"

"I can decrease the number of guests if needed. We've had this conversation before."

"I'll take a look around," I grumbled.

"Good. I'll cook lunch." His footsteps tapered off as he disappeared beyond a door.

I saluted his back and said, "Yes, sir." I dug the tape measure out of my bag and began working. By taking measurements of the room, I would know how many people could fit combined with just how many decorations I could use.

Half an hour later, I had a list composed. Instead of planning for the party, however, I noted every corner, crevice and room where I wanted to have sex with Royce.

I went to the kitchen to begin my seduction.

Unnoticed by Royce, I stood silently off to the side, watching him putter around. I couldn't help but notice the way his arm muscles flexed when he reached for bowls. The way he sucked in his upper lip as he concentrated. A rich, warm aroma floated past my nostrils and my stomach growled.

Royce placed a large dish on the table.

"*You* cooked lasagna?" I asked, incredulous.

"Are you kidding?" he said, flicking me a glance. "I didn't want you to suffer another bout of food poisoning." He grinned with wry humor. "I paid someone to come out here. She stocked the fridge, took care of the Jacuzzi. All that stuff."

I didn't care who made the lasagna, as long as I could eat it. My stomach rumbled again.

"Hungry?"

"Ravenous." In only ten minutes, I gobbled up the delicious pasta and consumed four glasses of juice. Royce had barely touched his food.

"Hurry up and eat," I told him. "When you're done, we can get naked." The last was spoken in a throaty purr.

"No thanks." He quickly turned his attention to his plate.

Everything about him, from the way he looked to the way he moved, promised pleasure, and I was going to collect.

When he finally finished eating, he stood and carried our plates to the sink. Once back at the table, he took me by the hands and pulled me up to my full height.

"Come on." He tugged me toward the door. "Let's go outside. There's a swing on the back porch."

"No, let's stay in." I focused my weight into my feet, bringing us to a quick halt. "I'd rather sit in the Jacuzzi. The bubbles will feel so good against my skin."

"I didn't bring a swimsuit."

I licked my lips. "Neither did I."

He jolted away from me as if I'd singed him. "I, uh, think I'll take a nap instead." He gave a feigned yawn. "I'm tired from all that driving."

"Don't be a baby. We're adults, and we can swim

together without it being sexual." If he believed that, he'd be inside me within the hour.

He frowned. "How do you suggest we go about this?"

"Nude, of course."

"I don't think so," he replied, folding his arms over his chest. "That's about as sexual as two people can get." A bead of sweat trickled down his temples as he stared at my hardened nipples. He gulped. "Yeah, bad idea."

I crossed my arms over my chest, too. The battle lines were drawn. "I thought you liked to be daring. We're boyfriend and girlfriend now. We can get naked together. It's acceptable."

"No."

"Where's your sense of adventure?"

"I left it at home."

I gave him a pointed once-over, even took a step closer. "*Tsk, tsk, tsk,*" I clicked under my tongue. "I think you're lying."

He continued to back away. This trip had been his idea. I hadn't wanted to come, but I think I'd successfully managed to switch our viewpoints. "Stop it, Naomi."

"Are you afraid you can't stick to your principles?" I reached out and traced a fingertip over his erection. "If you can't, I promise I'll still respect you in the morning."

The hard, thick length of him jerked at my first touch. He squeezed his eyes closed. "You're not playing fair."

"I want you to touch me," I said. "I'll do whatever it takes to make that happen."

"What happened to the woman who was determined not to sleep with me?" The lines around his mouth were taut, and he stretched his shirt collar with two fingers.

Daring, bold, I pressed myself against him fully. Chest to chest. Hardness to softness. "Please go swimming with me, Royce. I'm dying to get into that water, to feel it lap against me. It's not like we haven't seen each other naked before."

"That was different," he said, streams of sweat now dripping from his temples.

I placed a featherlight kiss on his chin. "Different how?"

"It just was."

My teeth ground together, and I released him, stepping backward. At this rate, the stubborn man might be able to refuse me all night. I had to try a different angle. "If you don't want to swim, why don't we play a game?"

His shoulders relaxed, and he even managed a half smile. "What do you want to play?"

"How about strip poker?"

Losing all traces of that smile, he paled and shook his head. "No."

"What about twenty questions?"

I could see the wheels turning in his head as he calculated just how sexual that game could be. Obviously (and foolishly) he decided I couldn't do much damage, because he nodded and said, "All right. Twenty questions."

Grinning internally, I led him to the only sofa in

the cabin. A black leather lounge made for pleasure. He claimed one side, I claimed the other.

"Why don't I go first?" I suggested.

He eased back and nodded.

I crawled my hands toward him and leaned over until I was merely a breath away. "If I take off all your clothes, will you let me lick you all over?" I whispered next to his ear.

He almost jumped off the couch. "No!"

Oh, this game was going to be fun. I smothered my smile. "It's your turn. Ask me a question. Anything you want."

A long while passed before he spoke, and he spent every second of that time studying me, looking for…something. "How long were you and your ex-husband together?"

"Which one?"

"You were married more than once?" he shouted.

I laughed. "No, I just wanted you to ask and waste another question. I was married only once, and that was for six hellish years."

"Why did you—"

"No, no, no." My words came out in a singsong taunt. "Your turn is over. I refuse to answer another question until you answer another one of mine." Nuzzling my cheek against his shoulder, I said, "What's your naughtiest fantasy?"

"Making love to my *wife*."

That wiped away my grin as he intended, I'm sure. The jerk.

"Have you dated anyone since you've been single?" he asked.

"Only you. It's hot in here, don't you think?" I asked next, removing my shirt and revealing my lacy pink bra.

"Is that your question?"

"Maybe." I tossed the material aside.

Shifting in his seat, Royce's eyes roved over my clothes. Or lack thereof. "No, it's not hot, it's cold. And is that strip of cloth supposed to be a bra or a Band-Aid? The fabric is so sheer I can see your nipples," he accused.

"I know."

"Enough games," he all but shouted. "I need something to drink."

He didn't wait for my reply. He just got up, strode to the bar and downed two shots of Scotch in quick succession. I loved the way his hands shook, as if he teetered on the edge of losing control. Made me feel powerful and seductive and all woman. Something I'd only ever felt with him.

When he returned to the couch, easing beside me, I said, "You finally up for that swim?"

His gaze raked over me again and he groaned. He tunneled a stiff hand through his hair. "Give me five minutes to change," he said. Shaking his head, he stormed into the bedroom. The door slammed behind him with a resounding thud.

I laughed, muttering, "Into what?"

Not feeling an ounce of shyness, I stripped down to the skin and entered the steamy, relaxing water. Another chuckle escaped when I imagined Royce in the other room, searching frantically for some type of swim trunks.

My grin disappeared the moment he opened the door, however. He had a white cotton towel draped around his waist. It was more provocative than if he'd emerged naked. Strength emanated from him. Strength and pure sex appeal.

His gaze met mine, making sure I was watching. And then he dropped his towel.

My breath snagged in my throat. Oh, my, but this man wanted me. He was rock hard, huge and as beautiful as a sculpture. "You look tense. Why don't you come over here and I'll massage your back?" I motioned to the water directly in front of me.

"No thanks." Slowly, so I got a view of every movement, he entered the water, the clear liquid caressing his skin the same way I wanted to. I guess he'd decided to play the game as unethically as I was. "I'm fine where I am." With that, he relaxed against the rim of the tub, his eyes closed, as if he hadn't a care in the world.

I frowned. "Then I'll just sit here all alone, thinking of things we *could* be doing. If you hear me moan, don't think anything of it. I'm probably in the throes of unbridled—"

He cursed and his eyelids popped open. "Damn it, Naomi. You win. I lose. Come here."

Well, well, well. My eyes widened, a thrill of anticipation and victory thrumming through me. I hadn't expected him to cave so early.

Obviously I didn't move fast enough for him

because he clasped me by the shoulders and jerked me into his body, turning me so that my back rested against his chest. His fingers glided over the sides of my breasts, plumping, then moved over my nipples, rolling. I bit my bottom lip.

He licked a drop of water from my shoulder, and I shivered with heat that had nothing to do with the water. "You were right," he said softly. "I can't fight you, knowing you're naked. Knowing you want me."

My head lolled back, onto his shoulder. I tingled. I ached. I desired.

I remembered.

He spun me around, water sloshing over the rim of the tub. "I need to hear you say this isn't just sex. I need to hear you say this is making love."

"I—no." I shook my head. "I can't say that." The more I admitted, the more eager he would be to convince me to marry him. I knew it, *felt* it.

A harsh scowl tightened his lips. "You're too stubborn for your own good, you know that?"

"So are you."

"If we're together tonight, I won't promise not to ask you to marry me," he warned.

I shook my head again, and this time my hair rippled over his shoulders and stomach. "My answer won't change."

"So you say."

"So I know."

"You changed your mind about being my girlfriend."

"Yeah, well…" I didn't know what to say to that. He was right.

He kissed my jaw. Our chests rubbed together, slick from the steam and water. One of his hands trailed down my stomach. His eyes gleamed with satisfaction and desire, and I'm positive they were a mirror of mine.

Using our positions to his advantage, he hoisted me onto his lap, my legs straddling his waist.

"No more talking," he said. "I've got a better use for our tongues."

"Prove it."

His mouth meshed with mine; his tongue swept inside and mine was there to greet him. I tasted the Scotch, but mostly I tasted Royce, a heady male flavor that was all his own. This is what I'd wanted. This is what I'd needed. To be with him. To lose myself and my fears in the pleasure only he could give me.

Water churned around us, lapping at my skin, acting as another stimulant. I tightened my legs around his waist and pressed intimately against him. His erection brushed the core of me, and we both jerked in blissful response.

My hands roamed over him, every inch. Sliding down his chest. Circling his nipples. Wrapping around his thick, hard penis.

"You're killing me," he growled. He nibbled my collarbone, sucking away every drop of liquid.

"What a way to die, hmm?"

His strained chuckle wafted over me, cool against my heated, wet skin. "You're like my kryptonite. I weaken just being around you."

"I'm glad." I nipped at his neck, all the while

rubbing myself against him. A moan slipped from my mouth. God, he felt so good.

"If it weren't for your four-hundred-dollars-an-hour lips, I might, *might* have been able to hold out another minute or two."

"Only four hundred?" The water and steam made his skin slick and sultry, and I slid down him until my mouth reached his nipples. I licked, circling the sensitive area with my tongue.

"Hundred thousand, sweetheart." His hands cupped my cheeks, forcing me to look at him. He gazed deeply into my eyes. "Your lips are four hundred thousand dollars an hour."

I grinned slowly. With my legs still anchored solidly around him, he pushed to his feet. My back straightened and I kissed him, and I didn't stop kissing him as he stepped out of the tub, groping blindly for the bedroom door. We made it inside and toppled onto the cool, dry sheets. We rolled and strained and writhed against each other, our excitement mounting, the tension building.

He pushed me to my back and crawled low, between my legs. His tongue licked inside me. I almost screamed. He brought his fingers into play, moving them inside me as his tongue worked at my clitoris. My limbs shook with the force of my pleasure, and I was just about to—

He sat up, his every muscle pulled tight. "Condom?"

"Yes," I quickly replied, though a part of me screamed no. I was going to have to have a long, stern talk with that ridiculous part of me.

"One sec," he said, his voice so husky and raw I barely heard him. He pulled away and raced to his bag.

"Why'd you bring condoms if you planned to wait until marriage?"

He smiled sheepishly, but never moved his focus from the bag. "I know my limitations."

I lay atop the bed, panting, needy, achy. "Hurry."

He was on top of me in the next instant, slipping, sliding inside me to the hilt. I welcomed him eagerly, crying out his name, arching my back, clawing at his arms. Oh, the exquisite pleasure of being with him.

He paused, staring down at me, the lines around his mouth and eyes taut. "Can you handle a rough ride?"

"I'm a Tigress, remember?"

He pulled back and slammed forward. I moaned in rapture. Over and over, he repeated the action, taking me higher, close to the edge.

"Naomi, Naomi, Naomi." He chanted my name as he moved. A prayer, or maybe a curse.

"Royce," I chanted back. Definitely a curse.

His tempo increased, and so did my pleasure. I was almost there, so close I would die if I didn't get there soon. Suddenly he reared back, then pounded forward and hit me exactly where I needed him most. My climax ripped through me. Stars winked behind my eyes; blood pounded through my veins. I think my soul even left my body for a moment.

As I spasmed around him, he roared loud and long. His body stiffened and he gripped my hips. He shouted my name again, and this time I *knew* it was a prayer.

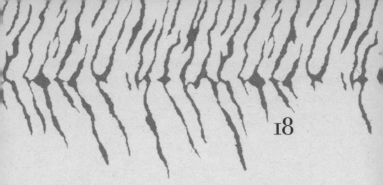

18

*If you allow another animal to have power over
you, you will slowly sink back to life as a depen-
dent cub. Your emotions will not be your own.
Your activities will not be your own.*

A LITTLE OVER A WEEK passed, and I used the time to
get used to being a girlfriend. Royce came to my
apartment every evening. First, we'd work on party
preparations. Then, we'd make—uh, have sex.

He didn't ask me to marry him, but each night I
went to bed in his arms (happily content, thank you
very much) and mulled the idea over in my mind. I
still broke out in a cold sweat, and I still wanted to
vomit. Just not as badly as before.

I wasn't the marrying kind of gal. Royce had never
done anything to deserve my distrust, but still, doubts

were stubborn things. Royce was a man. A beautiful, virile man desired by legions. Women of every age went crazy for him. And I had to wonder how long his fascination with me would last. One month? Two? Or until after vows were spoken?

Was happily-ever-after truly possible? I just didn't know. Before, I would have said hell no. Now... Mel and Colin were dating, much to Kera's glee. Mel had been unable to resist him that night at the club, and now they couldn't keep their hands off each other.

Would *they* last, though?

After breakfast with the twins, I'd climbed in this cab and was now headed toward Powell Aeronautics. Royce had offered me the use of one of his cars, but I hadn't accepted. I was holding part of myself back, determined to depend on him as little as possible. I'd buy a car soon, and then there'd be no need to borrow his.

When the cab stopped, I stepped onto the sidewalk and removed my sunglasses. The sun beat down, blinding me for a moment. I blinked rapidly, adjusting to the light, and pushed into motion. Like a steady heartbeat, my high heels thumped with every step I took. The security guard, Johnny, knew me by sight now and let me pass without a qualm.

Upstairs, Elvira, Mistress of the Damned, was boxing her belongings, and a tall, lanky, very feminine man was *unboxing* his. Today, Elvira wore a clean-lined black suit. Her hair was slicked back in its usual twist, but though she wore a bit more makeup than usual, she looked paler than ever.

Her lips pinched together when she spotted me. I wouldn't have been surprised if her nails elongated like a cat's. "What's going on?" I asked.

"I've been relocated," she said stiffly. "As I'm sure you planned."

"I'm taking her place," the man said, excitement bubbling from him as he fingered the necklace hanging around his neck. He had painted his nails pink. Smiling, he held out his hand and we shook. "I'm Weston Cross. Oh, it's so wonderful to meet you." He tapped a finger to his glossed lips. "You're Naomi, right?"

"Yes."

"I recognize the lips."

My features crinkled with my confusion. Royce had transferred Elvira and brought in an obviously gay man? For me? I couldn't help it. I grinned. What a darling, wonderful man.

"Wipe that smirk off your face," Elvira snapped. "So what if you won this round. Royce will hire me back when Idiot Cross messes everything up."

"Look, Elvira," I said, and she gasped. "Royce is never going to be yours. Deal with it."

She hissed.

Weston clucked under his tongue. "Should I ring security and have you escorted out, *Elvira?*"

Scowling, she grabbed her box and stormed out of the office.

"You're my hero," Weston said, grinning over at me. "Mr. Powell told me to let you go in without notice if you ever came up. So go on. Go in."

Practically floating, I entered Royce's office.

Royce glanced up from his desk when he saw me. He smiled in welcome, radiating warmth. "Naomi. What a pleasant surprise."

"As if you didn't know I'd stop by," I said dryly. "You're the one who programmed the BlueJay, gifting me with such a harmonious reminder that we were meeting today."

"Well, I'm glad you finally decided to heed it." His eyes twinkled with mischief. "Would you care for something to drink?"

"No, thank you." I settled in my chair, took out my notebook and pencil, and set my briefcase aside. "You've put this off long enough, and we're running out of time. Only a few weeks left till the party. You must choose a location. I need to get the invitations printed ASAP."

"I've decided."

At that, I glanced up. "You have? Remember you promised I wouldn't have to fly," I told him.

His smile widened. "I haven't forgotten."

"Then where will it be?"

"The Palace Hotel."

"Thank God," I muttered under my breath. I'd planned parties there before, so I knew the exotic hotel intimately. "I'll have to make sure the ballroom isn't already booked. We waited so long—"

"I've, uh, already booked it."

Something in his tone caused my back to straighten. My eyes narrowed on him. "How long ago did you book it?"

His cheeks brightened a little. "That's not important," he said.

"Uh, yes." I crossed my arms over my middle. "It is. When?"

"I booked it the day we decided on the *Arabian Nights* theme."

I could have gotten mad. I *should* have gotten mad. Honestly, though, I liked that he'd gone to so much trouble to take me on those trips. Maybe that wasn't the politically correct reaction, but I'd gotten multiple orgasms out of the deal, so who was I to complain? Still…

"You deserve some type of punishment," I said.

"So come by my house tonight and make me pay," he said, a seductive edge underlying the words. "I'll finally give you your present. And while you're there," he added, regarding me intently, "I want you to think about moving in."

Everything inside me froze, warmed, then froze again. So far, he hadn't pushed me for more. A part of me had known it was coming, that it was only a matter of time. "Royce—"

"Hear me out. I'm not asking you to marry me. When you're with me, I'm happy. When we're apart, I'm not. I don't mind going back and forth between our apartments, but I'd rather have you near me all the time."

"It's too soon."

"It's not too soon. Not when I love you."

Only the sound of my shallow breath emerged. No, no, no. I didn't want to hear those words again. Not now.

"I love you, Naomi," he said again.

"Don't say that." I had trouble drawing in a breath. "I don't want to hear those words. Love only complicates things."

"I love you, Naomi," he repeated, ignoring my words. "I do. I think I loved you the first moment I saw you. Since that day, I haven't been romantically involved with another woman. Only you." He moved from the desk and knelt in front of me. Reaching up, he caressed the softness of my cheek. "I love you. I love you so much I'm miserable without you."

By far, it was the most beautiful thing I'd ever heard. And the most painful. I couldn't give him the words back. I just couldn't. That would mean trusting him completely, forsaking my fears, and taking a dangerous, uncertain plunge. "Royce, I don't know what to say." My voice quivered.

"Say you'll give me a chance. Say you'll think about my offer."

Not knowing if I could tell him what he wanted to hear, I could only nod.

"Ah, such enthusiasm," he said, shaking his head and grinning. "But it's good enough for now. You'll come over tonight?"

I gulped and nodded. I could give him that at least, no matter how much the prospect scared me.

At the moment, though, I wanted to rush home, to bury myself under a mound of covers and think about nothing at all. Not Royce. Not moving in with him. Not his words. But I wouldn't. That wasn't the way I lived my life anymore. "About your offer… Give me a little time. Okay? I'll think about it. I promise."

"All right." Leaning down, he whispered in my ear, "While you're thinking about it, I want you to remember the way I made love to you against the wall in Colorado. I want you to remember the way I tasted between your thighs at the cabin."

My chin snapped up. He tugged me to my feet and gave me a gentle push, easing me into the hall. Then he promptly shut the door in my face.

Every muscle inside my body tensed. I went from conflicted to sexually charged to frustrated in less than one point two seconds. He'd done that on purpose, the jerk. Now I would be able to imagine nothing else but the way he kissed me. The way he used his tongue on me. The way he loved me.

Oh, God.

I scowled all the way home.

SECURITY ALLOWED ME TO GO to Royce's apartment without question or comment, even though I'd never been there before. I guess Royce had told them to expect me, had shown them my picture, or something.

All afternoon, I'd thought of only two things: living without Royce and actually living with him. I didn't want to do either, not permanently, but I had to choose one. Anything less was unfair to Royce. I realized that now. Unfortunately, I was no closer to a decision than I'd been earlier. My pro-and-con list balanced out equally.

Pros:

Unlimited sex with Royce.

Spending more time with Royce.

Eating breakfast off Royce's chest.

Cons:

Worrying about what Royce was doing if he came home late.

Worrying if Royce still loved me every second of every day.

Worrying if Royce would get tired of me sooner rather than later.

How did a person conquer their deepest fears? I'd searched my Tigress manual, but all I'd come up with was that I needed to kill them and feast on their remains. That didn't really answer my question, though.

After four hard knocks, Royce opened the door. When he spotted me, he smiled that seductive smile of his that drove me wild.

"Come in." He motioned backward with a wave of his hand.

"Thank you." I glided past him. I'd never been here, but I'd wondered about his place of residence. I drank in the details. The walls of the living room were painted in classic ivory. A white Tergal scarf was draped over each of the five windows. At first glance, every piece of furniture appeared to be the same monochrome shade of white. Yet at closer inspection, I saw pillows with cream-colored beaded jackets, wraps with eggshell trimming.

Behind the couch was a long, narrow table of dark wood. A chandelier boasting hundreds of tiny crystal raindrops hung over it. Chinese root tables flanked each side of the couch. It was a room that spoke of wealth, not comfort. I didn't like it.

"Who decorated this place?" I asked, not even trying to hide my distaste. Nothing about the place fit with Royce's open personality.

"My mother."

"It, uh, lacks warmth."

"So does she, for the most part. Fixing the place up made her feel wanted, so I let her do it." He clasped my hand in his. "Come on. I'll show you the rest."

I eagerly followed as he led me through a generously proportioned kitchen. High marble counters were scrubbed clean. No dishes sat in the sink. No pots or pans were out of place. In fact, the area looked as if it had never seen a meal prepared.

Next, he showed me the game room. It was nothing like the rest of the apartment. It had a dark, comfy couch, a large-screen television and more stereo equipment than I'd ever seen in one room. All of those gave it a nice, "lived in" feel. He spent most of his time in here, was my guess, and I doubted his mom had decorated it.

"And this," he said, "is my bedroom."

It, too, suited him, boasting deep blue and gold colors that spoke of warmth and masculinity. The decadent four-poster bed held my attention longest. Glossy wood, rumpled sheets. How I would love rolling naked on those Egyptian cotton sheets.

Sandalwood scented the air. Just the smell of it turned me on.

We strolled back to the living room hand in hand. I loved the feel of my hand in his. Where I was soft and small, he was calloused and strong. A delicious contrast.

"Where's my present?" I said. Was I too eager? Too go-get-it-now-or-I'll-die? "You promised to give it to me if I came over."

He grinned. "Give me a minute." He raced away and disappeared into the hall. He soon reappeared holding a medium-sized red box. "For you."

Too large to be a ring. Too small to be…anything else. My hands were shaky as I accepted the box and hesitantly lifted the lid. When I saw what was inside, I gasped. A glass orchid with blue petals sat in the center of pale green foam. It was the most beautiful thing I'd ever seen, delicate and almost dreamlike.

"I—I don't know what to say. I love it."

"I had it made for you."

The dainty petals glistened from the overhead light, shining like pearls. As I looked at it, my defenses crumbled faster than I could patch them. I gulped past the lump in my throat and forced myself to look up at him. "I'll, uh, have the party invitations printed and mailed ASAP," I said, bringing us back to the business at hand. I think I was pretty close to bursting into tears.

He drew me into his arms, but I kept the box between us as a shield.

His gaze was heavy-lidded and focused on my mouth. "You're pale all of a sudden. Why?"

My heart was inexplicably in my throat. "I—I have to tell you something."

Something hard and cold flicked in his eyes, followed quickly by determination. He pried the box from my fingers and set it on top of the coffee table. In the next instant, he had me pinned to the wall, his mouth on mine, his tongue taking possession. That's all it took. One touch, one caress and I wanted him with an urgency that never seemed to leave me. My bones began the slow process of liquefaction. Unable to stand on my own, I let him hold me up. Kiss me. Devour me.

A shiver rippled over me as his thighs trapped me further. I breathed in his scent, warm and male and all Royce.

His tongue battled mine. Hard. Quick. I didn't think I'd ever get enough of him.

"Royce," I said.

"No talking." He slowed the kiss down, making it soft and gentle. I pressed deeper into him. His arms braced around me, familiar anchors. He tasted hot, like sunshine and rain mingled together. His fingers cupped my jaw.

"Royce, I—"

"Love you." His lips lowered to mine, still a gentle conqueror, savoring the taste of me, taking time to explore every hollow of my mouth.

I shoved away from him.

"What's wrong?" he said, his expression filled with concern.

Everything! I almost shouted. Absolutely everything. How could I tell him he threatened me in a way no other man had? What a mess I had gotten myself into and now, I realized, it was do or die time. I had climbed out on a limb, and *I* was holding the saw. I had a choice—cut myself down or continue to dangle there.

The fire in his eyes vanished, leaving only that cold blue shield I'd seen moments ago. "If you're going to do this," he said softly, "you might as well do it while we're comfortable." He pulled me onto the couch.

I dragged in a deep breath and let it out. What the hell was I going to say to him? "I—"

He didn't even let me get the second word out before he said, "Damn it, Naomi. I can't believe you're going to push me away." Jumping up, he paced the room, stalking from one side to the other. "That's what you're about to do, isn't it? Tell me we're over?"

Sweat beaded on my palms. My throat was so constricted I couldn't get a word out. What would my inner Tigress do? What would she say? She'd never let a man tame her, that was for sure.

Marriage doesn't have to be about taming or changing, my mind whispered. *It can simply be about love. Some men* can *remain faithful. Let him try and prove it.*

"We belong together," Royce continued, barely sparing me a glance. "You love me. You may not admit it to yourself, but you do. You love me. You don't kiss a man like that unless you care for him."

"I do care for you." There. I'd said something. "I care for you a lot."

He didn't seem to hear me. "I can't believe you're willing to give up what we have because you're afraid. Well, I can't make a guarantee about the future. No one can. But I'm willing to try."

"So am I." The words left my mouth before I could stop them, and there was no taking them back at that point. I wanted him, and if I had to marry him to keep him, I would. Would I regret it later? Maybe. Would I be hurt in the end? Probably.

Did I want to give him up? No.

Relationships were about give and take. I couldn't take everything from him and give nothing in return.

"So am I," I repeated.

He whipped around and pinned me with a wide-eyed stare. "What did you say?"

Gathering my courage and forcing my fear at bay, I smiled shakily. "I'm willing to give it a try."

"What are you willing to try, Naomi?" There was fear in his eyes and a tentative kind of happiness. "Spell it out for me."

"Marriage." I closed my eyes, squeezing the lids tightly shut. "Marriage to you."

He watched me, still not approaching me. "Are you sure that's what you want? That you're not doing it because it's what I want?"

"Yes." No. "I'm sure." Kind of.

Finally he closed the distance between us and bent between my legs. He ran his hands up my thighs. "How long of an engagement do you want?"

"Two years?"

He chuckled. "That's what I'd thought you'd say.

That's a point we'll have to negotiate, then, because I want a one-day engagement."

Little flutters of fear and dread mingled in my chest. "No way. I can't plan a wedding in one day." My fingers gripped the fabric of my pants, twisting. "I need at least a year." Yes, a year sounded good. Surely I could conquer my doubts in twelve months.

"One week."

"Six months."

"Two weeks."

"Five months."

"Sweetheart," he said, his hands spanning the width of my stomach. His thumbs caressed back and forth. "I don't want to give you time to change your mind."

That was a very real possibility, and I couldn't deny it.

"I would never hurt you, never cheat on you. Let me prove it. I want to be with you, Naomi, and only you."

He kissed me then and the heat of his mouth sizzled hotter than flames. Rational thought skidded to a halt. My senses reeled. I felt transported on a soft wispy cloud of desire. Inch by inch, he was tearing down the stones I'd worked so hard to erect against him.

"I can't believe this," I said, pulling away and going cold with shock. "Shit. I'm getting married again."

His lips lifted in a slow, satisfied, triumphant grin.

I felt so vulnerable at that moment, but I knew that I wanted him. "Okay," I said. "We'll do the deed the day after your mom's party." Maybe that was for the best. Less time to worry. Less time to panic.

Leaning toward me, he softly kissed my lips. "You won't be sorry. I swear to you now, you won't be sorry. I have to go out of town for the next week, but when I get back—"

A cold chill slithered down my spine. God, the wifely what's-he-doing-while-he's-away worry had started already. "You're going out of town again?" I tried not to pout, tried not to cry. "So soon?"

"I'm looking at another plane." He kissed both of my hands. "You can come with me."

"No." I shook my head. "I have to stay here and plan the we—event."

I only prayed I could go through with it when the time came.

19

If you find yourself weakened, leave. Get away as fast as you can. Only after you've rebuilt your strength should you return.

MY MOM ALMOST DIED OF SHOCK when I called to tell her my news. The line went completely silent for several minutes before Jonathan came around and revived her.

I heard him say, "Gloria, Gloria, are you okay? Do you need to go to the hospital? You fainted."

"Naomi's getting married," she told him, trying to catch her breath.

"To a man?" he asked.

I scowled.

"Yes," my mom said. "A man. Royce Powell, actually."

"You're kidding," Jonathan gasped.

"How could I joke about something like this?"

"Mom." I pinched the bridge of my nose. "Focus on me. Your only daughter."

"Is this because of the triplets?" she asked.

Like I really needed a reminder that I might be pregnant. Thanks, Mom. I'd managed to block all thoughts of babies and diapers from my mind until now. Was I pregnant? So far I hadn't had any signs. Why couldn't I have a normal period? I had no idea when I should start.

I'd had no unusual cravings—for food, that is. Sexually, I was craving some pretty kinky stuff. My breasts weren't tender and my stomach was as flat as ever. Weren't those the only signs for the first month?

I knew so little about kids. Maybe I should have gotten a book on the subject or something.

"Well," my mother prompted. "Is it because of the triplets?"

"Of course not. There are no triplets. And he loves me."

She paused. "Do you love him?"

I wasn't ready to answer that, so I said, "Mom, you're losing focus again. I'm getting married. You're going to have a new son-in-law. Don't you want to meet him?"

"Dear God, yes. You have to bring Royce over tomorrow for a relaxing family dinner. I need to talk to him. He's got to be some sort of magician, making you forget about Richard and take another marital plunge."

My hand tightened on the phone.

"I need to give him my treat-her-right speech," Jonathan added, his voice floating over the line.

God save me. And God save Royce.

THE NEXT MORNING, Royce showed up at my apartment with an odd gleam in his eyes. I nervously let him inside, but kept my face toward the door, afraid to look at him again. What was going on in his head? Had he changed his mind about me? No, surely not. Look how hard he'd fought for me. Was he going to try and convince me to fly to Las Vegas?

Deep breath in, deep breath out. I turned to him, about to demand to know what was going on, but he was on one knee. "Ohmygod." My own knees almost buckled.

"Naomi," he said, holding up a black velvet box with a simple but elegant platinum diamond resting in the center.

"Ohmygod," I said again. This would make it official. *Ohmygod, ohmygod, ohmygod.*

"Will you marry me?" he asked.

I'd already said yes, so I hadn't expected him to do anything like this. Warm tears filled my eyes. How could one man be so wonderful? How could one man be so giving and charming and loving?

He was almost too good to be true.

Wait. Wasn't that a bad thing?

I gave him my trembling hand, anyway. He kissed my palm before sliding the ring on my finger. The platinum looked good against my pale complexion.

I twisted the band with my fingers, and it slid easily because I was sweating.

Royce stood, his eyes intent and filled with so much love and desire my stomach clenched. "It looks good on you here," he said, "but I want to see how it looks on you in bed."

Slowly I grinned. Now there was something guaranteed to drown out my fears.

HAVING SPENT THE DAY IN BED, Royce and I arrived at my mom's five minutes late for dinner. Yes, late. And I didn't even feel guilty. For the occasion, my mom had donned a formal, black sequined dress, two strands of pearls and all of her rings. Jonathan wore a suit and tie.

Royce and I were in jeans and T-shirts. "I thought this would be a relaxing family dinner," I said.

"I never thought this day would come," my mom said, grabbing Royce by the arm and leading him inside. "So excuse me for wanting to celebrate. Royce, come in, come in. I'm so pleased to finally meet you. Naomi has told me so much about you."

"Anything good?" he asked with a chuckle.

"Well, no," she admitted, "but you can't be all bad if you won her hand in marriage." She barely paused for breath. "I'd be so thrilled if you called me Mom. You are going to treat my baby right, aren't you?"

"Without a doubt."

The delicious scent of fresh-baked foods filled the house. I inhaled deeply and my mouth watered. I might be a nervous wreck, but I hadn't lost my appetite.

"Naomi!" Jonathan pulled me to him for a hug. "So glad to see you."

I returned the gesture, still not knowing what to make of his behavior lately. I continue to have no clue what he was doing with Nora.

He drew back, smiling, and turned his attention to Royce.

"It's nice to meet you," he said, holding out his hand. He and Royce shook.

"You, too. I've, uh, heard a lot about you."

"Did Naomi mention I'm a therapist? I'd be happy to give you both premarital counseling. Not enough couples do that, you know? Which is why divorce is so prevalent."

"We don't need counseling," I said. "Really. We get along very well."

Disappointment washed over Jonathan's features. "I doubt you've overcome all your relationship fears, Naomi, and being as Royce is nearing forty—you are under forty, aren't you?"

"Yes," Royce answered, clearly fighting a grin.

"And hasn't ever been married," Jonathan finished, "I think it's safe to say you could both use some professional help before you say your vows."

I rubbed my temple. *Dear Heavenly Father. Strike me down. A few locusts will do the trick. Or a plague.*

"My Lord," my mom suddenly cried. "Your ring. Look at your ring, Naomi. It's lovely. Not at all like that fifty-pound monstrosity Richard gave you. I know how you hated that thing. Didn't it cause carpal tunnel syndrome? This one is perfect. It's a good size, but won't cause any muscle damage."

I almost covered my hand; it felt odd having people stare at one finger as if it were a priceless object. But I didn't. I allowed Mom and Jonathan to look, oohing and aahing. Royce *had* picked the perfect ring for me, and I was proud of it. Proud of him.

"Naomi," Jonathan said, "you really should consider keeping a wedding journal."

I'd seen brides writing in their wedding journals, and had always thought it kind of silly. I wasn't a sentimental person. I didn't want to write about my feelings. "We'll see," I said noncommittally.

"You'll be so happy you did," my mom said. "You'll be able to savor the memories forever."

"And work through some of your problems," Jonathan added.

"Everything smells wonderful, Mrs.—Mom." Royce wound his arm around my waist, drawing me into the warmth and strength of his side. "Is it time to eat?"

"Yes, but…I thought we'd all sit and talk first. Have a drink, maybe. Oh, maybe I'll break out my own wedding journal that Jonathan gave me when he proposed. We can read some of the passages."

I massaged my neck.

"First, we have some questions for Royce," Jonathan said, giving her a pointed stick-with-the-plan glance. "We'd really like to get to know him better."

"Please, guys. No." I almost groaned. "No interrogation."

Royce laughed, taking everything in stride. "A chat would be nice." He gave me a comforting squeeze.

Sometimes, having him near me was the equivalent of swallowing a bottle of Xanax. I began to relax, all my troubles seeming to dissolve. Maybe because he smelled so good. Or maybe because I knew what he looked like underneath his clothes. Pure sex. Maybe because I knew he was mine.

For the moment, a fearful voice piped in.

I gulped. Stupid fears. We adjourned to the study, Royce and I taking the couch. Jonathan poured everyone a brandy. I accepted my glass and pretended to sip. No way I'd bring up pregnancy after the triplet fiasco.

"Royce, dear," my mom said. "I'm dying to know how you convinced my sweet Naomi to marry you."

"He sexed me up hard core, if you want the true version." My strategy was simple. To be so blunt my parents would decide not to ask another question. They might ask something I didn't want to answer.

My mom flushed, and Jonathan coughed and looked away. Royce pressed his lips together to smother a laugh.

"I'm glad to see I'm not the only one on the receiving end of that sharp tongue of hers," he said. "She isn't afraid to speak her mind, is she?"

"Is that the reason you picked her out of all the other applicants, then?" Jonathan asked. "Her... bluntness?"

"Naomi didn't have to fill out an application." He was a little embarrassed, I could tell. His cheeks were flushed and his voice cracked. "She became the only possible choice the first moment I saw her."

My chest constricted, just like it always did when he said such sweet things. Even my inner Tigress purred like a contented kitten.

What are you going to do when he realizes he's fooling himself?

The ugly question whispered across my mind. Another fear. I hurriedly shoved it aside, refusing to dwell on it.

My mom's hands had gone to her mouth, and I think there were tears in her eyes. "That's the most romantic thing I've ever heard. Did you hear that, Jonathan? Did you hear what he said about my baby?"

Yes, definite tears. As I watched, she crumbled in her seat, uttering great, gushing sobs. Snot soon poured out of her nose and heart-wrenching cries exploded from her mouth. I scrambled to my feet and raced to her. My heart thundered in my chest. "Mom, what's the matter?"

"Don't do it, darling. Don't marry him."

I shook my head, unsure I'd heard her right, and clutched her knee. "I thought you wanted me to get married and give you grandchildren."

"You really should become a lesbian and do the artificial insemination thing. You won't get hurt that way."

"Mom," I said, helplessly looking to Royce.

"He'll cheat on you like the rotten dog he is." Her

head popped up and she glared over at Jonathan. "They all cheat. And I hope they all burn in hell like the male prostitutes they are."

"What are you talking about?" Jonathan sputtered as he stood. "Gloria, what's wrong with you? I'm seriously considering doing a mental evaluation on you. I've never cheated. Whatever gave you that idea?"

Sparks of fury lit inside me. "You've been going over to your secretary's house," I said, pointing to his chest. "You've been coming home late, lying to my mom about your whereabouts. You've been making secret phone calls, and your dirty clothes smell like another woman's perfume."

"I—I can explain." He held out his hands, the desperate gesture of an innocent man.

"I'll just bet you can," my mom shouted. "I bet your car broke down and you had to wait for the mechanic. I bet a client swore to kill himself if you didn't stay and talk to him. I bet someone stole the money out of your wallet and that's why you're always short on cash. Is that right? Is any of that right?" By that point, she was screaming.

"No," he said, shaking his head. His skin was so pallid I could see blue veins. "That wasn't what I was going to say."

Shaking, I crossed my arms over my chest. That's when I felt a quiet presence behind me. Royce placed his hands on my shoulders and massaged the knotted muscles. I drew in an unsteady breath. I wanted to jump between them, but didn't. They needed to battle it out.

"Tell me the truth, Jonathan. I deserve that much, at least."

He slowly walked to her and dropped to his knees. "Gloria, I can't believe you'd think that about me. Why didn't you come to me? Why didn't you say something?"

"I shouldn't have to," she sobbed. "You should never have lied to me."

"You're right, and I'm sorry. So sorry."

She blew up again. "So you did it? You're admitting you slept with Nora?"

"No."

"No?" I said, eyes narrowing. Forget staying out of it. "You went over to her house." I'd never been in a fistfight before, but how complicated could picking up the lamp he'd bought my mom for her birthday and bashing him in the head be?

Jonathan sighed warily and got to his feet. "Give me a minute."

"You'd better be packing your bags," I said.

"Sweetheart, you're making this harder for your mom," Royce whispered. "Calm down." He kissed my cheek and nuzzled my ear with his nose. "She needs your support right now."

I drew in a shuddering breath. Royce was right. My mom needed me, and I was going to be there for her, hold her up emotionally for as long as necessary. I drew her to me and wrapped my arms around her. "I'm so sorry, Mom," I said. "So very sorry."

She wiped her nose on my shirt.

"This is what I've been doing," Jonathan said, striding back into the room. He handed my mom a glass bottle of what looked like oil. "Making you the perfect perfume."

"What?" I said, just as my mom said, "Perfume? For me?" She sniffed the bottle.

"Nora told me about this place she goes to, Body Electric," he rushed, "and how they make custom scents. I know how much you love lilies, and I wanted you to have your own scent. Something no one else in the world has."

I covered my mouth with a shaky hand.

"And I know how much you hated the lamp I bought you for your birthday. I know you wanted something romantic. I thought—I thought there was nothing more romantic than giving you your own perfume. *Gloria,* it's called. It's not perfected yet, not quite right, but…"

"I…I love it," she said, more tears swimming in her eyes. She clutched the bottle to her chest. "Oh, Jonathan."

"None of the scents were right. None of them were good enough, so we kept trying. I'm so sorry you thought I was cheating on you. I'd never do that, Gloria. Never. I shouldn't have lied, but I wanted it to be a surprise. I know how much you love romantic surprises."

Shame washed through me. My mom threw herself in his arms. I closed my eyes and buried my head in Royce's shirt. Dear God, I'd almost broken up my parents' marriage. For nothing. Nothing! Tears streamed down my cheeks. Jonathan loved my mom, had been faithful to her all along.

They had the kind of marriage I'd always wanted

for myself, but hadn't thought truly existed. And I'd almost destroyed it. "I'm such an idiot," I said brokenly. "This is my fault."

"You did what any other daughter would have done," Royce said, kissing my temple. While he spoke, his hands moved up and down my back.

"Don't make excuses for me." I pulled away from him and dragged my feet to my mom and stepdad. They were kissing and hugging and crying all at once. "I'm sorry. I'm so sorry. Please say you'll forgive me."

Jonathan didn't look at me, but reached out and gripped my arm. He tugged me into their loving circle. The tears poured from my eyes. I'd almost ruined him, and he forgave me so quickly and easily. He'd always been that way. He'd tried to be a father to me, but I'd always held a little resistance against him.

"Well, then. Now that that's settled." My mom disengaged from us and wiped one of her hands on her dress. She still clutched the bottle in the other, holding it tight to her chest. "It's time to eat. Royce," she said, as if we hadn't all engaged in an emotional breakdown, "I hope you like glazed ham."

"I—love it?" He glanced at me, clearly confused by her sudden change from psycho-wife to mushy-wife to perfect hostess.

Feeling giddy all of a sudden, I laughed and launched myself in his arms, planting a hard kiss on his lips. "God, I lo—like you." I lost my smile. *What are you doing, dummy?* "I really like you."

He chuckled and held me tight. "I'll get you to admit it yet."

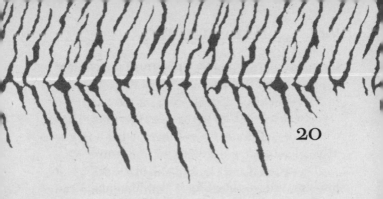

20

Beware of the scrumptious treat lying in the open, waiting to be eaten. A Tigress knows that traps can abound, sometimes invisible, but there all the same.

August 22
Dear Wedding Journal,
Jonathan surprised me with you today. I hate you, and I'm never writing in you again. Just wanted you to know that.

August 23
Dear Wedding Journal,
Fine, I'll give you a try. But don't expect me to gush on and on about my feelings. I do that enough in my own head, and I'm already sick

of myself. This morning I reserved the church, paid for the flowers and all that crap. The *Tattler* reporters followed me around, snapping pictures of me. Out in the open this time. They didn't try to hide. One of them, a balding guy with yellow teeth, called me the future Mrs. Royce Powell and I kicked him in the balls. Not my fault, I promise you. I heard the name and just freaked out. Thankfully Royce is out of town, so he hasn't witnessed my behavior.

August 24
Dear Wedding Journal,
I bought a dress today. It's pretty. Very plain, very simple. No ugly bows or itchy lace. It's formfitting, ankle-length, with thin straps that crisscross in back. Oh, and it's a gorgeous ivory. Let's face it. Royce returned from his trip (early!) and rocked me like a porn star, so I can hardly wear white. I just hope I don't throw up in it. My stomach is hurting all the time now, and I can barely eat. Nerves or baby?

August 27
Dear Wedding Journal,
I had nightmares all night about Royce seeing me walk down the aisle and realizing he's making a terrible mistake. In the dream, he flips me off and runs screaming from the church. And when I woke up, I started hearing voices in my head. Not schizophrenic voices, mind you—I'm

crazy but not *that* whacked-out. All of my fears about marriage and infidelity and abandonment are clamoring to be heard and they won't shut up.

September 1
Dear Wedding Journal,
It's been a few days since we last spoke. Or wrote. Or whatever. I haven't been able to concentrate. Those voices… They're saying to leave Royce and get away now, before it's too late. Linda's party is only a few days away. That means my *wedding* is only a few days away. What the hell am I going to do? Women are still sending Royce wife applications. They are still showing up at the Powell building. What if one of them entices him?

September 12
Dear Wedding Journal,
I think Royce realized there's something wrong with me because he's been telling me he loves me a thousand times a day. I was even starting to relax—a little—until he took me to his parents' house for dinner. I've never met two people more in need of a divorce. They bickered and fought all evening. Royce said that's how they express their love. I don't believe him. I mean, please. You tell me if you feel the love from this conversation (written word for word as I remember it):

Linda: Elliot, be a dear and get me another drink.

Elliot: Get it yourself.

Linda: Get up and fix me a drink, you lazy man.

Elliot: Woman, don't push me on this. I've finally gotten comfortable.

Linda: (sugary sweet smile) I'll push you only when you're standing on a bridge.

Elliot: If I were standing on a bridge and saw you coming, you wouldn't have to push me. I'd jump.

See? Does that sound "loving" to you? Really, the man had worn a shirt with If You See My Wife Coming, Shoot Me printed on the front. What if Royce and I end up— Wait. Royce is coming down the hall. I hear him whistling. I better go.

September 12 (two hours later)
Dear Wedding Journal,
I just had two amazing orgasms so I have nothing more to complain about tonight. Thankfully my fears have been quiet. I just might be okay with this wedding thing. In fact, I'm not talking to you for a while. I think you're screwing with my head.

September 16
Dear Wedding Journal,
Ohmygod, ohmygod, ohmygod. I'm totally freaking out. Tomorrow is Linda Powell's birth-

day party. I spent today decorating the hotel and finishing up the last-minute details, so my worries have nothing to do with that. It's just, well…the day after her party is my wedding. My. Wedding. Do you hear me? Ohmygod, ohmygod, ohmygod. My fears have come back full force and won't shut up. What the hell was I thinking, saying yes to marriage? Ohmygod, I'm going to be sick.

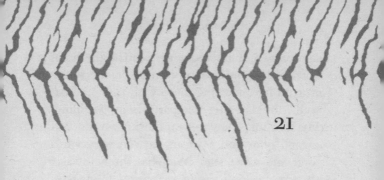

21

A true Tigress—ah, hell. If you don't know by this point, you're not a real Tigress. Take up gardening or something and call it a day.

THE DAY OF THE PARTY, I managed to pull myself together. Well, on the outside it appeared as if I'd pulled myself together. After hours of trying to find my happy meadow, and failing, I slapped myself across the face and joined Royce here at the hotel. Now I stood beside him, waiting at the door of the ballroom and waving guests inside. FYI, I wasn't dressed like a harem girl, but in a bright red sundress.

I must say, I did a wonderful job on the decorations. The area truly did resemble something out of *Arabian Nights*. There were belly dancers and magicians and multihued satin floor pillows. Jewels dripped from the tables and walls. Flowers abounded. There was a pink punch waterfall, and I'd even arranged for chocolate fondue. Soft, romantic music played in the background.

Six half-naked men were waiting outside the ballroom by a velvet lounge chair. When Linda arrived, they would place her on the lounge and carry her inside.

Kera and Mel were in their costumes, veils and barely there scarves, and were serving guests drinks and hors d'oeuvres as they meandered through the ballroom. Colin stayed by Mel's side, and neither of them could stop grinning. George Wilben stayed by Kera's, and *they* couldn't stop grinning.

Love was in the air.

Stomach cramp, stomach cramp.

Royce introduced me as his fiancée instead of the party planner. Everyone smiled at me and I swear to God they looked me up and down, trying to figure out what Royce saw in me, why he'd picked me. Honestly, I couldn't remember myself at the moment.

Stomach cramp, stomach cramp.

When all hundred and something guests had arrived—I'd made Royce narrow the list down—I helped them all find hiding places. Linda would arrive any moment, and this was a *surprise* party, after all.

"She's here," Royce said, a text message on his cell phone alerting him.

"Quiet everyone," I said.

The murmur of the crowd tapered to silence.

We dimmed the lights, letting the candles flicker

and illuminate. A hush went over the crowd, and we even heard Linda giggle outside. Giggle! Royce closed in beside me and chose that moment to kiss me. I was helpless to resist him—I was always helpless to resist him. When his lips were pressed to mine, nothing else mattered but the two of us. Not the past. Not the future. Not the surge of fears that refused to leave me alone.

Gong. Gooong.

The doors were thrown and staunch, sophisticated Linda Powell was carried in by her half-naked slave boys. Royce and I laughingly pulled apart. Linda wore a conservative brown pantsuit, I saw, her silver bob perfectly in place. Her husband trailed behind her, and he was grinning ear to ear.

I watched the byplay, but Royce hadn't taken his eyes off me. "I can't wait to make you my wife tomorrow," he said tenderly.

I stilled, the words pounding through my mind. *Wife. Tomorrow.* Words I'd managed to push to the back of my mind—well, for a little while, at least. *Wife. Tomorrow.*

"Surprise!" everyone yelled.

I didn't move, didn't speak.

Even draped across the lounge as she was, Linda acted appropriately shocked. She put her hands over her mouth and muttered, "I can't believe you did this."

Everyone laughed.

Not me. I stared up at Royce now, at his strong chin, his cheekbones, his straight nose. His soft lips.

His bright, bright blue eyes. He'd been inside me so many times over the last few weeks I hardly knew who I was without him there.

He kissed me softly on the lips. "I have to speak with my mom. Will you be okay on your own?"

"Yes," I said softly.

He kissed me again, a little harder, and walked away.

I watched him go. I'd tried to deny it, tried valiantly, but I couldn't deny it anymore. Couldn't fool myself, or pretend all I felt was lust. I loved him. I really, truly loved him. In that moment, my entire body pulsed with the knowledge. Roared with it.

My stomach cramped, hard. Love was dangerous. Love was messy, could ruin me. *Wife. Tomorrow. WIFE. TOMORROW.* All of my fears spoke up at once.

You'll love him forever, but how long will he love you?

He's too good to be true.

He'll get tired of you soon after the wedding.

He'll cheat. Men always do.

Jonathan hadn't cheated on my mom, I reminded myself, desperate. And Royce had done nothing to earn my distrust.

Not yet, that is.

I had trouble drawing in a breath. I felt like I was trapped in a small, airless box, no way out. Spinning round and round, helpless, screaming but remaining unheard. Hurting, sick. Frantic.

You're going to get hurt, and you'll never be able to recover.

Royce travels all the time. He might not mean to, but one day, somewhere, something will happen…

You'll be left as a shell of a woman.

Even now there were women dressed in green and camped outside the hotel.

I couldn't do it, I thought, shaking my head. I just couldn't do it! I couldn't be a forgotten, unwanted wife. Not again. If I hadn't fallen in love with him, maybe I could have gone through with it. If I hadn't given him my whole heart, maybe I could have risked it. Not now. No, not now.

Ohmygod, ohmygod, ohmygod. What was I going to do? How was I going to get out of this? *Ohmygod.*

"Breathe, Naomi, breathe."

The rest of the party passed in a haze for me. Royce mingled with the crowd, and I stood off to the side, wondering what the hell I was going to do to get out of my own wedding. I couldn't give Royce the chance to break my heart. I couldn't let another man destroy me.

I couldn't live through another divorce.

And that's what will happen if you marry him. He'll divorce you, take you for everything you've worked so hard for.

Shut up, I wanted to scream. The fears… I had to silence them. They'd won. They'd defeated me. I couldn't marry him. Why wouldn't they shut up now?

"Are you okay?" Kera asked, suddenly in front of me and holding out her tray of…whatever it was. It was brown and gloppy. "You look pale."

I ignored the offered food. "I'm fine, thank you. You?"

"I'm good." She paused. "Are you sure you're okay?"

"Yes."

Pause. "Maybe George should—"

"Leave me alone, Kera." I didn't want to see her with George. I didn't want to talk to George. They were a happy couple. At the moment, I hated all happy couples and the people who were part of them. Those people had something I didn't—the courage to work through their fears.

"If you're sure…" Frowning, she padded away from me.

"Are you okay?" Mel asked a few minutes later. She held out her drink tray.

"I'm fine." I ignored the offered drinks.

"Kera says you were short with her."

"I said I'm fine, okay."

She studied me. "What's going on, Naomi? You look like death. Colin can—"

"Leave me alone, Mel. Please." My voice cracked, sounding more tortured than I'd ever heard another human being. I was breaking inside. Crumbling. Dissolving.

Dying.

"Don't talk to Colin. Don't talk to anyone about me."

Without another word, she backed away from me. The traitor walked right over to Colin, even though I'd told her not to, and said something to him. He looked at me and frowned, then walked right over to Royce and said something to him.

Royce, who had been in the middle of a laughing conversation with his mom, turned toward me and frowned. Concern darkened his eyes. In the next instant, he began walking toward me. It happened in slow motion, each step a hollow thud in my ears. My heartbeat quickened its pace and my blood chilled. My skin heated.

Too good to be true.

Cheat.

Hurt.

Heartache.

I didn't give him a chance to reach me. I ran. Just ran. Out of the ballroom, out of the hotel and down the street. I think I heard Royce call my name, but I kept running. I had to get away. Couldn't face him right now.

Toward the end of the block, I was out of breath. Tears burned my eyes and streamed down my cheeks as I hailed a cab.

At home, I quickly changed out of my dress and packed a bag. Royce called six times, but I didn't pick up the phone. The first message was a concerned, "What's going on? Why did you run, sweetheart? Do you need time alone?"

The second: "Call me when you get this, sweetheart. Where are you? I'm worried about you."

By the sixth, he uttered a guttural, "Damn it, Naomi. Call me."

I heard cars in the background, and knew he was on his way to my apartment. *He only thinks he loves you,* my deepest fears said, still clamoring to be heard. *One day he'll be happy you left him.*

"Shut up. Shut up, shut up, shut up." Those voices were making me crazy, were spinning my world out of control. I had to get out of here. Had to be alone. Had to find peace.

I went to the only place no one would think to look for me. The airport. I bought the cheapest ticket possible—which happened to be to Oklahoma City, the place Royce had taken me last—and waited in the terminal.

My blood cooled with every second that passed.

When they finally called my flight, I began shaking. I got on the plane, though, one step at a time. *You're doing the right thing. A marriage to Royce would never have lasted.* I clenched the armrests as we took off and cried silently as we soared through the air. My shaking never ceased, and yes, I threw up in the barf bag. Several times.

Surprisingly, I made it to Oklahoma City alive and well. I plopped in the first unoccupied chair I came to, trying to breathe. Trying to calm my nerves. *Now you don't have to deal with Royce. Now he can't hurt you.*

"Shut up," I screamed.

Several people whipped around to look at me, but no one approached me or commented. And I found, as I sat there, that the ringing in my ears was slowly dying. My fears were finally quieting.

And for the first time in hours, I began to breathe. In. Out. I took in as much of the precious air as I could. All the while, people maneuvered around my seat, hustling past me. I watched them. Couples, singles, children. They were all headed somewhere, going about their lives and living as best they could.

Yes, they were living.

I hadn't been, I realized in a sudden burst of clarity. Not really. Only with Royce had I come truly alive. In fact, before him, I'd been living in slow motion, going about my daily life but never forging a real future for myself.

Like my fear of flying, my relationship fears had weighed me down and kept me in one place. Always that fear of crashing and burning—in a plane or out. Didn't matter. I'd been afraid. I'd let the fear rule me.

What a coward I was. Not a Tigress. Not even a whole woman.

Did I want to live the rest of my life that way?

No. God, no. Hell, no.

And if I died today, I'd go to my grave with so many regrets. That's what fear/worry/anxiety, or whatever name I wanted to give it, did. Made a person stagnant. I didn't want to be stagnant anymore.

Richard hadn't broken me.

It was true, I realized. I slowly grinned, realizing, too, I hadn't wished my ex to everlasting hell as I usually did when I thought of him. He hadn't broken me. In a way, he was the reason I'd met Royce. If Richard and I hadn't split, I wouldn't have opened my own business. And if I hadn't opened my own business, I wouldn't have met Royce.

Royce... Sweet, tender, loving Royce. He was honorable. He desired me. He loved me. He was nothing like Richard, so why had I let the fears Richard had caused in me affect our relationship?

Coward, idiot, dummy.

"Not anymore," I said firmly, not caring who heard me.

Maybe I couldn't predict what tomorrow would bring, but I knew I would always love Royce. And loving him didn't have to be the bad thing I'd feared. It hadn't been so far. So far it had been wild and wonderful, amazing and joyous.

Being hurt was a part of life. I couldn't keep myself from it, no matter what I did. Without the voice of fear to distract me, I recognized that for fact. Knew it. Allowing myself to experience good things— love—could only help me when the bad times rolled around.

"I'm going to be okay," I told the lady striding past my chair. "I'm really going to be okay."

She gave me an odd look and hurried on.

I stayed at the airport all night, awaiting my morning flight home. I didn't sleep, but remained awake and made a list for Royce. With every item I added, I felt stronger, more assured that I was doing the right thing.

In fact, the only thing left to do was tell him what I'd decided—if he would even speak to me. I wasn't going to be afraid, though. I was marching onward. I'd *make* him listen if I had to.

No more fears for Naomi Delacroix. I was finally a Tigress. I would tackle life as it came. I would love and be loved.

My return flight was delayed due to rain, and when the death trap did finally take off, the ensuing turbulence almost killed me through a heart attack—and

I almost killed the woman seated next to me by squeezing her too tightly. But I made it. I lived. I even flipped the plane the bird as I departed.

I hefted my bag over my shoulder and sprinted down the terminal. Outside, I hailed a cab and climbed inside. "Haul ass!" I told the driver.

He peeled out.

Thankfully Royce's apartment wasn't too far away. When we stopped abruptly, I threw the cabbie a ten and raced inside the building. But…

Royce wasn't home. And he didn't answer his cell.

Think, Naomi. Think. Where was he? I searched my place—nothing. I called his mom—no answer. I called Kera and Mel—no answer. I called Colin—no answer. Not knowing what else to do, I hailed another cab and drove to the church I'd reserved for our wedding. That would have taken place hours ago if I hadn't chickened out.

Maybe he was there, explaining to the guests that I was a flake who'd run out on him.

When I arrived, I threw open the double doors. "Royce," I called. I don't know what I expected to find inside, but what I found wasn't it. "Royce?" My shocked gaze scanned the building and tears welled in my eyes.

Everyone stood in place, and they were staring at me expectantly. There had been no cars in the lot, but everyone was here.

Mel and Kera were at the altar on Royce's left and Colin was on Royce's right. My mom and Jonathan smiled encouragingly at me. Even Rachel was there.

And Jennifer. She blew me a kiss. Royce's mom and dad nodded at me, and I noticed they both had tears of happiness in their eyes.

"About time," someone muttered.

"Quiet," someone else scolded.

I clutched a hand over my stomach and stared down the aisle. Royce's expression was neutral and didn't change when our gazes locked. He was in a tux, so unbelievably handsome, while I was in jeans and a wrinkled T-shirt. My hair was in complete disarray.

Determined, I strode to him. Gulping, heart hammering, I handed him the list I'd made. "Here," I said. "This is for you."

He didn't say anything. Just read over it, expression unchanged.

"Why are you here?" I asked him quietly, my gaze never leaving his face.

"I decided to take a chance that you'd come," was his only response. Still no change in his expression. "Why are *you* here?"

He'd decided to take a chance. God, I loved this man. And I, well… "Didn't you read the list?"

Fierce now, his dark lashes swept up and he met my gaze. "I need to hear you say it, Naomi."

Tears spilled from my eyes. My chin trembled, making speech difficult. "The list tells all the reasons I can't live without you. All the reasons I love you." I was going to take a chance, too. "You're smart. You're honorable. You're funny. You're passionate. And you're…you. You're mine."

I turned to the crowd. "I love this man," I shouted.

"I love him, and I want to marry him. I want to have his babies."

Several ohs and sniffles drifted from the crowd.

Royce and I might stumble along the way, but the journey would be worth any hardships. Slowly I faced him. "I love you," I said. "I love you so much, and I want to be with you, as your wife, forever. It might have taken me a little while to figure it out, but I still made it to the church. Consider this my application."

He grinned, his lips inching upward, and he dragged me into his arms with a murmured, "Thank God."

"Do you still want to marry me?" I asked hopefully.

He palmed my cheeks. "Well, your BlueJay says we've got an appointment today."

I grinned, too. "Give me the words."

"Yes, Naomi," he said, placing a soft kiss on my lips. "I still want to marry you. I'm nothing without you. I've loved you from the moment I first saw you. You were wearing green, and I've been obsessed with the color ever since."

His words hit me full force, and I thought back to all the women in green who had camped out in his office. All the women who had sent him pictures of themselves wearing green lingerie—or green body paint. I was the reason for that. Me. I covered my mouth with a shaky hand, more empowered in that moment than I'd been my entire life.

If I'd had any lingering fears about Royce's commitment to me, they vanished instantly. This man loved me so much he remembered the first outfit he'd seen me wear and wanted everyone else in the same color. He was crazy-insane in love with everything about me.

Like I was with him.

I lowered my hand and beamed up at him.

"Then may we at last begin?" the pastor asked on a sigh.

My smiled widened. Royce kissed me again. "You may begin," we said simultaneously.

EPILOGUE

September 14

Dear Wedding Journal,
Guess what? I've been married a full year now, and I'm happier than ever. Oh, and I'm also pregnant. The first go round was a false alarm— to my and Royce's disappointment. So, after the wedding, Royce and I hit the sheets as much as possible to rectify that.

We've barely gotten out of bed since.

Three months into our marriage, Royce got tired of leaving me to buy planes, so he handed that aspect of the job to Colin. Much to Mel's fury. She soon came around, though, and now travels with him. Yeah, they're still dating. I'm as surprised as you are. I think they got married in Vegas a few weeks ago, but neither one of them will say for sure. They just smile mysteriously. Neither wants to give up the image of being a player, I guess, but neither wants to give up the other, either.

Kera, too, is now married. She and George tied the knot mere weeks after me and Royce. They now have twin girls. Cutest little things ever.

And I'll soon have my own little bundle of joy. I can hardly wait!

I still can't believe I once resisted Royce. Can you? The man adores me. Truly. It's sickening sometimes, the way he loves me. He can't get enough of me. All right, all right. I can't get enough of him, either.

Anytime my old fears try to resurface—which is so rare now, it hardly bears mentioning— Royce spends hours and hours (and hours) reminding me (naked) of all the reasons he loves me.

Is he a dear or what?

Well, I better go. It's my turn to remind him of all the reasons I love him (naked, of course).

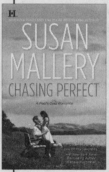  

REQUEST YOUR
FREE BOOKS!

2 FREE NOVELS
FROM THE SUSPENSE COLLECTION
PLUS 2 FREE GIFTS!

YES! Please send me 2 FREE novels from the Suspense Collection and my 2 FREE gifts (gifts are worth about $10). After receiving them, if I don't wish to receive any more books, I can return the shipping statement marked "cancel." If I don't cancel, I will receive 3 brand-new novels every month and be billed just $5.74 per book in the U.S. or $6.24 per book in Canada. That's a saving of at least 28% off the cover price. It's quite a bargain! Shipping and handling is just 50¢ per book.* I understand that accepting the 2 free books and gifts places me under no obligation to buy anything. I can always return a shipment and cancel at any time. Even if I never buy another book, the two free books and gifts are mine to keep forever.

192/392 MDN E7PD

Name	(PLEASE PRINT)
Address	Apt. #
City	State/Prov. Zip/Postal Code

Signature (if under 18, a parent or guardian must sign)

Mail to **The Reader Service:**
IN U.S.A.: P.O. Box 1867, Buffalo, NY 14240-1867
IN CANADA: P.O. Box 609, Fort Erie, Ontario L2A 5X3

Not valid for current subscribers to the Suspense Collection
or the Romance/Suspense Collection.

Want to try two free books from another line?
Call 1-800-873-8635 or visit www.morefreebooks.com.

* Terms and prices subject to change without notice. Prices do not include applicable taxes. N.Y. residents add applicable sales tax. Canadian residents will be charged applicable provincial taxes and GST. Offer not valid in Quebec. This offer is limited to one order per household. All orders subject to approval. Credit or debit balances in a customer's account(s) may be offset by any other outstanding balance owed by or to the customer. Please allow 4 to 6 weeks for delivery. Offer available while quantities last.

Your Privacy: Harlequin Books is committed to protecting your privacy. Our Privacy Policy is available online at www.eHarlequin.com or upon request from the Reader Service. From time to time we make our lists of customers available to reputable third parties who may have a product or service of interest to you. If you would prefer we not share your name and address, please check here. ☐

Help us get it right—We strive for accurate, respectful and relevant communications. To clarify or modify your communication preferences, visit us at www.ReaderService.com/consumerchoice.

MSUS10R

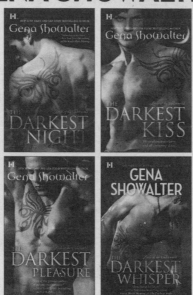